SYMPTOMS of a HEARTBREAK

SYMPTOMS of a HEARTBREAK

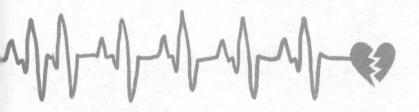

SONA CHARAIPOTRA

{Imprint}
MAKE YOUR MARK

New York

[Imprint]
MAKE YOUR MARK

A part of Macmillan Publishing Group, LLC
120 Broadway, New York, NY 10271

SYMPTOMS OF A HEARTBREAK. Copyright © 2019 by CAKE Literary, LLC. All rights reserved.
Printed in the United States of America.
Library of Congress Cataloging-in-Publication Data is available.

ISBN 978-1-250-19910-2 (hardcover) / ISBN 978-1-250-19911-9 (ebook)

Our books may be purchased in bulk for promotional, educational, or business use. Please
contact your local bookseller or the Macmillan Corporate and Premium Sales Department
at (800) 221-7945 ext. 5442 or by email at MacmillanSpecialMarkets@macmillan.com.

Book design by Elynn Cohen

Imprint logo designed by Amanda Spielman

First edition, 2019

1 3 5 7 9 10 8 6 4 2

fiercereads.com

A pox on the book thief who's stolen these pages:
Hope this story breaks your heart.

To my mommy, Dr. Neelam Charaipotra, for always setting the example.
And for pushing me past my limits

And to my papa, Dr. Kamal Prakash Charaipotra. I miss you every day.
I hope I can make you proud

SYMPTOMS of a HEARTBREAK

GIRL GENIUS DONS DOCTOR'S COAT

TIME MAGAZINE, JUNE 16

The University of Medicine and Dentistry of New Jersey graduated its youngest MD yesterday, conferring a doctor of medicine degree — with highest honors — to New Jersey's "Dr. Girl Genius," as she's been dubbed. Saira Sehgal, 16, joins Princeton Presbyterian — where her mother, Dr. Rana Sehgal, heads the pediatrics department — as one of three pediatric oncology interns in the teaching hospital's pre-residency training fellowship, a feeder for their oncology program.

Dr. Alfred Charles, the hospital's chief of staff, said he's thrilled to welcome Sehgal to their facility. "I first had the pleasure of meeting young Dr. Sehgal when she was eight, as a friend to an oncology patient," Dr. Charles said. "Even then her immense potential was blatantly apparent. In fact, she helped us diagnose her friend and even consulted on treatment strategies. I'm proud she's chosen Princeton Presbyterian as the place where she'll begin her medical career."

Sehgal is humble about the high expectations she faces. "It's an honor," she said. "Princeton Presbyterian is a top-rated teaching hospital, and the internship program has graduated many well-known doctors. I'm thrilled to work with Dr. Charles, chief resident Dr. Arora, and the staff at Princeton. I'm sure it will be a challenging and exciting opportunity."

Sehgal got her GED at 10, earned her undergraduate degree from Princeton and completed med school at 16 with honors and on full scholarship — all rare feats. She said she was inspired to pursue medicine when she saw how carefully the hospital's staff treated her friend Harper Rose Strich, who succumbed to acute leukemia at eight. "She got the best treatment, and Dr. Charles, who was the attending oncologist at the time, made sure she was very well taken care of. He tried new treatments that gave my friend a fighting chance. Sadly, she died of her disease when she was eight. I fight on in her honor."

CHAPTER 1

It's 7:30, and it's all going smoothly.

Paperwork: done.

Shower: complete.

First-Day Pants and Blouse selected: clean and classic.

White coat: ironed and safe in its dry-cleaning bag.

Loafers: stiff and polished.

Laptop and phone: charged.

Briefcase: prepped.

Everything just right. Or it was, anyway.

And then, there she is.

Mom. That familiar knock. Only about an hour too late.

I've just slicked down my hair again—this July heat triggers the frizz, inevitably—when she starts pounding on my bedroom door.

I look at my smartwatch. Yup, 7:43. If I actually relied on her to get me up on time, I'd be so very late.

"Saira, beta! Time to get up," my mother singsongs just outside my door. "Dadima made paranthe!"

"Mom, I don't have time."

"Of course you have time. Your dadima made you a special first-day breakfast, and you absolutely will eat it."

I sigh. I better get dressed. I've already been up for hours—three to be precise—but I didn't get dressed yet because I don't want to wrinkle my clothes. I mean, it's my first day. I've had a lot of first days on my path to becoming a doctor, but this is a pretty damn important one. I want to be ready. I *need* to be ready.

I walk over to the bed where I've laid out my perfect First Day as a Real Doctor Outfit: a mauve button-down shirt and gray slacks—a picture of Harper tucked into the left back pocket as a reminder—along with black loafers and the same plain, small gold hoop earrings I always wear.

But my outfit's not there. I mean, like, it was there twenty minutes ago when I got into the shower. And now it is GONE.

"It was just so wrong."

I turn around and my big sister Taara's standing in the doorway to the jill-and-jill bathroom we share—or did, before she left for college last year—a smirk on her already-glossed lips as she holds up a shopping bag.

"Taaaaara," I say, lunging forward, trying to find my clothes, but she blocks my path.

"Nope," she says, and I sigh as I take the bag.

"I mean, just because you're a doctor doesn't mean you want to look like you're forty," she says, taking things out of the bag and handing them to me. A soft, satiny black-and-white polka-dotted blouse, black tailored-but-casual capri-length pants, strappy black sandals. And some cute dangly earrings that I'll totally lose by the end of the day. "The white coat should do the trick."

I pull on the clothes and follow her back into the bathroom so she can do my makeup. There's no use fighting it.

"Aren't you supposed to be in class, like, right now?" I ask her as she lines my eyes with kohl. Taara's a sophomore at Rutgers. Premed, following in our mom's footsteps. This year should be pretty intense for her.

"No talking."

She works for a few minutes, frowning the whole time.

"What?" I say.

"We should really do something about those brows."

4

"I thought thick brows were in now."

"Thick brows, yes. Bert brows, no." She waves a pair of tweezers in the air, and I smack her hand away.

"No time."

"All right, but I'm warning you now." She grimaces and gets back to work, lining my eyes with kohl. She hands me lip gloss and I dab some on.

"There." She grins at me in the mirror, satisfied. "But it'd still be better—"

"No." I take a quick look. I do look cute. The problem: I also look so very sixteen.

"I told you . . . ," she says, preempting my complaint.

"I know, I know," I say. "The white coat should do it."

Should. But it won't. I know from experience.

Breakfast is a spread. Dadima went all out. There are aloo ke paranthe and egg bhurji and samose and of course chai.

And there's Vish, tucked into the booth right next to my dad, talking about cricket or Bollywood or some other boyfriend-father bonding topic. Here's a thing you should know about Vish: Technically, to everyone else, he's my *boyfriend*, one word, and has been pretty much forever. Like since we were twelve. But to me he's my *boy friend*, two very separate words, and decidedly platonic, because he's probably, definitely, totally gay. He just hasn't told anyone besides me (and his boyfriend, Luke) yet. He will when he's ready.

Here's the other thing you should know about Vish: He's half-Punjabi, half-Gujarati, and fully vegetarian. Read: hard to feed. Which sort of puts him on Dadima's shit list. (Granted: It's quite a long list.)

That's why she frowns and scowls when he playfully swipes the fresh, hot parantha she's just carried over from the stove.

"That was for Saira," she says, hustling me toward the breakfast nook. "Extra chili. You will regret. Saira, sit, eat. Quickly. Otherwise you're going to be late."

5

Taara and I squish into the booth and dig into the crispy potato-stuffed bread my grandmother has laid out, dipping it into cool yogurt and spicy mango achar.

"Are you nervous, Guddi?" Vish asks, taking a sip of chai. Guddi is his old nickname for me. It means doll.

I shake my head, my mouth already full of food.

"She's got this," Taara says. "She's only been preparing, like, her whole life."

"Where's Mom?" I wonder aloud. But I already know, because she's decidedly not in this room.

"In the shower," Taara mumbles.

"But she's fast," Papa says, and they all laugh.

I don't. Because this is no joking matter.

"I mean, if she's running behind, I can drop you off," Vish says, and I can feel the little dents on my forehead collapsing into those familiar creases. "Like, we can leave right now."

Dadi starts clearing away plates, and pours me another cup of chai. "Relax. It's not even eight yet. You have time." She plonks a grease-stained brown paper bag onto the table. "Treats. For your big day."

I sigh. It's inevitable. I'm going to be late. On my first day. Because of Mom. As usual. All my life, my mom has made us late. She's known as the local pediatrician in our neighborhood—and has been for nearly thirty years—and so every time she steps out of the house she has to look perfect. And as junior representatives of her, so do Taara and I. For Taara—all long, lean, and flawless, like Katrina Kaif—that's pretty easy. For me? Not so much.

Mom walks into the kitchen, her shoulder-length bob freshly set, her burgundy blouse a perfect match to her burgundy pants (and burgundy lipstick), her black patent loafers freshly polished. You'd think it was *her* first day.

But it's mine. And we're late.

"Ready?" she asks. Like I'm the one who's been holding things up. Dadi, prepared as always, hands her a muffin and her to-go chai.

And a full twenty minutes behind schedule, we're finally headed out the door.

We should be okay. Barring any other incidents.

But as soon as we step outside, we're surrounded. By thirty members of the extended Sehgal-Kapoor-Dhillon clan, along with a few stray cousins thrice removed for good measure. The whole paltan, as my dad would say. Except for my friend Lizzie, who'll be sleeping till noon.

Vish's mom stands front and center, of course, a puja thali prepared with the glow of a lit diya and a small bowl of vermilion.

"Pele pait puja, abh asli puja," Vish says, laughing, and I shoot him the glare of death.

"Oh, Saira, we all just wanted to come to show our support and offer our blessings," his mom—forever known as Sweetie Auntie to me—says, waving the tray around near my face in a precarious circle. She dips her ring finger into the vermilion and pokes a little tikka of red onto my forehead as they all lean in close to peer at me. My dad glares in annoyance. He thinks Vish's parents are too religious. But that's probably because we're hardly religious at all. Too many doctors in the family.

"We should get going—" I start, but the expression on Mom's face stops me cold. I rub my cheek. "What?"

"You can't go to the hospital with your eyebrows looking like that," she says, her voice stern and worried.

"I mentioned it this morning, but Saira said we didn't have time," Taara says in her told-you-so voice.

"We still don't have time."

"Of course we have time," Sonia Mamiji says, stepping forward with authority. It's barely eight a.m., but she's all dolled up, her face made, her hair curled. "I even have my kit in the car."

And that's how I end up in the passenger seat of Mom's car, the seat reclined, as Mamiji uses her quick-heating wax strips and professional tweezers to coax and refine those suckers into shape as an audience of twenty—most of the men wisely bailed when the brow talk began—watches with smug satisfaction.

"You really should get them done every two to three weeks," Mamiji says as I yelp with pain. "Otherwise they're out of control."

"Yeh tho main hamesha isko kethi hoon," Mom says. "But she never listens to her mother."

"Or her sister," Taara adds with a grin as I fire death rays from my eyes, framed by newly impeccable brows.

When we finally start the car, it's already 8:45. Thank gods the hospital has that rule that mandates doctors live in a fifteen-minute radius. Because we are SO. VERY. LATE.

CHAPTER 2

It's 9:04 when we finally pull into the staff parking lot at Princeton Presbyterian.

I hate being late. Loathe it. It literally gives me hives. They're psychosomatic, obviously. Physical manifestations of emotional stress are usually fascinating. Except when it's the first day of the rest of your life and you've got roses blooming on your arms and face.

By the time I climb out of the car, it's already 9:06.

Mom and I race to the main lobby and barely make it through the elevator doors as they close. I stab the button for the eighth floor as the people inside—a nurse, another doctor, a couple of civilians—frown or fret.

Except for one, tucked away in the corner—a boy about my age, tall and lanky, skater shorts and board, his hair flopping into his eyes as he stares at his phone. He brushes it away with his free hand, and I notice the freckles on his nose.

My stomach does an odd flip.

Weird.

I look down at my brand-new feet-pinching, old-people loafers, trying to focus. But there's something about him that makes me look again.

He catches me staring and grins. I look away quickly, blushing, the brief erythema warming my cheeks.

He's busy with his phone again, that smirk still on his lips. I wonder what's so funny. Especially at 9:08 in the morning at the hospital.

There's only one reason someone his age—well, my age—ends up at this part of the hospital. Someone's really sick. Or, like, having a baby or something. I wonder who.

He's cute, if somewhat unkempt.

Cutie McFreckles sneezes, and I automatically say, "Bless you." He grins at me again, then looks back at his phone, the moment over.

"Code blue! Code blue!" As the elevator doors open, the alert sounds on the intercom, shaking us all awake. That familiar hospital scent fills the elevator as one of the doctors on board rushes out, frantically punching at his phone. Not good news, clearly.

I reach for the photo I keep in my back pocket, and that's when it hits me. It's in my other pants. *Shit.* No Harper. How am I supposed to get through today?

A lump forms in my throat as her little face pushes its way into my brain. Every inch of this place reminds me of her. Those big blue eyes, rosy cherubic cheeks, that funny, familiar, hiccupping laugh that would crack me up and get us shushed by the nurses.

I close my eyes and can almost feel her by my side.

I shiver. I count to ten, then reopen them.

I can do this. I have to do this.

Focus, Saira, focus.

As we continue up, the elevator's half-empty now and the skater boy has moved closer to the doors, pretty much right next to me. He's tapping away on his phone, the clicking echoing in the silence as we continue to whoosh up past three, four, five.

I wonder where he's going.

My mom catches me looking at him. She nudges my shoulder and raises one perfectly groomed eyebrow.

The door opens and others step out, but he stays. It's the three of us now: me, Mom, and him.

I jab the eighth-floor button again for good measure. I check my watch.

It's 9:11 a.m. Catastrophically late.

This is all Mom's fault. And Taara's. And Sweetie Auntie's. And Sonia Mamiji's.

And okay, maybe just a bit mine. I should have gotten my brows done last week because this was pretty much inevitable. Or maybe I should have worked on getting my license this summer like any normal sixteen-year-old.

Then I wouldn't have had to have my mommy drive me to my first day of work.

She grins at me as I glare at her, and raises her brows comically.

Gods, I really do need a license.

As we get off the elevator on eight, I steal one more look at Cutie McFreckles (because for some reason, I can't *not* look), then bolt out, rushing down the hall toward oncology.

"See, I got you here, safe and sound and in one piece," Mom says, trailing behind me, her arms full of stuff. Why is she following me?

"Yes, but I'm late, Mom." I flash my smartwatch her way pointedly. She's supposed to be at pediatrics on the eleventh floor already, not here with me. "And aren't you late, too?"

"What, half the place is Desis!" she says with a grin. "We're always late."

"Mother, Indian Standard Time is an excuse manufactured by chronically delayed brown people like you." Mom's looking me up and down, "from tip to toe," as she always says, pausing at my earlobes. *Damn. I forgot my earrings.* She reaches up toward her own ear, ready to remove one of her ruby studs.

I stop her before she can get it out. "Yes, I forgot them. And no, I don't want yours."

I hear laughter, and that's when I see him. The guy from the elevator. McFreckles. He's standing near the registration desk, still on his phone, skateboard on the floor beside him, all casual like he's got no place else to be. Except maybe the oncology floor. And he's laughing. At us.

I glare at him, then at my mom, check my smartwatch one more time, and start walking toward the main oncology door.

Mom grabs my arm before I can storm off.

"Not another hug. I can't take it anymore, Mom."

"Did you remember your lunch?" she asks, and I can feel her mentally checking my briefcase.

I nod at her, raising my newly perfect eyebrows so she'll take the hint and leave. Instead, she steps closer, spits on her hands, and starts to smooth them out with her fingers. "Sonia Mamiji made this one a bit thicker—"

I shove her hands away. Hard. *"Mother!"*

The guy laughs again. Louder this time. He's not looking at his phone anymore, just staring right at us, like we're a part of his favorite sitcom or something. Mom notices him and frowns, but turns her focus to me.

"I knew we should have waited for Reshma to return," Mom says, and she can't resist one last eyebrow stroke even as I'm backing away toward the wall. "She's the only one who really knows how to do them properly."

My phone vibrates in my backpack. Lizzie, likely. If she's up early.

"Mom, I'm late!" I basically shout this time, making a move toward the door. My stomach is about to boil over, like an overdone pot of chai. This is pretty much the most important day of my life so far, and I am SO LATE. "I'll see you at lunch."

"Wait," she says, shoving the greasy brown bag toward me. "Don't forget the samose."

"I don't want them."

The guy laughs again, and I hear him say under his breath, "I'll take them."

"But, beta, your friends will enjoy them—"

"No."

"Acha," she says, tucking them back into her bag. "Have a good day."

She gathers all her crap—the carryall, the samose, three other random bags—and heads back toward the elevator. As it dings, I take a deep breath, then exhale.

"I've never witnessed anyone so violently reject samosas," the boy says to me. "I mean, I've never seen anyone reject samosas at all."

My cheeks are blooming again as he waltzes right up to me, just a few inches away. He's a good foot taller, and he smells familiar—like crisp citrus and something sweeter, maybe cinnamon. His dark hair flops forward into his eyes as he looks down at me, a dimple denting one cheek and that smirk playing on his mouth again. He looks mostly white, but there's a hint of something else, like that guy from my best friend Lizzie's favorite K-drama.

"You new?" he says when I don't answer. "You've got that new-kid vibe."

"You could say that," I say, picking up my briefcase. "And I'm late."

"So I heard," he says with a laugh. It's rough around the edges, like it could turn into a cough pretty quick, and he clears his throat to stop it. "Big appointment?"

"Yes," I say, looking at my smartwatch again. "And I really am super late now."

I rush off.

But I can't help but look back one last time.

He's still standing there, his phone at his side, staring after me with a wide grin. "Maybe I'll see you around. Give you the tour. Or something."

"Maybe!" I shout, then nearly trip over my own two feet as I head toward the oncology double doors. I catch myself, and for reasons I can't explain, I take a little bow, like some nerdy, uncoordinated ballerina, and push on through.

His laughter follows me through the door, and that tingle rushes up my back again, making me want to stay, to chat another minute. But I know I can't—my smartwatch tells me it's now 9:18. I'm a whole eighteen minutes late. On my first day of work.

So very late.

CHAPTER 3

I stride into the administration office, as grown-up as I can be, my hair in a fancy Taara braid, my polka-dot blouse paired with some tailored black pants—I just couldn't do the capris—and my new cherry lip gloss adding just the right hint of color and shine. (At least according to my sister.) Professional, but not stiff. I hope.

All eyes land on me—because, of course, I'm the last one here. And I'm sixteen, so, you know, I stand out. A blush warms my cheeks. The erythema again.

I pull my shoulders back, take a deep breath, and try to focus on the details instead of my anxiety. There's too much to look at, too much to think about. *Breathe, Saira, breathe.*

The rest of the group is already gathered, and there's a woman taking attendance. "Glad you could make it," the woman says sternly. Dr. Davis, the hospital administrator, I guess. She's tall and blond, with Texas curls and an accent to match. But there's not a touch of softness to her. Which works, since she's like the boss of this whole place. If doctors worship medicine, and the hospital is our church, this lady is like the pope. You don't want to mess with her. She decides who gets to stay—and who has to go. I've heard terrible things about her. Mostly from Mom—who's now standing next to her, waiting, expectantly. She's got Dadi's sack of samose in one hand. And my dry-cleaning bag in the other. *Wait, what?*

Oh yeah, that.

"How did you get in here?" I ask, my voice croaking.

Mom points. The stairs, obviously.

"Your white coat," Mom says brightly, shimmying the dry-cleaning bag. She hands the sack of samose to Dr. Arora, the chief of residents, whom I met at my interview, and he smiles graciously as Mom ignores the fact that *everybody* is staring at us. Arora's the guy I'll be working under in oncology. Mom's invited him to dinner several times—I think she wants to set him up with Taara—but he keeps politely declining. Which makes me like him already.

"Mom, get out of here!" I whisper-shout, but she's beaming at me as she unzips the dry cleaning.

My coat. It's so crisp and white, I want to touch the collar in awe. No more wearing my mother's white coat and following her around the office like a little kid playing doctor. I mean, I've worn an actual lab coat since the White Coat Ceremony last year and all, but this one is brand-new, and marked with the Princeton Presbyterian logo, all official.

This is it.

This is real.

I suddenly feel super nauseous.

There are snickers among the group. Except for Davis, who clears her throat loudly.

"Just a minute, Davis," Mom says to her. A mistiness coats Mom's eyes, and I'm as red as that gross chicken tikka masala at the Indian place at the mall, but I have to let her have it. This is a moment she's been imagining for years—and so have I. "You know this has to be done properly. Come on, beta, let's get you ready."

Mom holds up the coat for me like she did with my coats when I was small.

I slip my arms through the sleeves, button up the front. Smiling, my mother smugly pins my ID to the front pocket, then straightens the collar. Part of me is mortified at all the witnesses, but I can't help but relish this moment a little, too.

My mother raises a hand, giving into her urge to smooth my

French braid. I duck and bump into one of the other interns, a young black woman with springy, dark curls and glasses. She grins.

"Mom, I think Dr. Davis is waiting," I say, trying to usher her to the door. "I'll see you at lunch."

"Okay, beta." She waves to Davis and the others. "Enjoy the samose!" She wanders off toward the door, empty dry-cleaning bag in hand.

"Well, now that drop-off is done, maybe we can get this show on the road?" Davis says. "Given that we're a good half hour behind, thanks to Sehgal here."

"Sorry about that," I say.

Davis grimaces at me. "First things first." She passes around folders of paperwork. "Welcome to the Pediatric Oncology Fast-Track program here at Princeton Presbyterian. It is unique, and you are lucky to be here. These folders will contain all the information you need to acclimate yourself to the hospital, including maps, log-ins, and passwords for the electronic records system, your intern lounge and cafeteria pass, and other details. And here's Dr. Arora, whom you all met at your interviews last month."

Arora clears his throat, as if he's about to give his Oscar speech, and turns to address the three of us, young, new, naive, and ID'd as interns by the pink strip on our badges. "Dr. Sehgal, Dr. Howard, Dr. Cho," he says. "Welcome to Princeton Presbyterian, your home—and I do mean you will pretty much live here—for the next year."

My fellow interns are the young black woman, who seems friendly, and a scowling twentysomething Asian man who's wearing a tailored suit—complete with an oversized Winnie the Pooh tie—under his lab coat. Is he a doctor or a clown?

"Princeton Presbyterian is one of the most renowned teaching hospitals in the United States. This is the inaugural year of the Fast-Track program, a specialized residency year designed as a filter program for the award-winning pediatric oncology program here in Princeton. As you all know, the three of you were selected from among hundreds of applicants based on your stellar records of academic merit, recommendations from your clinical and rotational supervisors, and your previous research. As interns, you will be competing for two coveted spots in our pediatrics program, which feeds our renowned pediatric oncology fellowship—of which I am a graduate myself. As you know, our fellows have gone on to practice and teach at many esteemed institutions, including Harvard, UCLA, Hopkins, and others.

"Once we fill out some of the paperwork, Dr. Davis needs to set up your night calls, and I'll give you guys a tour of the pediatric oncology ward."

I scan the packet in my hands, reading through the schedule—state-mandated forty hours a week for me, to start, and nearly double that for the other interns—the rules and regulations, the criteria that we'll be judged on, and information about board certification, which I'm already studying for. I scrawl some notes in the margins of the pages.

"Seagull! Sara Seagull!" Davis yells my name (or her own slaughtered version of it, anyway), then taps me.

"Here!" I say, like she's going through the class roster.

Davis raps on her clipboard like it's a clock that's stopped working. "Sara Sehgal, if I could get your rapt attention for a moment."

Apparently, she doesn't like to repeat herself.

It makes me feel like the bad kid in class—which I've never experienced before.

"Sorry, Dr. Davis, it's actually Saira. Like Sigh-ra Say-gull." My words rush out in a whoosh when I'm nervous.

"What?"

"Saira, you know, with an *i*. Sigh-ra. Etymologically, it's of Arabic origin and means 'traveler.' There's also a Hebrew version that means 'princess.' But my parents named me after Saira Banu, the Bollywood starlet from the sixties, known for her roles in classic films like *Junglee* and *Padosan*. There are more than sixteen hundred Sairas in the United States, all of whom spell their names with the aforementioned *i*."

Cho rolls his eyes with a scoff. He's tall and well built, with pitch-black hair and wire-rim glasses. Arora smiles. I wonder if people butcher his name a lot, too.

Davis sighs. "Look, Sara. Sigh-ra. Whatever. I understand that you were late, that your mommy brought your lab coat and your lunch because you forgot them, and I know you don't have your license yet. But—"

"I have my permit," I tell her. "And I'm preparing for the practical exam, too."

This does not seem to impress her.

"What I was going to say, Sehgal, before I was so rudely interrupted, is that I really don't care for excuses."

"Neither do I, Dr. Davis. And I'm not making them. But you know how it is, learning to drive."

She frowns.

"Or not," I add.

"In any case, punctuality is a vital facet to your employment here at Princeton Presbyterian. I expect you to be on time, and fully committed while you're here." She looks haughtily at the three of us and clicks the clipboard again. "Understand that this will be trial by fire—you will be assigned a supervised caseload and will be expected to pitch in wherever you are needed within the department. All three of you. And by the end of the year, only two of you will remain for residency. If today is any indication, it won't be much of a challenge to eliminate one of you, and while Dr. Arora has the majority say, nothing is finalized here without my approval." She looks pointedly at me. "Now, once you've filled out your paperwork, Dr. Arora will lead you through the different sections here in the children's oncology wing, introduce you to the nurses and staff, and give you your schedules for the coming weeks, which are subject to change."

She turns her attention back to me. Which is unfortunate. "Sehgal, I understand, too, that you're temporarily excused from night rotations due to your . . . circumstances."

"Ah yes, I'm age-challenged."

"If that's what you want to call it."

Mom and I negotiated—as soon as she's comfortable with me driving solo, she'll notify the state to green-light overnights. Who knows when that will be, though. Since I'm still nowhere near getting my license.

Davis marks something down on her paper again. I rarely dislike anything or anyone. It wastes too much energy. For her, maybe, I'm making an exception. She could be a nemesis.

"Cho, Howard. The two of you will be working five sixteen-hour shifts per week." The other interns are trying—and failing—to look unbothered. Davis continues. "While Sehgal, of course, is exempted." She turns to address me. "For the moment, we have you working four ten-hour shifts per week, which is less than half of the usual workload. I guess it helps to have your mommy on the hospital board." Her eyes are narrowed, and she's practically snarling.

Howard and Arora look alarmed. Cho's entertained, like he's binge-watching his favorite TV doc drama.

I try not to suck my teeth. "Yes, that's a state mandate, actually, for this kind of situation—for which I'm the precedent. My mother has—"

"Convinced the state of New Jersey that you only have to do half the work to become a whole doctor?" Davis delivers this casually, while scribbling on her ubiquitous clipboard.

Cho actually cackles, but the others look on in stunned silence.

"My *mother* actually had nothing to do with the decision," I finish, trying to keep my voice steady. Yes, she's a senior attending in pediatrics at Princeton Presbyterian. But that has nothing to do with me landing *my* spot here. Or the special rules the state makes for minors. "New Jersey decided that all on its own."

"And I'm sure she doesn't iron your lab coats, either," Davis says, leaning in close to flick an imaginary piece of lint from my shoulder.

I take a step away and smile. "Nope, we have our coats dry-cleaned at Schroder's on Elm. Organic and lavender-scented. My favorite." I take a deep breath. "In any case, I'm happy to discuss this in private if it's something you'd like to explore further. In fact, I'll stop by later to see if I can get on your calendar." *Maybe we're getting off on the wrong foot. Maybe—*

"That won't be necessary." I swear there's fire flashing in her eyes. "My calendar is pretty full. Some of us are here to actually work, Sehgal."

"*Dr.* Sehgal," I say, smiling so I won't scream.

"Excuse me?"

"I'd prefer you call me Dr. Sehgal, Dr. Davis."

"That's a title you'll have to earn from me, Sehgal," Davis says as she's walking away, waving her clipboard in the air as she goes. "All the interns have to. You've got a year to prove yourself."

Diagnosis: Hate her.
Prognosis: War!

CHAPTER 4

"Don't take it too personally." Arora walks up to me, clipboard in hand—they're all about the clipboards in this hospital. He tucks a pen behind his ear. "She's like that with all of us." He's so tall, I feel like a little kid standing in front of the Empire State Building, staring up at him. "Especially the Indian doctors. There's too many of us or something."

So the rudeness is because I'm brown? "She seems to like you just fine," I say with a frown. "Maybe it's because of Mom. She's always saying that the Sehgal name means something. I always thought she meant in a good way."

Arora laughs, so I decide to work it. "And, given the population density of the state and the regional demographic, we may actually be underrepresented here," I say. "I mean, we're in the thick of Central Jersey. If anything, there should be more brown people. And don't white people, like, love our food? I should be the most popular intern here." I point to the samosa bag.

"Ah yes, the infamous Sehgal samosas," he says. "Classic. So, your mom has told me a little about the root of your passion for pediatric oncology. Very interesting."

"Yeah, I've wanted to do this since I was, like, eight." I can almost see him wanting to roll his eyes. "And I've been working toward it for a long time—just as long as anyone else. But because I'm sixteen, there are rules, like they have for kid actors and stuff. I didn't ask the state to regulate my hours. I mean, I graduated magna cum laude from

Princeton and from UMDNJ. I'm perfectly capable of handling the workload."

"I wouldn't have hired you if I didn't think so, Girl Genius," he says with a smile as I cringe. "You are too modest, but your mom makes up for it. And you're not much older than some of our patients here in pediatric oncology, as you'll soon learn." He leans back against the counter, resting his clipboard on it and scrawling something else on the first page. "You know, back in the day, I was sort of a protégé myself. That's how I got to be the youngest chief resident in New Jersey. I think you'll shatter my record, if things work out well here. Although that Varun Khanna kid might beat you to it. I'll try not to hold that against either of you."

Gah. Why'd he have to bring up Varun Khanna? At nineteen, he's the second-youngest doctor in America. And decidedly my nemesis. Although we've only met twice. I wonder if he was up for this internship. In any case, I'm the one who got it.

Howard walks up to us, carrying two cups of coffee, and for once, I'm not the only one blushing. I swear, Arora stands a full three inches taller all of the sudden. And I can't really blame him. Howard is adorable—light brown skin scattered with freckles, with these teal-blue-tortoiseshell cat's-eye glasses, her pink-streaked brown curls held back by a red polka-dot scarf. A look Taara would appreciate, even if it is a bit too hipster for my sister's posh style. I stare down at my stiff doctorly loafers and frown. I should have gone with the sandals.

"Hey, is this a private conversation?" Howard says in a flirty tone, handing one of the coffees to Arora.

I must look shocked, because she sticks out her hand, suddenly formal. "I'm Sam. Samantha Howard. Your competition." She winks. "Georgetown, magna cum laude. But you knew that already, I'm sure."

"You might be right," I say. "That Kids Caring for Kids program sounds amazing."

"It's now pairing up kids with shared cancer diagnoses from all over the world."

22

I've got my work cut out for me between Howard and Cho, who, as uncharming as he might seem, graduated from Yale, also magna cum laude, with a year in adult oncology already under his belt.

This isn't going to be easy.

"Nice to meet you, Dr. Howard," I say.

"Call me Sam!"

"Okay, Dr. Howard."

"No, really, you're making me feel old."

Well, you are old. She must be, like, almost thirty. I can't say that, though. "I, uh, okay, Dr. Sammy."

"Okay, then." She laughs, and it's this light, tinkling thing, and I kind of feel like I want to be her. "Just so you know: We're gonna have fun this year." Her eyes twinkle as she grins at me. "Think of it as a year-long slumber party. With less sleep and more blood."

Diagnosis: A unicorn in scrubs.
Prognosis: Could be trouble!

We roam through the main oncology floors—all linoleum and antiseptic, the same beige concrete-block walls and hunter-green pleather waiting room chairs that I remember from my mom's office in pediatrics. There's the constant thrum of nurses on rounds, chatting as they wheel patients and do paperwork. Orderlies run cleanup duty, and staff start the next batch of lunch deliveries. Every so often, the background beeping of an alarm goes off and running, the specter of death reminding us why we're all here. I try not let it throw me, the way it used to when I was here for Harper. But my heart races every time it happens anyway.

After some paperwork, Arora gives us a tour of the children's floors. There are three of them (one of which my mom is in charge of—pediatrics, hence the nepotism worries), but in this special program, we'll be focusing on the subspecialization of pediatric oncology, which has a separate wing. It's where the really sick kids are. The cancer kids.

The doors to the ward are stainless steel, cold, and foreboding. And familiar.

"You need a special ID card to enter this area. Access is limited to those working or supporting children in the wing. They're too fragile for us risk exposure," Arora says solemnly. "And it's not a fun space to spend a lot of time in if you don't have to. Unfortunately—or fortunately?—for you all, you do have to."

We walk through the double doors and scrub down immediately, washing our hands and arms before moving forward.

"The children in this ward are facing forms of cancer including melanoma, leukemia, sarcomas, and carcinomas, and especially localized disease, which we are seeing a significant rise in recently," Arora says, drying his hands. Howard hangs on every word, while Cho makes frantic notes on his phone, and I hold my breath, bracing for memories of Harper. "The hospital is one of the premier centers on the East Coast for treatment of such pediatric ailments, with a forty-bed in-patient facility and an eighty-person out-patient capability. We meet state and federal requirements for the utmost in pediatric care, and some of our doctors have even been awarded the Pediatric Oncology Award by the American Society of Clinical Oncology. Make no mistake, being here is a privilege. Understand, too, that the competition here makes this already stressful experience all the more so. Remember this: While the people in this room right now are your rivals, they're also the people you will need and learn to rely on."

My heart flutters—palpitations. The oncology wing looks the same as it did when I was six and here visiting Harper during her treatment for acute lymphocytic leukemia.

The walls are painted a bright, cheerful but chipping yellow, with images of balloons and circus animals on murals here and there. The furniture and cabinetry haven't been updated in a decade or more. The clown mural near the nurses' station—with its blue hair and red nose—still scares me a little. Harper used to make me hold her hand and close my eyes when we walked past it. The hair on my arms stands.

Harper was my first-ever diagnosis. She'd fallen off the swing after school at our neighborhood park. Her big purplish bruise wouldn't heal, so I researched it online, then cross-checked it against my mom's medical books. I remember calling her mom and insisting that Harper go to a special doctor called an oncologist. I even spelled it for her.

We pause at the entry desk. I met Dr. Charles, the current chief of staff, for the first time when he was the surgeon supervising Harper's chemo treatments. He called me a little doctor and took me seriously when I brought in information about treatment options. In the end, it didn't matter. Harper died anyway.

Arora continues on, telling us that the wing admits patients as young as three months old and as old as eighteen years old, and has a recovery rate of 90 percent. "That's a number I'm pretty proud of," Arora says, "and one that we will work really hard to maintain and improve."

"We're playing God here," Cho says gleefully. He's slick, self-assured, maybe a touch too excited. Too thirsty, and always back for refills. "Controlling life and death." It's almost like he can feel the thrum of power, the way he's drumming on the counter. "Each new technology brings us that much closer to giving every kid—even the worst off—a fighting chance at survival."

"That's right, Dr. Cho," Arora says carefully, like Cho might explode. "The technology is critical. But one of the biggest and best tools in our medical arsenal is hope."

"We have the power to shape things and shift things," Howard adds, leaning in close to Arora. "A small sliver of light can lead the way. Our patients need our optimism."

I thought that, too, once. That hope would be enough. But now all I can really see is Harper's face in my head. It takes hard science, the work of medicine, to really give a patient any chance at all. I ponder opening my mouth to tell them so, but Arora steps forward then, all business again.

"Okay, time for us to get your system access sorted," he says, taking a pointed step away from Howard. "You'll get your rotation schedules this afternoon." He heads into the administrative office, leaving us behind to worry in his wake. Well, I'm worried anyway.

And like he can sense it, Cho pounces. "So you're the genius, huh?" Cho asks, a weird smirk snaking across his face. "Can I offer you some advice?"

I frown at him. Cho-splaining is clearly going to be a thing. Howard grins. She's clearly reading my mind.

"Do your best to stay on Davis's good side. Oh, too late! Seriously," Cho says, and in my head he's hopping up and down like a leprechaun in a suit and tie, full of malicious glee. "She's notoriously difficult. And we all know why you're here—especially her. So I don't think it will take much for them to cut you."

"And why do you think I'm here?" I ask. "Because I thought it was the advanced medical degree I earned. You know, like the one you have."

"Your 'degree'"—oh my gods, he literally air-quotes the word "degree"—"might as well be in finger painting for all the good it'll do you. You won't last a month."

"Go ahead, Cho. Underestimate me. It'll hurt that much worse when I kick your ass." I feel weird about cursing in front of all these adults, but I have to show them I can hold my own.

Cho does that weird smirk thing again. A list of things I'm going to tell Lizzie about him grows in my head. *Like a tumor.* Uh-oh. Med student syndrome is setting in already. My mom warned me that doctors tend to be the worst hypochondriacs.

"Leave the kid alone, Cho," Howard says.

I appreciate her coming to my defense—but "*kid*"?

"Oncology is difficult and exhausting—mentally, physically, and emotionally," he says. "An eidetic memory is hardly going to be enough to get you by. You're clearly too young for it."

"I don't think you're qualified to make that judgment. After all, my UMDNJ degree would state otherwise," I say. "And I agree that my memory won't be enough, so I'll be using my intellect, too. It's

26

not about memorization. You have to be able to *extrapolate* and take decisive action."

"Listen, little girl, you think you get it," he practically spits. "This job takes more than smarts. There's an emotional maturity needed that can't be taught."

"And are you going to be the big bad emotionally mature wolf of this whole thing?" I say. It's like he's reading from some script, eager to play the villain.

"It doesn't take a genius to see that you're gonna crash and burn. After all, Mommy can't save the day every time."

Grrrr! "You leave my mom out of this," I say, seething.

"I would, but then who'd drive you home when playtime's over?" He grins like the wolf baring fangs, gleeful.

Howard flashes us a serious look, one that warns us to stop.

"Guys, this is going to be the hardest and most exciting year of our lives," Howard says. "We're in this together—the three of us. This is work, yes. But we're in the business of healing, of saving lives. And having enough room in your heart to care is a big part of it. That's something that can't be taught. It can be grown, though. That starts with us. We're going to need each other." She side-eyes Cho big-time.

Cho grimaces, and I try not to laugh. Or cry. Like it or not, I'm going to spend my days with him for the next year. We've got to get along. Or kill each other.

Diagnosis: Standard narcissist.
Prognosis: Going down.

CHAPTER 5

The Pizza Hut waiter sets a pie down on the table between me and Lizzie. Ugh, mushrooms. I definitely didn't order mushrooms. I glare at Lizzie, who's oblivious, staring down at her phone, and probably responsible for the offending topping. Yuck.

"Into fungi today, are we?" I say to get her attention while I pick off the endless mushrooms, stacking them up on the side of my plate, leaving the good stuff, like peppers and pepperoni.

Lizzie—Bizzie Bopper, as I've called her for the ten years I've known her—is my best friend, and one of only two non-Desi people here. (The other is my cousin-in-law Lisa, who's Taiwanese and married to Sunil, my cousin twice removed.) But she fits right in, and she's family, pretty much. Which is good, because she's an only child.

One of my little cousins races through the restaurant screaming, "You're it, you're it, you're it!" Sonia Mamiji and the other aunties dig into a pile of garlic bread, ignoring their kids and the chaos they make, but my aunt Anya—Dragon Auntie, we call her—shouts at them to bring the volume down.

I know this scene by heart, I've lived it so many times. Thirty-five of us are crammed at six big tables, piles of cheese and meat congealing in front of us, my mom standing at the center of the room waving her arms like she's conducting an orchestra.

This, in the Sehgal clan, is what you call "a small family party." Meant to celebrate my first official day as a real doctor.

I cringe. The sheer number and noise we bring confuses and

confounds other unsuspecting diners, especially with all our musical chairs–ing around the room.

"Ralphie!" Papa shouts to the manager from two tables away. "Can we get another jalapeño-and-onion pie?"

"And a just pepperoni for the little ones," Anya Auntie yells from across the room, glaring in our direction. She's always glaring. Mom is annoyed that she didn't show up for my big send-off this morning, but I was grateful to not deal with her disapproving grimaces so early in the a.m. "Those kids swiped the whole pie."

The frazzled manager hands off extra napkins and straws, then bustles toward the kitchen. Papa leans over Raju Mamaji's Sprite with some vodka from his water bottle, pretending no one notices, even though the waiters know exactly what's up, since we're here at least once a month.

My dad and uncle slap at each other, laughing, and Raju Mamu takes a big swig of the "water."

Vish slides into the seat across from me and starts inhaling his meatless thick-crust extra-cheese monstrosity.

"Well, hi to you, too," I say.

"Too hungry for hellos." He sets his new digital SLR camera on the table. He's a wannabe photographer and filmmaker, so he never travels without it. Even to Pizza Hut.

"Move over," Taara says as she shoves into the booth, picking up a slice from her thin-crust veggie pie (because she doesn't do grease). "This is pretty much the unhealthiest thing you could ever eat. You'd think a family of doctors would know that."

We all ignore her, not wanting to trigger the usual rant. Taara shoots a glare around the room, clearly wishing she was somewhere else.

"Sit down. Stop running," she barks at our six-year-old little twin cousins Dolly and Molly (yes, rhyming is a thing), five-year-old Shaiyar, and the baby of the group, Pinky, who's two. They're racing around the tables like they're working a giant obstacle course, and the waiters bearing trays of pizza are just another hurdle in their game.

They take one look at Taara, still glaring, and erupt with laughter as one of them crashes into a table or chair.

My mom directs waiters balancing more pies to other tables, and my dadi and all the aunties sit at the outskirts of the group, gossiping as they pick at their pizza, ignoring the chaos, along with their kids.

"Arre, beta, why are you eating Lizzie's supreme?" Mom hovers over my head, waving her arms around, and the thick, musky scent of Shalimar and sweat descends like a storm cloud. The clang of the bangles she wore to match her fancy gold-worked salwar kameez, all for an outing at Pizza Hut, echo loudly over our family's din. "Where is your barbeque chicken pie?"

"Mother, it's okay. I can pull the mushrooms off." I use my arms to cover my plate, blocking her invasion.

"No, I'll get it, and let's order another one. Onions, peppers, chicken?" She looks from me to my sister to Lizzie. "Do you need more garlic bread?"

Nobody ever really needs more garlic bread. But those are apparently the magic words.

"Yes, please," Vish says, not looking up from his phone. "With cheese!"

"Okay, two more pies and two orders of garlic bread. I'm on it." My mom rushes off to go order more death on a plate.

"I can't believe Davis called you out," Lizzie proclaims for the sixtieth time. She's looking at the camera in her phone, inspecting her new look: a lacy shirt and black leather skirt, her blue eyes lined with kohl (Taara gleefully taught her how to do it), her usually stick-straight hair curled in big blond ringlets. "Dr. Davis is going down."

"Well, Saira was late," Vish says, trying to be the voice of reason. He's conflict avoidant.

"She's brown," Taara adds, reaching over for more thick crust. "We're always late."

"Not all of us," Vish says, then turns to me. "Keep a low profile for a minute. Let it blow over. Davis's rec—"

"Is a big part of my grade," I interrupt. "I know. She pissed me off."

"Yeah, but you're a professional now," Vish says. "Gotta get it together. And besides, you just started. Maybe all the doctors in training *do* have to earn the title. Like JV versus varsity, ya know?" He takes another huge chomp of his pizza.

Lizzie flashes the phone at me again. "The white coat pic I posted for you got like two thousand hearts," she says. "And I remembered to tag Princeton Presbyterian!"

"That's great," I say. Lizzie's been doing my social media, and as far as I can tell, she's pretty good at it.

"Yeah, I think it should be a good mix of doctor Saira and teenager Saira," she says. "So we'll get some good shots to post at the Fourth of July party, too." She grins. "Maybe of you and Vish, lovey-dovey."

Vish and I both groan. I am so not going to that party.

"Oh, and once you finally have your license, let's do a shoot of you going car shopping for something super fancy," Lizzie says. "Like an Alfa Romero or something."

I frown.

"I mean, what's the point of living at home and making all this money if you're not gonna blow it on something sexy and slinky?"

Of course that's when my older cousin Arun strides in from outside, shouting to my mother, "You want me to get the cake, Masi?"

"Ohhh!" My mother spins around, frantic. "No! Don't you dare. Nobody touches the cake but me." She glares at my dad. "Especially not your uncle! Remember Taara's twelfth birthday, when he dropped it?"

"You're the one who ordered slippery ice cream cake instead of platters of jalebi, like I told you to!" Papa shouts, then guffaws, as if what he said actually made sense and was funny. Raju Mamaji joins him, apparently already tipsy.

Arun laughs—at them, not with them—then tucks into our booth, squishing Vish in farther. "You bring it up anytime there's cake!"

And there's cake *every* time.

Arun towers over us now. He grew like a foot after his freshman year at Rutgers and is very Ranbir Kapoor these days—all lean brown muscle and close-cropped hair. Lizzie's already batting her eyes from across the table.

"Eat, eat," Mom says, rushing toward the restaurant door. "I will go get it!"

"Arun, did you see that new Deepika movie they just released online?" Lizzie leans forward, showing too much cleavage, eager for his attention.

He turns to Vish, already distracted.

"I mean, she's no Madhuri—" Lizzie continues. She's nothing if not determined.

"I haven't seen it yet. I'll check it out." He jostles Vish's shoulder. "I saw your game last week," he says.

Vish turns beet red.

"You gonna play college lacrosse?" Arun says. "I could put a good word in at Rutgers."

"Dunno yet," Vish says, scooting away, though there's nowhere to go. "I'm thinking California, maybe?" He points to the camera. "Hollywood and everything."

"I wanted to go to Cali, too. Mom wouldn't even let me apply." Taara pouts and shreds the wrapper from her straw. "But Rutgers isn't so bad."

"Actually," I say, "Rutgers is ranked among the top hundred public universities in the nation, and its affiliation with UMDNJ makes it a very logical move for you, Taa—"

A sudden crash silences the restaurant noise. Oh no, the cake? Again? But Mom's not back yet.

It's my little cousin Pinky, who's collapsed onto the dirty linoleum floor. Vomit spills from her little lips, and they're turning from pale pink to blue. Her eyes roll back in her head.

I jump up and rush over to her.

"Pinky!" Anya Auntie shouts, letting out a peal of anguish unlike any sound I've ever heard before.

Pinky's body flops and goes stiff, then starts flopping again. I drop down next to her, my eyes on my smartwatch, counting. My uncle Ramesh scoops her up, trying to hold her quaking body still.

"Turn her on her side," I say.

He doesn't hear me, his body frozen with panic.

"Her side, please. It's important!"

Fluid spills out of Pinky's mouth and onto the floor.

He nods and does it. The shaking doesn't stop.

"Don't touch her," Anya Auntie keeps yelling at me. "And someone call 911!" Anya sobs. "Please! My baby!"

I kneel closer, peering at her to see if she has food in her mouth. *Nothing.*

"Does Pinky have any allergies?" I ask. I try to remember—nuts, soy, shellfish, but Pinky eats anything, as far as I know. Not that Anya lets us see her all that often.

He looks at me with a stunned expression.

"Ramesh Uncle," I say gently this time, trying to calm him down.

"No, no, nothing that we know of," he says, his voice panicked.

I lean in, undoing the ribbon and zipper on Pinky's frilly dress, trying to give her as much breathing room as possible.

Anya Auntie pushes forward again, eager to shove my hands away from Pinky. "The paramedics are coming."

"This could be a reaction to nuts or honey," I say.

Ramesh Uncle is still frozen in his stupor.

"Taara, move the tables and chairs away!" I yell out, and she and Lizzie follow orders for once.

"What's wrong with her?" Ramesh Uncle asks, anxious.

"How about low blood sugar levels? Any known history of that?" I ask. "Has she had a high fever? A recent head injury? Has she been around other sick children?"

He shakes his head.

"Does she have medication? Prior history of seizures?" I already know the answers. She's been perfectly healthy—until now.

Ramesh Uncle shakes his head again.

"Don't touch her. Don't touch her!" Anya Auntie shouts, her voice frantic and full of sobs.

Sirens wail outside.

My mother marches back inside and makes eye contact with me, instantly mirroring the worry she sees on my face. She drops the cake and rushes forward, trying to make her way through the crowd. "What's going on? Saira!"

The cake box is splayed open and thick white frosting is splattered everywhere. She kneels down beside me, looking from me to Ramesh Uncle, and touches Pinky's forehead.

Pinky's shaking stops, just like that, like when the washing machine is done with its cycle.

"She's okay, Mom," I say. "For now."

The paramedics push through.

"Step back, step back, move!" a female paramedic shouts, parting the crowd, kneeling down next to Pinky. "Miss, I need you to back away," she tells me.

I don't move. She tries to push me away—physically. I catch her hands. "Seems like a seizure, first known incidence, clocking at three minutes before resolving itself," I say calmly. "Her lips turned blue before going pink again. I'd take her in and do a full workup and—"

"Step away from her. Now."

"I know what I'm doing," I say.

"Yes," Ramesh Uncle says. "She helped my baby. She saved her."

"You did the right thing by clearing the space and not moving her, but knowing how to manage a seizure doesn't make you a medical profess—"

"I know that. Being a doctor does."

She stares blankly at me, her eyebrows drawing together.

"I am a doctor."

She flinches.

"I'm at Princeton Presbyterian. But you're right. She should definitely have a formal follow-up, and we can run some tests to see what might have caused this. I'd do a pulse ox, maybe a dose of Diastat to be sure. With no prior history, I'm a bit worried. My mom will know more, but right now Pinky needs medical attention."

The paramedic is unimpressed. "Well, we intend to give it to her."

I turn to Ramesh Uncle. "The emergency room will run some tests, but she's awake and alert, which is a good sign. Go with her now. I'll check in at the hospital tomorrow for an update." Anya Auntie pushes forward, trying to shove me away again, but I hold firm. "It's important." I don't dare look away from Anya Auntie's face. I need her to take me seriously, to trust me. "Did you hear me, Anya Auntie? Take her to the hospital. Now."

Ramesh Uncle squeezes my shoulder. Pinky's breathing steadies and she lets out a wail. I take a deep breath, relieved to hear her crying. Anya Auntie leaps forward to hug her baby. Both the paramedic and I pull her back.

"She needs breathing room right now," I tell Anya Auntie. "They'll take her in—you can ride with her. I'll be there first thing in the morning to check on her."

"No, you won't," Anya Auntie says. "I want her to see a *real* doctor." She looks around the room, hoping to pick another fight with my mother.

It stings like a slap to the face. My cheeks burn hot as everyone stares. This isn't the first showdown Anya Auntie and I have had—she's never quite bought into the Girl Genius thing, and never lets me forget it. But this definitely hurts the worst.

"Saira is a real doctor," Taara says. "And either way, Pinky needs medical attention."

"We'll make sure she gets it," Anya Auntie says, her shoulders squared as she hovers between me and the paramedics, who carefully lay a whimpering Pinky on a gurney and buckle her in.

"Thank you," Ramesh Uncle says as they start to follow the paramedics out.

"I'll be there—first thing," I say. "I promise."

"And I will, too," my mom adds.

Ramesh Uncle nods and races out after the stretcher.

The din starts up again, slowly at first. Soon, people are talking, laughing, focused on their families and friends. I'm sort of lost in it, standing in the spot where Pinky collapsed, trying to figure out exactly what just happened.

My dad marches into the room from the bathroom. "What happened?"

"Oh, nothing!" Lizzie says with a grin. "Just Saira, saving lives and taking names."

Papa laughs, murmuring something about cake, but I can't stop thinking about Pinky. Whatever that was, it wasn't good.

TEEN DOCTOR SAVES TODDLER—AT PIZZA HUT

The Girl Genius is at it again. Everyone's favorite real-life *Doogie Howser, M.D.* — teen doctor and Princeton-native Saira Sehgal — was at it again this weekend. Ralphie Higgins, the manager of the Pizza Hut, reports that the 16-year-old Dr. Sehgal, who recently started as an oncology intern at Princeton Presbyterian, performed emergency care on an unidentified 2-year-old who had a seizure on the premises on Thursday evening.

"She cleared the space, checked the child out, and did some medical stuff," Higgins said. "I can't even tell you what she did, really. In the end, the girl was A-OK. It was magic to watch — a child saving a child." The 2-year-old is reported to be in stable condition, though further information about her diagnosis was unavailable.

Sehgal's mother, a prominent local pediatrician, runs her own practice affiliated with Princeton Presbyterian, but Higgins says she wasn't in the room when the incident happened. "The teen was perfectly capable of handling the situation on her own. She's a real doctor!" Higgins said.

Stay tuned for more on Dr. Girl Genius — we're sure she'll be saving more lives around town.

CHAPTER 6

If yesterday felt like the first day of school, today feels like the SATs—when you haven't cracked a book all summer. Not that I *actually* know what that would be like. It seems apt, though.

Today's our first day of rotations, and I made Mom leave the house super early so we don't have a repeat of yesterday.

The oncology floor is bustling, with kitchen staff serving in-patient breakfasts, nurses making their morning rounds, the chemo lab doing the a.m. shift for kids who can still handle going to school.

I swing open the intern lounge door to meet Arora for rotation, and Cho and Howard are already there. One of the bunks is still sleep-rumpled, so at least one of them spent the night. Show-offs.

Before I can make my way over to them, a nurse with a stack of folders steps into my path.

"So you're her, huh?" the nurse says. He's tall, with light brown skin and thick, wavy dark hair, and dressed in scrubs. He gives me a proper once-over, all obvious and dramatic, and it would make me cringe if it didn't make me giggle. He has a stack of files in his hands—for today, I'm presuming—but he doesn't seem ready to hand them over.

"Dr. Saira Sehgal, Girl Genius. Have you trademarked that yet, by the way? I read about you in the *Star Ledger* a couple of years ago. So intriguing. Been following your career ever since," he says, and a bright, toothy grin plays on his face. "I'm José Gonzalez-Martin, your nurse practitioner extraordinaire. I work frequently with Dr. Arora, so I'll be on your rotations, as well as Howard's and Cho's." He frowns at this. "That Cho, such a sweetheart."

"A peach," I reply, and put my hand out for the files. I notice the little flag pin that he wears on the collar of his scrubs. "Dominican Republic?" I ask, and point.

"How dare you?" he says with a mock gasp. "Puerto Rico!"

I laugh.

"I wear it so my Spanish-speaking patients know immediately that they can talk to me."

"Nice."

"Do you still read tarot cards, too?" he asks.

"That was a really old article," I say, and he laughs.

"Yeah, you were, like, twelve then. I guess in teen years that's, like, decades ago. Maybe we can get a deck to play around with on breaks."

"I'll be honest: They wanted something to 'soften' me for the story," I say, wondering why I'm telling this guy the truth. "My best friend Lizzie is still very much a believer, though. She can read your cards." I try not to roll my eyes as I say it. Lizzie's into tarot; Taara's into astrology. Delusions. Pseudoscience.

"Well, maybe I'll manage to convince you. But in the meantime, we've got work to do." He heads toward the computer, and I follow.

We both sit, and he logs on. "Let me introduce you to your first caseload. You'll be doing rotations on eight of Abhi's—that's Dr. Arora, I mean—patients, along with Dr. Cho and Dr. Howard. You'll each be assigned specific cases, but for the purposes of training under this special program, you'll be rotating as a group so you'll all be up-to-date on everyone." A wrinkle creases his forehead as he clicks into a screen. "Get ready; this is going to be fun."

"Oh, I've already been through it—I logged into the online system first thing this morning," I say as my phone buzzes in my pocket. I ignore it. Lizzie's finally up, I guess, and harassing me again about the pool party tonight. No thank you. The last thing I want to do with my Friday night is hang out with a bunch of drunk teenagers. "I prefer the neatness of computerized records. I computerized all of my mom's records when the hospital demanded she be up to code with her electronic medical records system. It was very relaxing."

"Sounds like it," José says. I follow his gaze and realize he's looking at my hands. I raise an eyebrow, and he grins. "Very nice. Neat, clean, no polish. Dull, but super professional. You don't want to give them any more reason to distrust you than they already have. These people are putting their kids' lives into your little hands. I'm glad they're well manicured. Some of the other interns have got to clean up their act." He steals a glance at Cho, who's looking at a stack of files. "Especially their cuticles."

I grin at him. He's definitely got a point. "Have you met my mother yet? She would love you."

"Oh, Dr. Sehgal Senior, you mean? Who do you think she brings all those samosas for? I'm her favorite child, not you." He shuffles through a bunch of papers. "Okay, let's get to it. So you interns have eight new admits assigned to you. Abhi will supervise your work. One day soon, you'll each be doing some of those solo, while he and the others observe and offer second opinions." He leans in close and whispers, "This place is no joke. I've seen interns flee the hospital in tears, never to return. I'm rooting for you. I have been since you were twelve." He glances back at the others again. "Although Cho is fun to look at, when he's not chewing his fingernails." Ouch.

Diagnosis: Charming—and he knows it.
Prognosis: Future hospital bestie.

He runs through the protocol—paperwork first, which is mostly complete, our initial visit and confirmation of diagnosis, prognosis, and strategy. All of which I already know. Then plotting out a chart of treatment and procedures.

"You got this already, but we're also scheduled with tech for a run-through on the EMR system, too. They're obsessed with record-keeping here, especially Davis. I presume you won't have this issue. People have been fired more than once for being sloppy about it."

"Yeah, my mom's told me about the drama with that doctor who got kicked out. She's glad that I can help her with some of that stuff."

"I'd believe it. She keeps saying she wants to recruit you for primary pediatrics—then you can work under her at the hospital and take over her practice."

I frown, and he laughs.

"She didn't mention that to you? Family practice and all."

"She's mentioned it to me a million times, and I've told her a million and one that I'm oncology all the way. Whether she likes it or not."

"Oh, you're in for a mess of trouble with your mama."

"I can hold my own."

He grins. "I can tell." He looks at his phone. He stands and claps twice, startling Howard and Cho. "All right, let's go. You guys are officially on call!"

Right before we go inside, Arora gathers us for a pep talk. It seems to be his MO, and I actually kind of like it. "So today is a big day. You'll be introduced to your current caseload, which is mostly new admits. Unlike some residency programs, our approach is more team-based. I'll observe your interactions the first few weeks, then assign you each specific cases to manage. So while one of you will be assigned as the primary intern on each case, I expect all of you to be informed and up-to-date on each case. Under my supervision, of course."

Howard opens her mouth to say something but thinks better of it. Not Cho, though. "Doesn't that limit our ability to really learn to lead?"

Arora frowns. He's clearly proud of his strategy, and didn't expect questions. "No, quite the opposite. I think it simulates the experience of taking charge and leading while getting active feedback. And sometimes contradictory feedback. I've tentatively assigned each of you a patient, so let's see how it goes this week. Regarding Brendan Jackson: Sam, you're up."

Howard steps in. "Yes, Brendan Jackson, age eight, diagnosed with Stage One non-Hodgkin lymphoma, a type of cancer that develops in the lymph nodes and begins to grow and spread quickly," she says all formal, as Arora watches and takes notes on her performance. The attending already knows the diagnosis—but we're graded on our assessments and delivery, like this is a practical exam. "It was discovered as a small swelling on his abdomen and caught pretty early because it was causing him stomach troubles."

We walk into the first patient room as a group and are greeted warmly by an older black woman with a shock of graying curls. She's sitting in a chair, knitting what looks like a blanket in pinks and reds—a clash my mom would surely appreciate.

"Hello, hello!" she says, standing as we walk in. She marches right up to Howard and shakes her hand, then turns to me and embraces me in a bear hug, even though we're strangers. "I'm Ruby, Brendan's grandmother, and this is my daughter Ericka."

A younger woman who's an echo of her mother—the same dark brown skin and hazel eyes—smiles tightly and nods toward me, worry lines marring her otherwise smooth forehead. She's wearing a suit and her exhaustion like a coat. "Hello," she says, offering a firm, formal handshake.

"You must be Saira," Ms. Ruby says. "Your mama's told us so much about you, ever since you were knee-high."

Before I can speak, Cho shoves himself in the space between the Jacksons and I. "I'm Dr. Cho." Then he points to José. "And that's Nurse Gonzalez-Martin. Nice to meet you, Mrs. Jackson."

"That's Ms.," Ms. Ruby says with a big grin. "I'm quite single. A longtime widow."

Cho blushes, and José laughs.

"Well, Ms. Jackson, let's get started," I say, following toward the bed, where a little boy lies.

"Call me Ruby, dear. And say hello, Brendan."

I wave at Brendan, who looks so small in the oversized hospital bed.

He's got bright brown eyes that almost match his skin color and flashes of his grandma's smile, except a missing tooth or two. He's got a tablet on his lap and earbuds in, which his grandma pulls out casually. Ericka busies herself rearranging the bedsheets and Brendan's things.

"Hello," he says, then pops the earbuds back in, his eyes settling back onto the screen.

"Lovely to meet you," I say. "I understand from the file that Brendan is one of my mom's patients?"

Ericka nods. "And I was, too, before him."

"Yes, dear," Ms. Ruby adds. "We've been going to your mama since my own babies were born. Your mama's like a member of our family."

My phone starts buzzing and I rush to silence it. Cho shoots daggers at me, his eyes tattling. "If I recall correctly, you're the maker of those amazing sweet potato pies we get every Thanksgiving."

Ms. Ruby laughs again, and it's lovely. "That would be me! Ericka's got no baking skills—she's too busy lawyering—but Brendan here's been apprenticing with his grandma, reluctantly."

"Back to business," Ericka interjects. "Dr. Sehgal—your mom, I mean—says we caught it early and that perhaps things are salvageable."

"He was barely eating, and when he did, he couldn't keep anything down, not even water," Ms. Ruby says. "Complained about stomachaches. Poor boy. Got so bad he couldn't go to school for days on end. We spent a lot of time praying on it. And he was already a skinny little thing. Look at him now."

Brendan focuses harder on the screen—I see flashes of an old *Power Rangers* cartoon. He hasn't said more than a word the entire we've been here. I make a mental note to try to chat with him one-on-one.

"Why don't we step outside so we can discuss some options," Howard says, and the group follows her to an office suite.

Ms. Ruby trails behind her, still talking. "Then we found the swelling. It was bad." Ms. Ruby turns to me. "Dear, your mama said you'd take good care of my grandbaby, and I believe her."

"Of course, Ms. Ruby," Howard says, hiding annoyance. "The

main treatment for lymphoma is chemotherapy, which is intense for the patient—and for the family. Because his cancer is spreading quickly, we need to move fast. There will be four phases of treatment: first surgery to remove the growth; then radiation treatment and chemotherapy to eradicate any future growth; and then maintenance. Unfortunately, this may take several years, and it's not an easy process. But we want to make sure we get it all and prevent recurrence."

"Years!" Ms. Ruby says, and her eyes go misty. "My poor boy."

Ericka frowns at her mother but doesn't say anything.

"He's in good hands here," Howard says. "And he has a loving support system at home—which is critical."

"That he does," Ms. Ruby says. She takes my hand, and Howard's. "Thank you for taking this on, my dears. I know it seems like Brendan isn't listening, but he's absorbing everything. It's too much for him." Then she hooks a finger under my chin, lifting it. "And you, sweetheart, you're the spitting image of your mother. With you, he's gonna feel safe."

I nod, and we say our goodbyes—for now. "We'll be back later this afternoon with further information about Brendan's treatment plan," Howard says. "Brendan's got a long road ahead of him. So for now, the best thing he can do is get some rest."

That's definitely what he needs. But as I steal one more glance at Ms. Jackson and her frowning daughter, I sense some familiar mother-daughter tension simmering between them. I don't think this case (or any of them, really) is going to be as straightforward as it seems.

CHAPTER 7

I quickly check my phone as we follow José to the second suite. Lizzie, as suspected. Sending me pictures of her new bathing suit. "Saira, this one is all you, so if you could focus, that would be appreciated," Arora says, and Cho nearly guffaws.

Guiltily, I stash my phone. "Of course, Dr. Arora. Alina Plotkin, age twelve, facing acute leukemia." Which is what Harper had. And died from. I swallow hard, bracing myself.

"Transferred over from Philadelphia Children's because her family is supposed to be back at work and school this week—"

"That's not really relevant, is it?" Cho interrupts, but Arora shakes his head.

"That's the thing about oncology," he says. "You're not only dealing with a sick kid—you're treating the whole family. Because they're all dealing with the fallout of the diagnosis, and that can take a heavy toll on a family. So while technically it's not 'pertinent,' it is something to note."

I continue, my voice steady, as if Cho hadn't interrupted. "Alina's cancer was caught early, thanks to a sunburn issue this summer, and the prognosis is strong," I add. "Suggest straightforward approach of chemotherapy followed. So the standard procedure in a case like Alina's— which we've caught relatively early—is to begin with chemotherapy and see how effective it is before we consider other options, which might include targeted testing and trial-run medications to reduce growth, surgery to remove the affected cells, and in some cases, stem cell transplants, which is a newer methodology we can certainly discuss. Beyond that, worst case, would be radiation."

Arora nods in approval. "All right, let's go."

As we enter the room, Arora stands beside the bed, holding a chart and chatting with an older, balding man. The dad, likely. He smiles at our little group, then takes a small step back, settling into observation mode.

She's small and blond, with cherub cheeks and bright blue eyes—a baby face that makes her look much younger than the twelve years her file claims. She smiles when we walk in, big, white Chiclet teeth fill her tiny mouth. It's a wide, misfit grin that reminds me of Harper's, whose grown-up teeth hadn't even finished coming in before she died.

As we gather around the bed, she sits up straight, careful that her cotton medical gown isn't revealing too much. I remember watching Harper do the same thing when she used to come here.

"Hi there, lovely! I'm Nurse José," José says chirpily, walking right up to the girl and arranging pillows and blankets to give us easy, discreet access to the patient. "You must be Alina."

The girl beams at him, then looks to me, her eyes curious. I probably don't look all that much older, to her at least. Even though she seems like a baby to me.

"And I'm Dr. Cho." He sticks his hand out to the father, who shakes his hand firmly. "I'll be part of the team taking care of your daughter."

Howard introduces herself, too, and then the man turns to me. "And what are you, a candy striper?"

I want to hit him.

"If I am, I'm definitely wearing the wrong outfit," I say with a laugh. But no one quite gets it.

"I'm Dr. Sehgal," I say to the man, whose face wears what I presume is a permanent grimace. "Another intern. I'll be the part of the team handling Alina's care here at Princeton Presbyterian, and the primary resident on her case."

"No, I think there's been a mistake here. We were told that Alina would have the best doctors in the country. I don't think a teenager qualifies." The man's frown deepens.

I make my voice as strong as possible, despite Cho's not-so-discreet sneer and Howard's worried frown. Arora looks concerned, too, but doesn't step forward.

"I assure you, Mr. Plotkin, that your daughter will receive the utmost in care here at Princeton Presbyterian." I put on my warmest smile. "I'm part of a carefully vetted team, and between us, we've got degrees from Princeton, Georgetown, and Yale, and training in some of the finest medical programs nationwide. I graduated top of my class at UMDNJ, in their prestigious seven-year program, completing it in four. I have a photographic memory, which means I can recall every single detail of everything I've ever read or procedure I've seen or done. I've also completed preparatory rotations at private facilities, including Princeton Pediatrics & Adolescent Care, and served on Doctors Without Borders missions for two summers and counting. I'm also dedicated, focused, and well versed in the literature in oncology, as I'm preparing for the boards already. And because I'm closer to your daughter's age, I promise you, I understand what she's going through."

"Listen, kid, you may have the MD or whatever, but this my child's life on the line here," Mr. Plotkin says, still frowning. "We need the best. That means experience."

"Yes, I understand. But I have experience. In fact, she reminds me a lot of my own best friend, who had cancer and was treated at this very hospital." I pause for a second and swallow hard. Part of me wants to pull out that tattered photo of Harper from its spot in my back pocket. But that might cause tears: "I helped diagnose her."

José pumps his fist in the air on the other side of the bed, and Alina looks up at me, her smile hopeful. Harper's face flashes in my head.

"I'd really like it if you could stay," Alina says, soft but determined. "Actually, if all of you could stay. I want to hear my options. I want to be involved. Okay, Dad?"

Her father looks startled but nods.

I smile at Alina and then turn to the father. "I looked at your daughter's chart and came prepared to discuss some new and advanced strategies that may be highly feasible and successful in a case like Alina's," I continue, my voice strong and steady. "However, I understand if you're not comfortable with me here. If you'd like me off the case, I can step outside right now."

The man touches his forehead. "No, I think we should proceed. Alina's right—she needs someone who knows what she's dealing with. And your background is certainly impressive. For a teenager." He smiles at me in apology.

"Thank you, sir." I smile back. "Let's get started, then."

As Cho and Howard make notes at the monitor, I walk over to Alina's bedside. She's barely five feet tall, and her pale white skin is marked with blue bruises. She's got a broad forehead like her father's, and round cheeks that will probably slim down into high cheekbones with age.

"How are you feeling, Alina?" I ask her.

She shrugs. "I've been tired, and I kind of want to go back to school. It gets boring being in the hospital after a while."

"Have you been in pain?" I ask. "Could you tell me how much, on a scale of one to ten?"

"Define the scale—like a banged-up knee is one, and having your tonsils out is ten?"

"Have you had tonsillitis?" I ask her.

She nods. "When I was little—like eight. It was the worst. I had, like, a sore throat for a whole month. Then I got to eat lots of ice cream."

I grin at her. "Well, there's this really awesome ice cream place called Thomas Sweet's down the street from me—maybe we can get you a pint when you're feeling better."

"Maybe," she asks, a thoughtful expression on her face. "What's your favorite flavor?"

"Peach in the summertime and candy cane in the winter. What's yours?"

"Strawberry cheesecake."

"I'll make a note of that on your chart," Howard says, and we both laugh.

Cho clears his throat. "Can we get on with it?"

"Yes, I'd like to hear about the treatment options," Alina's father says, his voice stern and rough, like my old organic chem professor's.

"Yes, sir," I say, then cringe at my use of the word "sir." "I mean, of course. So the standard procedure in a case like Alina's—which we've caught relatively early—is to begin with chemotherapy and see how effective it is before we consider other options, like surgery or radiation."

"Yes, well, hopefully it won't get to that," Alina's dad says with a laugh that slowly turns into a cough. Then all his words come out in a rush. "We've got other kids at home—that's why my wife's not here, actually—eight-year-old twins, and we thought it best not to expose them to all this, if we can. We'll be trading off, you see, and I want to make sure Alina is comfortable, and that, despite her being here, treatment remains as painless and manageable as possible. Her bubbe may come down from Brooklyn to help, if that's necessary, as her mother can't lose any more time from work. We know the prognosis is good—at least that's what they said in Philadelphia. We've never dealt with anything like this before, and hopefully won't again."

"That is the hope," I say flatly. The prognosis is strong, straight-forward. But the flash of Harper's grin on Alina's face reminds me that it's not always so easy. We're not allowed to say that, even though it pinches me to keep the bright white of the lie going. "And of course we'll do the absolute best we can. One other thing we can explore—"

Arora steps forward at exactly that moment—the wrong moment—and says, "All right, guys, let's wrap it up." Like it's my first day scooping ice cream or something.

"Yes," I reply. "We're about ready to begin Alina's blood work, aren't we, Dr. Cho?"

Cho waves toward José, who brings over a fresh, sterilized workup kit to get things moving. Howard hovers too close.

My phone vibrates again, wrecking Cho's concentration, and he glares at me as I fumble to silence it. Once it's quiet, he turns his attention back to Alina and the needle.

Nurse José sets up the blood tubes, and prepares the needle and IV, Cho watching the intake as I watch the monitors to make sure Alina's doing okay.

"Okay, Alina, I know you're an old pro at this by now. Dr. Cho's going to start the blood work. You can hold my hand while he does it, if you'd like," I say, offering it. "I always prefer that when I'm getting shots."

She takes my hand and smiles. "Okay," she says. "Thanks."

"So," I say, distracting her, distracting myself. "Strawberry cheesecake, huh? In ice cream? I've never had it."

"I've always stuck to plain old chocolate," Howard adds. "Maybe with rainbow sprinkles. You've got a sophisticated palate, kid."

"Yeah, I want to be a chef when I'm older," Alina says, "so I like to try all different kinds of food. When I can keep it down. Strawberry cheesecake is amazing, and they've also got blueberry in season."

"Have you ever had lychee?" I ask. "I had it at this fancy place in DC on one of my Hopkins trips and it was like this slow-churned fruit and cream—"

Cho clears his throat, pulling the needle and closing the tubes. "Well, that was easy, wasn't it, Alina?" Cho says, swiftly labeling each one with Alina's details. "We're all done."

"You're a pro," I tell Alina. "We'll get this blood work done and then figure out a plan. In the meantime, I'm going to monitor how you're doing on the current schedule of meds. Anything bothering you right now?"

"The blue ones make me nauseous, I think," she says in a voice that's tentative, unsure she's allowed to complain. "The yellows were better. The other doctor said they weren't strong enough."

"Unfortunately, there's not much to be done about that," Cho starts in an unforgiving voice. "The pills you're on were carefully calibrated to ensure that you'd be getting the right combination of medications to address the growth—"

"Actually, Dr. Cho," I cut him off, "can I talk to you for a minute?" I gesture to the hallway. I wave him out of the room, taking Alina's chart with me, doing math in my head.

Howard steps out and looks at me, incredulous.

"We may be able to fix that." I show them the chart. "We could swap back, try a different antiemetic, increase liquids and simple sugars to get the same impact without as many side effects."

"No way," Cho insists. "She needs the anti-nausea meds to get through it. Without it, she would—" I know what he's thinking. This one should be simple, but it's the complications that could cause trouble.

Howard interrupts. "No, Saira's right. That could totally work."

"It's too big a risk," Cho says, looking from me to Howard and back again. "She's already deteriorating. You're putting her life on the line."

"It's a risk worth taking," Howard says, her voice low. "And she'll be more comfortable in the meantime."

Cho shrugs. "The insurance is going to balk. You watch. You can talk to Arora, but keep me out of it." He glares as he's heading back into the patient room. I can almost hear him say, *It's your funeral.*

Back in the room, José's wrapping up blood work, and Cho's whispering with Arora. He shoots a little sneer my way.

But I won't give him the satisfaction of a response.

"We'll be back this afternoon to check on you, okay?" I tell Alina. She nods.

"And I might not be able to score you ice cream yet, but I can definitely get you some real strawberries tomorrow."

She grins. "Cool."

José tucks her in, and her dad waves ever so slightly at me as we walk out.

Two down. Six to go.

Nurse José gives me a thumbs-up and runs ahead. Cho does this weird, curt nod before we move on to the next.

I can hear my aunt before I see her. She's in the room two doors down, and shouting. As expected.

Arora is already in there, and facing the wrath of Dragon Auntie.

"I don't want her on the case. Period." Anya Auntie glares at us— well, at me—as we walk into the room. "She's too young, too inexperienced, and too bold. I told you. Get her out."

The others are startled—and Cho looks positively gleeful. He can't stop the grin from taking over his face.

Arora is still hoping for reason to prevail. "Ms. Sharma, I understand. But as Dr. Sehgal bore witness when the incident occurred, it makes sense to have her present, at least for now, as we work toward a firm diagnosis. She *is* a doctor, after all."

My neck burns and I'm sure my cheeks are a livid red, but I don't let my expression betray my humiliation.

"A sixteen-year-old should not be a doctor!" Dragon Auntie shouts. "I don't care what the state says."

How my cousin Pinky can sleep through all of this, I'll never know. She's slumped on the exam table, drool pooling, her chest rising with mild snores. I want to pick her up, cuddle her, and whisk her away from all of the pain she's about to endure—her ranty, ridiculous mom the least of it.

Or maybe I'm being too harsh. After all, her kid is sick. But Anya Auntie's been my nemesis ever since I yelled at her at a family party for pinching my cheeks every time I saw her as a kid—"so cute, so chubby"—so rude! She didn't like being called out on her bad behavior, and it blew up into this really messy thing about "respecting your elders." I was fourteen, though. So don't touch my face.

"Ms. Sharma, protocol dictates that Dr. Sehgal be here, at least for the intake portion of Priyanka's evaluation," Arora says. "Then we can decide—"

"I've already decided. I don't want her on the case."

My mom pokes her head into the room, her white coat wrinkled and stained with I don't want to know what, her mouth trying to smile instead of pucker. "Anya, I thought I heard you. Ramesh told me you were here with Pinky." My mom rushes over to the baby, lifting her for a cuddle even though she's still asleep. She sits, tucking the child into her lap like the pro she is—at mothering and at doctoring. "What's happening? Do we have a diagnosis yet?"

"We're getting started," Arora says, his voice ever patient. He's so not cut out to tackle dragons and lions. "It seems Ms. Sharma would prefer that Dr. Sehgal, Junior that is, be taken off the case."

"Hanji, then that is what needs to happen," my mother says, decisive.

"Mom!" I say. "I have information that could be pertinent—critical—to the diagnosis."

"So list that information in detail on the chart and go."

"Mother." I clear my throat. "Dr. Sehgal, I have just as much right as Drs. Cho and Howard to be present for this evaluation. I have the same medical qualifications and am an intern in the same program. And, in fact, I have more right—even need—to be here, if you consider that I was present for the actual incident."

"You don't have the same rights because the patient's guardian hasn't granted them to you," my mother says tersely. "Case closed."

"But—"

"Dr. Sehgal, I'm telling you as a member of the board at Princeton Presbyterian—and your mother—that you must abide by the patient's wishes. And in this case, the patient is a minor, so her parents' wishes." She looks at Arora scoldingly, and Dragon Auntie nods vigorously. But what pinches the most is Cho silently laughing behind us. "You know that."

"She's right." Arora shrugs, defeated. He turns to me. "I can't override the patient's request—even if I do think it's in her best interest to keep you on the case. Dr. Sehgal, will you note your findings on the file, per the consulting physician here's recommendations?" Then he nods toward the door. "And in the meantime," he says, "step outside."

I do my best not to suck my teeth at Arora or my mother, and head toward the door, feeling the heat of Dragon Auntie's glare burn my cheeks as I walk out.

Patient Name: Priyanka "Pinky" Sharma
DOB: December 22, 2015
DIAGNOSIS: Aggressive high-grade medulloblastoma
PROGNOSIS: 20 percent success rate with surgical
treatment

Priyanka "Pinky" Sharma, 2. Of Indian descent, Punjabi. Family history of heart disease and diabetes, late onset manifestations. Child experienced a grand mal seizure at a local restaurant and was attended by oncology intern Saira Sehgal, who requested a follow-up visit. Emergency admitted the patient and ran a battery of tests, including blood work, a pulse ox, CAT scan, and an MRI, which revealed a coin-sized tumor. Dr. Abhishek Arora and team diagnosed this as an acute growth occurring, aggressive high-grade medulloblastoma in the rear cerebellum region.

Dr. Arora suggests transfer to a facility with comprehensive molecular profiling options before an invasive procedure is planned.

CHAPTER 8

We're in the intern lounge, wrapping up patient paperwork, and I can feel Cho itching to pat me on the head every time I get an answer right, like a kitten. But I'm not a kitten. I'm a lion. And I'm about to roar.

"And why would you use this methodology?" Cho says, quizzing me on the patient chart we're going over like a tutor instead of my peer, my equal.

"Cho, you don't have to quiz me. We both graduated med school, remember?"

"What, so no one's allowed to question the great Girl Genius? Guess you only take orders from Mommy."

That hits—my mother's interference earlier still stings like that jellyfish that got me when I was ten.

"Better than sucking up to Davis and company twenty-four-seven!" I say. "But I guess that's part of the curriculum at Yale."

José dramatically takes a seat and makes popcorn-eating motions.

Cho peers down at me, grinning. "If you were actually smart, you'd realize that you should be doing some sucking up, too."

Howard shimmies her way into the little space between us, putting a hand on each of our foreheads and pushing back. "All right, all right," she says. "Break it up." She's actually an inch or two taller than Cho, so she stares him straight in the face. "You, pick on someone your own size." Then she turns to me. "And you, go take a break."

José busts out laughing. "I haven't seen drama this good since *Grey's*

Anatomy," he says. "Which is the reason I became a nurse. I thought there'd be more hot docs."

Cho frowns, not sure whether to be pleased or insulted. Then remembers his mission: "Yeah, Saira. Time for a time-out!"

I storm off without another word. I do need a break. A long one. That's the thing about being an intern: You're on. The whole time. For, like, ten hours straight. Well, actually, ten hours for me. Sixteen for the others. I don't know how the other interns hack it. Because after eight patients in two hours, I'm exhausted.

"I'll bring you back a double espresso," I say to Howard, and grab my bag. I can feel my phone vibrating in it. I'm not ready to face Lizzie and her mounting demands about evening plans. I want to crawl into bed and sleep through the weekend.

Maybe I underestimated how much work this is going to be. My mom makes it look so easy—she does rotations, runs a private practice, and manages a household with three kids, a dog, a demanding mother-in-law, and a very messy husband. All without saying so much as *oof.* Maybe that's why she needs twelve cups of chai a day. I could use one myself now. My mom has a secret stash of actual chai in her office, along with a contraband hot plate, and I think about swiping some, but I'm just too mad. She's being a total daayan lately. (Dadi would roast me for calling my mom a witch, even though she would, too, if she could get away with it.)

I text Lizzie. She's only got a few weeks left before her summer acting camp. Maybe I should ask her to meet me for pancakes at the diner down the street. But I know I won't actually have time to sit and eat. Maybe I'll go grab a real coffee, though. Their hazelnut brûlée is amazing.

I head to the lockers and I stash my coat and scrubs, changing into jeans and Taara's super-soft vintage Nirvana shirt, which she doesn't know I stole from her closet. Then I start toward the back elevators so none of the other staff will spot me.

I drum my fingers against my legs, trying not to look to the left at that darkened hallway. The one that's been beckoning. But it's inevitable. Harper's face pops into my head.

The elevator dings and opens, but my feet have other plans. I walk down to the far end of the hall, past the patient rooms, away from the nurses' stations. Away from the administrative offices, in a wing only the janitors really ever visit. Or at least that's how it was back then.

Harsh, flickering lights flash overhead. The eerie, dark quiet of the hall sends a shiver through me.

This is the one place I've managed to avoid so far in the week I've worked here.

The place where Harper and I hung out the most when she was sick.

I stand in front of the door for a minute—dull gray steel, a square window makes up the top half, covered over with privacy paper that's thinned with age and holes. A small sign calls it the patient lounge, and a keypad sits untouched above the handle. I punch in the numbers from memory—one-six-two-six—not expecting the door to open.

But it does.

I hesitate for a minute, then shake it off, trying to laugh. It's just a room. A dusty, old, underused room. A place to take a real break.

I step through and pull the door closed behind me. It's like walking into the past, like maybe some part of Harper is still here. Or some part of eight-year-old me.

My heart is racing—sinus tachycardia, I self-diagnose, an accelerated beat due to emotional distress or excitement. I take a few deep breaths and focus, the way Mom taught me, and wonder if I should maybe step right back out that door. Clearly, my body's telling me I'm not ready for this.

But my mind floods with memories of the hours Harper and I spent here, playing endless rounds of Monopoly with our earrings as the game pieces, since the original ones were all missing, or watching old movies—actual video tapes—like *Anne of Green Gables* or *The NeverEnding Story* on the VCR that was never upgraded. The deep breaths don't help at all.

I flip on the light switch, and the brightening reveals a pretty non-descript room, beige, concrete-block walls, a couple of rows of waiting room–style chairs, a sofa that's seen better days, an ancient big box TV on a black console table, and, in one corner, a little kitchenette with a sink, a coffee maker, and small fridge, brown and noisy, like the ones they had in the studio I shared with my dad during my first summer at the Hopkins gifted program. There's the bulletin board near the window, still filled with photos of patients, some healed and moved on, others dead and mourned. Right there in the corner is the one we stapled up there together taken just before she died. Her parents kept in touch for a while after they moved away, but I haven't heard from them in years, and I can't find them online. Mom says they split up. The thought hurts my heart.

I touch the image, thick with age and dust, and uncover a memory of me and Harper, age eight, bright-eyed and flashing our gap-toothed grins.

Before she lost her hair, and her will.

Before I lost her.

It's all exactly the same, like we were here yesterday.

A part of me is relieved, and a part of me is disappointed.

I sneeze. Once, twice, three times. A fine dust coats pretty much everything in the room, and as I head toward the window to open the shades, I can see it come to life, particles twirling in the sun like they're doing a little dance. Harper and I used to spin in the sunlight here, my dresses and her little-kid robe flaring around us, the beams hitting our faces. She missed the sunshine when they stopped letting her leave the hospital.

I twirl a few times, and then I'm sneezing again, one, two, three, an endless fit of them, giving way to tears.

They've just started streaming when I hear the word.

"Gesundheit."

"What?" I freeze. In the glare of the light, I can just make out the shadow of a figure at the door.

"Salud?" A male voice, amused.

"I'm sorry?"

"It means bless you. They both do."

The owner of the voice steps forward out of the shadows and peers at me, and I wipe at my face, trying to erase the tears.

"Or maybe I should say jai mata di? Or waheguru? You okay?"

It's him. Cutie McFreckles. The guy from the elevator.

I take a step back, right into the wall and the window. "Yeah, I uh—how did you know that?" My left hand automatically grasps the silver kara that circles my right wrist. "Waheguru" is what the Sikh side of my family says when I sneeze. Even Taara and I don't use it very often.

"One of my lacrosse buddies, Tarun, is Indian. His family says it whenever I sneeze. Which is a lot. Like you." He eyes me. "Hey, you're that girl. From the other day. In the hall. I saw you with your mother. She's hovery. Like mine." He steps forward, offering me his hand to shake, like we're grown-ups. "I'm Lincoln. Link Rad. You're the new kid." His eyes travel to the image I was just looking at. The one of little me and Harper. "Maybe not so new?"

I take his hand. It's cool and strong. A ladder of bruises climbs his arm. When I look up, he's smiling, and there's a tiny gap between his front two teeth.

Little bursts of energy fire through me like static electricity, zinging all the way to my toes. The small hairs on the back of my neck stand straight and tall, and I pull my hand away too quickly.

His hand travels toward my face, then into my hair.

I step back.

"I'm not contagious. But you've got this"—he flashes me two fingers coated with dust—"in your hair. That explains the sneezing." One half of his mouth lifts into a practiced smirk.

This is the first time I can really get a good long look at him. He's like someone right out of Lizzie's favorite fansite: lean and tall, with floppy black hair that falls into hazel eyes that are sunlight bright against pale skin. Actually, it's a little orangey. He should be checked for jaundice, maybe? He's wearing a Beatles T-shirt, skater shorts, and kicks. His face is all planes and angles, long forehead, sharp cheekbones. And then there's that tiny gap between his two front teeth. The little flaw in an otherwise perfectly straight, white, toothpaste ad–worthy smile. The thing that makes him human. Well, that, and the cancer, of course, which has made itself known with small bruises along his jawline.

He's got a guitar case slung over his left shoulder, which is the thing that usually seals the deal, right? I should be swooning—if I did things like that. Or maybe not. He seems like trouble.

Diagnosis: Heartbreaker.
Prognosis: I'm in trouble now.

I stare so long, he finally says, "What's the diagnosis? Are we both doomed?"

I almost bite my tongue—literally. It's like he's in my head.

Then he adds: "My cancer is probably worse than yours."

Oh. He thinks I'm a patient, too.

And I'm starting to feel like one. My skin is clammy and my palms are slick with sweat. I'm definitely having some kind of reaction. Chemical, or maybe allergic. I sniff. The cologne maybe—it's fresh but spicy, cinnamon and oranges. I take an involuntary step closer, then back, bumping into a nearby table. "Uh, I—"

He mistakes my incoherence for emotional trauma. "Oh, too soon. Can't deal. That's okay." Then, "You want some coffee?"

"There's coffee?"

"Don't get too excited. It's not very good. And powdered creamer. We keep a secret stash, along with other contraband—cookies, Twix, beef jerky. The Korean BBQ stuff is mine, but it hardly tastes like the real deal. What're you gonna do? Anyway, you gotta replace what you take. And don't eat any of the cake donuts. Tommy's very possessive."

He puts the case down and rummages through one of the cabinets near the windows. "So were you just admitted? Haven't seen you."

"N-no," I stammer. What is wrong with me?

He frowns for a second and looks me over. "Oh, a readmit, huh? You look like you're holding up pretty well."

"So do you," I say. I don't know why I don't correct him. Only that I'm not ready to reveal any truths.

"Yup. Prognosis: seventy-eight percent. Decent odds. Especially for take two. Metastatic leukemia, first recurrence," he says, pulling out two strips of beef jerky and standing. He offers one to me. I shake my head. "Take two, essentially. If they're talking marrow—which is likely next—I'm screwed."

When I raise an eyebrow, he explains: "My mom's Korean, and my dad's Scottish and Dutch. A rare mix for sure." He shrugs. "Not much to choose from, gotta be hopeful. What did you say your name was?"

"I didn't. Saira. Like Sara, with an extra *i*. Sigh-ra."

He grins. "That's a great name." He leans down again and pulls out a bag of mini chocolates. "Twix? Nah, I peg you as a Kit Kat girl." He offers it again, and this time I take it, our hands grazing for a second too long. And then I start rambling.

"My parents were obsessed with this sixties Bollywood star named Saira Banu. My sister is named Taara, which actually means 'star,' and she could be one. I mean, she's gorgeous." I'm babbling now, talking about her first year at Rutgers and missing her and I don't know what else.

"That's cool. I'm not going to college. When I bust out of here, I'm going to audition for *Rock Star Boot Camp*. Have you been watching the latest season?"

I shake my head. I haven't seen the latest season of anything, except for maybe Dadima's new favorite Hindi soap opera. It makes for soothing background noise.

"There's not a lot of real talent out there. I've been working on a new piece. Want to hear it?" he says, gesturing to the guitar case. "Unless you've got an appointment? I need to get more practice in front of strangers."

I should find his confidence annoying and overbearing, but he kind of reminds me of myself, and it doesn't feel forced or fake like Cho. Or maybe it's the way his eyes are taking me in, intent, looking for telltale signs of cancer, lurking, looming, like a shark in placid waters. I've seen people do it again and again—I did it endlessly myself this morning. I should tell him now, because the chances are almost 100 percent that he'll end up on one of my rotations this week.

But I can't.

I don't want to.

He's pretty much the only person who's talked to me like a normal person in years. Because he doesn't know me as "Girl Genius." To him, I'm just a girl. And maybe a patient.

"Yeah, I've gotta go in, like, five." A weird high pitch elevates my voice, and heat climbs up my neck and cheeks. What's wrong with me? "Maybe another time?" Then I add, "I heard this is the place to be when you're not hooked up to machines."

My phone vibrates. And he looks at me like, *You gonna get that?*

I press the buzzer to shut it up without checking. I know it's Lizzie again, yelling at me for ignoring her texts, but I want to keep talking to him. "You in here a lot?" Maybe this place has changed after all, if the kids are actually using it.

"Yeah, I've been hiding out in here between sessions. I'm outpatient right now, I think they're going to readmit me as in-patient in a minute," he says, looking at his arms, touching some of the bruises. "It'll get worse before it gets better. But it will get better."

His nostrils flare, pink around the edges, and I can tell he's due for a nosebleed in a second, so I grab a tissue from my bag and hand it to him.

"Oh, thanks." He dabs at his nose, completely unselfconscious. "Guess you're used to that, too, huh?"

My phone buzzes again. "Something like that," I say. "Anyway, gotta run. Someone's waiting for me." Did that sound weird? "Nice meeting you, Link."

"You too, Saira with an *i*," he says, and grins.

I walk super carefully toward the door, waving as I step out of it. Once it's closed, I lean against it, and try to calm myself down. My pulse is still racing, there's a trickle of sweat settling into the small of my back; my cheeks and neck are flushed and warm to the touch. Why am I so worked up? Must be the dust. Or a potential cologne allergy. I should do an allergy panel. Or something.

My phone buzzes again. I can't answer. I can't do anything at all, really. I hear him behind the door, muffled sounds slipping through and then the low, slow strum of a guitar. It's a gentle thrum, his voice quiet above it, hushed, like a lullaby, even though I can't quite make out the words. The rhythm of my heart mellows to the music, and I take a deep breath, then another, letting the sound settle deep into my muscles, easing my body in a way it hasn't in days, months, years. Exhaustion washes over me, making me want to slip out of this body entirely, the way Dadi always says old souls can, and back into that room. Just to listen.

I can't believe myself. I'm totally my mother's daughter, eavesdropping on a clearly private moment. And not able to walk away.

I will myself away from the door, catching my reflection as I'm about to step away. There's dust in my hair, and my eyebrows are still too much for my small face, and the T-shirt looks old and tattered instead of vintage cool, like it would on Taara. My jeans have a ketchup stain—or is it blood?—faded and pink, on the left thigh, and my sneakers are so close to death that Mom would command me to bury them already if she saw them. But maybe she's right. Maybe it's time for an upgrade. Of all of me.

Quietly, I tiptoe away. I have to get to a mirror. Or a shower. Or call my sister. Yes, Taara. She'll help me figure this all out. Stat.

Saira: Hey.

Saira: Hey, you there?

Saira: I called you. Like three times.

Friday, June 29, 1:48 p.m.

Taara: Can't talk. Studying for biochem midterm.

Saira: Oh, need help?

Taara: I have a study buddy!

Saira: Something weird happened.

Friday, June 29, 2:55 p.m.

Taara: Oh yeah?

Saira: I met this guy. A patient. And I was like all sweaty and nauseous.

Saira: And frantic.

Saira: Hello?

Taara: A patient? Isn't that, like, against the rules? And what about Vish?

Saira: I'm not gonna do anything. It was weird. Different.

Friday, June 29, 3:04 p.m.

Taara: Aw, my little Saira's finally hitting puberty!

Saira: Shut up!

Taara:

Taara: Look what I made!

Saira: Sure you don't need my biochem notes?

Friday, June 29, 4:20 p.m.

Taara: Nope!

CHAPTER 9

It's nearly seven p.m., and I've been waiting for forty minutes. Almost the end of my second week in, and this has become the usual. Mom's late. Of course. She's been texting me, but I'm still mad, and deliberating calling a car service. I'm sick of sitting in the intern lounge, where Cho is hovering, itching for another argument, so I stash my doctorly stuff in my locker and head downstairs for some fresh air. I head to the main hall elevator bank, and there he is.

Link.

Waiting by the elevators, humming to himself with his headphones on, his guitar slung over his shoulder.

I haven't seen him since that day in the lounge, almost a week ago. And, I'll admit, I haven't stopped thinking about him since.

I freeze, wondering if I should wait and let him get on and avoid making a fool of myself again. But something makes me take one step and then another and then another until I'm standing next to him, absolutely quiet, staring at the ratty Chucks on my feet. Hoping he'll notice I'm standing there, but not quite ready to, like, you know, say something.

Like maybe: *So what kind of guitar is that?*

Or: *Fancy meeting you again. You come here often?*

Or even: *Man, these are the slowest elevators known to humankind.*

Or: *What med sked are you on for the recurrence? You think it might help if they ramp up the methotrexate?*

Okay, maybe not that.

Instead I drop my backpack, and my tablet and a copy of *Living with Childhood Cancer: A Practical Guide to Helping Families Cope* fall out of it and onto the floor. Oops.

"Hey!" he says, slipping his headphones down to his shoulders. "How's it going?"

I stumble as I reach to pick up my bag, and when he does the same, we bonk heads.

"Ouch," we both say at the same time. "Sorry," we add, rubbing our heads. Then he laughs, and so do I.

I grab my bag and my tablet, and he picks up the book, peering at it curiously before he hands it back to me. "They're still making the newbies read this, huh?" he says with a grin, that dimple denting his cheek again. "You'd think someone would have written something new by now."

"Someone should." I shrug, then add: "I guess it's considered a classic."

"Yeah." He looks down at his shoes, frowning suddenly. "I think they're gonna readmit me." Then he looks up and smiles. "I'm about to live it up while I can."

"Oh yeah?" I say, and look at my smartwatch. Force of habit. "Wild weekend plans?"

He grins. "Yeah. You?"

"Pj's and old Bollywood films with my dad." I grin back. "I like to party."

"I love Bollywood movies! I've watched a few online. You'll have to rec some. What's your favorite?"

"Two: *Bobby*, which is, like, way, way old. And *Dilwale Dulhania Le Jayenge*. Which is, like, slightly less old."

"Shah Rukh Khan, right?"

"Yeah, one of his early ones."

"Maybe we can watch sometime," he says, then bites his lip, so the dent in his cheek digs deeper. "I mean, like, in the lounge or something."

I smile. "Sure. My . . ." I swallow Vish's name before it slips out. "I can get a copy on my laptop."

Howard walks toward the elevator, fresh from a shower in the intern lounge. She's ditched her lab coat and work wear for a slinky summer dress that shows off all her curves. She sashays over and strikes a pose, waiting for me to comment.

"Sizzling," I say, obliging.

Link nods in agreement. "Hot date?"

"Damn straight," she says, laughing.

Then she grabs my arm, leaning in close. "You did great today, by the way."

I turn beet red. "Thanks."

The elevator pings. Link and I step into it, but Howard stays, looking at her phone. "Oh, I forgot my keys." She waves and runs back toward the intern lounge.

"She's new, I think," Link says after hitting the button for the lobby.

"Yup," I say, looking straight ahead. Withholding is not lying, right?

"Seems nice."

"She's amazing," I say, still not looking at him.

"Good. It's important to like your doctors," he says, all Obi-Wan in his wisdom. "You'll be spending a lot of time with them."

I nod. "A lot."

When we get to the lobby, my mom's still not there. But Arora is—and dressed in a suit. It's the first time I've seen him without his lab coat, and he looks very dapper. Do all doctors dress like this off-duty? I definitely missed that memo.

He waves, and my first instinct is to duck, or leap away from Link. "Hey, Link. Saira." Arora grins at me and at Link, and we both wave back awkwardly.

I decide to be busy, focus on my phone, and text my mom.

I can still feel Link watching me, though.

"You need a ride somewhere?" Link says.

"Nah. My mom's driving me home. She's perpetually late."

Link smiles again, the light in his eyes and his smile blinding me. "I remember."

I can feel the heat at my throat, the erythema coloring my cheeks. *Breathe*, I remind myself. "She writes it off as a brown-people thing, but it's signature Rana Sehgal."

"Sehgal. Saira Sehgal. I like it, Saira with an *i*," Link says. He pulls keys from his pocket, then heads toward the door. "See you around."

That's the problem, I realize with a thud in my stomach. He definitely will.

And that will ruin everything.

I wait for an appropriate moment or two to pass, look at my smartwatch again, wave at Arora, and run out the door to wait at the car. Too. Much. Stress.

It's nearly eight by the time we pull up in front of the house, and I'm exhausted. We rode home in silence, which was fine with me. All I want now is my dadima's thari chicken, then a piping hot cup of chai and my pajamas in front of the TV while I binge-watch old Amitabh movies with Papa. (He likes to school me in the classics.) Lizzie's been texting nonstop about yet another pool party at Cat's house, and as I climb out to follow Mom up the front walk, my phone buzzes. I send it to voice mail, then it starts ringing again. Lizzie is relentless.

"Lizzie again?" my mom asks irritatedly as she unlocks the door. "Pick it up already." She bustles inside and I follow as I answer.

"Hello?" The scent of Dadi's thari chicken—thick with cumin and cinnamon—fills my nostrils as we step into the front hall.

"Hey, where are you?" Lizzie's voice is nearly drowned out by the din of the party in the background—bass thumping, poolside shrieks and splashing. I can see the scene in my head, and it looks miserable.

"I just got home." I kick off my shoes, phone glued to one ear, and head to the bathroom to wash my hands. Dadi doesn't like us bringing germs into her kitchen. "About to eat."

"Thari chicken?" Lizzie says, and I can almost hear her drooling.

"Of course." I scrub my hands with soap and dry them on the pale blue hand towel. I look at my face in the mirror. It's been just over a week, and it's already showing the wear and tear of forty-hour weeks. How will I ever manage sixty? "You wanna come eat?"

"No, actually, I need you to come here." She's shouting into the phone, so I put it on speaker. My mom's already puttered away, out of earshot.

"I told you I couldn't."

"Vish's wasted. Like, trashed. For real."

"Uh-oh."

"And he's being totally handsy with everyone. Not a good look."

"Can't you drive him home?"

"Uh, I would. Except I don't wanna leave. I've been flirting with Eric all night." I think she can feel me frowning, because she adds, "And, okay, I'm trashed, too."

"Call a car service."

"His parents would slaughter him." Even though they're vegetarians. But dammit. She's right.

"Okay, I'm on my way."

I run up to the kitchen, and the proximity of the thari wala chicken that I'm about to miss makes me want to cry. My dad has piled his plate high with chicken and a stack of ghee-slathered rotis; the pungency of the fresh onion, sprinkled with vinegar, lal mirch, and chaat masala, the mix of spice and sour, is making my eyes—and mouth—water. I reach over and pop a few cherry tomatoes in my mouth, pondering how to handle this.

"Is Lizzie coming?" Dadima asks, excited, as she brings another fluffy roti over. She offers it to me, but I wave toward my mom, who's settling in at the kitchen table, already in her nightgown. "Shall I make her a parantha?"

Dadi loves Lizzie and her unabashed appreciation for Indian food. She doesn't love Vish nearly as much because, in Dadi's not-so-humble opinion, he's half-Gujarati and vegetarian and therefore his food choices are decidedly wrong.

"No, I have to go there. She needs, uh, homework help." I suck at lying. But I do it so rarely, no one even looks up from their plates. "I mean, she's at a study group. They need help. With chemistry. Nonorganic. Substitution reactions." Do they study those in high school? "Vish's there, too."

"Good," Mom says. "It's Friday night. You should see your friends. People your own age."

I ignore her. "I could just stay home, though." I yawn. "I'm really tired." I shoot a glance at my watch, then daggers at my mom. "And I have files to catch up on, since, I was, uh, dismissed from a case today."

"It's protocol," Mom says, not looking up from her plate. "We can't make exceptions for you or anyone else. People already complain about nepotism and—"

"It's ridiculous. Anya Auntie says jump and you—"

"Enough," Mom says, glaring now. "Go. Be a kid. Have fun with your friends."

"But be home by eleven," Papa says, his mouth full of chicken and roti. "And I'm going to rewatch *Sholay* without you."

"Okay," I say, pseudo-reluctant. We've seen it, like, fourteen times already. I'm not missing much, except dinner.

Dadi must've read my mind, though, because she walks up then with a little foil packet—a makeshift kati roll of thari chicken wrapped up in a parantha, still steaming hot.

I beam at her. "Thanks, Dadi!"

She hands me a plastic bag. "I made more for your friends. And egg-only for Vish. He still eats eggs, right?" She's frowning.

I nod and head up the stairs, my mom shouting behind me. "Wear something presentable!"

Twenty minutes later, I round the corner toward Cat's house. I could hear the music from five blocks away, this deep, relentless bass and

71

what sounds like wordless shrieking over it. The cul-de-sac is crowded with Mercedes and BMWs, all very Princeton prep.

I spot Lizzie's perky pink Fiat, which she says she picked because it defines her as quirky and cute. Vish's navy-blue Jeep is parked not far from it, the little Ganesha sitting stoutly on the dashboard, as if his mother's protective gaze is following the boy's every move. Most of my friends have been driving for almost a year, but I still haven't passed—or even taken—the test. I keep meaning to get my license. But at the rate I'm going, my cousin Pinky will have hers first, and she's only two. Right now it feels like one thing too many on my overloaded to-do list. Even though my work fate depends on it, if Davis has anything to say about it.

As I walk toward the back gate, I tug at my dress and peer into the side mirror on one of the cars, making sure I look okay. Walking was a bad idea. My summer dress—stolen from Taara's closet and decidedly snug at the chest—is already drenched with sweat. I pull my hair out of its usual ponytail and try to pat it to submission, the curls unruly in the mid-July humidity. I wish it would rain already. Maybe I should have put on lip gloss. Or eyeliner. Or something. I dig through my purse, find my ginger mints, and pop three, hoping to cut some of the onion breath.

The last time I was here, I was twelve. Cathleen lives in a big, sprawling modern mansion, lots of lofty ceilings and exposed piping. There's a massive kidney-shaped pool in the back, complete with a hot tub and outdoor showers. Cat's house is always the place to be, I guess. I mean, even in the winter when the pool is heated. Or at least that's what Lizzie says. I haven't been to one of these parties. Yet.

Cat used to be my friend, sort of, way back in the day, before Harper died. But she was always really Lizzie's friend. So she bailed when Harper was sick. And so did Lizzie, to be honest. Now Cat is Lizzie's "official BFF" at school. Even though Lizzie always insists that I'm her *real* best friend. That's the thing about being a genius—you completely miss out on that whole normal school experience with your friends.

As I open the black wrought iron gate and walk down the path of bluestone pavers, I wonder if I might see Link here, and my heart does this weird leap. He's probably, maybe, definitely in high school, and it could be East Princeton, so there's logically a decent chance I'd bump into him here. Which would be—probably not that great at all, actually, I tell myself, thinking of Vish.

My heart is in my throat as I scan the backyard, which is all lit up and magical. Strands of fairy lights crisscross the emerald grass from one end of the football field of a yard to the other, twinkling like the stars that are missing from this suburban Jersey sky. The pool is the centerpiece, set back from a two-layered redwood deck, where the caterers have laid a spread of snacks and pitchers of peach and berry sangria—which Lizzie told me Cat's parents allow, since they don't consider it to be real alcohol.

There's a DJ set up on the higher deck, and the pounding of the bass works its way in through my toes and right to my heart, the thump, thump, thump of it shaking me like a defibrillator. There are a hundred ways that I'm not ready for this—not nearly at all. In that moment, though, there's a small voice inside of me saying, yes, maybe I am. Maybe Lizzie was right. Maybe this is what I've been missing all along. As shallow and insipid as these things look on TV, maybe there's a reason they've been happening for a thousand years and will, barring the apocalypse, keep happening for a thousand more. Maybe high school parties can be fun.

Kids are everywhere—in the pool, playing water volleyball, piled thick in the hot tub, or drying off on the deck with drinks and snacks. The living room's wall of glass has been opened to the upper deck, and a few VIPs wander in and out of the house, too, where Cat's probably holding court.

I see a few familiar faces. But no Link. A girl whose name I forget stops me to say hello. "So you're, like, a real doctor, now?" she says in that annoying, upspeaky voice that makes me sure I know her. "Can I, like, show you this sore on my toe?"

"What insurance do you have?" I ask, but she doesn't laugh. That's when Lizzie finds me.

"There you are!" I say as she drips all over me, fresh from the pool. "I was just talking to, uh—"

"Yeah, you don't want to get stuck with that. Let's go get a drink. Don't worry, it's just sangria," Lizzie says, but I can tell she's already had plenty. Her blue eyes are totally dilated, and she's got this too-wide grin plastered on her face. She's shivering in her new two-piece, bright red with black piping along the edges, emphasizing the right spots. She looks gorgeous in it, and fits right in here, among the pale, golden Princetonians. I didn't even think to bring a suit, not that I'd have the nerve to rock it here.

"I don't think you need any more to—" But she's busy. She snaps a quick smiley picture of the two of us, and has it up and posted within seconds. She's good.

Then this boy comes up from behind her, his arms lacing around her bare stomach like one of those generic letches from '80s Bollywood films, and they're making out before I even know what's happening. I realize I'm staring, so I focus on the bar, pouring some sangria into a red plastic cup. I take a sip and grimace. Lizzie said you can hardly taste the alcohol, but I must have a refined palate or something, because I definitely notice it. Still, it goes down okay. One cup. Maybe two.

She grins at me as she finally comes up for air. "This is Eric. You were in third grade together." Eric and I both shrug. He's about to kiss her again, but she's still talking. To me. "Good stuff, huh? Go easy, though. It'll hit you quick."

She pours me another cup, then downs one herself and refills her own. We cheers, and she takes another photo.

"Don't post that one," I say as she clicks away on her phone. "My mom—"

74

"Doesn't follow me on Twitter." She waves her phone at me. "It's only on mine."

"Okay, but don't—"

"Tag you, I know." She frowns. "Wouldn't want to make it look like Saira Sehgal, Girl Genius, actually knew how to have any fun." She turns back to Eric, and I take that as my cue.

It's like the bubbles are filling up my head, anyway, all of the logical thoughts just floating away in them. I ponder wandering, because the idea that Link might be here, somewhere, has taken hold of my heart and won't let go. I have to go find him. I must.

Or at least, like, Vish.

I walk toward the back, where the barbeque is going, and the scent of grilling meat makes me queasy, so I turn and head the other way to where the fire pit would be going if it wasn't July. There's a group gathered there. A bunch of guys and girls. And guitars. That's it. That's where he'd be. I head toward them, peering confusedly, and one of the guys looks up. Swim trunks, pale skin, floppy hair. My heart leaps.

"You lost, princess?"

Not him. I must be frowning, because the guy makes a sad face back, standing.

"You okay?"

"I think . . . I'm looking for my friend."

"Oh yeah?"

"Link."

"Oh, Link Rad! Yeah, he was supposed to be here. But he bailed." The guy whispers something to the girl who's leaning possessively on him now. I think I hear the word "cancer." "Want me to text him?"

My heart sinks, but one thing is confirmed: He's not a figment of my imagination.

"I know you, right?" I shake my head again, but the boy's still talking. "You're that girl genius doctor. I saw you on CNN."

"Tonight she's just Saira Sehgal, party pooper," Lizzie says, her arm snaking around me from nowhere. The guy laughs, and Lizzie steadies her gaze on me, all serious. "Pool?"

"I am not a party pooper." It sounds silly when I say it. But honestly, the thought of getting into actual water right now makes me want to throw up. I wonder if I'd float.

"Did you bring your suit?" Her tone is stern.

I shake my head, and she purses her lips. "You could probably borrow one from Cat." She shouts toward the pool. "Hey, Caaaaat—"

There's Cat. Perched on some guy's shoulders in the pool, playing volleyball.

No, not some guy. Vish. My Vish.

"SAAAAIRA!" He's shrieking from smack-dab in the middle of the water, drunk, her arms resting lazy on the top of his head.

"Hey!" Lizzie shouts toward the pool. I can barely hear her, but somehow, all eyes are on us now. "Look who's here!"

"My girlfriend! My girlfriend's here!"

He dumps Cat into the pool and she shouts with a mix of horror and glee, watching my reaction as she tries to latch back on. Vish's already pulling himself up and out of the pool, water splashing everywhere, and within seconds his arms are wrapped around me, soaking my dress.

"Saira's here!" He's sweaty and slick from the water, but the worst of it is the stench that's seeping out of his skin—beer and something a gazillion times stronger than the sangria, which is enough to make me tipsy, apparently, even though I'm Punjabi and we're known for holding our liquor. Though clearly I can't hold mine. Like, at all. Tomorrow's gonna suck.

"Oh man," I say, "Lizzie was not kidding."

"I missed you, Guddi," Vish says, sloppy as he purses his lips and takes aim.

I move just in time, and he makes contact with my ear.

"Get off, Vish," I say, shoving his arms away.

Vish falls toward Lizzie, who can barely support his weight with her stick-straight frame. She giggles as he shakes off water again, like a sheepdog that's recently had a bath.

"Come on, we're going home." I hit home on the car service app and turn to Lizzie, who staggers under the weight of Vish's arm. "Where're his clothes?"

Lizzie shrugs. "Jeep?" Then her eyes light up. "You gonna drive?"

I flash my phone at her, shaking my head. "Three minutes until the car service gets here. I gotta find his clothes."

"I think I might be sick," Vish says. His face is scrunched up like a squashed almond muffin.

Ugh. The car pulls up, and the driver honks. Lowering the window, he smiles at me, then panics when Lizzie hoists Vish, still clutching his stomach, toward me.

I take his other arm and Lizzie and I drag him toward the car, his wet shorts dripping a trail of chlorinated water down the path.

"No! No way!" the drive says, hopping out of the car, and crossing his arms to block our path.

"Please, sir," Lizzie says, her pout practiced. "He needs help."

"No!" He shakes his head. "He'll puke in my vehicle. I won't allow him to ride."

"Sir, seriously," I say, putting on my most professional tone. "He's not capable of driving, and should something happen, you'd have that on your conscience." I look at my phone and note the name. "Mr. Kershaw. You wouldn't want that, right? I mean, I'm happy to cancel. I'll just tell the car service you weren't willing to drive a couple of brown kids home."

Mr. Kershaw looks pissed, but he also looks torn. The belching noises Vish's making aren't helping. But it seems my twisty legal intimidation may have done the trick.

"Okay," he says. "Wait."

He runs toward the back of the car, and for a minute I think he's going to get in and take off anyway. Then he pops the trunk and pulls out a giant blue tarp, the kind my dad uses to cover our outdoor furniture during a storm. He lays the tarp across the back seat and motions at us.

Lizzie and I drag Vish over, and haul him into the back of the black sedan. He sprawls across the seat like he's on his couch at home, falling asleep while binge-watching *The X-Files*. He's a big Mulder fan. The belching turns to snoring.

I slam the door shut and head to the front seat.

"Hey, hey," Lizzie shouts as I crack the window. "You coming back?" Her face is red, splotchy, and so very hopeful.

"Of course," I lie. Then I close the window. Then open it again. That's better.

"Thanks, Mr. Kershaw. I appreciate your cooperation." The guy nods, staring straight ahead, silent as he drives the five minutes it takes to get back to my house.

The house is nearly dark when we get there. Mr. Kershaw is kind enough to help me drag a still-snoring Vish up the path. I perch him seated against the porch railing and ponder my options.

I need to focus, to figure this out before I get caught, but my brain feels fuzzy.

Getting him up the stairs to my room seems pretty impossible, given physics, my body strength and the fact that Vish has about ten inches on me. Plus, my parents are probably still watching movies.

I could take him to the garage. But it's ninety degrees out at 10:46 p.m. The best bet: the basement. Dadima's bedroom is down there. If she wakes up, I'm done for. But she sleeps with old Bollywood songs playing at top volume, so maybe it'll be okay. It's not like I have that many other options.

I unlock the door, drag Vish in as quietly as I can, and seat him up against the wall near the basement door.

I'm still dripping with sweat when I climb up the front stairs to the foyer. I open and close the door loudly. Then I hang up my keys and take off my shoes, stomping up the stairs to scope things out as if I just got back. The TV room lights are dimmed, the light from the big screen flickering.

I poke my head in. "Hey." Am I slurring?

"That was fast," my mom says, her voice sleepy. They're curled together on the sofa, her head on Papa's shoulder, a blanket spread across their laps because the AC is blasting. She always zonks when Papa does Bollywood-movie Fridays. She says it's okay, though, because she's seen them all before.

"Stay," Papa says, patting an empty spot on the sofa. "I skipped *Sholay* because I know you love it. So tonight is *Laawaris*, in which a young, orphaned Amitabh Bachchan once again does the angry, young, and frequently drunk man thing that's a signature of his early days."

"Sounds thrilling, Papa, but I'm so tired. And I've got files." The lies slip out hot and melty, like butter on Dadi's fresh paranthe. Too easy, too fast, almost mindless, like they always do when it comes to Vish. "Actually, I'm hungry." The munchies? Or wait, is that pot? Yes. But I'm still snacky. "I'm going to get a treat and head to bed."

"I can't hear Amitabh over your chatter," Papa says, suddenly cranky. "And bring me a snack, too."

I putter around the kitchen, hand my dad some chana chor garam and a fizzy Limca, ice cold and still in the bottle (his Bollywood-night staple). I make a little bowl of chor garam for myself and Vish, too, in case he wakes, and pop a few of the spicy chickpea bites into my mouth on the way back downstairs to the front hall. Vish is still slumped asleep near the door, his snores tapering as his torso slouches downward. Time to get back to work.

He swats at me, mumbling, "Five more minutes, Ma," as I hook my arms under his and drag him through the basement door. It reminds me of playing toy soldiers at the park when we were six, rolling down the hills, our moms yelling about the inevitable grass stains that ruined countless pairs of pants. Harper would always play the sergeant, and Vish was always super patient with her. We nearly tumble down the stairs as I slide him down, though I manage to get to the bottom without too much clatter or pain. Dadima's golden oldies are playing—at the moment it's "Yeh Raat Beeghi Beeghi"—so she's still out cold. And thank gods for Papa's insistence on tacky-but-soft ultra-plush carpeting. Although it now probably stinks of sweat and chlorine.

I fumble around in the dark, wondering where to stash Vish. Dadima's room is tucked in one corner, and the TV area in the middle is the most obvious and inviting—the couch is the perfect place to sleep off a hangover.

Or, it would be if:

(1) you were allowed to be at your girlfriend's house at nearly midnight.

(2) you were allowed to drink.

(3) you were allowed to be drunk off your ass.

Since all three of those things are resounding NOs, the couch is out. The laundry room? The steady thrum of the washer warns me that he'd be quickly discovered there.

"I think I'm gonna be sick," Vish grumbles, and I run back toward the base of the stairs, where he still lays, his head at the bottom, his legs still elevated. He slides down and looks confused.

"How'd we get here? Toilet!" He shoots up and runs toward Dadi's bathroom, shoving the door open. He hurls his body toward the throne, which wears a fancy electric bidet—or butt washer, as Taara and I like to call it—as its crown.

"Wait, lift the seat!" I whisper-shout.

Then he throws up on Dadi's pale blue handwoven Indian cotton bath mat, which she brought with her from her old house in Delhi. *Of course.*

I grab a bunch of towels from the rag stash Dadi keeps under the sink and clean up the area—and Vish—the best I can. He reeks of sweat and vomit, and it triggers my gag reflex, so I stop and splash water on my face and then scrub him down with a damp towel.

"Saira?" I hear Dadi shout from her adjacent bedroom, over the swell of music. "Is that you?"

Shit. She's up.

I rush out, shouting so she won't come looking.

"Yes, Dadi, peeing. Go back to bed." I hold my breath, hoping she will. I count to sixty. She doesn't stir again. Thank gods.

"Come on," I say to Vish, who's whimpering and rubbing his face. "We've got to get out of here."

He stands, bleary-eyed, and looks around. I grab the towels, the rug, and any other evidence and race out of the bathroom, motioning him to follow. We tiptoe across the basement to the other end, where I open the laundry closet door. It'll have to do. I shove Vish inside, and he crashes on top of a pile of blankets. He's already snoring as I empty the freshly done laundry into the dryer and dump the dirty towels into the washer.

I pull my phone from my pocket and text Taara.

Two things!

(1) How do you cure a hangover?

(2) How do I get vomit out of organic cotton?

I want to text her a third: *(3) Do you believe in love at first snooze?*

The three little dots appear, but no actual response.

I slide down beside the machines, letting them rock me, and sigh. I can feel a migraine coming on. I glare at Vish, watching as his chest rises and falls, peaceful despite the snores. I kind of hate him right now. I've known him since I was six, and I've saved his ass a million times now. I mean, I'm saving his ass even by just being his girlfriend at all. The thought burns as soon as I think it, or maybe it's just kati roll reflux. Or, like, alcohol poisoning?

I stare at my phone again. Still no response from Taara. I open my phone's browser and google vomit and organic cotton. Apparently, vomit is a protein stain. Ugh. Definitely no bleach. Enzymatic cleaner? Do we even have that?

Still no response from Taara. Sigh.

I open another window and find myself typing the words before I even realize what I'm doing.

"Link, Princeton."

Golf course. Nope.

"Link Rad, Princeton."

Nothing.

"Link Rad, Princeton. *Rock Star Boot Camp.*"

Boom, there he is. An online video. He's smiling, playing his guitar and singing. The dimple dents his cheek, and his mouth makes a little *O* when he croons the chorus, even though I can't hear it because it's on silent.

I watch it on a loop, over and over again, until I fall asleep.

Online Search Results

SEARCH

Link
Link 16
Link Rad Princeton Rock Star Boot Camp

GO

RESULTS
Link Rad, 16, Princeton NJ
Click to open video
Viewed 83586 times
Click to Vote for Link Rad

IMAGES
Link Rad: Singer, skater, cancer kid
1453 Followers
Follow?

CHAPTER 10

On Saturday morning, I awake to a migraine—or is it a hangover?—
and the mingling scents of detergent, freshly brewed chai, and aloo ki
tikkis—the crispy potato cakes are my absolute favorite. That means
Dadima's up and didn't come into the laundry closet last night—which
is good news, because Vish's still sleeping on a pile of dirty bedsheets.
But she:

1. likely did use her bathroom.
2. knows the rug is missing.
3. probably heard him snoring through the door.

The question is, is she going to give me away?

I pull myself up and off the floor, and poke at Vish, who has dents
in his cheeks from his uncomfortable bed.

"Hey, Guddi," he says, bleary-eyed. "What happened?"

"You were drunk. And threw up. On Dadi's rug." I grin. "She's
never gonna make you egg bhurji again. And you owe me like a gazillion rupees because it's from that old flea market in Delhi and priceless.
You're very lucky I didn't use bleach."

"Oh no!" He jumps up, apparently not hungover at all. Of course.
I put my hand to my throbbing head. Two cups of sangria? That's all?
Never. Again. "Yeah, that sangria was spiked with tequila and rum."
Oh. "And I had a few shots."

"You okay? Need water? Juice?" What do they give people when they're, like, totally drunk? I'm itching to look it up. I could really go for some guava juice right now, but the thought also makes me strangely nauseous. "You were so wasted last night." And apparently, so was I.

"Did I make out with anyone, though?" he asks with a laugh, all wide-eyed.

I grin. "Not that I know of. But Liz Biz definitely did."

"The drama." He leans in close and gives me a peck on the cheek. Ugh, morning-drunk dragon breath. I shove him away. "Should I sneak out?"

I shake my head. "No, Papa will be back from his run in a second. He popped out exactly fifteen minutes ago." I grab a clean sweatshirt from the basket. His shorts are dry, so they'll do. "Put this on, then sneak through the back and ring the bell. You're here to give me a driving lesson."

He grins. "You asked for it." He pulls on my sweatshirt—thankfully a generic Princeton one that everyone in town has—and my phone falls out. It hits the floor and starts blasting the video I downloaded last night—of Link. It's even better with the sound on.

"What's that?" he says, his eyes flickering from the video to my face. "Lizzie's new fave?"

"Actually, a patient. At the hospital. He's trying out for *Rock Star Boot Camp*."

"He's good."

And hot, I think.

Vish hands me my phone. "You should introduce him to Lizzie. Totally her type."

Or mine. Maybe?

I laugh, then open the laundry closet door, peering into the basement. Sunshine streams in, but it's quiet and empty. I take Vish's hand, and we tiptoe to the back door. I unlock it and push him through.

A minute later, the doorbell rings. I hear Papa's voice booming in the hall as he answers.

I sneak upstairs and change, and by the time I come back down, everyone's at the breakfast nook, eating tikkis. Vish's already got his mouth full—breakfast is one meal he and Dadi can usually agree on, because it doesn't involve chicken or lamb.

"Driving lesson canceled!" Papa says with a snort, as if it's the funniest joke he's ever played. Thank gods. No drunk driving for me.

"Aaja, Saira," Dadi says, and ushers me toward the table, laden with treats. "Sit, sit. Time for choske." She shuffles around steaming plates of tikkis, golgappa, chaat, samosas, and lots of tandoori maal, like chicken and kebabs; the yummy street food she grew up with in her down and dirty Delhi neighborhood.

"Reminds me of home." She piles a potato cake on my plate, dousing it with spicy, tangy chickpeas slathered in brown gravy, then tops them with cool yogurt, fresh onion, and mint and tamarind chutneys. It all looks delicious, but one bite may just take me out.

Dadi's peering at me, all curious and judgmental, though, so I stuff a bite into my mouth before I take my seat, squeezing in next to—but not too close, because my parents are watching—Vish.

"How's it going with Elliott Cho?" Mom asks me.

"Well, the scene with Dragon Auntie definitely didn't help," I say, glaring at her.

"Oh, come on, Saira," Mom says, spooning up some chole. "You can't make mountains out of small battles. You have to win the war."

Huh? "Mom! You're just giving them more ammunition—"

Dadi shushes me. "Nashta time," Dadi says. "Eating. No working. Chai?"

It's not really a question. No one in the Sehgal household functions—even on Saturdays—without chai.

Dadi pours chai for everyone. It's super strong and milky, spiked with ginger and spices. "Too strong, too sweet," Dadi says, pinching her nose as I dump three spoons of white sugar into my cup. "Rail station chai."

The chai actually seems to help take the edge off. So I slurp it loudly, and Vish starts. Dadi silences us with a glare. Does she know about last night? I can't tell, since she's always sucking her teeth at Vish anyway.

"Te Rhona di shaadi da kya?" Dadi says, looking straight at Mom. My cousin Rhona's wedding isn't until January, but Dadi's been trying to get an answer about going to the wedding in India for weeks. "Tickets book karay? Twenty-nine!" Dadi adds with disgust. "Finally, she has relented."

"Maybe you and Pash can go early," Mom says to Dadi.

"No Pash," Dadi says. "Pashaura."

Mom ignores her. "Then Taara and I can join you. It'll have to be a short trip, because she has school." She looks at me. "And I don't know if it will be possible for Saira to go. This internship will be relentless. And difficult. It's an important time."

"She hasn't been in years," Dadi says, the disappointment slipping out and layering us all like a too-warm blanket.

Vish clears his throat and pours himself some more chai.

"And she probably won't, Biji," Mom says in her "I'm the grown-up" voice. She's all about making decisions for everyone. Especially me. I seethe. "She's made a commitment—she understands it."

I haven't been to India since I was nine, just before I started skipping grades and doing the genius track at Hopkins. So part of me wants to quit completely, be a kid and go to India and doll up in fancy new lenghas for a favorite cousin's wedding. Even just to piss Mom off. But most of me knows Mom is right. I have to finish what I started, and I *want* to. I asked for this, begged for it, really.

"Mom's right, Dadi. I can't leave. Not now. So I'll miss this one. You and Mom have to promise to get me as many lenghas as you get for Taara."

"And some new kurtas for me, too," Vish adds.

"Tell your Gujarati nani to get them for you," Dadi says.

Ouch. "Dadi," I scold sternly, but she pours more tea, unfazed. She holds fast to her preconceptions and prejudices, no matter what we all say.

Vish bubble-faces at her, blowing his cheeks full of air like a balloon. "Did I thank you for the kati roll you sent?" he says too loud. "Eggs and achari potatoes are a brilliant combination. You should have a restaurant."

"Home food is the best food," she concedes, then turns her attention to me, cupping a frail, paper-skinned hand under my chin. "And lenghas, suits, maybe even a sari for you, guriya. You've outgrown all of your old things, and you're too big for Taara's old ones already." She means it as a compliment, I'm sure, but it makes me pause before grabbing a second cookie. Only for a minute.

"Are you guys going to homecoming this year?" Mom asks Vish, and Dadi tsks.

"Phir se ye dating-shating," she says, walking away in a huff.

"If she'll come," Vish says. "You know Saira." Then he and Papa start talking about the school's chances at state, and the rest of us zone out.

I think about homecoming and wonder if Vish will make me go. We've only been to two dances so far, in the whole time we've been "officially together," or whatever. I wonder what my Dadima would think of Link. I don't know why he pops into my head. But he does. I can still feel the tingling when he touched my hand, like when you hit your funny bone—which, of course, is not a bone at all, rather the ulnar nerve vibrating—on something. He was so odd, strange and familiar all at once, like the first bite of a new Dadi dish I know will become my favorite.

I wish I'd had a chance to get my hands on his patient file. Even though that would maybe go against the oath I've taken. Besides, I've got the weekend off and no excuse for quick drop-in at the hospital. I shake the thought away. I've got lots to do. Charts and a driving lesson, and the boring mall with Lizzie. Dammit. I forgot to call her back, watching that video on repeat all night.

I tell myself it's only a medical interest in his case, but my stomach's doing this weird flutter—it's a fight-or-flight response, which is odd. It means reduced blood flow, no doubt, thanks to a release of adrenaline, which means I'm stressed or excited. Or both. Yes, both.

I take another cookie. Maybe that will help.

I dip it in my tea, and watch it crumble and collapse into the cup.

"What do you think, Saira?" Mom says.

I have no idea what she's talking about.

I look at Vish, and he shrugs.

"Huh?"

"Regarding Taara?"

"It's a good rishta," Dadi says, hoping for a yea from me. Even though I never back her up when she tries to talk Mom into these arranged marriage scenarios. "A good family to build a relationship with. A doctor boy from Canada. Family from Delhi. They'll be in India when we are."

"It couldn't hurt to introduce them, nah?" Mom says.

I'm already shaking my head. "Nope, nope, nope," I say, slurping the last of my chai, crumbs and all. "And nope. You need to stop making decisions for people. You're asking for trouble, and Taara's fine. She's smart, beautiful, relatively tall—and really young. She'll find her own husband."

Dadi tsks again. "When? You girls are so busy focused on work this, study that—"

"No, Biji, Saira's right," Mom says, and I nearly drop my teacup. "They should be focused on work and studies right now. They are very young, and we are rushing for no reason. Love can strike in the oddest of ways, when you least expect it. We need to give it time and space, room to grow. Like with you and Vish."

My cheeks are on fire now, and Vish's staring down at his plate. Awkward.

"You always buy into this Amreeki drama," Dadi says, abruptly standing and gathering teacups and kettles on her big golden tray. "You'll see, Rana, one day, the error of your ways." She bursts out of the kitchen in a mood, leaving the rest of us sitting in silence.

Mom giggles first. It's catching. Soon we're both laughing so hard, we're near tears.

"She's like a Desi soap opera," Papa says, hugging my mom. "And you are the willful daughter-in-law. Next it be smashing plates and fainting spells."

Mom laughs. "Yeah, Taara's the only one who can match Dadi's drama." She grabs another cookie from the tin Dadi forgot, and then says, "And I will stay out of it. Last thing I need is the wrath of Taara." Then, "Is she dating anyone, by the way?"

I shrug. Taara's been dating the same guy on and off now for three years. But I'm the only one in the family who knows about him. And this much even I can tell: He's so not a suitable boy. But she's only nineteen. So she's got time. (Just don't tell Dadi that.)

Vish looks at his phone, afraid to get involved. Smart boy.

"How are you guys doing, Vish?" she asks. His mom and mine believe we're totally PG, which works for them. And for us.

"We may go see the new Ranveer film this afternoon," he says, which is news to me.

"Not too late, though, acha?" Papa says. "I heard it was very good. Lots of action."

And romance. Why can't I stop thinking about Link? A thought pops into my head.

"Hey, Mom, I have an idea," I say, startling everyone. "You know how you're always saying everyone needs an escape?"

She nods, tentative, not sure exactly where this is going. I can see she's worried it has something to do with me and Vish. And so is he.

"Well, that's just it—these kids, the cancer kids at the hospital, they don't have that. Not when Harper was at the hospital, and not now, eight years later."

"It must be so weird being at that hospital all the time without Harper," Vish says, squeezing my hand.

I know he misses her, too, but the scar has healed for him.

90

Mine still feels like a fresh wound. And maybe, working with these kids at the same hospital, I'm a glutton. But I have to help them. "Yeah, and that's why I need to do something," I say. "The lounge is the least of it."

"Yes," Mom says, still confused. "That's true."

"They should." I take a deep breath. "So maybe I can help with that. You know that old, stuffy patient lounge I used to hang out with Harper in?"

Vish's grinning. "I can't believe it's still there. And the VCR? The old movies. We should go watch them!"

I nod. I know he can already see where I'm going with this. *"Anne of Green Gables!"*

He tugs at my hair. We both swooned over Gilbert Blythe. "Carrots! Carrots!"

"How dare you!" I shout, and we both dissolve into laughter.

"Nobody uses that lounge anymore," Mom says with disgust. "I can't blame them."

"They could—if it was nice again. I could do that, pretty easily. A little paint, update the furniture, buy a flat screen and a new fridge. Make it brighter, more livable."

Vish's nodding. "I could help paint and get a discount from my uncle's store on the flat screen."

"It's not a bad idea, really," Mom says, "and living at home, you could certainly afford to give back some." Then a wide grin spreads across her face. "Only one problem, and it's a big one: Davis."

Saira: Heads up, Dadi's at it again.

Taara: 😌 What is it this time?

Saira: Some guy who's gonna be in India for the wedding.

Taara: Yuck. Did you shut it down?

Saira: Of course I did. You owe me a Princeton pie, yo.

Taara: 😌

CHAPTER 11

The mall is bursting with teenagers. Like me, I guess. But I feel like I'm in a foreign country where I don't know the language. I haven't been to an actual mall in maybe five years, nearly a third of my life now. It's so easy to order necessities online.

"Sasha's first, then that little boutique next to the Gap, then Lolita's for some new underwear," Lizzie announces to the twenty thousand people in this squishy, trendy store, because of course they needed our itinerary. "I know you definitely need some."

She winks at me and drags me toward the fitting rooms. "Can I get these pants in a six and an eight? And does that cover-up come in blue?" Lizzie's my tour guide, and luckily, she speaks mall.

Moments later, we're locked in a changing room at one of her favorite stores, a stack of "party wear" a mile high sitting on a chair next to me.

"You've got to stop stealing from Taara's closet," Lizzie says. "None of her stuff fits your boobs." She points to a blue dress, then shakes her head, then points to the red. "Not that one. Try the other." She shakes her head again as I hold it up against me. "No, take off your grubby T-shirt and actually put it on." It doesn't budge once it hits my boobs, so I pull it back up.

Nothing fits me: big Punjabi boobs, not quite skinny waist, short torso, long limbs. My body's built like it was Frankensteined together with spare parts. Lizzie, on the other hand, is long and lean, with fluffy blond hair, big blue eyes, and the kind of small, perky breasts that you could totally go braless with. Yes, I'm jealous.

She tosses me a bigger size of the same dress, which fits over the boobs, but is too roomy everywhere else. I sigh. That one hits the floor, too.

"Too bad," Lizzie says. "It was super cute."

"So, I, uh, this weird thing happened at work—"

"Try the blue one on now," she orders, ignoring my hemming. "I think it suits you more than the yellow."

I pull a floral dress on, and Lizzie's already shaking her head. I toss it off, and she hangs it back up, handing me a striped dress. I frown at it, but she nods, in charge, so I pull it on anyway. "This store doesn't get my body," I say, tossing the latest onto the floor. "I quit."

"Don't give up. We've only just begun!" she sings. She sings a lot.

"Dresses never fit me right," I complain. "Except for that one place online. It's meant for girls with big boobs."

Lizzie ponders, a finger to her lip thoughtfully. "Maybe a skirt and top would be better. And you could mix and match, so you'd have more options." That sounds like a disaster waiting to happen. She scans through the stack, tossing aside this and that any which way. We go through the same cycle—try, whine, defeat—a half a dozen times before she finally throws her hands up.

"Okay, time for lunch," she says. "You're treating, Moneybags."

We head to the food court, go our separate ways to place orders, then stalk the tables until we can snag an open one.

"So how was the matinee?" she asks.

Oops. "I would've asked you, but we went on a whim." It was the new Ranveer Singh, and he's, like, Lizzie's fave, but I mean, it was Vish's idea, a just-the-two-of-us thing. "And it didn't have subtitles."

"New Brunswick would've had subtitles," she says, then races off as a table opens.

I follow her, take a napkin, and scrub the surface down before we sit, laying our food out.

"I can smell those onions," Lizzie says, scrunching up her petite, freckled nose.

"Yup, they're delicious," I say, taking a bite of my sub from Larry's bulgogi with extra kimchi and the offending onions (which I asked them to add, naturally), and salt-and-vinegar potato chips crumbled on top. She's got her usual, plain old roast beef with mayo. "Enjoy your bland white-people food."

She chomps hard, then opens her mouth to reveal a disgusting glob of white cream. I giggle, and toss a potato chip at her mouth. She catches it and claps like a seal. I laugh, nearly choking on my lemonade, which I've doused with black pepper, Desi-style.

She swallows and takes a sip of iced tea. "Did you hear that Cat's dating Brian?"

"The one who used to eat chalk?"

"No, the other one, Brian F. Not Brian H. The one who is the lacrosse captain now."

"Oh," I say, "that's nice."

"She's applying to Stanford." She pauses, waiting for me to say something. "And Yale."

"Well, good for her."

"Maybe you can help with her apps," Lizzie suggests.

"I think she's got it handled."

"She was asking about you and Vish." She eats a potato chip, and we sit in awkward silence for a second before she starts on about Rebecca and Lisa going off to college on opposite coasts. They've been together for two years. About as long as Vish and I. Well, technically. "I mean, California. That's, like, thousands of miles. Are you upset?"

"I don't think long distance is a big deal," I say with a shrug. "And Vish and I are good. For now. I mean, only two percent of teen romances lead to marriage or any kind of serious commitment. We'll live. And so will they."

There's dead silence for a second. I have to actually look up from my sandwich to make sure Lizzie's still there. Her mouth is a thin, straight line, and her eyes stare straight ahead, avoiding my gaze. "You could show a little interest. I mean, they're your friends, too."

"They were. I haven't talked to most of them in months. Some more than a year."

"That's your fault, not theirs."

When I open my mouth to defend myself, she cuts me off. "You make time for the people you want to make time for. Like Vish. And sometimes me. If you want to have an actual life—and not endless hours in some lab coat at the hospital—then you have to make an effort. Even with me."

"Ouch. Okay. Are you excited about camp?" I ask her, too brightly. Maybe she'll let it slide. This time.

She swallows a big bite of her sandwich. "I'm nervous."

Lizzie's hardly ever nervous. "Yeah? Why?"

"Madame Yulia—she's old-school Russian method acting. Like a starlet from the fifties who's still channeling the throwback vibe. So she doesn't care about soap operas or reality TV or any of the things that would constitute a big break for wannabes like us. She wants us to cut our teeth in theater or indie film. Serious stuff." She takes a sip of her iced tea. "This program is hard. Really hard. I mean, it's Yale. I'm not sure I can do it."

I swipe a chip from the pile. "You wouldn't have gotten in if you couldn't. I know you. You're smart and determined and plain old good."

"Yeah, but I'm a generic blond girl, one of, like, sixty in the room." She lifts up a strand of her golden locks. "Maybe I should do something to my hair?"

"Hey, I know you!" a voice interrupts. I recognize it. I turn to look behind me, and there he is.

Link. Skateboard, ski cap—even though it's July—shorts and Hendrix T-shirt, ratty Chucks. Bright eyes, and that flawed yet perfect grin as he walks over.

I panic. I wonder if that kid mentioned the party. That would be beyond humiliating. My body's fight-or-flight response is in overdrive—my heart thumps in my ears, my stomach flutters, and for a second I forget where I am. He's standing in front of us, his board on the floor next to him, his hands grasping the empty chair in front of him, a question. I should say hi or introduce him to Lizzie or something, but I forget how. Or why. Or anything else.

"Saira with an *i*, right?" he says. "They let you out of the cage."

The cage? Oh yeah, he thinks I'm a patient.

"Oh, the hospital. Yes, out on good behavior." My voice sounds funny, breathy, almost giggly.

Lizzie's mouth twists in amusement.

"Back on Monday."

"Sucks," he says, and then gestures to the chair he's been leaning on.

I nod, and he swings it around so he can sit leaning forward on the back of it. Like his body needs the extra support. Of course. Muscle atrophy is pretty common at this stage, and he's probably exhausted.

"I'm Lizzie," she says, and Link sticks out his hand. She's confused for a second, then she shakes it.

"Oh yeah, I'm so rude. This is my best friend, Lizzie."

"Nice to meet you, Saira's best friend Lizzie. I'm Link," he says, then turns back to me.

"Is that Larry's Korean BBQ sub?" I nod, offering a chip. He takes it and our hands touch. That little buzz zips through me again. "Girl after my own heart. Have you tried the chicken tikka one?"

"Yes," Lizzie says. "Yum."

"But it can't compare to my dadi's," I add.

"Yeah, well, home food is the best food," Link says, and I almost leap out of my chair. "That's what my halmeoni says."

"My dadi, too!" We beam at each other.

He steals another chip. "So remember I was telling you about *Rock Star Boot Camp*?"

I nod again. The reality show. Maybe I should watch it. Lizzie watches it.

"Oh yeah," Lizzie says. "I submitted once. Nothing."

"Yeah, I sent a tape. They asked me for another—that means I'm doing the second round." He lifts his hand for a high five.

I give him one, and I can feel the tingle again as soon as our palms touch.

"That's actually, like, my favorite part," Lizzie says, "the little documentaries." He nods, and she adds, "It's Saira's favorite, too, right, Saira?" Or it would be, if I'd ever watched the show.

"Oh yeah, of course, you can really get to know a lot about someone through a mini documentary." I sound clueless even to myself.

He looks confused but smiles anyway. "Yeah, so here's the thing," he says, looking intently at me, "and you would know, maybe. Do you think I should tell them about the cancer? In the video? Because that would, like, totally make me the underdog—"

"And who doesn't love an underdog?" Lizzie adds.

He doesn't look away from me. "It's also kind of weird, having a camera in your face. And I don't know about playing the cancer card. I don't want them to pick me as a Make-A-Wish kinda thing, you know? The Pity Pick. I want to get there on my own merits."

He's staring at my face, waiting for me to speak, and nothing's really coming out of my mouth. Lizzie's about to chime in again any second, and she's so much better at this stuff. Like, for real, she can talk to anyone.

He's not anyone.

He's Link.

And he's asking me.

Me.

"You know—" she starts, and I kick her under the table. Not hard. But enough. So she gets it.

"Yeah, I know what you mean," I finally say. "You can't play it halfway. And being the cancer kid sucks. But you have a dream. You don't have to let cancer steal that from you."

"You know from experience," Lizzie adds helpfully, and I grimace.

"Here's the thing: It's a part of you," I say. "I mean, physically and all. Also mentally. You went through it once. And you're still here. How many sixteen-year-old rock-star wannabes can say that? You can do this."

He grins at me again, and it's different this time. Truer somehow. Like I know who he is. And maybe he knows me, too. Which kind of sucks, considering.

"Maybe you're right. And honestly, I may not have a choice." He swallows hard, and the fresh bruises on his arms jump out at me, suddenly too obvious. He notices me noticing. "Yeah, I think I'll be back soon." He's quiet for a moment. "The good news is, maybe we can hang out. Maybe you can even help me shoot my tape. I mean, since you'll be around and all." Then he grins again. "We'll have to be stealthy about it, though. Davis already hates me."

I can't stop myself from beaming in that moment. "She totally hates me, too," I say with too much pride.

He stands then, kicks his skateboard up so he can grab it. "Anyway, see ya at the hospital."

"Yeah," I say, lifting a hand awkwardly. How do goodbyes work again? "See ya there."

With one last look back and a quick wave, he's gone, just like that.

I stare after him, into the space where he was, until I feel a hard pinch on my bare thigh. "Ouch! Lizzie!"

"Who was that?" she says. She twists her lips.

"Link. Link Rad." I grin.

"Okay, so this guy's a patient? Like, your patient?"

"Yes, a patient. Not *my* patient. I ran into him in the patient lounge. The one we used to go to with Harper." I trip on the words, that sinking feeling hitting me again, and realize I stopped thinking about Harper as soon as Link walked into that room. "It looks exactly the same."

"Oh man, that's weird. Was it weird?"

"Yeah, I was in there, pretty much sobbing. And sneezing, and he walked in, like, guitar and all, and said bless you. And salud. And gesundheit. He really wants to be the next *Rock Star Boot Camp* hero."

"Yeah, I got that," she says with a practiced pout. "But it's harder than he thinks."

"I think he could actually do it."

I know what she's thinking—*unlike me*. But she says: "Even with, like, cancer and all?"

"It's not a death sentence, Lizzie," I say, and I can't help feeling annoyed. "Even though he's got leukemia, and it's recurring. And mixed-race kids have a much harder time finding a viable donor."

"Downer. Especially because, dude, you are so smitten."

"I'm not smitten."

"You are so totally smitten. And he seems kind of smitten, too." She whistles. "Which could be a big problem."

"No, it's not smitten. Smitten means you're, like, laid low, struck down with the feels. Like, suffering for love. That's not me. I'm interested. I'm curious."

"Whatever, you're smitten. Like, smote, even."

"Smoted."

She grabs a handful of potato chips and pops a few. "Here's the thing, though: He thinks you're a patient, and you totally let him keep believing it."

"I know. He's, like, the first person who ever talked to me like I was normal."

"Dude, what am I, chopped liver? And he's not talking to you like you're normal. He's talking to you like you're a cancer kid. Like him."

"Yeah, maybe."

"Saira."

"I mean, technically, I didn't lie. He just assumed."

"He's going to find out." Her voice is harsh and a bit pouty, like when we were little and I told her I was quitting ballet to spend more

100

time with Harper at the hospital. She always hated how much I went there. I always hated how she never came with me.

"Maybe." I shrug. "Maybe not."

"Saira, you're going to have to tell him. Before he, like, actually finds out."

I know what she's really worried about. Vish. I wish I could tell her he'll be just fine. I wish I could tell her why. But it's not my place. And anyway, she's *my* best friend, right? So what's with all the judgment? I haven't actually done anything wrong.

"For all I know," I say, swiping some chips, too, "he's fine and he never comes back and the next time I see him it's on *Rock Star Boot Camp.*"

"Nuh-uh. You two? Star-crossed. Watch. I called it." She swallows another bite. "Poor Vish."

"Vish's a big boy. He'll be just fine. Besides, it's not like I'm gonna actually do anything." I sigh and stand, bussing my tray and not looking Lizzie's way. She can read every emotion on my face, even the ones I work hardest to hide. "Should we get going?"

"No way. You might not want anything, but I need new stuff for camp. You are totally coming with me."

"Okay," I say. "And maybe we can look for some work stuff for me? Everyone else at the hospital is all, like, dashing and dapper. I need to step up my game."

Lizzie grins, one eyebrow perched, amused. "You're so on!" She takes a last sip of her iced tea and gathers her stuff, too. We throw everything in the trash, and she links her arm through mine, leading me down the path to some other trendy shop. "Here's the thing, though. If it works out with Link, I'm so setting Vish up with Rubina. She totally has a crush on him."

Olive+Aby
Sales Receipt

ITEMS:

Silver Smash Pleated Midi Skirt	$86
Ink-Blue Keyhole Blouse	$54
Black-and-White-Striped Blouse	$54
Editor Slacks, Black	$108
Editor Slacks, Red	$108
Minimizer	$56
Summer Dreams Dress	$127
Lynley Dress	$98

- - - - - - - - - - - - - - - - - - -

SUBTOTAL:	$691
TAX:	$45.78

- - - - - - - - - - - - - - - - - - -

TOTAL:	$736.78

SHOE STOP
Sales Receipt

Flower Power Chucks	$83
Maria Sandals	$34
Tanya Flats	$52

- - - - - - - - - - - - - - -

SUBTOTAL:	
TAX:	$169
	$11.20

- - - - - - - - - - - - - - -

TOTAL:	$180.20

Diagnosis: Smitten Saira = Spendy Saira
Prognosis: There goes that first paycheck!

CHAPTER 12

I'm lying in my bed, my laptop in front of me, watching the video of Link on *Rock Star Boot Camp* for the fortieth time when the door flies open.

"Papa!" I shout, slamming my laptop shut. He's standing in the doorway, keys in hand, driving cap on.

"What? I knocked three times. You don't answer. Time for your lesson."

"I can't today."

"Saira," he says, walking right over and tugging at my blanket. "That's three lessons you've missed so far."

"I have paperwork to do."

"On a Sunday morning? That's unhealthy." My dad's a big believer in leaving work at work. Mom, not so much. Like, at all. "Do it tomorrow."

"I can't, Papa. I'm drowning. Okay? Just please understand." I get up and usher him out. "Next Sunday for sure."

"Okay," he says, still frowning as I close the door. I climb back into bed and watch the video again, another forty times. Am I a stalker? Maybe. But I can't stop staring at it and grinning like a fool, addicted to the odd flip-flop my stomach does, the way the synapses fire in my brain when I see that dimple and those eyes.

When I finally come downstairs, Taara's at the kitchen counter rolling out paranthe. Every attempt she's made at making them so far has been a resounding mess. So Dadi hovers nearby, tossing salt and cumin and other spices into the dough, and reshaping as Taara rolls out the flatbread, stuffing it with filling. Aloo ke paranthe are usually my favorite, with their savory mix of potatoes, onions, and chilis. But seeing Taara make them makes me nervous. She'd probably use sweet potatoes instead of regular ones, which makes me cringe.

"They'll be delicious," she says, wagging a finger at me accusingly. "Wait till you taste." She takes a doughy hand and tosses her phone at me. "Ready? Record. I'm going to put these up on my blog. I did a couple of takes. Dadi's not a reliable camerawoman."

I hold the phone up, the camera rolling, and she does this practiced spiel. "Hi, I'm Taara Sehgal, and you're watching *IndiEats*! Today, we're in my dadi's kitchen in sunny Princeton, New Jersey, and she's teaching me how to make aloo ke paranthe—crispy, buttery, and rich potato-stuffed flatbread, best served with yogurt, mango pickles, and ginger-spiked chai. Come on in for a closer look!" I focus on Taara, who overacts as she rolls out another parantha, and then lays it down onto the sizzling, ghee-greased pan. She lets it cook for a minute, then flips it over, the surface turning golden and crisp, making me drool despite myself.

I zoom in close, narrowing on Dadi's hands as she rolls and stuffs. But Dadi turns directly toward the camera, rolling pin in hand threateningly, glaring. "I am not one of your Bollywood stars," she says, waving the belna at the camera like a sword.

"Cut!" Taara says, and snatches the camera away. "Dammit, that would have been a good one."

"Vish can edit it for you," I say, peering over her shoulder at the footage. She's smiling, all clean and crisp, then there's flour-covered, scowling Dadi, weapon in hand. "Actually, it could be really funny."

When we turn back, the parantha's about done, and Dadi flips another one onto the pan, shooing us away with a flying towel. "Chalo, bacha log, both of you! Sit. Eat. I will make the rest."

We curl up in the little breakfast nook, which is my favorite place in the house, and dig into the spread that Dadi has set out. Taara shoves her phone in my face as I'm spooning yogurt into the stainless-steel divided plate that sits in front of me, and I nearly pour some right onto it.

"Look it," she says, pressing play on a FoodTube video. There's a quick logo—IndiEats, it tells me, and then there's Taara, in her little dorm room, with a hot plate and a bunch of bowls set up on her desk. She's behind it, stunning as always, her long, wavy hair pulled back into a loose low ponytail, a tiger-print dress grazing her lean frame. Gold bangles clink on her wrist. "Today we're making one of my family's favorites—the classic Mughlai vegetarian specialty, matar paneer. It's decadent cubes of mild chenna cheese and sweet peas in a savory onion-and-tomato-based sauce. The wonderful thing about matar paneer is that it feels rich and hearty, even though it's a relatively healthy vegetarian dish. Carnivores will love it, too."

She puts oil and spices into a pan, then starts on about making a traditional Punjabi masala—"the spiced onion and tomato base we use for pretty much everything. Make a big batch and freeze some so you can turn out fresh, exciting meals within half an hour, even in a dorm-room kitchen like mine."

Cut to reality and Taara looking at me expectant and hopeful. "What do you think?" she asks, super earnest. "Not bad, huh?"

"Yeah, it's making me hungry," I say, reaching over her to grab a parantha from the pile. "Did it turn out good?"

"Of course," she says.

I'm already distracted. I poke at the hot, stuffed flatbread, filled with potatoes and onions and chilis and dripping with ghee. I dip little bites of still-sizzling parantha into the homemade creamy homemade yogurt. Taara makes her own plate, pools of buttery ghee leaving traces on the metal and our hands and the table.

Her mouth full, she adds, "It was like Mom's! It was amazing. Can you believe I can cook up these awesome Desi dishes right there in my dorm room?" She sounds like a commercial.

"How's biochem going?" I ask.

She doesn't answer. "Check it out: three hundred views and counting, and I posted it last night," she tells me, sticking her phone in my face again. "Pretty cool, huh?"

I give her a thumbs-up, my mouth full.

"I'm gonna be a FoodTube star!" Maybe I should get Liz Biz to do her social media.

"You sure are." I stuff more food in my face as Taara swipes half the parantha from my plate instead of waiting for the next one. I frown, but Dadi brings another one seconds later.

"This is one of the ones I made," Taara says excitedly. She grabs it and digs in. "Exactly like Dadi's!"

We eat in silence for a minute. It is not exactly like Dadi's. But not terrible, either.

"I miss you," Taara says. "You should come up to Rutgers. We can cook in the dorm, and I'll take you to your first-ever real college party."

I nod, not really listening, still focused on my plate.

"Chai?" Taara asks.

I nod, and she pours the strong, milky, ginger-spiked tea into my cup. I dump three heaping spoons of raw sugar into the cup, and Taara frowns at me, but she doesn't say anything.

"So come," she says, again, "like, maybe in two weekends? When the summer session is wrapping up. You can help me move to the new dorm, and maybe we'll go shopping."

"Sounds thrilling," I say, shoving the last bite of parantha into my mouth.

"It will be," she says, ignoring my tone. "A sisters' weekend. We need one."

She's right. We do. It's only been two weeks since she left for summer session, and so much has changed, so much has shifted. There are parts of my life she knows nothing about. Like work. And Vish. And Link. I open my mouth to say something, to tell her.

I'm not sure where to start.

CHAPTER 13

"Did you download the app for the EMR system?" I ask Howard, who's grinning and staring off to space. Smitten. Yep, that's what it looks like. I poke her, and she snaps to. It's bright and early on Friday, but she's really out of it. "I can't believe we've been here three weeks already. Did you do anything fun this weekend?"

"Hey." She looks down at her phone and grins again for a moment. Looks in the camera app and adjusts her hair. Then turns to face me, taking me in as if she's just seeing me. She shakes her head like she's clearing it. "Cute dress."

"Thanks!" It's one of the new ones I got with Lizzie, professional but sassy, she called it. A deep red with small white flowers—poppy and colorful, but not loud. And thanks to the minimizer we bought at Olive+Aby, it fits perfectly. I've got my white coat over it, and paired it with my new flats, which might have been a bad choice, since I'm nearly a foot shorter than everyone else around here. Even some of the patients.

"So, the app?" I wave my phone at her again.

"Nah," she says, logging into the laptop. "I'll use the computer here. I don't want to bring my work home with me."

She may have a point there. I've been stalking the system in my off-hours, looking for information on one particular patient. But it hasn't popped up. And I can't bring myself to actually put his name in the system. It would be totally unethical, for one thing.

But there's something else inside, this weird thrum of energy, that won't let me do it, either. It's like I just want to hold the moment the way it is, the flip-flop of my stomach, the way my mind buzzes when I think about him, without ruining it with the messiness of reality. That hasn't stopped me from googling, though. I've checked the social media apps on my phone, looking up the words "Link" and "Rad" and "Princeton." That brings up random tech sites and other crap. There's the photo app and the *Rock Star Boot Camp* site. That's it.

I'm starting another search, when I hear a loud rap, rap, rap, on the desk, right near my arm.

I look up, startled, and Davis whacks the table between me and Howard with her pen. Like an old-school teacher with a ruler. Rude.

"You may have noted the multiple signs requesting that cell phones be put away while in the oncology ward, no?" Crankypants says, looking over her glasses at me. "They cause cancer."

"So does everything else, right? It's what keeps us in business." *Ouch.* I regret it instantly, without even having to see the horrified look on Davis's and Howard's faces.

She points, and I follow her gaze. Howard works hard not to crack a smile. Yup, there are signs, for sure, tacky white ones with bright blue writing and a frilly border, one of those old clunker cells pictured below the bellowing text. They're posted everywhere—on the wall behind the nurses' station, on the opposite wall heading toward the patient rooms, wherever you look. In fact, I've memorized them. That doesn't seem like the wisest thing to say.

"I thought they were for patients and parents," I say.

"Get off your phone this instant. You're here to work, Ms. Sehgal. Need I repeatedly remind you of that?"

"*Dr.* Sehgal," I spit back. "Need I repeatedly remind you of that?" As the words leave my mouth, I kind of want to duck and hide. If she could give me demerits or detention, she would, I'm sure. Or she could fire me. Like, right now. And I'm fed up. So I flash the EMR app on my phone. "I am working."

Davis peers at it for a second, then turns on her heel and storms off with a harrumph. I'm sure she'll make note of the incident in my file. She's gathering them all rabidly, the way Lizzie and I used to collect unicorn stickers, waiting for the day she can show off her collection and kick my ass out of here.

"You know that's a losing battle," Howard says. "She doesn't *have* to call you doctor when not in front of patients."

"Yes, but it sure is fun to poke her." Howard and I dissolve into giggles, and she peers at me over her glasses, like Davis did.

"What are you all laughing about?" Nurse José asks, walking up with files in hand. "Was Cho snoring again?"

"No, Dr. Davis. I do like pissing her off." I flash my teeth at him in glee.

"Keep it up, and we'll both end up on her hit list," Howard says. "Where's Cho?"

"He's been asked to consult on a new case. I'm sure you'll hear all about it as soon as he sees you."

"No doubt. Should we get started?" I say, and he starts to hand me the files. "Nope, let's do them one at a time."

We run through the list, checking in on the usual suspects.

I prep myself as we head into Alina's room. Her big blue eyes and bright demeanor remind me so much of Harper—and so do her symptoms. I take a sip of water and a deep breath. My stomach flips as I walk into the room. Clearly psychosomatic, but it still hurts. Literally.

"It's that Sasha, I tell you. Always talking, saying 'so pretty, so sweet.' She cursed that child with the evil eye." The voice is coming from a small, weathered woman, a crown of white tufts on her head, her face wizened like a golden raisin. "I tell you, Vanya knows that healer in Brooklyn, we should bring her in. What can it harm?"

"You must be Bubbe," I say, standing in the doorway, and the lady grins, perfectly straight teeth. Dentures, like Dadi's.

"Ah, the girl doctor." The woman reaches up and touches my shoulder. I'm taller than her at five foot two. "Alfred told me of you. But you are very young." I laugh, and she grins again, but when I offer my hand, she backs away. "Well, child, come in. Don't stand in the threshold." I follow her into the room, and she leads me to Mr. Plotkin, rather than Alina. Because in Russia, like in India, children should be seen and not heard. Not listened to.

And the news we bring isn't good. Her white blood count is low. She's struggling.

Deep worry lines indent Mr. Plotkin's face, and I know he can tell, too. He stands near the bed, dabbing her forehead with a cool compress and giving himself an ulcer.

I take one look at Alina and start worrying about congestive heart failure—a side effect that's killed plenty of patients. She's a twig, collarbones jutting from her hospital gown, bruises marking her cheeks and arms, her eyes sunken and bulging, her cheeks swollen from the fluid retention. The blue bruises are spreading across her pale white skin like a raging river flooding its banks. It's only been a few days since we last met, but already the change is drastic.

"I'm okay," she says as her grandmother frowns. "I had ice cream for lunch. Plain old strawberry, better than nothing," she says, then waves me over. "I would die—pun intended—for some good pad thai. Do you think you could make that happen?"

I laugh. "I'll see what I can do."

Cho glares my way, then proceeds with updating vitals. "You're handling chemotherapy well, and we're thinking about trying an even stronger dosage to be more aggressive with our treatment."

"I don't want to be more aggressive," she interrupts. "I don't want to do this at all."

Bubbe grimaces, but she's nodding. "She doesn't need a doctor. She needs a healer."

"I need a break," Alina says, and I can feel her wanting to roll her eyes at her grandmother. "I need it to be over. Either way."

"That would be ill-advised." Cho doesn't quite look at her, instead focusing on making notes in his folder.

So I have to chime in. "You've got to get better if we're gonna stuff you full of Thai food and ice cream," I say. "And I'm waiting for the day when you'll cook for me." I lean down close and whisper, "In fact, remind me to show you my sister's FoodTube videos. I bet you could do some, too."

She cowers into the bed and winces—in pain and something else— and I realize how insensitive my comment was. The cancer is literally eating her alive. The last thing she wants right now is witnesses.

"I can't cook. I can barely eat," she says, bursting into tears. "I can barely get up to go to the bathroom, and every time I brush my hair, it falls out in clumps." She runs her hands to show us, strands of it spilling into her palms. "My friends are back from their vacations and having pool parties and I'm stuck here, all by myself."

I swallow hard. "I'm sure they can visit," I say. My voice sounds defeated, even to me. In the end, it was just me and Harper all the time. Because Lizzie bailed early. And then even Vish stopped showing up.

"Yeah. I don't want them to come here and see me like this," Alina says. "I can't blame them for not wanting to be here. Can you?"

Yes. Yes, I can. And, I realize with Lizzie, I still do.

But I don't have time to worry about that right now.

"Well, you need to focus on getting better," Howard says.

"As I said—and I'll discuss this with your father—a more aggressive treatment is probably the smartest option," Cho adds.

When she looks at me for my take, I bite my lip and nod. He's right. Even though it kills me to admit it.

Mr. Plotkin sighs. "Can I talk to you guys for a second outside?" he asks. Bubbe starts hovering and fussing as soon as we head to the door, waving us away, dismissive.

We follow Mr. Plotkin out, the worry in his voice unsettling all of us. As soon as we're a few feet from the door, he breaks down, a shudder moving through his thin frame. "My wife lost her job last week," he says. "Which means we have one month of insurance on Cobra, and then we're—"

"Shit," Cho says, then catches himself. "I mean, that's very unfortunate. Does your work provide any kind of coverage? Maybe we could talk to someone—"

"I'm a professor," he says. "I mean, adjunct. There's nothing. She was the stable one. But all the time away, here with Alina, made them think she wasn't taking the work seriously. How could she? This is life or death. Don't they understand?"

I step forward, putting a hand on Mr. Plotkin's shoulder. "We'll call the insurance and see if they can extend the Cobra out. Legally, they have to provide a year and a half."

"We just can't afford it." Mr. Plotkin looks grim. "We won't be the first to lose someone because of this. Or the last."

"We'll do everything we can to prevent that," I insist. "We'll fix this, Mr. Plotkin. Do you trust us?"

He nods as he clasps my hands, but his are shaking.

Our next stop is little Brendan Jackson, and his grandmother.

"I asked them to discharge him this week," Ms. Ruby says, her voice full of conviction. "This is all too much for him, really. I think the best thing is to just to keep him home, to pray on it. But Ericka insisted we keep him here. She won't quit until there's nothing left of the boy," she adds, her voice dropping, even though Brendan's got his earbuds in, his eyes focused on the game he's playing on his phone.

"Frankly, Ms. Ruby, I tend to agree with your daughter," Cho says too harshly. "I do believe his condition is deteriorating, and treatment is critical."

"I'd like to see evidence that this is medically necessary," Ms. Ruby says, her chin jutting. "Show me the proof that he's improving. I think all these chemicals are just making him worse."

That's when I notice the tears slipping down Brendan's face. He's still staring at the screen, silent, seemingly unaware. The salty streaks marring his still-round cheeks betray him.

"You see, Saira, dear," Ms. Ruby says. "My boy's tired. Exhausted. He can't take much more of this."

If he doesn't, he'll die, I want to say. But I don't.

"These things take time, Ms. Ruby," Howard says. "It's always darkest before dawn."

Ms. Ruby nods, but I know what she's thinking: Her grandbaby's life is at stake here, and time is the one thing they really don't have.

We go back to the intern lounge between patient check-ins, and while Dr. Howard inputs chart updates, José plops himself down in cushy papasan chair I've stuffed into the far corner.

"This was a good decision," he says, removing his loafers and curling up into it. "Can we take twenty before the next go? I'm going to close my eyes a minute."

How can he sleep when the world's falling apart? I log on to my laptop. I use the intern landline to call the Plotkins' insurance company and ask about an ETA for the transfer paperwork, on speaker, so the whole team can hear.

"The Cobra extension is pending approval," the woman tells me in a nasally voice. "They have another insurance option available."

"No, they don't."

"Yes, through the father's university job," the woman says.

"I don't think that's a feasible option," I say.

"Hold, please."

While the Muzak plays, I watch the video of Link again—on silent, of course—on my phone. I've been watching it nonstop for days, like a total stalker. I haven't seen him since the mall.

"Dr. Sehgal?" The nasal lady's back on the line.

"Yes, ma'am," I say. "All set?"

"No, actually, we're not," the woman says. "Cobra is pending approval provided they prove the university insurance is not an option. In the meantime, the other issue is on your end. The hospital administrator says they won't readmit the patient until prior invoices are paid. Dr. Davis, the head administrator, declined approval."

"What?"

"Dr. Davis—"

"No, I mean, I heard you. I don't understand."

"It seems, Dr. Sehgal," the woman says, all snark, "that you have been overruled. So I suggest you take it up with her."

"Oh, believe me, I will." I slam down the phone without saying goodbye. It gives me no real satisfaction. Alina needs this treatment. *Needs.* Or she will die. I have to do something about this.

José perks one of his perfectly groomed eyebrows at me. He stands, towering over me, and tries to place a calming hand on my shoulder. "Breathe, Saira. Now, I know, I know. You're mad. Don't go storming in there like this. It'll only make things worse. Let's figure out what to do." He ponders for a second. "Maybe a GoFundMe?"

"We can't do that," Howard says, shaking her head in disbelief. "I mean, maybe I can walk Mr. Plotkin through the process, but legally we have to stay out of it, per hospital rules."

I'm shaking, I'm so mad. I have to get myself together. José's right. I have to stop, breathe, think. "I know what to do. I'm going over Davis's head—I'll speak to Dr. Charles, the hospital chief, about this directly."

Howard's about to lecture, but Cho steps into our little circle then, his face grim. "Come on," he says, completely ignoring my rant, as if nothing's wrong, as if this is business as usual. Which I guess it is. "We've got patients."

I nod, and José gives me one more encouraging pat on the shoulder. Then he passes us each the new patient file.

I take one look at the name on top and nearly pass out, dropping the file. Paper is everywhere, and José drops down to gather it up as I blubber incoherent apologies. My cheeks are blazing and my neck is slick with sweat.

It's him.

Link.

Lincoln Chung-Radcliffe.

He's been right here all along.

And then I realize what that means. A readmit. That can't be good news.

"Shit," I say. "I'm sorry. Shit."

"You gotta watch the mouth," José says. "Davis is definitely not gonna be pleased if she catches that."

"Uh-huh," I say as he and Howard head out. "Hey," I call, hanging back. "I'm too wound up. Maybe I'll go see Dr. Charles." Or Davis. "Can you guys can do this one without me?"

Nurse José walks back to me, takes his little flashlight and checks both of my eyes. Then he takes my stethoscope and tries to place it over my heart, although my white coat's in the way.

"What are you doing?"

"You must be sick," José says, incredulous. "Do you want Davis to fire you? Because missing rounds is a smart way to do it."

"Yeah," Howard says. "Besides, Cho's already winning—and you know we can't have that." She heads out the door, fully expecting me to follow.

I sigh. This was inevitable, of course. The odds that he'd be admitted to my very small department and not have me on his case were minuscule at best. And aside from dropping dead this very second, there's nothing much I can do to change things now.

Patient Name: Lincoln Chung-Radcliffe

DOB: February 11, 2001

DIAGNOSIS: Acute myelogenous leukemia, metastatic

PROGNOSIS: 30 percent success rate with chemotherapy; 50 percent if a donor match is found

NOTES: Lincoln Chung-Radcliffe was admitted to Princeton Presbyterian for acute leukemia, metastatic, his first recurrence. He was previously treated at Princeton Presbyterian with a similar diagnosis at age 13 via CAT scan, blood count, and bone marrow biopsy. Treatment via chemotherapy eradicated the growth, sending the patient into remission, though follow-up care was continued.

Relapse occurred when the patient was 16, after two years cancer-free. Dr. Arora, who supervised the patient's care during his initial occurrence, admitted as inpatient for an aggressive plan including chemotherapy, to stop myelogenous growth from progressing in his bone marrow. However, Dr. Charles observes that perhaps the best course of action is immediate mandate for bone marrow transplant, as this is a recurrence.

CHAPTER 14

My heart drops as I read through Link's chart. I knew it was bad, but I didn't know how bad. He's been putting on a brave front. Which is good, in a way, staying upbeat. But also terrible.

I'm not ready—for any of this, really, at all—but I know the time has come. I have to face him. And I have to tell him the truth.

But I'm a mess, in all ways. I stop in front of the mirror by the sink on the way out and take a second to smooth my hair—and my eyebrows, which are at it again. I rush out the door and catch up with the others.

I head toward Lincoln's hospital room, my body heavy with dread. The dress under my lab coat is drenched with sweat, and even my feet in my flats feel sticky and gross. The worst part is the way my heart is racing, a too-fast thrum I haven't experienced since I took the MCAT—severe heart palpitations, generally a signal of intense anxiety or stress. Usually harmless. Except when you're about to face the boy you kind of, sort of like and clearly shouldn't like, who thinks you're a kid, like him, and not the Girl Genius who's officially about to be one of his cancer doctors. Who needs to tell him that his diagnosis is pretty grim.

I take a deep breath outside the door, then push it open. Howard, Cho, and Arora are already surrounding the bed—and Nurse José is giving his usual chipper introduction. A woman—she looks a lot like him, of Korean descent with dark hair and tired brown eyes—so I assume she's his mom—stands lean and tall at the edge of the bed next to Howard.

I tuck myself sort of behind Howard, slightly out of sight, and hope to get through this unnoticed.

"You're in great hands here at Princeton Presbyterian," Nurse José says. "Drs. Cho, Howard, and Sehgal here will be working with Dr. Arora—who's familiar with your case from the last time—to plot out a course of action."

"Dr. Cho, will you outline your proposed treatment strategy for Lincoln's case?" Dr. Arora says, looking at his own patient file. He looks exhausted, too, but flashes me a bright smile.

Cho clears his throat, then starts outlining his proposal. "As you know, a recurrence can be alarming, and sometimes more difficult to treat than the first, given an already weakened immune system and some built-up resistance to certain treatment strategies, which is why we proposed in-patient treatment at this time. We're working as a team to ensure the utmost in care. I propose that we start with a softer course of chemo—not as invasive as the previous one—to see if that reduces or stops the spreading of the cancer. That way, we can also ensure that Link's body can tolerate the treatment. If it works, we can eliminate the damaged cells pretty quickly and stop the recurrence completely. If not, we'll have to look at more exhaustive options."

Howard clears her throat and pulls me forward by the arm so I can actually see the patient.

Link sits perched up in the bed—his cheeks more hollow, his hair thinner than it was just a week ago at the mall. Or wait—the ski cap. It was strategic.

He's focused on the big box TV set to a music channel, his eyes still on the screen for a second before they turn to us, finally. And then they narrow. And then widen. And then narrow again. It's enough to make a girl dizzy. Or maybe that's the heart palpitations, which are still going strong and oh so fun.

"Wait a minute—" He looks confused. Which makes sense.

"Hi," I say weakly.

"Saira with an *i*?" he asks. "What are you doing—" He sits straight up in the bed now, completely focused on me, as if he can't quite see me clearly or something. As if his eyes are deceiving him.

"I'm actually Dr. Sehgal."

"Girl Genius," Cho adds with a smirk. "You know, the real-life Doogie Howser?"

"Doogie who?"

Of course he doesn't know. The show is ancient. Why would he? Why do I even know?

"Oh yeah," Lincoln's mom chimes in. "I read about you in the paper. I'm Maggie Chung-Radcliffe. Link's mom." She's smiles as she shakes my hand. "I'd love to hear more about your Doctors Without Borders trips to Mexico. So fascinating."

"Yup," Arora says, annoyed. "Girl Genius. Anyway. Dr. Sehgal is an intern here, like Dr. Cho and Dr. Howard, and she'll also be part of the team on your case. Tell me, Lincoln, are you in pain?"

"No, I'm all right," he says, still staring at me. "Seventy-eight-percent prognosis. Decent odds. Especially for take two."

The same thing he said the other day. He opens his mouth again, then shuts it, like a fish, confused and swimming in circles. His eyebrows rise, then fall, then he opens his mouth to speak, and I think he's going to say something about me, about us, about the fact that I'm not a patient. Instead he says, "But they're going down fast." He looks me square in the eye. "My odds. Am I right?"

Cho presumes the question is addressed to him. "Unfortunately, we're not legally at liberty to discuss a prognosis—things can change so quickly, and of course there are no guarantees. You should know, yes, that we're at the stage where a marrow transplant in the strongest option, and given your racial background, the chances of finding a perfect match are slim. However, we've only just started, and we have a few resources to exhaust, especially within the Korean community, which gives us the strongest chance of finding a solid match. Getting the word out, to family, friends, and the larger community, will be key."

Link's mom nods. "We've already started reaching out to our church group and other local organizations within Princeton. I guess it's time to broaden the search."

"I've begun reaching out to Asian-and Korean-specific cancer organizations who help draft up a campaign to reach donors," Cho chimes in—and it suddenly becomes clear to me why he was asked to consult. He's connected to this community in a way the rest of us aren't. "Social media is critical here," he adds. "And the hospital's PR team is already working on press releases and some news placement to get the word out."

"All right, time for blood work," José says. "Saira, you're up this time."

"Yeah, actually, if we could have some privacy, that would rock," Link says, surprising everyone. That's not usually how this goes.

"I don't think that's a good idea," Arora says.

"I can handle it," I say. "Maybe Link wants to chat with someone, uh, closer to his own age?"

I have to explain. I have to fix this. If I can.

Arora reluctantly nods. "Clear out. José will be right outside if you need help, Saira. And Mrs. Chung-Radcliffe, if you come with me, I can go through some of the donor drive paperwork with you in the meantime."

They all shuffle out, Cho looking particularly irritated.

My hands shake as I prep blood tubes, and the clatter of glass against glass startles both of us. Link purposefully doesn't look at me, instead staring up at the TV screen, or at his arm as he lays it flat, elbow down, at his side. The median cubital vein—that bright blue one in the forearm—beckons, awake and ready for the venipuncture.

I can't bring myself to do it. Not yet. Not without saying something, anything, first.

"This might hurt a little," I say. Or a lot. Which I don't say.

"It always does." His voice is bitter, not mean.

I open my mouth to speak, but I don't know what else to say. I take the alcohol swab and set my mind to the process, step-by-step, familiar and mindless. My heart rocks from side to side, thumping so loud I can hear it in my ears, like when Taara used to bounce tennis balls off the wall between our rooms, out of control and unignorable.

I reach over, trying to stop the tremor in my hand before I clasp his arm.

"Go ahead and do it," he says, and we both look up at the same time, our eyes locked in this weird game of seesaw, where the other will go flying if either one of us shifts our weight.

Link flinches as I insert the needle, and then again as I attach the blood tube. Then I start the fluids, flicking the bag with one hand the way Dr. Arora taught me to ensure there are no air bubbles.

"Cold," he says. "I always forget."

"Yeah, you think you get used to it—"

"So you're not a patient, I take it?"

"Actually," I say, looking down at the patient file and avoiding eye contact, "I never said was. You presumed it."

"Yeah, because you were, like, in the patient lounge. And, you know, sixteen. Like me."

"I can see what might have given you that impression."

"And yet you let me assume it."

"Well, you know what they say about assumptions."

"Yeah, well, if I'm an ass, so are you."

I pull the tube out—a little too hard, I'll admit—and he flinches again. "Ow," he says.

"Sorry," I say.

"I'm sure you are," he says. His eyes are back on the screen now, not looking at me, and his energy has completely shifted.

I don't exist at all. I feel the cold of the fluids rushing through my veins the way they are through his right now. Like ice. Despite the sweat pooling at the small of my back and at the nape of my neck. Despite the fact that my hands are still shaking and that electricity, that light, is still bolting through me like thunder.

"All set," I say.

"Good," he says, not taking his eyes off the screen. "Let Dr. Arora know I'd like to talk to him please."

"Will do," I say, gathering the blood work kit and packing up. "See you later."

"Uh-huh."

He wants to talk to Dr. Arora. And he definitely does not want to talk to me. This is it. The end. It's all over. Me and Link, 100 percent. But maybe all the rest of it, my career, too. I knew I should have fixed this. Now it's too late.

Diagnosis: Disaster.
Prognosis: Chance of survival, slim to none.

CHAPTER 15

When I walk out the door, it's clear that, as much as Link wanted privacy, we've had an audience the whole time. Howard and Cho are all standing right outside, staring expectantly, while José paces, the anxiety an exclamation point between his eyebrows. As soon as I walk through, he races toward me, grabbing me by the arm and leading me away.

"Why didn't you tell me?" he whisper-shouts as he leads me toward the intern lounge. "I mean. This is serious."

"I know. I'm about to get fired, right?"

"No, I mean—he's adorable! But yeah, you're in trouble for sure. Davis does not look favorably upon, uh, patient-staff relations."

"There have been no relations!" I nearly shout. Not that I maybe wouldn't want there to be but . . . "Just, like, a few conversations."

We both frown.

"And he thinks—" José's eyebrows are jumping.

"Thought," I interrupt.

"That you're a patient." Howard invades our little circle, and she's grinning despite my trauma. "Oops."

"Yeah, not a good look," Cho says, pushing his way into the group. "This could mean serious trouble."

"But nothing actually happened," I say with a sigh. "Like, at all."

"That's not what it seemed like in there," Cho says, and he can't keep the smirk off his face.

Howard frowns. "Yeah, that chemistry? Mind. Blown."

"And in front of his mama, no less," José says with a laugh.

I grin for a second. I can't help it. So it wasn't just me imagining it. But maybe that makes things worse. "Yeah. So I mean, nothing happened, and nothing can happen. Nothing will happen. I'll just make that clear. To everyone involved."

"You can start right now," a deep voice says. Arora towers over us all, and for once in his life, he's not smiling. "Come with me, Dr. Sehgal. The rest of you, back to your rounds."

He starts walking toward the oncology administration office, his strides so broad I can barely keep up. I practically run behind him, trying not to drop my files—or break a sweat.

He stops abruptly in front of his office door, and I crash right into him. He still doesn't crack a smile.

I look up, wearing my best "who me?" expression.

He opens his office door and gestures for me to step inside. "Have a seat, Dr. Sehgal."

I can see the creases in his forehead—all I can see above the big screen of his computer—working as he ponders an email or something. I know he's still frowning.

I clear my throat a bit to get his attention. "So, am I grounded?" I say, a little too bright.

"If Davis gets an earful—which is super likely—then you'll be way more than grounded. Do you care to explain what that was all about?"

"Uh, I, uh . . ."

"Gave Lincoln the distinct impression that you were a patient, that much is clear. Did anything else happen?"

"Absolutely not, sir." I flinch at the word "sir." How old am I? "I mean, I ran into him here, and at the mall and stuff. And we talked about food and our grandmothers and music and Bollywood movies, but, like, that was all." Even though it kind of feels like that was everything.

"And what about that day in the lobby?"

"That was nothing. He offered me a ride. I didn't accept." See? I can do this.

"Well, in any case, you will remain in the employ of Princeton Presbyterian—for now. I—despite my better instincts—will refrain from reporting this to Dr. Davis. But this ends here and now. Got it?"

He sounds like my dad giving me a lecture when I miss curfew. Good cop to Mom's bad, but with a measured sternness to keep him from cracking a smile. He frowns, clearly unfamiliar with the extended internal dialogue of teenagers. "Got it?" he repeats.

I nod gravely, just like I do when I convince Papa not to report back to Mom. "Oh yeah, of course. I mean, I know the rules. Doctor-patient interactions are to remain strictly professional. And they will. And they have been."

"Yes, they will," Arora says. Then he clears his throat. "Especially because Lincoln—and I—have decided it's best that you be removed from his case. His mom has reluctantly agreed. You're lucky that Mrs. Chung-Radcliffe was impressed with you and your résumé. It seems she's your saving grace here. Because while Link has asked me to remove you from the case, his mother asked me to not send details of this further up the chain. Yet. But trust me, Dr. Sehgal, if Davis hears a peep about this, from you, Link, or anyone else, there will be nothing I can do to prevent her from dismissing you."

"Thank you, Dr. Arora."

He nods, then looks back to his computer. When I don't move, he raises those bushy brows again, perplexed. "Anything else, Dr. Sehgal?"

"Well, yeah. I mean. I know Link doesn't want me on the case. But hear me out. I can still help. And I don't even have to be in the same room with him."

"I don't understand." His eyes are drifting back to the screen, so I've gotta make this good.

"Listen, I'm a teenager. And a doctor. The only teenage doctor. A curiosity. The Girl Genius."

"Don't we all know it?" he says, a little too cranky.

"So we can *use* that."

He looks at me blankly. "I don't get it."

I try not to sigh. For a doctor, he's kinda not very quick. "For the marrow campaign."

Still blank.

"For Link. Lincoln. Chung-Radcliffe." He's already shaking his head. "What Link needs right now is a match. Given his genetic background, the chances of finding one are slim. So we need to get the word out as far and wide as possible. Now, I don't really do social media much, but my friend Lizzie made me sign up on all the sites—and people just follow me. Because, Girl Genius. So she, like, tweets for me. And she's pretty awesome at it. Like, she has even more followers than me, and this kickass Instagram fashion page and stuff. So we can use that—my social media—to get the word out."

He shakes his head again, his mouth a grim line. "I told you, you're off the case."

I lean forward, trying to make him see. I can do this. "I don't even have to be on the case. I just—I just want to help him." I'm blushing, I know, and suddenly I can't look away from my hands. "I know it's a bit of a mess, but won't you let me help, at least in this small way?"

One side of his mouth has perked up a little, the left brow perched to match it. He's gonna say yes. He has to say yes. He's just about to speak, when there's a rap on the door, fast and furious. Uh-oh.

Arora literally jumps out his chair. It has to be Davis. She knows. We're doomed. Well, I'm doomed.

"Come in!" he shouts while running to the door to open it. I flinch as it swings open, expecting the worst.

But it's not Davis. Standing just outside, looking abashed and agitated, is a man, about six feet tall, dark brown hair, pale white skin, worry lines making the frown on his face so much more pronounced. He's wearing pristine tan pants with super-sharp creases and a brown corduroy jacket, complete with elbow patches, even though it's the thick of August. Which would explain why he's so sweaty and panting.

"I'll sue this hospital for millions," he says, his finger jabbing the air. "Just you wait."

Link's mom steps out from behind him, her hand on the man's shoulder, trying to calm him down. "Lincoln, relax." She's trying not to grin.

"Professor Radcliffe, Maggie," Dr. Arora says. "Please, come in. Have a seat. Let me explain."

"I don't want to hear it!" the man yells, though he actually comes in and takes a seat next to me. Link's mom hovers behind him. "Maggie already told me everything. An affair? With a doctor? Unacceptable."

He's drumming his fingers on the desk, his eyes taking in every inch of the room, as Link's mom stands behind him, rubbing his shoulders soothingly. She smiles at me.

"It was hardly an affair. Barely a flirtation," Dr. Arora says. "And a terribly mild one at that, as far as I can tell." Womp womp. "And while doctor-patient interactions as such are never appropriate, I'd like to introduce you to the doctor in question, Professor Radcliffe." He waves toward me and I stand to shake his hand. "This is Dr. Sehgal. Saira Sehgal."

The man just blinks at me, not quite comprehending. "Is she a candy striper?"

"No, sir," I say, sticking out my hand. "UMDNJ grad, oncology intern, Bollywood film fan. Can't say I've ever been a candy striper, though." I smile, then pull it back a little. Too much teeth. I sit, turning a bit toward Link's dad, trying to seem friendly. And smart.

Still, confusion rules the man's face. "I don't get it. She's a kid."

"I told you she was a kid," Link's mom says. "But you were too busy ranting."

"Yes, Dr. Saira Sehgal, Girl Genius," Arora announces, a little too dry for my taste. "She's sixteen. Just like Link. He mistook her for a patient."

The man speaks slowly, as if we're perhaps not quite speaking English. As if I'm not even in the room. "A doctor? Not a patient? And she's sixteen?"

"Yes," I say, exasperated. "A doctor. Do you want me to have them fax my diploma?" Okay, maybe I shouldn't have snapped. But Link's mom giggles a little.

"In any case, Professor Radcliffe," Arora says, his voice patient but tired, "we've removed Dr. Sehgal from Link's case—"

"But I have an idea," I interrupt. "I can help!"

"Yes," Arora says, weary. "Perhaps you could. But that would entirely be up to Link and his parents."

"I fail to understand." Professor Radcliffe looks confused, and maybe just a bit exhausted. "We are pushing forward with the search for a donor, correct? That is the next best step?"

Link's mom whispers something in his ear, and the professor seems to relax ever so slightly. "Lincoln seems pretty reluctant to have you involved," she says to me. "Of course, you understand why things might be awkward."

"I do understand. Just hear me out." I have to make them see how this could help. "I have a plan."

Arora sits back down at his desk, frowns at me, then shrugs. I take that as my cue. "See, as I was telling Dr. Arora, as the youngest doctor in the United States, I have a bit of a following. Like, on social media. My friend Lizzie, who's like a social media rock star—she wants to be an actress—she runs my Twitter and Instagram and stuff. And it's more than thirty thousand followers on Twitter. Plus, every so often, news media likes to check in to see 'what I'm up to.'"

The professor looks more confused than ever, but Link's mom is nodding, her smile getting wider as I continue. She has the same dent in her cheek that Link does.

"We can channel those resources as we kick off the hunt for a donor for Link. Start a social media campaign, do a TV spot or three. I mean, I'll help however I can, even if you don't want me on the case."

Professor Radcliffe is about to open his mouth. Another zillion questions, I'm sure.

But Link's mom gets there first. "I think it's a great idea. We need to use every resource we can find. And Saira, your celebrity status, at least in the medical community, might just give us the edge we need."

We beam at each other for a second.

Then she says, "Now we just need to convince Link."

I'm showered, changed, and waiting for Vish to pick me up so we can go see the new Shah Rukh Khan thriller. He's late, naturally, and Cho is on night call, so he's grumbling around the intern lounge, waiting for something to happen and generally being a nuisance. He's been lounging on the couch, his laptop open, perusing Grubhub for dinner options for the past hour.

"So this boyfriend of yours know about your, uh, thing with the patient?"

"It's so not a thing. In fact, it's absolutely the opposite of a thing." It's been eight hours since Link found out, and six since I floated my genius plan, as I like to call it. But I haven't heard word from anyone—including Davis, thank gods—about it since then. And my mom hasn't come roaring in and torn me to shreds, which 100 percent means she doesn't know. Yet. I hope it stays that way. But somehow I doubt it.

"You doll up for the cancer kid but not the boyfriend?" Cho's smirking, and it makes me want to smack him. "What happened to that flowery thing from before?"

I look down at my clothes. Capris and a raggedy old T-shirt from the Shah Rukh show Vish and I went to when we were twelve. Super appropriate. "He likes me the way I am," I say with a shrug. "And he would definitely approve of this T-shirt. It's sentimental."

"I'm just saying."

"Yeah, yeah," I say. I think about plopping down on the couch to wait some more. My feet are itchy again, though. I kind of know where they want to take me. And I don't have the power to stop them. I weave through the halls, waving to patients and nurses in a daze, and find myself right back where it all started. The patient lounge.

I don't even have to open the door to know he's in there. I can hear the music, plaintive, lonely, lovely, as he strums his guitar, and the hitch in his voice as he tries to lift himself above the pain.

I lean against the door gently, trying not to give myself away as I peer through the small gap between the layers of paper (and grime) that cover the window.

He's sitting on a stool by the window, the last rays of sunlight and dust swirling, just like they did that first day. He's in hospital-issue sweats, and the IV bag has followed him here on a cart, constant company, just like it was for Harper in those later days. It makes my stomach jump in this odd, jittery way, familiar and excruciating. There was nothing I could do for Harper then, but that doesn't have to be the case this time. Not with Link. I can help him, I know I can. I just have to convince him to let me.

And maybe, just maybe, I know how.

Dear Link,

I'm the ass. I admit it.
So hear me out. Please?
Meet me here in the patient lounge, Monday, 4 p.m.
Worth your while. I promise.

Saira

CHAPTER 16

"Can you drive me to Lizzie's?" I say as soon as I climb into Vish's car.

"Well, hello to you, too," he grumbles. "And I thought we were going to the movies? I bought the tickets."

"It's urgent." I feel guilty. I mean, it's Shah Rukh Khan. "I'll get us tickets for the eleven p.m." He opens his mouth to speak. "I'll convince Papa. Promise."

"All right," he says, shrugging as he starts the engine. "What's this about?"

I turn to look at him as he pulls out of the parking lot, then take a deep breath.

"Do you think we should tell her?"

He hits the brakes. Hard. "Why would we do that?"

He's clearly not ready. I'm going to have to tread carefully.

"You remember that guy?"

"What guy?" A horn honks behind us. He starts driving again, but everything about him is tense now.

"The one I showed you. On my phone the other day."

"Your patient? The rock-star wannabe?" He's trying to focus on the road, but also keeps glancing my way, trying to read me. It's making me nervous. I put a hand on his knee, but he shifts, tense. "What about him?"

"So I need to help him."

"Yeah, you're his doctor."

"I'm not. They took me off his case. But I can still help."

"How?"

"He needs a bone marrow donor. And one of the best ways to find one will be via media. And social media."

It's like a light bulb goes off, and I can see his shoulders slump back, his breathing go easy again. "Oh, of course. That's perfect. She can totally do that." But the bulb flickers. "What does that have to do with me? With us?" He peers over at me, pausing at a red light, trying to catch my eye, to unravel what I'm saying. "Wait. You."

I'm sweating now—my palms, my neck, my back slick—even though the AC's blasting.

"Oh, Guddi," he says, his face falling a bit. But he recovers quickly. "You like him."

I nod, but I don't know if he notices it, because his foot is on the gas now, and we're moving too fast, pulling onto Lizzie's street.

"She knows?"

"Yeah. Well, sort of. But it's not like I did anything." And it's not like this, us, is real anyway. Right? "And I mean, you already have a boyfriend."

"That's not the point. It's just—I mean, obviously it looks really bad. It looks like—"

"I'm cheating."

He actually cracks a smile then, pulling into park, and rests his forehead on the steering wheel. He's sweaty, too. "Yeah, which, of course, is ridiculous. But, Saira. Guddi. I—"

"You're not ready."

He looks at me again, and shakes his head. "Not yet."

"Okay. We'll play it strictly professional." I take a deep breath, my hand on the door handle, ready or not. "But just so you know: It's gonna be weird."

He nods.

"So, whatever I say, just back me up."

Lizzie's in her pj's when she answers the door. Weird. No plans on a Friday night? She looks shocked to see us. And that makes me feel so much worse. Because we were totally going to go to the movies—Shah Rukh Khan, no less—without her. Again.

"What are you guys doing here?" The house is quiet, which means her mom is out.

"Need your help."

She looks alarmed but opens the door wide, and we walk right in.

It's been a while since I've been to Lizzie's. She always came to my house, instead of the other way around, but when her parents split, her mom—a literature professor at Princeton—moved them to a smaller house closer to campus. She stayed in the same school, but she wasn't just a few blocks away anymore. We made it work. In fact, for a while, she slept over my house a few times a week. Until middle school, anyway. And, well, the genius track for me.

"What's going on?" She looks from me to Vish and back again, worried. "Is Dadi okay?"

Dadi? Why would she think that?

"Of course," I say, too abrupt. "She's fine." I take a deep breath, then decide to sit first. Vish settles in next to me, and I follow Lizzie's gaze from the couch to the kitchen, wondering if she should offer something. "We're fine. We're all fine. Except. Remember that kid?"

"What kid?"

"Link. The guy from the mall."

Her eyes light up for a second, but she tempers that fast, looking at Vish. "Yeah. The guy who did *Rock Star Boot Camp*. The cancer kid."

Vish raises his eyebrows, his mouth doing a weird pursing thing. Like he's afraid of what I might say. Of what Lizzie might think. But he's got nothing to worry about.

"Yeah. He's sick again. And it's bad this time."

"Oh," she says, her face falling a little. "I mean, you said he proba-bly was. So he's officially your patient now?"

"Yeah, sort of. I mean he's admitted. But not my patient. Technically." I take a deep breath. "And that's why I need your help."

"Do you think I might be a match?" she says, tentative, not quite sure how she feels about that.

"No. Maybe. It definitely doesn't hurt to get tested. But I thought you could help in another way."

Her eyes are on Vish now, waiting for his reaction, his worry or approval. Waiting to take her cue from him. Instead of me. I guess I really would be the bad guy in this scenario. Even though I haven't done anything wrong. Right?

"So the hospital is gearing up this campaign. To find a match. I mean, it's a long shot. A really long shot, given his background. But the key thing is to get the word out, to get the story out, to make people want to help him."

She nods, still confused. What does that have to do with her?

"So I thought, maybe, you could like do some social media for him. Set up an account across on all the platforms. Build a following. Like yours. Like mine."

She's still looking at Vish, unsure. Is she betraying him by helping Link. By helping me? He nods. "He needs our help. And you rock at this."

"Like, he has a few followers on everything—@linkradrocks—but it needs to be more. It needs to go big. So we can use my accounts. And blow out his." She opens her mouth to speak, but I plow forward. "We can get access. His mom's on board."

"His life depends on it," Vish says, his voice all thick and nasal. He takes my hand. "We have to do what we can."

"And technically, I can't," I say. "I'm not on the case. But I told them that I could help. That you could help. It has to be sort of officially unofficial. Though they'd pay you, probably." Or I could.

"And you're cool with this?" she asks Vish, which annoys me. But I get it. Sort of.

"Why wouldn't I be cool with it?" he says. "He's a patient. He needs help. We can help."

She nods, and I can see the wheels in her head turning already. "Yeah, I think I know how to do this. Video is key," she says, looking right at Vish. "Because he's got a look. And already the sympathy thing is working for him." She pauses, struck by something. "But you know what would *really* help? *Rock Star Boot Camp.*"

Of course. That's it. But how do we make that happen, now that he's in the hospital?

I frown. "Yeah. I don't know if that's possible now. But we'll figure it out."

"Well," Liz Biz says, "count me in. #TeamLink."

"Awesome, cool. Amazing," Vish says, standing. "Now, Lizzie— you down for some Shah Rukh Khan? Complete with subtitles?"

CHAPTER 17

Monday morning dawns hot and sweaty. And while all I can think about is Link, I've got a lot on my to-do list. Starting with Alina and the money situation.

I've been at the hospital now for nearly a month, but I still haven't stopped on the top floor to see Dr. Charles—the man who was Harper's primary oncologist, and my mentor on the path to medicine. He's the one who actually heard me out when I first diagnosed her black-and-blues as something more than your usual bruises, then helped me comb through those big fat medical encyclopedias to pinpoint it was cancer. He's the one that wrote recommendations for me for the Hopkins' Genius Program, then Princeton, then UMDNJ. His word weighed heavily on my landing the internship here at Princeton Presbyterian—which will never cease to annoy Davis. Essentially: Without his guidance, I'd still be your average high school junior, fretting about SATs and junior prom. But I'm not. And I have him to thank for it.

Which is why this conversation is not going to be easy. But I have to do something about Alina's insurance, and I think it's better to go to the source than have Davis cut me off at the knees. A patient's life is at stake here. I have to do what I have to do.

I knock on Charles's door once, twice, three times, fast.

"Come on in, Saira!" Charles stands as I enter his office, and waves me over for a hug. He looks far older than the last time I saw him, his hair fully gray instead of its former salt-and-pepper, and face far more wrinkled than I remember. "Or should I say, Dr. Sehgal!"

"You should, though Davis won't."

Charles laughs, and it transforms him into the man I remember— usually so stoic and serious, but just a giant teddy bear when he was around kids. Mom always said that's what made him the best pediatric oncologist—he didn't seem cold and calculating while delivering often devastating prognoses. Which is critical when you're talking about the lives of children. "Davis doesn't make it easy," he says. "But with good reason. We want only the best of the best here at Princeton Presbyterian. That has to be earned."

"Yeah, well, I'm trying. But she seems to have it out for me in any case."

Charles grins. "Believe it or not, you remind me of her when she was younger."

"Decidedly not," I say. *Yeah right.*

"Trust me, Saira. You'll do just fine."

"If you say so. Anyway, there's something I wanted to talk to you about."

"A patient, so I've heard." Uh-oh. What has he heard?

"Yes, a patient. Alina Plotkin."

"Plotkin. Ah yes, Davis did mention her. The situation seems pretty dire."

"Yeah, the insurance has dropped them, which means that we can't proceed with treatment. But it's critical that we not stop right now. She needs all the support she can get, and when I talked to the insurance company, they were totally unreasonable. They said that Davis—"

"I'm sure Davis is doing the best she can in this situation. We have the best intentions for all of our patients, of course, and I'd hate for you—or anyone—to think that wasn't the case. But these days, the way things work, sometimes it's out of our hands."

I want to speak but I'm too busy lifting my jaw up off the floor.

The Dr. Charles I knew would never dismiss a patient's situation that way—especially not one in crisis. He reads the expression on my face, reaches across the desk, and takes my hand, trying to soothe me. But I pull it away.

"Understand this, Dr. Sehgal: We are doing our best. Sometimes situations are out of our control. Dr. Davis knows this case and this scenario intimately, and she will ultimately make the right decisions for both the patient and the hospital. It's not up to you—or me—to second-guess her thinking. This is what she's paid to do, and she's an expert."

"But Alina's family—"

"Will get through it. There are other resources available. St. Jude's for one. Or private or crowdsourced funding. This is not a rare situation in medicine these days, unfortunately, and a counselor here at the hospital has been in touch with the Plotkins to provide some guidance. They are already behind on their bills, the insurance has dropped them, and they need to regroup and rethink their strategy. This is the reality for many cancer patients—and others—these days. But you need to focus on what you're here for, and that is to learn the process of treating the disease. Of course, the family's situation is tied to the outcomes here, but there is a dedicated staff to handle these matters, and it is not your place to interfere in these intimate family matters." He clears his throat. "Here or elsewhere."

I jump. I wonder what he knows, what he's heard—and who told him. If he knows, Davis must know, and my mom, too. But I push forward, because I have to do something, anything, to help Alina.

"But—"

"You know, Saira, one of the things I've always admired about you is your passion. But you are very young. If you want to be taken seriously in this world, in the medical community, then you must learn to balance the passion with the practical, and to keep it in check when necessary."

He stands, my cue to follow him to the door. "Now, if you will, I have a meeting at ten—and I understand that you do, too." He opens the door, and I step through it, turning to look back at him. "I do think you can thrive here. You may be young and idealistic, but you're very smart, and you have a keen sense of responsibility. But the trick to a long career in medicine is to learn how to compartmentalize. You won't survive without doing so. I know you have it in you."

As he shuts the door and I start to walk away, I wonder if I do. I need to calm down. I need to compose myself. But my heart is racing, and I'm not sure where to put the anger. If I head to the intern lounge now, Cho will be the recipient of my wrath, this much I know. But if I want to help Link, I've got to stay on his good side.

I have twenty minutes before the meeting, so I head to my mom's office to grab a cup of chai. I knock a few times, but she doesn't seem to be around, so I let myself in.

My mother's office is small and cluttered—shelves full of old patient files that she insists on holding on to even though the hospital staff went to the electronic record-keeping system this summer. There's a large, bulky faux-wood desk, and two pleather chairs for patients to sit in during consults. Her chair, behind the desk, is a fancy peacock-blue velvet armchair—completely out of place here, but she insisted on buying it when she saw it. "One day, it'll go in my library," she said. She reads everything, from medical journals to pulp novels in Hindi to bodice rippers. "It's my escape," she always says.

Maybe I need to find one, too. I've been coming to this office for as long as I can remember, and spent hours here as a kid, coloring in her big fat medical books before I started reading them myself.

I get out the Quik Tea chai mix and put the kettle on. It's not anywhere near the real deal, but it will do in an emergency, and this definitely is one.

While the water is heating, I plop down at her desk and log in to her computer. I google the words *Rock Star Boot Camp*, and the show's website pops up. I click on the contestants page and there are thousands and thousands of entries. But I don't care about the rest of them I look up the words "Link Rad," and there he is, grinning back at me. His profile has been clicked some two thousand times, and it has about eleven hundred likes. We can definitely do better than that. I sign into my social media account—though it takes me a few tries to remember the password, which Lizzie set to SairaAndVishy4Eva, no exclamation point, apparently. But it has a *y* from when we were little, when Vish was still Vishy. I copy the link to Link's page and try to think of the perfect message. I type, then delete. Then type, then delete. Then type again. *I'm all about Princeton's own @LinkRadRocks for #RockStarBootCamp! Who are you rooting for?*

Yes, that seems about right. I note the number of votes he's got now, and set my smartphone to remind me to log in this afternoon to check. I don't know if this will work, but it's worth a shot. And Lizzie will know exactly how to blow it out.

I ponder tweeting about Alina's case, too, or maybe setting up a GoFundMe account myself. But that would be asking to get fired.

I get to the admin office a few minutes before the meeting's set to start, and the room is quiet—Howard and Arora are sipping coffee and chatting, while Cho's scrawling notes in a file.

I pull out my notepad and start scribbling some action items for helping Link and Alina. Social media is a start—but it's not nearly enough to make a dent.

A shadow falls over me just as I'm doodling his name into the edges of the page, and I try to cover the page with a palm. Davis.

Oh no, she knows. It's not enough that I'm off the case. She's about to fire me.

Instead, she says, "Distracted as usual, huh, Sehgal?" Loud enough that all eyes are now on us.

"No, doodling actually helps me think, Dr. Davis. I can be a bit scattered, so I use it as a strategy to help me focus so that I don't go looking for distractions." ADHD, likely, undiagnosed. But she doesn't need to know that.

"Oh, you mean like that scene you made in Dr. Charles's office?"

"I was just trying to help—"

"Am I to understand, then, Sehgal, that you went *above* my head and straight to Dr. Charles regarding matters that have absolutely nothing to do with you?" she spits. Like, literally.

"I, uh, I just thought we should do something to help the Plotkin family get through this," I stammer. "A girl's life is at stake."

"That is not the way this works, Sehgal," she says, her hands leaning hard on the table. "We are doing the best with the resources we have been given, but this hospital is not a charity. This family is already extremely behind on their payments—to both the hospital and the insurance company—and that is why the insurance company has dropped coverage. I was working with the company to try to reduce some of the debts they owe, but the agent said someone called and snapped at them, undoing all the goodwill I've managed to arrange thus far. I've also got some calls to nonprofits to arrange possible grants, but they are contingent on a clean track record and verifiable health insurance. In other words: I had things handled. But by getting Dr. Charles involved, you've set in motion a process that could unravel everything. Then the Plotkins really will have to rely on a public funding site and the goodness of strangers' hearts."

"I'm sorry," I say, still in shock. "I didn't know."

"You don't know a lot of things," Davis says. "You are always overstepping, just like your mother."

I rise at that. I am nothing like my mother. Right? I look around, but Cho is nodding and Howard is awfully focused on her coffee mug.

"Get it together, Sehgal. Every misstep you make—and I hear there have been quite a few—is a mark against you." She looks around at the others bitterly. "And need I remind you, your competition here is fierce."

With that, she turns the meeting over to Arora, who clears his throat and begins updates on the patients for the team. "The Plotkins"—he looks from me to Davis as he says this—"are planning to pull Alina from Princeton Presbyterian as soon as they can get a spot at St. Jude's," he says, "but that may be weeks or months."

"I have arranged for two weeks' extension on a shared room for Alina," Davis says, "but I can't push it further at the moment until they meet minimum balance requirements."

"Could they do a fund-raiser?" Howard says, overeager. "Maybe a bake sale or something? Or an online thing?"

"People have fund-raiser fatigue," Cho says, dismissive. "There are too many patients in need, and not enough bleeding hearts to take on the cause." I'm expecting a sneer in my direction, but for once it doesn't come. "I can further research some grants, but I think we need to push the family to remove the malignancy now. The longer they wait, the bigger the risk. They don't have the money—or the time."

I want to say something to help, offer some magical solution, but in this case—and it seems, in every case, when it comes to oncology—there simply isn't one. So I just sit and stew, listening to the whirl of useless ideas swirl around me, and doodle Link's name in the margins of my notepad.

"Sehgal." Davis's harsh voice slices through my thoughts, rushing me back to the cold, dreary reality of the hospital. "If you can't be bothered to pay attention, much less contribute, I suggest you pack up your stuff and step outside."

It's like a sock to the stomach. But she's right. I'm being pretty useless right now. I pack up my things, trying not to suck my teeth, and leave the office.

I head straight for Alina's room, and where she's watching *The Great British Bake Off.*

"Hey," I say. "Mind if I join you?"

She nods.

"Is Jessica Park on this one? She's my favorite!"

"Mine too. Those scones."

"And cupcakes."

"Perfection."

I plant myself in the chair next to Alina's bed and stare at the screen until she drifts off, trying to figure out a solution for a problem that doesn't have any easy answers. It feels too familiar, as the tears sting at my eyes. Like when I sat here for hours on end with Harper. Because sometimes all you can do is just be there. Hopefully, that's enough.

CHAPTER 18

I don't know when I fell asleep, but I awake to Bubbe snapping her fingers in front of my mouth.

"Careful," she says as Alina laughs. "You'll swallow a fly." I yawn, and she snaps some more. "Someone needs a nap," she declares, and drags me out of the chair. "Off you go. You're no good to anyone in this stupor."

Bubbe's right, so I get up and zombie over to the intern lounge, wishing I had thought to leave pj's here for these kinds of emergencies. I guess scrubs will have to do. But first, a shower.

The lights are out, and it's quiet, thank gods. I head over to the lockers and grab a pair of scrubs, stepping into the bathroom to change. But as soon as the steam hits my face, I realize someone's already in the shower.

"Sorry!" I call out, but all I get in response is a groan. A decidedly male groan. Oops. I'm about to jet when I hear a voice.

"Saira, that you?" It's Howard. Definitely not whom I was expecting.

"Dr. Howard?"

"I'll be right out!" she calls, and then steps out of the stall, her hair pulled back, a towel wrapped around her. "I thought I locked the door."

"I'm sorry. I needed to wake myself up, so I thought I'd—" I step toward the shower, but she steps in front of me.

"Let me clean it up a bit first," she says, all casual and calm. Except for the rose of her cheeks, of course. Because she definitely caught me looking at the very male (read: hairy!), very brown feet that are still in the shower, exposed to the knee, where the curtain ends.

"Okay," I say. Stepping back toward the door. I can hear Howard—and her companion—sigh in relief. "I'll see you later, Dr. Howard."

"Yep."

"And you, too, Dr. Arora."

"Sure, Saira."

Howard isn't quite sure whether to laugh or cry, so she just shuts the door, and I can hear them scurrying behind it, whispering in too-loud tones.

"You should have kept your mouth shut."

"The girl's a genius!" Arora says. "I'm sure she figured us out by now."

"Abhi, she's sixteen. This is so totally inappropriate, genius or not."

"You're the one who was all about 'getting caught cuz it's hawt.' Well, congratulations. You got your wish."

"I can still hear you!" I shout through the door, and then there's dead silence. The shower starts up again and Howard, now dressed, comes carefully through the bathroom door. She's still flushed pink, from the heat, humiliation, or maybe something else.

"I'm sorry you had to witness that," she says, sitting on the arm of the sofa, where I've plonked down with my stuff.

"Me too, believe me." I've gotta get out of here. I definitely don't need a confessional from Arora after his lecture. "You guys should be more careful."

"Oh, we're very careful." She pauses. "That's not what you meant."

"Nope."

"Yeah, I know. I mean. God, this is embarrassing. It's just, we can't get enough of each other. And we're just always here, you know? But if somebody were to find out—"

"Nobody's going to find out. At least not from me."

"Oh, thank god, Saira. I guess you know how it is, though, right?"

"Not really."

The bathroom door starts to open, and I take that as I my cue to bolt, jumping out and heading straight for the door.

Wow. Howard and Arora. Maybe some part of me suspected it that day, when she was all dolled up and he was all suited up for his date. I mean, the math makes sense. But still, I'm floored, not quite sure what to do with myself. Yes, they're consenting adults or whatever, but interpersonal staff relations are definitely not allowed. It's in the handbook and everything. And Arora is her boss. But then again, Link is—was—my patient.

I mean, is it a tactic to get ahead? No, she wouldn't do that. She must really, actually like him. I mean, he's handsome, smart, kind. What's not to like? But he is her boss. And she is my competition. Maybe sixteen-year-old me *is* unwise to hold on to this information. After all, what would Cho do? I know exactly what he'd do. Which means that's exactly what I shouldn't do.

I stop stewing and marching to find myself standing in front of the door to the patient lounge. This is becoming a habit, and a bad one at that. But today I'm here with a purpose. It's almost four o'clock, and even though I know, deep down, that he won't show up, I have to try.

I can feel that weird flutter in my stomach as I hover near the door, that anticipation that I'm getting kind of addicted to. I can almost already feel the disappointment that always follows, too, the heaviness of it nesting along my shoulders and my back. I hold my breath and push the door open, hoping for the best. And expecting emptiness. The space is quiet and dark, but there's a light snore coming from the patchy old corduroy couch that's been there longer than I've been alive. And even though we've barely touched, it's a body I'd recognize anywhere. Link.

He's here. I haven't seen him since the day they took me off his case, and I realize now that this fatigue I've been carrying is because of that. It slides right off me, and suddenly every synapse in my body is firing on overdrive, my heart racing like a champion, my nerves tingling with the desire to reach out and touch him.

But he's fast asleep, his IV bag trolley hovering over him like an overzealous nurse, one sockless foot dangling off the side of couch, the other overshooting right off the end. An arm is thrown over his eyes, hiding them from the last rays of sunlight seeping into the room, and he looks so peaceful, he could be dead—a thought that makes my heart stop—except for the slight snore. It's soft and comforting, like a glitch in a record, and I'm sure his mother appreciates it in moments like these, when it feels like a short nap could easily give way to an endless slumber.

I sit on the table across from him and take him in. He's wearing a hospital gown and sweatpants that are a few inches too short, revealing bruises that have spread, the black-and-blues deepening into purple swirls here and there. Needle pricks mark his arms, and I can tell now where he's experienced José's gentle touch versus Cho's more clinical approach. I even find the spot from the day he found out I was a doctor, not a patient. It's nearly healed now, but surrounded by more recent punctures, like the soft center of a blooming bud. Before I can stop myself, I've leaned over to touch it, and Link shocks awake, his dream stupor making him blink.

"You're here."

"Hey," he says, a slow smile spreading, then ending abruptly when he remembers he's supposed to be mad at me. "What do you want?"

"You got my note?" My eyes wander to the clock above the door.

"Yeah." He sits up, composing himself, pulling the hospital gown closed a bit. "I still haven't decided if I'll bother to show up."

My eyes wander to the clock above the door. "It's four now."

"Well, I'm not here for you," he grumbles, his voice still sleep-rumpled. "For that. I just . . . I needed a break. From José. And my mom. And everything. Including you."

He starts to detangle himself and cringes away when I try to help him. Ouch. "I just . . . I don't understand why you're so mad at me."

He sighs, but it's jagged, like a cough. He's getting worse. "Of course you don't. And that's exactly it. When I met you, I got my hopes up. I got excited. I thought you might be someone."

"Someone?"

"Someone who'd understand."

Oh. I get it now. Kind of. The way he talked to me, I thought he might be someone, too. I want to tell him that I am someone, that I do get it, but I'm not quite sure that's true.

"So anyway, you're not."

"What?"

"You don't get it. So nobody gets it. Again." A trickle of pain flashes across his face. I reach to help, but he leaps out of my grasp, his IV trolley tugging at him like a nosy Dadima, and starts for the door.

"Wait!" I jump up, beating him to the door. Blocking his path. What's wrong with me? "I just wanted to say—"

"You should have said it earlier," Link says, his eyes shining in the dim light. "Before we both made asses out of ourselves."

I grin for a second, and so does he, sheepishly. But then it fades again, and he shoves forward with his little trolley.

"I'm sorry. In any case."

He turns back to look at me, his eyes daggers now. "That's your apology?" I want to hang my head in shame. "I thought you were supposed to be some kind of genius, Saira with an *i*. Couldn't do better than that?"

"I'm—"

"Save it. I'm due for meds."

I nod. "See you round?" I try not to let my voice rise with hope.

"Doubt it," he says, shutting the door behind him, quiet but firm, in a way that shatters my heart into a million pieces.

CHAPTER 19

My hands grip the wheel, sweat slicking them away from two and ten, even though the AC is blasting.

"Relax, we're nearly there," Vish says, his voice too cheerful for eight a.m. on a Saturday morning. I should know this trip by heart—we're headed to my alma mater, Princeton University, for Vish's obligatory "sure, I'll apply" tour. But I've never actually driven here before, because I was twelve when I attended, and chaperoned by my father or Taara every day. It's essentially a waste of a trip. Vish's big plan—much to his parents' eventual surprise and chagrin, I'm sure—is to jet off to Los Angeles and study film and photography at USC. They'll be horrified when they find out, and that's not the worst of it by far. But for today, we're doing our duty as good Indian kids by checking out the local Ivy.

"Wait, wait, wait, Guddi, you're about to hit that lamppost." We ping it ever so slightly, but luckily Vish's Jeep is sturdy, and it's taken bigger hits. "Want me to park?" he asks as I drop my head down onto the steering wheel in sweaty a mix of humiliation and grief.

I nod onto the wheel and mumble yes. He pops out of the passenger side and makes his way over, opening the door to let me climb out and stand in shame by the side as he pulls the Jeep into the teeny tiny parking spot, one, two, three, like it's nothing.

"I mean, there are lots of different kinds of intelligence," Vish says, laughing as he climbs back out of the Jeep. "You can't be a genius in every aspect of your life, after all."

I *dishoom* him—fake punching like Akshay Kumar, this uber-macho action hero Vish had a crush on when he was thirteen—and he ducks and kicks back, nearly catching me on the shin for real. Then he headlocks me from the back, wrapping one arm around my neck and the other around my waist, then twirling me until we're facing each other, forehead to forehead, except he's leaning about eight inches down because I'm so damned short.

"Hey."

"Hey."

"You ready?"

"I guess," he says. "Breakfast first?"

"Yep."

We walk over to the student lounge, which is barely bustling on a sleepy summer Saturday. The only signs of life are eager wannabe Princetonians and their even more eager parents, poring over Viewbooks and campus maps as they munch on croissants and down lukewarm lattes. Ah, I remember when this was me. A rush of nostalgia hits me, but it's weird. Today, I actually fit right in with this mix. Sixteen going on seventeen, the thrill of my whole life ahead of me. Back then, I was the nerdiest of them all, barely five feet tall (though I'm only five two now!), a twig, and decidedly a child. Everyone thought I was Taara's kid sister, along for the ride as she looked at schools. But while all those kids were hopeful of their chances at Princeton, I was the sure bet. I kind of want to shake them all now, tell them to stop and enjoy the moment, not to take it all so seriously. But I wouldn't have listened to anyone who said that to me six years ago.

Vish walks back with two white-people chais—vanilla and cinnamon, so not the real deal—and a sesame bagel for us to split. He watches me as I butter it, scowling.

"Dude, can you get a little excited?" I say.

"I know. This isn't me. Nothing I've done this year is me at all. I'm, like, going through the motions."

"It'll come together."

"No, it won't. Things like this don't just happen, Saira. You know that better than anyone. You have to *make* them happen. And I'm too busy hiding to do anything about it."

"So do something."

"Like what?" he says, then takes a big chomp of bagel, little flecks of butter caught in his twelve o'clock shadow. I know he shaved this morning, but the pricklies are back already. The few times we kissed, even when we were younger, they always used to scratch. He watches me watching him, and then his eyes widen, going big, bigger, biggest, like someone's suddenly given him an IV of caffeine. "Wait. I know."

"What?"

"The perfect project to submit for my USC app."

"Oh yeah? Something set in Princeton?"

"Yes, at Princeton Presbyterian, actually."

I narrow my eyes. I'm not sure I like where this is going.

"'A day in the life of Saira Sehgal, Dr. Girl Genius.' It's perfect." I'm shaking my head, but he plows forward. "C'mon. Who else has that kind of access?"

"Cameras in the hospital suites? Davis would fire my ass. Like she needs another excuse."

"Eh, she's probably gonna do that anyway. Why not help me get into USC in the process?"

"I'm not that interesting."

"Oh, but you are. You're smart, you're funny, you're caring, you're charming. You are. And you're a certified genius. The youngest doctor in America. Come on, I already have footage from your White Coat Ceremony, and that interview thingie we practiced for MedNet. We could do this. It could be kick-ass. And maybe it would be good publicity for the hospital."

Hmmm, maybe not just the hospital.

"I could make it happen," I say slowly, dragging out the tension. "On one condition."

"What condition?"

"Link Rad. Lincoln Chung-Radcliffe." I've only caught glimpses of him since that day in the lounge, because he's decidedly avoiding me. But I can still hear the grumble in his voice, all sleepy and rough. And it makes me miss him. Can you miss someone you barely know?

Vish is smirking in a way that makes me want to punch him. "Him again? I thought you were already on it. With Lizzie."

"Yeah. But you can help, too."

"By getting tested?"

"Yes, definitely. It never hurts to do that, and you could actually save a life. But in Link's case, like I told Lizzie, we'd be unlikely as matches. He's half-Korean and half-white, like a mix of stuff. So that combination is pretty uncommon, which makes the whole thing harder."

Vish drums his thumb on his chin, pondering. "So we could do like a little docu segment on him, and Dr. Girl Genius to the rescue maybe?"

"Yeah, sure. But that's not exactly what I had in mind."

"Oh yeah?" he takes another bite of bagel.

I raise my eyebrows and grin. This whole fake-boyfriend-with-a-camera thing could be useful.

Thankfully, Vish lets me off the hook when it comes to driving home. My dad is out front as we pull up to the house, sweat dripping down his face and soaking his T-shirt as he pushes his puttering old mower around the front lawn. He's probably the only one in the neighborhood who insists on doing his own yard work—this is Princeton, after all. But I can hear the refrain now: "Paisa vasul." Get your money's worth. And he counts every penny.

"What happened to your driving lesson?" he calls out, cutting the motor on the mower. "Vish, I'm counting on you."

"Hanji, Uncle—she did the drive there this morning, because the streets were quieter then," Vish says, leaping out of the driver's seat and rushing over to where my dad stands. "But let me take over here. You look like you could use some nimbu paani."

Lemonade does sound good right now. I bet Dadi's already got some ready and waiting, the sweetness cut with sour pucker of chaat masala. I realize I'm ravenous, as usual. "Did Dadi make paranthe?" I ask my dad.

"Better! She made chole bhature. Come on!" He heads toward the front door. "Veggie-friendly, Vish!"

Vish rigs the motor in response, and it roars back to life. "Let me finish up here first."

I follow my dad inside, the scent of the curried chickpeas making my mouth water. I hug Dadi, pour myself some chai and am ladling up a bowl when Dad reappears, freshly showered. That was fast.

I pass him the plate I've been filling, and Dadi brings over a hot, freshly fried bhatura, the puffy, crispy bread releasing steam as he pokes it.

"Vish nahin aya?" he asks as he stuffs a bite into his mouth.

"He'll be here in a second," I say, dipping my bread into the chickpeas. "Dadi's chole are his favorite."

Papa ducks his head a bit, leaning closer to say, "I think she makes them just for him. Even though she'd never admit it."

"The grandson she never had," I say, and burst into laughter.

"Or son-in-law," Papa adds, and that shuts me right up. He chews for a second, and I can almost see his brain unraveling how to ask what he wants to know. "So, are you guys pretty serious now?"

I frown and take a sip of chai, the ginger hitting my throat just right. "Papa, we're too young to be serious. I mean, he's still in high school."

"And you would be, too."

"I know."

"He's still got college; you've got your internship. You may feel like a grown-up, but you're both still kids." Then he adds: "You're both still figuring yourselves out."

I blink, shocked for a second, and wonder what he knows. But then he shoots a look toward Dadi, who's still at the stove, frying up bhature. "So you have plenty of time. No matter what anyone else might say. Got it?"

I nod. "Got it."

"Good."

CHAPTER 20

I spent Sunday reading and watching everything I could about *Rock Star Boot Camp*, and I think I'm nearly ready to put my plan into action. In the meantime, Monday looms, long and tedious, and I'm on the early shift for rounds, so I take a car service to the hospital to clock in at six a.m. There's no way I'm relying on Mom for that one.

Everything's still dim and quiet, and I stash myself in the intern lounge—thankfully empty—with a thermos of chai Dadi made me, reading patient files and making notes. I keep coming back to the one for Pinky. I know I'm not supposed to be on the case—which seems to be true for every case, lately—but she's my baby cousin, and I can't not help. But while Cho and Howard and Dr. Arora seem to be doing everything right, something's not quite adding up.

I log on to the American Journal of Clinical Oncology site to read up on her previous diagnosis of medulloblastomas—abnormal, possibly malignant growths on the cerebellum, the back part of her brain. Maybe something there will help me unravel this.

José comes bustling in a few minutes later and gives me a crouched hug, peering over my shoulder at my files as I pour him a mug of chai. "Girl, you need to leave that case alone. That old auntie will have your ass if she sees you in Pinky's files." He's right. It's none of my business. But she is my little cousin.

"Well, thankfully, she'll never find out," I say, raising a now-bushy brow (yes, again) at him. "But maybe I found something?"

"What?" he says, overeager.

"Give me a minute. I've got to make sure I'm on the right track."

"Yeah, that's smart. By the way, you free now?"

"Sure, why?"

"Ericka Jackson—Brendan's mom—has been here all night. Something's on her mind for sure."

I stand, closing the thermos and draining my cup in one gulp. "On it!"

I grab my white coat and head out onto the floor. The hospital is slowly awakening as sunlight seeps in here and there, and the nurses begin their morning bustle. Breakfast trays float past, mostly uneaten, nurses shuffle through their rounds, and orderlies push beds from one place to another.

I poke my head into Brendan's room—he's in a private suite, which means his mom or grandma can crash on the lounger in the corner.

Brendan's in there, wide awake, watching cartoons on his iPad and eating Lucky Charms—which I'm pretty sure are contraband—just like any kid.

"Hey," I say, and he frowns immediately. I don't blame him. He's probably sick of doctors. "What you watching?"

"Yo Kai Watch," he says, all excited, and then frowns some more at the confusion on my face. "It's this anime about this kid, Nate, who can see these troublesome spirits that are up to no good through this watch that lets him communicate with and capture them. If you've got a problem, maybe a Yo Kai caused it." *Like even cancer,* I can almost hear him say in his head.

Oh. "That sounds pretty cool." I'm at a bit of a loss then. I hold up a test tube, and he nods, all solemn, because this is old hat. "Where's your mama?" I ask as I start the blood work. "And your grandma?"

"Mom's on a work call with Japan. She's got to catch up when she can, you know. Because of me." He takes a slurp of cereal. "And Grandma, well. She's pretty mad."

Uh-oh. "Mad? Why?"

"You'll find out soon enough." He grins when he says it.

"How are you doing, Brendan? Like, really, actually doing?"

"It's not fun." He sighs. "They fight a lot. About me. And I still don't feel good. Ever. But Mom said that maybe—if it works—I will. So I'm just trying to focus on that. Because I want to feel better." He shrugs, like all that talking has exhausted him. Or at the very least, distracted him from his show. But then he looks up at me again, and I notice he's lost another tooth. "The only downside?"

"What's that?" I ask.

"When I'm better, I'll have to go back to school."

That makes me laugh, and he grins. I pull the last tube, and he's absorbed by his show before I can say another word.

I'm labeling blood work, when his mom, Ericka, walks in, all raring to go. She looks like she's had more chai than I have. And I had a thermos full.

"There you are, Dr. Sehgal," she says as soon as I walk in. She takes my arm and leads me back out the door. "Let me buy you a cup of coffee."

I grin. "I guess I could use some more caffeine."

"I'd IV it, if I could," she says. "I can't really sleep when I'm at the hospital. Or when I'm at home, really. Too much on my mind." She pauses in front of the elevator, and my heart stops for a minute, half expecting Link to be standing there when the doors open. But, of course, it's empty.

We step off the elevator and head to the patient café in silence. I fret over what she's going to say. I can't afford to have more parents pushing me off their kids' cases. And I know Grandma Jackson's been pretty adamant about the toll this is taking on the family—I hope she hasn't convinced her daughter to discharge Brendan.

The café is busy. Seems a lot of weary relatives need sustenance this time of day. I remember coming here in the mornings with Harper's mom when Harper was sick to pick up banana muffins, and find myself reaching for one now. Then I grab some coffee—dumping so much hazelnut creamer in mine, it looks like chai—and take a seat.

We're barely seated, before Ericka jumps in. "I wanted to talk to you about something. But I need to ask you first: This can't get back to my mother."

My eyebrows leap—Mom says that's how she could always tell when I was up to no good when I was little. I look around, as if we're about to get caught, and pick at my muffin. I tastes the same—bananas and whole grain and something slightly metallic.

"She helps me with Brendan a lot, but I'm his mom. I'm his guardian. And it's my responsibility to make these medical decisions—possibly life-saving decisions—on his behalf. I have to do what's best for him. Even if she disagrees with it."

"But don't you think talking to her could—"

"I already know what she's going to say, and we can't afford to lose any more time. Brendan can't. We have to act now."

I nod.

"I talked briefly to Dr. Howard about this, but she was reluctant to discuss it further with Dr. Arora. I thought you might be more open."

"What did you have in mind, Ms. Jackson?"

"Call me Ericka." She pulls some paperwork from her purse and passes it to me across the table, her coffee untouched. She waits for me to read.

It's about a medical trial—an inhibitor meant to block oxygen access to the cancer cells—that could address the aggressive growth Brendan's been experiencing. The company's successfully done three similar trials before, and the results, while not unanimously positive, are encouraging. Brendan fits the profile for the next round of trials, the first the company will do on children under twelve. I can see why Ruby would be concerned. But also why Ericka would be hopeful.

"It might be his only shot, Dr. Sehgal."

She waits for me to respond. To say yes. To say I'll fight for him. But I'm not sure I can. "The risks—"

"The risks are far greater if we just allow this cancer to continue to grow. We have to do something, anything. We have to try."

I nod. She's right. Brendan needs at least a fighting chance. This may be the only thing that could give it to him.

My next stop is a quick visit with Alina, so I grab an extra muffin from the cafeteria on the way out. The cocktail of drugs we've got her started on seems to be helping—she looks brighter and more alert, she can breathe, and she's been gaining weight. Plus, happily, her appetite is back.

She beams at me when I hand her the muffin, peeling the wrapper away and taking a quick nibble as her dad hovers. He gives me a half smile in thanks for the muffin, but stress racks his body: His eyes are bloodshot, his shoulders tense, and he can't stand still. I know he wants to talk to me about the insurance situation, and I'm trying my best not to bring it up myself. There's not much I can do at this point, aside from get myself in deeper with Davis. And I have to take care of all my patients, not just Alina, so it would behoove me not to do that. Though the thought of Alina being kicked out of here, just when she's starting an upswing, it pretty much kills me.

I'm done checking her vitals and am about to draw some blood, when Howard walks in. She's on second shift today, but I was hoping we wouldn't overlap. No such luck.

"Hey, hey!" she announces to the room, then huddles in a corner with Mr. Plotkin, whispering for a few minutes. I know I should go download Alina's information to her right now—because it's my job—but I don't know quite what to say after that scene on Friday. Do I act like nothing happened? Do I confront her about it? Either idea makes me sick to my stomach, so I focus on Alina, who's a pro at blood draws by now. She barely pays attention, nibbling her muffin as she watches *The Great British Bake Off* on the small screen in front of her.

"That looks yummy," I say, motioning to the screen with my head.

"It's a cake made out of layers of crepes," she says, grinning. "They pump it full of cream. I bet it's so extravagant, you can only take two bites."

"I'm gonna be honest: I'd eat the whole thing," I say, and she laughs.

"Dr. Sehgal, can we see you for a moment?" Howard interrupts, her tone stern, like she's my teacher and not a fellow intern.

"Yeah, give me one sec," I say, pulling the needle from Alina's pale arm as the tube fills with blood. I snap off the tourniquet and slap on a bandage that has Strawberry Shortcake grinning on it. Alina polishes off her muffin, so I grab the wrapper and hand her a napkin. "All set." She smiles and turns back to her show.

I head to the corner table, where Howard and Mr. Plotkin are conferring over a computer screen. There's a fund-raising page on the screen—but only two thousand of thirty has been raised so far. Not a great start.

"We've got to do better," Howard says. "Alina doesn't have much time."

"Do you have any ideas?" Mr. Plotkin asks, his eyebrows veering from question mark to exclamation point. His eyes are damp, but he won't cry. Not here. Not in front of us. So I won't, either.

"No, but don't you worry, Mr. Plotkin. We'll come up with something."

We have to.

CHAPTER 21

As I knock on Davis's door, I feel like a lamb offering herself up for slaughter. I already know she doesn't like me, and this isn't going to help my case. But I need to do something—anything—to help my patients right now. And while I can't create any magical trial access or fund-raising miracles, I can do this. So I will.

"Come on in!" The voice that answers is upbeat and happy—so not Davis. I push the door open tentatively and take a step inside.

"She'll be with you in just a few minutes," a lady says, straightening pillows on a small spare sofa against one wall. "Would you like some coffee?" the lady asks, and I shake my head.

She waves toward one of the chairs by the desk, and I take a seat to wait. I drum my fingers on the table and look around. The room is bright but cool, with large windows filtering in sunshine, and the glass desktop taking over much of the space. There's a wall of glass shelves bearing books, framed certificates—from Hopkins, UMDNJ, and Penn—hang above the desk. On the table, there's just a single photo, which I turn to look at. It's of Davis and another woman, striking, with dark skin and long brown hair, along with two youngish-looking brown kids.

"Nosy much?" The voice makes me jump.

"Dr. Davis. I didn't—" She takes the frame and moves it out of my reach, then sits behind the desk. "I think we might have—"

"What do you want, Sehgal?" She doesn't waste any time, does she?

"Well, I know there's a lot going on right now with Alina, and

Brendan, and certainly Lincoln, and so much of it feels like it's out of our control, so I just thought maybe this could be a good opportunity to do one thing that we could actually control."

She stares at me blankly. I guess I should just spit it out.

"The lounge."

Still blank.

"The patient lounge."

"Be more specific, Sehgal."

"I think we should redo the patient lounge. It's in the same shape that it was in, like, eight years ago, when I used to come here to visit my friend Harper, which is to say it's in terrible shape. And I don't think it would cost very much at all to update it, and in fact, I could totally pay to update it as sort of a donation to the hospital. I think that the kids in oncology deserve a space to go that's clean, bright, and comfortable, with some amenities that would make it a far more welcoming space. A new couch and rug, Wi-Fi, an updated TV, maybe a box with Netflix and stuff?"

"Saira Sehgal," she says, a bit incredulous, and I want to cower down in my chair. But I can't. This is a good idea, a simple idea, a doable idea, and I need to make it happen. I need there to be one good thing right now. So this is the hill I will die on, apparently.

"I mean, it doesn't get much use. But it will. Once it's updated."

"I think the patients like the lounge just fine. In fact, I think they rarely think about the lounge at all. They have bigger problems to deal with. Like the specter of death, Ms. Sehgal."

I frown, trying hard not to suck my teeth. My mom hates when I do that.

"So if you're done wasting my time, Ms. Sehgal, I have other, far more important things to worry about." Then she smirks a bit, which catches me off guard. "And so should you."

I sit up straight. Is that a threat? My heart rattles in my rib cage, a frantic bird.

"You've been here hardly a month and already there's been more than one complaint about you, Ms. Sehgal. Not off to a great start, are we?"

A complaint? Mr. Plotkin, maybe? But he seems fine now. It has to have been Link. I swallow.

"Who was it from?" I ask, already knowing she's not about to give me the satisfaction.

"I'm not at liberty to say," she says, the glee in her eyes not quite hitting her mouth. "But I'd tread carefully if I were you, Ms. Sehgal. Not everyone is impressed with your prodigy status. I've got my eyes on you. And so does everyone else."

I nod and stand. Heading toward the door. Then turn back, and she looks up at me from over the rim of her glasses, like the principal who's had it with the bad kid. Annoyed. Exhausted. Resigned.

"So those are your daughters, Dr. Davis?"

"Yes."

"About my age?"

"One's getting her master's now, actually."

"And that woman."

"My wife."

"Oh."

"Goodbye, Ms. Sehgal."

I walk out, closing the door behind me.

She has a family. That means she must have a heart, somewhere in there, right?

I head straight to the patient lounge, more determined than ever. This is one thing I can fix. Right here, right now. And I refuse to let Davis—or anyone else—stop me.

I pull out my iPad and download a design app. It's a big square space. The kitchenette will do just fine with a quick cleanup and restocking. Some paint and a new rug and couch will make this place feel brand-new. Vish's cousin can get me a flat screen for cheap and set up the tech to include video games, the streaming box, and a DVR. I think about a thousand bucks and weekend's work should do it. And since my parents are letting me live at home, rent-free, I can afford to do it. If I have help. I grin to myself.

I know just the right coconspirator for this task.

CHAPTER 22

"That's what you're wearing?"

Lizzie's standing at my door, in a long, flowy strapless wrap dress, staring at me like I just climbed off a spaceship.

"You said it was a pajama party."

"Yeah, but you can't just wear pj's to the party now. Get dressed, and bring your pj's for later. Better yet, bring some of Taara's pj's instead," Lizzie says, wrinkling her nose.

I'm wearing an old Nirvana T-shirt—which actually belongs to Taara—and polka-dot pajama bottoms, which I guess are not on the approved list. I frown. "Do I really have to go?"

"Come on, Saira," Lizzie says, tugging my arm and leading me back upstairs. "It's literally been years since you've hung out with everyone, and I had to work really hard to get Cat to green-light this. She only agreed because it's my last big shindig before I leave for acting camp."

I really don't want to hang out with Cat. Or Emma. Or Julie. Or any of the other random girls from elementary school that Lizzie insists I should still be BFFs with. I barely knew them then, and I definitely don't know them now. I let myself be dragged up the stairs, but instead of heading to my bedroom, Lizzie pulls me into Taara's.

"Why don't we just have our own slumber party here? Vish downloaded the new Deepika movie for me. I heard she's, like, groundbreaking in it."

I can tell that Lizzie's ever so slightly swayed by that. Deepika is her Bollywood idol. But then she snaps out of it.

"Nope," she says, digging through Taara's closet for appropriate party gear. "There! This!" She holds up a long, lean T-shirt dress. "Comfy, casual, but party appropriate." She points to different parts of the dress like a car salesman. She tosses it toward me, then digs into Taara's dresser for pj options. "Voilà!" A matching pink floral set, tank and shorts. A bit skimpy. "It's perfect." Lizzie grins, satisfied.

It's going to be a long night.

Half an hour later, we pull up to Cathleen's house. It's much quieter than the last time I was here. There are only a few cars parked in the circular driveway, and no DJ or thumping bass, thank gods. But my heart's pounding enough to make up for it. I take a deep breath, trying to compose myself as Lizzie pulls her little Fiat in behind a Mercedes. Not only do all these kids know how to drive already, they all apparently got luxury cars as their sixteenth birthday presents. Which makes me the loser on both counts, I guess. Can't drive, no ride. *Oh well.*

The maid opens the door for us before we even ring the doorbell. "Ms. Austin is expecting you," she says. "The ladies are all upstairs." She takes our bags and hands them to a young man, who seems to be the butler. Like, an actual butler.

"Hey, Vincent," Lizzie says, leaning in to give him a hug—a seductive one, I think—and giggling. "You gonna come up?"

"Not tonight, lovely Lizzie," he says in a British accent. "Though I will send some treats for you guys in a bit." He winks and walks off with our bags.

Lizzie swaps her sneakers for cozy slippers that the maid offers, so I do the same.

When we get upstairs, it's just Cat, Julie, and a few other girls I don't recognize, all in summery dresses like Lizzie's. They're sprawled out on a bunch of recliners in what seems to be the screening room, with some white-lady road trip movie playing in the background, though they're barely paying attention.

"I thought they broke up three months ago?" Julie is saying, incredulous. She's still got the dewy brown skin she's always had, her glossy, dark hair in Leia buns, freckles scattered across her pert nose.

"Well, apparently so did he. Because he was hooking up with this girl the first week at film camp. But when she found out—oh, hey, Lizzie." Cat jumps up and gives Lizzie a kiss on the cheek, hugging her like she hasn't seen her in ages. Even though she saw her at school this morning. She's more tentative when she reaches over to hug me, and I'm not sure whether to hug back, so the whole thing is awkward and forced. "Glad you could finally make it, *Dr.* Sehgal."

The others laugh at that, and I try to think of a witty reply, but the moment passes before I can come up with one. Instead, I just take a seat on one side of the couch, wondering what to do with myself.

Cat leans in toward me, over Lizzie, her eyes curious. "So I heard Vish is headed to California for school," Cat says, and I try not to look surprised. Did Lizzie tell them? "You guys gonna stay together, you think?"

"We'll figure it out," I say, trying to keep my voice light. "I mean, it's long distance, which is hard. But Vish and I have known each other forever. So it's not like we'd just end things."

Cat raises a brow. "What if he meets someone else?" She sips her drink, sly. "Or you do?"

I turn to Lizzie again, but she and Julie are whispering about something else, distracted. "Where are you going to school, Cat?"

"Early decision to Yale. Pre-law. Didn't Lizzie tell you?"

I shake my head. She might have, though. "I've heard good things."

"But it's no Princeton, right?" There's a challenge in her voice. "Lizzie said you started your residency. How's it been going?"

"It's intense. And weird. I don't know, exactly." I'm not sure what I'm trying to say. "I mean, I'm the youngest one there by, like, a decade, and some of my patients are, like, my age, which is strange. And I'm, like, responsible for their lives and all. And so much of the time, I look at them—at this one girl in particular—and I see her. Harper. And it's like it's happening all over again, you know?"

Harper's name sort of shocks us all into silence. Not where they thought I'd go with that, I guess. Not where I thought I'd go, either.

"Must be rough," Cat says. "Want a drink?" She pulls over a little cart that's piled down with vodka and all the fixings—I know because I recognize them from my dad's bar. A variety of juices, some wine coolers, cherries and stuff.

Oh no. Not doing that again. Not after last time. "I'll just have some pineapple juice, I think."

"I thought you were off duty tonight, Doc?" Julie says, then dissolves into giggles.

"So, Queen Saira, we were taking bets on whether you'd actually show up today," Cat says, a bit too sharp, as she pours me a plain old juice. "Guess I lost."

I try to smile, even though I know it must look as awkward as it feels. Lizzie's thrown herself on the couch between Julie and one of the others, and they're whispering about something they apparently can't share with the group.

So I just stand there awkwardly, drink in hand.

"Sure I can't offer you something stronger?" Cat asks, pouring a big swish of vodka into her cup, along with a splash of cranberry juice.

"I'm good." Except that I'm not. Maybe I should just have a drink. It's not like I haven't had one before—and I'm not even talking about the party. My dad will sometimes offer me a glass of champagne or whatever when we're celebrating. But I don't want to give in to Cat. "Maybe I should go change?"

"Sure, if you want," Cat says. "Come with me. I'll get you a towel."

I close the door to the bathroom—which is about the size of my entire room—and stand there for a second, staring in the mirror, reveling in the quiet. I can hear the girls yapping outside, and I'm grateful to be alone for a second, away from the noise. I've never felt more out of place in my life, and I went to medical school when I was twelve. This is so not where I belong.

It makes me wonder if Lizzie and I would still be friends at all if I'd been just regular old Saira Sehgal, junior. Somehow, I doubt it.

"Come on, Saira!" Lizzie shouts through the door. "We're about to start the show!"

I change quickly into the too-tiny pj shorts Lizzie picked out for me, wishing I had my robe or pajamas. I take another deep breath, then make myself open the door.

When I walk back in, Cat hits play on the big screen, and a familiar instrumental tune beeps out. "Do, do, do, doh, doh, doh, doooh, doh, do, do, do, do."

Doogie Howser, M.D.

"Ha-ha," I say, unable to fake the smile as they all crack up at my expense. I try not to glare at Lizzie. Did she know about this? Did she just go along with it?

"Our very own Doogie," Cat says. Then she offers me a tiny glass. I see everyone else is already holding one.

"Oh, come on, Sai. Lizzie says you're officially an MD, so aren't congrats in order and all?" She holds it out to me again, and I feel silly saying no this time.

"Cheers!" They all raise their glasses, then slam them in a single breath. But I'm still holding mine.

Cat looks at me expectantly.

"I can't. I've got a lot to do—"

"We all do. We're celebrating you here. Live a little."

"Yeah," Lizzie chimes in. "It's sweet, Saira. You'll like it."

"Come on, guys," Julie says. "It's no big. I'll drink it if you don't want to, Sai."

I hand the glass to her. But Cat is frowning. "You know, Lizzie was all like, oh, you'll see, she's so the same—just like she used to be." This isn't going her way, and she's not used to that. She snatches the glass from Julie and downs it, the sticky liquid dribbling down her chin like a toddler's. "And she was right. You're exactly the same. Still a stuck-up bitch, too good for any of us. Well, have it your way, Saira. You can have Lizzie all to yourself."

Cat storms off, taking two of the girls with her. Except for Julie, who's shocked. And Lizzie.

"Oh, you know Cat and her tantrums," Julie says, her tone hushed and apologetic. "She's just had a rough week. Wanted to celebrate. And always has to do it her way. No big deal. She'll be back in a minute." She keeps talking, but I barely hear her. Because I'm too busy watching Lizzie, who's turning bright red. Not a good sign.

"I think I'll walk home," I say, turning to leave, but Lizzie grabs my arm before I can. Julie takes that as her cue to bolt.

"You better, because I'm never taking you anywhere again." Lizzie has tears streaming down her cheeks. "Cat's right. She's been right all along. You think you're so much better than everyone—than me. 'Oh no, *I* can't be inebriated. Do you know the ratio of alcohol to water in that, and how it impacts your body?' 'Oh no, I've got to be mentally and physically at my best at all times.' Or 'Teenagers are so vapid these days.' News flash: You are a teenager! But you'd rather claim to be an old soul and hang out watching ancient Bollywood movies with your dadi. Anything but actually give your best friend the time of day." She's shaking now, but the tears have stopped. "And then you come here and act all high and mighty? And everyone was just trying to be nice to you."

I open my mouth, but she plows forward. "Don't deny it. I know exactly what you were thinking. You always have to be the downer. Well, I'm done with it. You're on your own."

She takes off, headed upstairs where the rest of the girls are.

That's when that British dude shows up, holding a tray of brownies. "Oh, hey, lovely. Where are the girls?" He winks. "Brought your treats."

"They went upstairs, but I'm headed home."

He hands me a brownie wrapped in a napkin. "One for the road then, miss. *Enjoy* it." I nod, and take a nibble. Mmm, coffee-flavored. At least something good came out of this horrible night.

Saira: Lizzie, you there?

Saira: Can we talk?

Saira: Look, I'm sorry.

Saira: I was being a brat. But I was tired. And I'd rather just hang out with you.

Saira: I'm really sorry.

Saira: Want me to come back?

Saturday, August 18, 12:48 a.m.

Saira: Are you still at Cat's?

Saira: I'm so sorry, Lizzie.

CHAPTER 23

"Saira, utja! It's already nine forty. You're going to be late!" Papa's rapping on my door, his knock insistent and urgent. I look at my smartwatch, and sure enough, it's 9:43. On Saturday. Wait, I'm not scheduled to work today. I look at the calendar app and there it is: the dreaded driving test. Which I totally would have missed if I'd stayed at the party. But which I have no excuse to miss now. Dammit. I'm so not ready.

My dad opens the door a crack, peering in at me. I duck farther under the covers.

"Papa, I can't," I say, making my voice as nasal as possible. "I think I'm coming down with something. Feels like a head cold with a looming sinus infection, maybe. Definitely going around. That summer cold thing. Not prime conditions under which to take such an important exam."

Papa raises an eyebrow. He may not be the doctor in the family, but he knows a faker when he sees one. "Saira, for the record, I'm not pleased with this. At all. You, of all people, know how important it is to take this test and get it out of the way. But if you're really reluctant, I give you permission—this once—to call and cancel. But make sure you reschedule for the next available date. And then come downstairs. Dadima made paranthe and chai.

"Dramaebaz," Papa calls me. I peer over my comforter at him, and he grins. "You know you get your acting skills from me, right?" He chuckles and closes the door.

Before he was forced to become an engineer like his father and grandfather before him, my dad was quite the rising star. He was in all his high school and college productions, and even spent a summer in Mumbai, hopeful, before his dad ordered him back to school. Now he just watches old Bollywood movies and reminiscences about the roles he would have been perfect for—much to my grandmother's chagrin. She's all about being smart and practical. Though, not quite secretly, she's a big Rajesh Khanna stan.

I ponder climbing out of bed—the lure of chai and paranthe is strong—but then I remember last night. Ouch.

I check my phone. Lizzie hasn't responded to a single one of my twenty "I'm sorry" texts. *Sigh.* I mean, I get that she's mad or whatever, but I'm mad, too. And I still apologized. Well, two can play this game. I shut my phone off and storm to the bathroom. I brush my teeth, take a quick shower, and change into clean pajamas. I'm taking the day off. From everything.

Mom's in the front hall, all dressed and ready, when I pad downstairs in my pajamas. I kind of want to tell her about last night and Lizzie, to ask her what I should do. But she's putting on her shoes, all rushy and late.

"Patients," she says. "Back around four. Go eat nashta."

"Is Pinky coming? Can I—"

Mom shakes her head. "Anya's going to be there, and I can't take the tamasha today."

"You have to convince her to push forward with the surgery," I say, my voice breaking a bit. "Without it, Pinky doesn't have a shot at all. I know it's scary, but—"

"But you are not her mother. And neither am I. But I am yours. Now stop thinking about work. Eat. Lounge. Watch movies. You need the day off."

I'm about to protest, but she's already out the front door, closing the door behind her, before I can open my mouth. It's been like that ever since I started work, ever since Pinky got sick. Like we're just not allowed to talk about it—about anything—anymore. It kind of sucks. But she's right. Time to take a day off.

Papa's long gone by the time I get to the kitchen.

"Jogging," Dadi says, then makes a face. She doesn't get exercise for the sake of exercise. She grew up on a farm in Tarn Taran, in Punjab, where they earned their paranthe by working in the fields. She's got a batch sizzling on the stovetop now—potatoes, onions, and chilis stuffed into a crispy whole-wheat flatbread, pan-fried with ghee. Yup, a farmer's breakfast for real.

I take a seat and she places a plate in front of me—paranthe, yogurt for dipping, and a few extra green chilis for good measure. My mouth is already full when she starts her lecture.

"Thu nahin gayi nah, driving test?" she says. She tsks. "Khi gal si, Saira?"

I've gotten countless scoldings from Dadi. But this one is unexpected. "I wasn't ready."

"Well then, get ready. You've done everything else ahead of schedule. Why are you letting this one thing hold you back?"

"I'm not—I'm just tired—"

"No."

"I haven't had enough time to practice."

"No."

"I just . . . I don't want to right now. Okay?"

"Not okay." Dadi takes a seat across from me and pours chai into two mugs. I take the sugar and start dumping spoonfuls into my chai, breathing in the gingery aroma. "Saira, you need to learn to drive."

"Why?" I stuff more parantha into my mouth, hoping for a reprieve, but Dadi stares at me. "Everyone else drives. I can take a car service. It's so not a big deal."

"It is a big deal, puth."

"You don't drive. You never did."

"I am old and weary."

"Whatever, Dadi."

"That's exactly why you should drive." She takes a sip of chai, and her voice sounds a bit faraway when she talks, like she's talking to herself and not me. "When I was younger, your age, there were so many things I wanted to do. I used to play field hockey in school in Patiala. Did you know that?"

I didn't.

"We had these old wooden sticks and pucks, and played in a field just outside the boys school. Me, and five other girls. We were pureh palvans. Real athletes. We'd have our lassi and paranthe for breakfast— and two full mangos each, always—and play for hours. In our kurta pajamas, all dirty and dusty. I would forget my studies for field hockey. But in the end, it was pointless fun. No one took a group of girls playing seriously. They wouldn't even entertain the idea."

"That sucks, Dadi."

"That's just the way the world works. Worked. Back then. I didn't learn to drive, I didn't go to college. I didn't continue to play field hockey. I got just enough education to be marriageable, and then I was wed. I didn't complain."

"You could have complained."

"It would be no use." She refills my chai cup, staring into it like it'll reveal something big. "But you, puth, you have all the freedom I never did. Sometimes too much freedom." I know she's thinking of Vish. I wonder what she'd think of Link. "I never did, beta. So it hurts me when you choose to throw that freedom away."

She cups a hand under my chin, making me look at her. "Women like your mother, as bold as she may be, they fought for that freedom. They earned it. So that it is a given for you and your sister. You have to honor that."

I nod.

"So go reschedule your appointment for the driver's test, puth. And change out of your pajamas."

I bubble-face at her, filling my cheeks with air, and she pops the bubble like a balloon, with a single finger poke.

I rush up the stairs, taking them two at a time, and throw myself onto the bed, pulling my laptop open. I'm about to go to the DMV site to reschedule. But instead, I head to the *Rock Star Boot Camp* website. The deadline for round two is a few days away. If I'm going to make this happen, it has to be fast.

I call Vish.

Saira: Wanna come over and watch "Dilwale Dulhania"?

Vish: Yes!

Saira: Will you ask Lizzie to come?

Saira: She's still not talking to me.

Vish: Uh.

Vish: She left for camp last night.

Vish: She didn't tell you?

Saira: 😠

CHAPTER 24

I grip the steering wheel and my own sweat makes the leather slippery. The tendons in my shoulders bunch—anxiety muscle tension. Nonsevere, but recurring. Taara's slightly new car is spotless, and smells like a perfume shop—flowery and sweet—and if I wreck it, she's warned me a thousand times that she'll make me buy her an upgraded version, with a leather interior. Because, you know, doctor's salary and all.

"Turn right here," Taara says, her left hand firmly on the gear shift, her arm taut and stretched with worry. "And then make a left three blocks down."

If Mom knew she was letting me drive to our favorite non–Pizza Hut pizzeria, the Princeton Pizza Palace, she'd take away Taara's keys and ground us both. At first, I didn't get it. I mean, on the one hand, it's all *pass your road test!* On the other, it's panic about highways. But with demon drivers going eighty an hour, I'm starting to understand the conflict.

The faster we get there, though, the faster we eat. My stomach grumbles.

"Hungry? It's been so long since I've had good pizza," Taara says. "I've been making pizza bagels in the dorm, but the jarred sauce sucks. Maybe I'll make a batch before I go back down to school tomorrow. I'm going to try putting cumin in it. And maybe shallots instead of onion to make it a bit sweeter. You wanna help me?"

"You should try hospital cafeteria food. Yuck," I say. "I've got rounds tomorrow."

"Exit right here," Taara says, her left hand firmly on the gearshift, her arm taut and stretched with worry. "Quick, or you'll miss it. And then make a left three blocks down. Is it weird being in that hospital again?" Taara asks. "I mean, you must see Harper everywhere."

I swerve a little at the mention of Harper's name.

"Be careful," she says, then asks me another question about Harper.

Definitely not going there. I wave an arm to shut her up. "I need to focus on the road."

"You need to go faster. The speed limit here is forty, you're barely doing fifteen."

"There's no law that says you can't go slow."

"Yes, there is. It's the law of the starving sister." She laughs at her silly joke, rolls down her window. "Actually, it's called the minimum speed limit. You'd know that if it hadn't been so long since you looked at the DMV booklet, smartie-pant." She peers ahead, squinting into the distance. "Half a mile down and then a right." She frowns over the dash.

My hands get even more gross and clammy. Cars honk and pass me on the left, and another driver shakes his fist at me on the right. Driving isn't any harder than medicine, but people forget that you can kill someone with a car just as easily as you can with a scalpel.

I make a left and then a right, following her instructions perfectly. But every time I go a smidge over thirty miles per hour, I fret a little. It just feels too fast.

"Hurry up and make the next right," she says.

My whole shirt is soaked through by the time I pull into the pizzeria's parking lot. I stop the car. "You park the car."

"Nope. You've got to learn how to do it sometime," Taara says, disapproval twisting her mouth.

"But not today," I announce, turning the car off and unlocking the door. The spots in this lot are parallel, and the last time I tried parking with Papa, it didn't go well. "You do it."

She frowns and sighs, but gets out and comes around to the driver's side. I stand near the restaurant door as she parks the car.

I hold the door open for a young couple on a date. They can hardly keep their hands off each other. It would be cute if it wasn't gross.

My phone buzzes. There's a text from Vish about our plans for tonight. We're going to go to the movies, then go over our plot to convince Link to make another tape. If he'll even talk to us at all.

I sigh and follow Taara as she walks into the restaurant, the sharp, spicy scent of garlic hitting us. It's old-school Italian and very charming, all white-and-red-checkered tablecloths and waiters with chef's hats on. It's always bustling, and there's hardly a free table since it's a Saturday night. We claim an empty booth near the windows, and order garlic bread with cheese and a large pepperoni and veggie pie.

The couple is in the next booth, sharing one seat, the girl's legs thrown over the guy's. They pause their making out to order a sausage-and-peppers pie.

Taara looks at them, then at me. "So how's it going with Vish?" she asks before I can even take a sip of my lemonade. "It's been, like, two years, right? Serious stuff."

"I mean, I like him all right," I say, wondering if I'm giving myself away. The garlic bread arrives then, gooey and sticky, and I attack it, breaking off a piece and dunking it into the spicy marinara. I take a big bite, and when I look up, Taara is watching me really intently, her forehead lined with seriousness.

"You know you can talk to me about that stuff, right?" she says, her mouth a grim line. She hasn't touched the garlic bread. "Like, I know Mom wouldn't talk to you about it—she never talked to me, even though she's a doctor. But I'm here if you need me."

I try not to laugh. "It's mostly just Bollywood movies and ice cream. No biggie."

"It is right now, maybe. But at some point, you know, things might get a little more intense. And if you need to talk about birth control or any of that stuff—"

"I definitely do not need any," I say, my voice a little too loud. "And, dude, I'm a doctor, too. I know all about that stuff."

"Yeah, technically you do. But you're a kid. This side of it is new. And weird. For everyone. Even Girl Genius doctors."

"Well," I say, stuffing my mouth with garlic bread and avoiding her gaze, "we're not having sex anytime soon." Which is totally the truth. I take another bite. "And if we were, I think I'd have it handled."

"All I'm saying is, I'm here if you need me." She finally takes a small piece of garlic bread, removes some of the melty cheese, and nibbles at the edge of it. "And I want to be. When Marc and I started—"

I nearly spit out my garlic bread. "I do not want to hear about you and Marc."

Taara laughs. "Okay, okay. You don't have to be such a prude about it. As a doctor, I'm sure you know that it's all perfectly natural." She pauses. "And healthy."

"It's just not something that's happening between us," I say, and regret it instantly.

"Why? Is it the chemistry? I mean—"

"I like him a lot." *But not in that way.* Or, correction: *There's no point in liking him that way.* In any case, the way I feel about Link, I can tell the difference. "I'm not ready. And Vish's fine with that."

"Well, if you won't talk to me about it, I hope you're at least talking to Lizzie," Taara says, and I nod, even though every single thing Lizzie believes about me and Vish is a lie. It has to be.

"Here you go, ladies!" The waiter arrives with our pizza, placing it in the center of the table. It's steaming and melty, with crunchy burnt cheese toward the edges, the pepperoni crisped and beckoning.

"There's nothing to talk about," I say, digging in for a slice, and this time Taara does, too, picking off a few pieces of pepperoni and popping them into her mouth. "And everyone's always all up in my business— including you. It needs to stop. I mean, you don't like it when they're always trying to marry you off."

"Yeah, but you and Vish give them hope. Visions of future grandkids or something. But if you want privacy and freedom, you need to get your license," she says. "So you can actually have some control over your life."

"That's what Dadi says." Taara raises an eyebrow. "There's always car service. But I will. I'm just . . . busy."

"Well, you have to log those hours with Papa," she says. "And really practice. It's the only thing you're not that good at."

I scoff, then shove at her arm. She laughs. We both know she's right.

She nods, then focuses on her pizza, taking a bite and then another. "I've missed this," she says, her mouth half-full, and I don't know if she's talking about pizza or us. "Rutgers would be so much more fun if you were there."

"I've got to study for my boards."

"Dude, you're always studying. What's the point of being sixteen if all you're gonna do is work?"

I stare at her from over my slice, taking another bite. Work is *fun* for me. But I don't know how to explain that. It doesn't seem like something Taara would understand.

"College is weird," she says. "I mean, the hanging out and stuff is cool. But my classes are so boring, I can barely keep my eyes open. Especially biochem."

"Is it Tarcher?" I say, and she nods. "I had him, too, when I took the summer intensive at Rutgers." When I was eleven. "I might still have my notes, if you want them."

She shrugs. "Would it be like beyond horrible if I dropped the class?"

I nod my head and swallow a bite of pizza. "Better to knock it out early, because all the other chem classes will build on it. We could always do a study group or something if you want. I thought it was fun."

"Of course you did," she says drily. "But I have a tutor. This kid George. He's Greek. And hot. He's in my lab group."

"Well then, I guess you're all set." I guess little sister tutoring big sister would be a bit weird anyway.

"But really," Taara says, her voice all serious all of the sudden. "I think I'm gonna drop it. And premed."

"What?"

"Two doctors in the family is plenty, right?"

I nearly laugh out loud. But I manage to control myself. "Nope. The more the merrier. For real, Taara. Mom would flip." After all, if I don't take over the practice, Taara's next in line. Though I realize why the weight of that obligation might make her run. I take another nibble of my pizza. "And besides, what else would you do?"

"I dunno. A lot of things. I was thinking about maybe taking some nutrition classes. That's sort of sciencey, right? Because I could add real, practical information to my FoodTube videos. And I joined this drama troupe on campus. We're doing an updated version of *Hair*."

I nearly spit out my bite. "Wait, isn't that the one where they're all naked onstage?"

Taara shrugs. "You make it sound so scandalous. I mean, it's about art and expression."

"Tell that to Dadi, dude."

"Don't you dare tell Dadi!"

"I won't if you won't."

She reaches over, and we pinkie swear on it. I hate keeping secrets from everyone. But if I have to do it, having Taara on my team definitely helps. But the secret she's keeping could blow up big-time. All I know is, if it does, I'll stand by her side.

And if she can go after what she wants, so can I.

183

CHAPTER 25

Monday morning, and I am nothing if not determined. This is happening. I mean. I'm sixteen. I'm the only teen doctor in the known world. I'm a goddamned genius. I can do this. I know I can.

But there's sweat pooling in the small of my back, and glistening above my—recently groomed, thanks, Mom—eyebrows. My heart is racing and my palms are so clammy, I nearly drop my clipboard. Why does he manage to make me feel this way? There's no rational, medical explanation for it. Some would call it lovesickness—in Hindi they call it prem rog, an actual affliction caused by lust and longing, that can manifest itself in symptoms like nausea, mental anguish, and even depression. Not fun. But this feels like something way worse. And I'm worried there isn't a cure.

Checking to make sure none of my superiors—or snoopy fellow interns—are around to watch me make a fool of myself, I rap gently on the door, and hear a mumbled "Yeah, I'm up."

So I push back the curtain and step in. "Morning," I say, my voice squeaking with false cheer and bravado. I've got to tone it down. "How are you feeling?"

Link frowns from his prone position on the hospital bed, then immediately reaches for the call button to summon a nurse.

"Wait, wait, please, just give me one minute. Hear me out for a second."

"You're not supposed to be in here."

"Just—I have something to tell you."

"No."

"Your tape. I have an idea. A really good idea."

"No tape."

"Listen—"

"Saira with an *i*, can't you see I'm, like, pretty much dying here? I don't have the energy for a tape. I barely have the energy for anything."

That's not super surprising, but it is somewhat alarming, given the new treatment they just started. Which I'm not supposed to know about because I'm no longer on his case. Hippocratic oath and all that. But I can't help it if Cho and Howard keep talking about it, right? "Oh, have they been keeping an eye on the jaundice? Because that's worth investigating." He does look even more pale than before. And the bruising has spread and darkened, marking every visible inch of skin now.

"I don't know. I just want to sleep. So get out. Please."

"I—"

He reaches for the nurse call button again, pressing it firmly this time, once, twice, three times for good measure.

"Go. Please."

Resigned, I turn to leave, but then the curtain flies back. It's Howard, looking concerned.

"Everything okay, Link?" She stops short, startled when she sees me. "Dr. Sehgal, you're not supposed to be in here."

"I know."

Her voice is terse when she responds. "So I'd suggest you step outside. Now. Before I'm forced to report this to Dr. Arora."

"Oh yeah, that's right, I'm sure he'd love that. Go report to him."

Howard takes my arm, firmly. Ouch. "Let's go, Dr. Sehgal. Now."

Link's thrown his IV'd arm over his eyes, trying to block out our drama.

"Dr. Howard, can I get another dose of morphine? I need it."

"I'll look into that, Link. Be right back."

She drags me out of the room.

"Have you guys explored the option of a stem cell infusion while we wait for the marrow to pan out? I mean, I know it's controversial, but honestly, it might buy us some time."

"Thank you very much for your insights, Dr. Sehgal, but lest you've forgotten, Lincoln Chung-Radcliffe has expressly asked that you be taken off the case. Which means we can't incorporate your feedback into his treatment, and we certainly can't have you hovering in his room and harassing him."

"I was not harassing him," I say, my voice rising as I speak. Nurses hover nearby, but José shoos them away, even as he pauses to listen in himself. "I just had something to tell him."

"He clearly did not want you in there."

I pull myself up to my full height. All five foot two of me. She towers over me by a good six inches. But I have to stand up for myself. "What gives you the right—"

"I'm his doctor," she says definitively, her voice cold. "And you are not. That's what gives me the right. I can't believe you'd cross such boundaries—"

"You're one to talk about crossing boundaries! You're really using your assets to your advantage with Dr. Arora, aren't you?" I spit, too harsh, and immediately regret it, though I can't admit that.

Howard's face goes pale, and she flinches, like she's been slapped.

The rest of the hospital continues its bustle, but José looks shocked, and I know I've done real damage. But I can't apologize. If I do, I'll cry. So instead I just walk away, leaving her standing there in the hallway, stricken.

Five minutes later, I find myself in baby Pinky's room on the other side of the hall. Another patient I'm not supposed to visit. Another patient I can't stay away from. What's wrong with me?

"She's been crying nonstop," Nurse Ibarrando says. "It's a whimper if I'll hold her, but as soon as I put her down—even if she's asleep—she starts again."

"I'll take her," I say, reaching out for little Pinky, and the nurse looks so relieved as she passes her tiny body to me. She's a small sack of skin and bones now, Pinky. She curls into me, her thumb tucked into her mouth, her breathing ragged and shallow.

I pace the room and look at the scans that are pinned to the backlit scanner. The tumors—medulloblastomas—have taken over the back, lower part of the brain, which affects function muscle and movement. They're growing at an alarming rate, and if they don't operate to remove them soon, it will be too late. They already know all of this. Arora repeats it during each staff meeting. And it breaks my heart every single time.

But Anya Auntie insists on no surgery. Which means she's pretty much given her two-year-old daughter a death sentence. I guess it's in the gurus' hands now.

There has to be something I can do to help. I stare at the scans and feel Pinky relax against me, her breathing going even and deeper. I walk over to the rocking chair in the corner and tuck myself into it, Pinky draped over my lap. I let the chair's sliding motion soothe us both for a minute, staring at the blur of her brain scans, trying to unravel the answer.

It's just after five when I clock out, showered and changed. Thankfully, I haven't run into Howard since the incident, but I'm not taking any chances, so I bail on the intern lounge as soon as possible, even though my mom's working till six. Paperwork can wait.

I have to try again.

I head straight back down the oncology hall to Link's room. Number eight-oh-two.

But before I get there, I hear him. He's in a wheelchair, in the hall, and shouting. Well, not really shouting. But talking loudly. To his mom.

I edge closer to the room, hoping to overhear a bit of the conversation. So what? He already thinks I'm an ass, right?

But he sees me and shuts right up, pulling his mom's sleeve, so she sees me, too. She frowns in my direction, then gets behind Link's chair and pushes him back into the room.

Dammit. There's no talking to him now.

I can't get anything right. I feel like a total and utter failure—as a doctor and as a human being.

If he won't talk to me, there has to be another way.

But how?

CHAPTER 26

We're gathered around the big table in the oncology office conference room, going over patient files. I admit, I've been distracted—and doodling—again. I can't help it. It's barely eight a.m., and if I don't draw, I'll fall asleep. Arora's been droning on and on about the possible expansion of pediatric oncology to occupy two full floors of the hospital.

"Numbers are up significantly—which is both bad news and good news—and we have been turning away patients who really need our care," he's saying now. "I've outlined a file on why this expansion should happen sooner rather than later. And I'm tasking the three of you with completing the report within the next two weeks, so I can deliver it to Dr. Charles and Dr. Davis." He pauses, takes a sip of his coffee, and looks at each of us intently. "As you know, the growth of this department is critical to these patients. But expansion here can also mean more opportunities for you guys—all of you, even. If I could keep all three of you on board with the hospital's blessing, I'd do it in a heartbeat." Is it just me, or did his eyes linger on Dr. Howard when he said that? "To do that, we have to knock this out and make it irrefutable. Don't let them say no to this."

Howard nods solemnly, and I almost want to laugh. I almost want to confess to oblivious Cho—as annoying as he is—that he might as well give up now. Howard's got it in the bag. It's him and me that are gonna duke it out till the end. But the selfish part of me wants to keep him clueless, work this to my advantage. But how?

"Dr. Cho, can you give us an update on Lincoln Chung-Radcliffe's case? When does the campaign kick off?"

Cho stands, flicking an invisible speck of dust off his white coat and straightening his tie—a Christmassy Mickey Mouse today, even though it's August. José catches my eye, and my cheeks burn. I know exactly what he's thinking. Maybe we should tell him. Even out the playing field or whatever.

"As you know, the campaign is set to launch at the end of next week. The publicity team has reached out to all major Asian media, and we've got some things lined up. We've also reached out to the local press here in Jersey, and we've tried TV and mainstream media, although we haven't made much headway there, unfortunately. The bottom line is, there's just too many kids with cancer. One producer told me if they were going to do a feel-good cancer story, it would be on a much younger kid. Teens don't buy much sympathy."

"My sister's boyfriend is a PA in Philly," Howard says. "Maybe he can connect us to someone?"

Arora nods. "Yes, worth trying for sure. But I think what we need is a hook." He looks at his file. "Something to make the story stand out. Bone marrow drive for a sixteen-year-old just isn't sexy, sadly."

"Right." Cho looks forlorn, as if this was his fault. "But in the meantime, we're setting up local donor drives in tandem with K for Kare, starting at the local universities, and setting up a street team to try to recruit and direct at grocery stores and churches. It's grassroots, admittedly, but we're hoping that will spread the word."

"What about online?" I find myself chiming in. I've been checking the stats on the account Lizzie set up—and shockingly, she's still posting for Link, even though she won't talk to me. His follower count is building, slowly but surely. "As I mentioned to Dr. Arora—"

"Thank you, Dr. Sehgal, but we've got it handled," Arora says, shooting me a pointed look. I open my mouth to speak again, but he adds, "As you'll recall, Lincoln and his parents requested that you be removed from the case."

If I could get up, run off to my room and slam the door, I totally would right now. But doctors aren't allowed to throw tantrums. So instead, I nod and go back to my doodling. Arora talks a big game about wanting to keep us all here, but right now it sure doesn't feel like it at all.

When the meeting's over, I rush out ahead of the rest of the team. I can't take any coddling "it's okays" from them. Not today. I'm not a baby, and I refuse to be treated like one, even if they did totally hurt my feelings. I quickly dump my files in my locker in the intern lounge, then head straight down to the staff cafeteria. I grab a muffin and some coffee, but what I'm really craving is some chai and samose. Where's Mom when you need her? She's at the private practice today, which means no treats for me. Unless . . .

Saira: No patients till two. Want to bring me lunch?

Vish: I'm in school.

Saira: ☺

Saira: What if I told you to bring your camera?

Vish: Did Davis say you could shoot at the hospital?

Saira: What Davis doesn't know won't hurt her!

Vish: Be there in twenty. Chinese?

Saira: Chai and samose. And paneer pakora. Double orders of everything, please.

Vish: Aye aye, oink oink.

Saira: 🐷

He'll be here in an hour. That's just enough time to set my plan in in motion. The first thing I have to do is recruit José. He already knows the basics about me and Link. Which is to say, there's not really a "me and Link." But if there's anything I've learned about José in the short time that I've worked at Princeton Presbyterian, it's that he's always down for the drama. So this mission is right up his alley.

He's changing bedsheets in Alina's room when I find him.

Alina beams at me, and I do a quick rundown on her numbers and meds while I'm in there, to make things feel all official.

I'm wrapping up my file update when she pulls up her iPad to show me her latest obsession: the British kids bake-off challenge. "If only," she says wistfully.

"That's funny," I say with a little smirk on my face. "I have a friend who wants to be a reality TV star, too—and he almost pulled it off."

I can almost feel José's ears perk up, and Alina leans forward, excited. "What show? Did they make a tape? Can we see it?"

I nod, and she hands me the iPad. José's already peering over my shoulder as I scroll through YouTube, typing the words "Link Rad" into the search bar. The *Rock Star Boot Camp* video pops right up, and already José's eyes are wide.

"Is that Lincoln Chung-Radcliffe?"

"It sure is!" I can't mute my grin. This is gonna play out exactly as I planned, and I barely had to do a thing. "He made it to the semifinals!"

"Oh, that means he can go to LA for round two, right?" Alina asks. She hits play on the video, and she and José watch, riveted, as Link belts out the Foo Fighters song "Everlong," all croony and groovy with his acoustic. "He's good. He definitely could make the cut."

"And he's got the look, too," José says, grinning at me, mischief in his eyes. "Well, except for the patchy-hair thing. But he can work it. He's gotta go to LA."

"I don't think he wants to do it," I say, solemn.

"He has to do it!" José and Alina say in unison.

"We have to convince him," José adds.

"You're right. And I just might know how." I turn to José, my face serious. "But I'll need your help."

"Girl, you know I'm Team Saira."

"Good. Here's what we're going to do."

CHAPTER 27

Twenty minutes later, Link's exactly where I hoped to find him: in the patient lounge. I asked José to hover and fuss and generally chase him out of his own room, and it totally worked. I can see his silhouette through the papered window and hear the thrum of his guitar as the melody slips out the door, which he left slightly ajar. I lean and listen for a minute, composing myself. I can feel the arrhythmia making my heart skip a beat, the restricted blood flow making my stomach flutter, the erythema coloring my cheeks. My palms are sweaty, and my throat is tight. This is my shot. If I blow this one, I don't know that he'll give me another. I have to make it work.

Vish will be here any second, so it's now or never.

I don't knock. Just push the door open and catch him off guard.

"Hey!"

He stops strumming and looks up, his smile flipping once he realizes it's me. He's already putting the guitar in the case, trying to unravel the IV bag from its entanglements. He can't get away from me fast enough. But I'm not letting him go. Not this time.

I step closer and try to help him disentangle. "Let me help."

"I don't need your help."

"I think you do. As a doctor. As a friend."

"You are so not my friend."

"But I want to be."

"That's just too bad." There's a hard edge to his voice. A bitterness that I haven't heard before, rock beneath the anger.

He's frenzied for a second, trying to get everything cleared out so he can bolt, and his breathing is rough, ragged.

"Stop," I say, reaching for his arm, wrapping my hand around his wrist, like I've done with a million patients. But this isn't the same thing. Feeling the thrum of his heart beat like this, frantic and fluttering, like hummingbird's wings, it's different, enthralling, strangely intimate. It's like the energy there is locking us into place together, and something in the world has shifted, and it can't be changed. Before I know it, he's free of his bonds, and his other hand is wrapped around mine, like he needs to feel my heartbeat, too. Like he needs to know it's beating just as fast, that the rhythm is the same.

We stand like that for what feels like a million moments, entranced.

"Hey!" The door opens again. And there he is. Vish. Samose in hand.

He looks from me to Link and from Link to me, and his face falls a little for a second. Then he grins. "You must be Link."

"Yeah," Link says, letting go of my arm like he's accidentally touched a hot chai pot. "And I must be leaving."

"Wait," Vish says, and lifts up the bag. "I bought samosas. And chai. And paneer pakore."

Link looks intrigued despite himself. And despite his stomach. I know from his chart that he isn't keeping much down. "What are paneer pakore?"

"They're amazing," I say, eyeing the bag. "Hand 'em over, Shah."

"Yeah," Vish says, gesturing to Link. "I brought enough for three. I brought enough for eight, actually. Saira can be a bit ravenous sometimes."

I stick my tongue out at Vish and snatch the bag, setting it down on the coffee table and removing items. A thermos of chai, cups, six samose, still greasy and hot, and the paneer pakore, crispy fried cubes of cheese battered in a thick, luscious chickpea paste. Yum. I pull one right out and dunk it in mint chutney, swallowing half of it in a single bite.

Link watches me eat, and he can't resist. "Okay, I'll stay," he says, then grins at me. Finally. "If it's doctor's orders."

"It is."

Vish makes him a plate with a samosa, some pakore, and three different kinds of chutney—spicy mint, sweet tamarind, and a kicky, bright red garlic—"Good for what ails ya," he informs us.

"I don't know how much it'll help me," Link says morosely, "but it's delicious."

"My dadima thinks food can cure everything," I say, swallowing a bite. "But I have to keep reminding her that too much deep-fried Desi food can also kill you."

"My halmeoni makes Korean BBQ every Sunday night and insists we come over," Link says. "My dad tried going vegetarian once. That lasted like three minutes before she said she'd essentially disown him."

"Half my family is vegetarian," Vish says gravely. "Including me. Saira's dadi hates me because of it. But it's okay, because I still love her. And besides, this whole spread is vegetarian and amazing."

We all ponder this for a minute, our mouths full.

Then Link asks the question I've been dreading. "So, are you Saira's brother? Or her boyfriend?"

"Boyfriend," I say.

Vish frowns, his eyes conflicted. "But not really," he says.

Link looks confused.

"I'm gay. But not out," Vish explains.

It's, like, the first time he's ever said those words to anyone besides me. And his boyfriend. He takes a deep breath. "Because my family's pretty old-school. And they wouldn't get it. I don't think. So when they just assumed Saira and I were together, I let them believe it." He pauses for a second. "And Guddi here let them believe it, too."

Guddi. "It means doll," I explain.

Link shoots me a look that could slay me. But I can't let this falter. Not now. "They pretty much have our wedding planned," I say, unsure of whether to laugh or cry. "Except for Dadi. Who would never abide by a half-Gujarati groom." Vish laughs.

And when I finally work up enough nerve to look at Link again, I see what seems like relief on his face. "She'd rather have a white boy than the wrong kind of Desi," Vish adds, a little too on the nose. I frown at him.

"Yeah," Link says, and I can see his brain working. "So you're not actually together?"

"I mean, she was my first love, my first kiss, my first everything. And if I was bi, I'd be totally into Saira. But I'm not."

I shove him. Hard. And he doubles over, laughing. Link still looks flummoxed, and just a bit green. I leap up, grabbing a plastic bag, and hand it to him. He races to a corner, his IV cart following him, and pukes into the bag.

Great. It seems every potential love interest I have has food issues.

"Well, there goes my appetite," I tell Vish, who's looking at me intently.

"I can see why you like him," Vish says.

I blush again and head over to help Link.

"Here," I say, offering him a cup of water.

"I'm sorry. The pakoras probably weren't a smart idea. Actually, none of this was a smart idea. I should head back to my room." He looks for his nurse call button. But then stops, exhausted.

"I'll help you get back. But I want to talk to you about something."

He looks over to Vish, who's still sitting on the couch, working hard to mind his own business and, not shockingly, still nibbling on a samosa. I see his camera bag stashed at his feet, ready for action. "I don't think that's a good idea."

"I do," I say, and sit him down on the armchair near the bookshelves. I perch on the edge of it, looking down at him. "Look, I don't know why I did what I did. Omitted information." He shoots me a look. "Okay, lied. Or whatever. It's just, I never felt this way before, and everything was weird, and I thought we had this bond . . ."

"I thought we had this bond, too. I did. Because you let me think it. Because I thought you got it. Got me. I thought you were my someone."

I swallow hard. "Yeah, I don't have cancer. I've never had it. But I'm a doctor. An oncologist. So of course I get it. Of course I get you."

He shakes his head and swallows hard, frustrated. "No, you don't."

"My best friend died of leukemia."

He actually stands, offended. "Your best friend? Your best friend!" He tries to throw his hands up, but the IV holds his arm down too much. "You mean the girl from the picture?" he says, staring right at the bulletin board, where the old photo has gathered dust again. "Look, Saira, I know how you feel. But you're not one of *us*, and you can only pretend to get it. It's like when those white ladies at yoga class tell you they did the ten-day Golden Triangle loop and the Taj Mahal, like, changed them, and now they're practically more Indian than you. Bull. Fucking. Shit. You don't get it. You can't get it."

Ouch. That hurt. I can feel my eyes misting and my mouth is dry, like that time I had too much of Taara's red wine. He's trying to get himself together to go again, but I have to stop him. So I step closer, and I take his wrist again. And there it is, that frantic bird thrum. It slows and calms as I hold his arm, and I look at him for a minute, noting all the small changes. The bruising on his jaw, the hollowness of his cheeks. The thinning of his hair, which still tries to flop into his eyes, but misses.

"Link, I need to help. And if it can't be as your . . . friend, then it will be as one of your doctors. Because I can. Help. And I may be the only one who can actually help in your particular case."

His eyebrows climb again, and he rubs his jaw. "What do you mean?"

"The reality is, the odds are not in your favor."

"Thanks. I already know that."

"So finding those few people who really could be a match is of utmost importance."

"Uh-huh."

"So the hospital's doing what they can: outreach to ethnic media, cancer orgs, all of that."

"Yup."

"But we need to do more."

"What more can we do?"

That's when Vish walks over with the camera perched on his shoulders. "You ready?"

Link looks from me to him quizzically. "What?"

"*Rock Star Band Camp*, right?"

"I told Vish here, who's studying film, that you made it to the semifinals."

"I missed the deadline."

"Yeah, you did. But we called them. And for you, Lincoln Chung-Radcliffe, they've decided to make an exception. We need to send them a new tape by Friday."

"I might be dead by Friday."

"As your doctor, I'm telling you: That's not going to happen."

"But like you said, my odds . . ."

"Are not great. So let's improve them, shall we?"

Link looks from me to Vish and back again. "I don't know why I'm saying this. But okay. Let's do it."

CHAPTER 28

"I think that's the one!" Twenty takes later, and we're finally done. Link is exhausted. His fingers are bruised and nearly bleeding from playing the guitar over and over, and I can see the weariness on his face and in his stance. Vish looks pretty tired, too, but he's so pleased with himself, he can't stop grinning.

"This is going to be amazing," he tells Link, putting up his hand for a high five. Link aims for one, but his IV tubes hold him back. "I'll try to edit tonight and bring you something to look at tomorrow. Then we can finalize the cut and upload it before the deadline."

Link nods and plops back down on the sofa. I press the nurse call button, and José is there in seconds with a wheelchair. He helps Link climb in, lifting him like one of those old ceramic figures Dadima collects. "He looks exhausted," José says, scolding.

"But just wait till you see," I tell him, and Link grins, too.

"Night, Saira with an *i*."

"Night, Link."

I'm blushing as José pushes him out the door. And Vish catches me shuffling my feet, takes my hand and twirls me.

"I've never seen you this way, Saira!"

"What do you mean?" I ask innocently. But I kind of know what he means.

"You got it bad."

"I do not."

"Yeah, you do." He shuffles his own feet for a second. "You remind me of me when I first met Luke."

I grin at him, and he starts packing up his camera gear while I clean up the food, putting some of the leftovers in the little fridge. I'll reclaim them as a snack tomorrow.

By the time we're done, it's dark out—and when I look at my phone, I realize I have a dozen text messages and missed calls from my mom, who was supposed to drive me home. She must be livid. I text her back immediately that I'm with Vish at the movies, and she responds with a flat-line emoji, meaning she'll deal with me later. And it won't be good.

Okay! Getting ice cream, then home, I text back.

We grab cones—chocolate chip with sprinkles for me, and rocky road for Vish—down the street at Thomas Sweets, then pause in the park at the old elementary school, where Vish and I first met. The tire swings—old and grungy and classic—are our go-to spot. That's where we had our first kiss—way back when we were, like, ten—and also where he told me he's gay a few years later. It's where he told me he was in love for the first time, too. Luke, this boy he met at lacrosse camp. They kept it a secret the whole time there—hard to do when you're stealing kisses in the boathouse. And he's only seen Luke, who's from Connecticut, twice since camp ended, but they talk every day.

"Is Luke still going to apply to USC?" I ask. I wonder if moving across the country together is such a smart idea—I mean, they're still just teenagers—but they both seem pretty set on it.

Vish nods.

"Did you tell your mom you applied?"

He looks down at his feet, kicking up dirt with his ratty Jordans, and I take that as a no.

When his mom does find out—about LA and USC and film school, about Luke and kissing boys—she's going to hate me. Because I've been complicit all this time. Keeping secrets, telling lies. I did it because I love Vish—not as a brother, as more than a brother. And because he needed me, too. Because I believe he has the right to be whom he wants, and to set the timetable he's comfortable with when it comes to coming out. But my lies will still hurt people, still break their trust. And I never know quite how to feel about that.

"What will she say?" I can't help asking aloud. I know he doesn't want to think about it. But he'll have to, sooner or later. Before the gap between the truth and expectations gets too unwieldy to manage. Maybe it already has.

"I'll deal with it when the time comes," he says, like always. "I have to. I know that. Just not now."

"I can't believe that by this time next year, you'll be gone." An unexpected tear slips down my cheek. "What will I do without you? I'll miss having a boyfriend."

"From what I saw tonight, that role has already been filled."

"Shut up!"

He laughs at me, at my cheeks burning, at the tears that run hot down them, even as I crack up, at the last bit of my chocolate chip and sprinkles managing to drip into my stray locks of hair, like it always does. "I'll miss you, too, Guddi." He looks down at his shoes for a second. "Is it weird that I'm jealous of him?"

My eyebrows fly up, like they always do. "Why would you be jealous?"

"It's not that. It's just . . . despite all of this, the fake dating, the faux-mance, I do love you, you know? You're my girl."

I nod.

"And with him, it'll be real."

"It won't. It's nothing." And what we have is real, too.

He spins his swing, then turns to look at me—sharp, knowing, so very practiced. A total Shah Rukh Khan riff. "Don't say that, Saira. It's real. I can see it. I bet José can see it. And your boss. Which is prolly why he flipped out. Why you were dismissed from the case. Sure as fuck Link knows it's real. That's why he shut you out. That's the last thing he needs right now: true fucking love."

"Always comes at the worst time, huh?"

"Damn straight. Or not so straight."

I laugh and lick my drippy cone again. "I think you have a very vivid imagination."

"And I think, Dr. Sehgal, that you sure are dumb for a genius."

I frown.

"Listen, all I'm saying is, he's working damn hard to push you away. And I know you're nothing if not tenacious or whatever, but this is new territory. Hold your ground. Don't let it go so easy."

"What do you know?"

"This is one place where I'm smarter than you, Girl Genius. Trust me, okay? There are only so many chances at love, whether you're eighteen or eighty. Especially for someone like me. But even for someone like you. You know what you want. Are you willing to fight for it?"

"I've got to get him healthy first."

"I know you'll pull that off. And I'll do anything I can to help."

I nod.

"Maybe we can double-date sometime, me and Luke, you and Link. You know, after we officially 'break up'!"

I grab his hand, and pull his swing closer, like I used to when we were little, when I thought maybe he could be a little bit in love with me, too.

"Whatever else happens," I say, "this, us, has always been real. Fauxmance, yes. But real love, one hundred percent."

He nods. Then spins me away. "That's what I just said, fool." He laughs. "Like I said. Girl Genius, sure. But not so bright at everything else!"

CHAPTER 29

All I want to do today is hole up in the patient lounge with Link, waiting for Vish to bring us his edits. But work beckons, and when it's literally life and death, you can't procrastinate. I'm scheduled for rounds this a.m. with Arora observing, so I took a car service in early—if I waited for Mom, I'd definitely be on Desi time, and I can't risk that.

It's still dark out when I get in. I head to Arora's office, but the door's shut, so I take a seat outside. The rise and fall of voices tell me he's not alone. Howard is in there, and I can hear her voice rise. "You can't be serious!" she's saying, her voice ragged and harsh. "I don't know if I can do this. I don't know if I *want* to do this. This is my first shot. Maybe my only shot. If this gets out—what will people think?"

"What are you saying?"

"You know exactly what I'm saying."

"Then what do you want to do?"

I hear footsteps, and there are more words, but they're muffled, like he's hugging her. I hope he's hugging her. She says something else, and I can sense movement toward the door, so I bolt. It's one thing to know. It's quite another to confront. I'm definitely not ready for that. Not yet.

I try to stay 100 percent focused on the patients as Arora and I do our rounds. It's clear Howard hasn't told him a thing about our, uh, altercation.

"How's it going with Vish? He decide on schools yet?" he asks, trying to be friendly. "Are you going to prom this year?"

I shrug. He keeps trying but then turns talk over to the patient files.

I guess he chalks my sullen one-word answers up to the fact that I'm a teenager. Or whatever.

First up is Brendan, who's still asleep. Ms. Ruby Jackson is hovering this morning, as usual, fluffing pillows and flipping channels when she's not working on her crochet.

She pauses when she sees us, and is far more curt than usual.

"Cookie?" She holds a tin out to Arora. But not to me. He shakes his head.

"You can deliver the news," Arora says to me, proudly. "Since it was your idea."

"Actually, it was Ericka's idea," Ms. Ruby says, hardly hiding her upset. "Despite my reservations, as you well know."

"Yes, about that," I say, trying to keep my voice stable. "He's been accepted to the trial. And the best news is, they'll send a consultant here to initialize the administration, and then we can observe him here. So we don't have to move him!"

"That's the best of both worlds, right, Mrs. Ruby?"

"Ms.," she says, still fussing. "And I suppose it will have to do. But I think this is all too much on the boy." She peers at him, readjusting his blankets. "Look at him. A wisp of a thing now."

"Ms. Ruby, this is an opportunity very few kids will get—I think it could really improve Brendan's chances in the long run." From my file, I pull out a copy of some stats on the trial's initial run and hand them to her. "I know Ericka's got all this information on her computer, but I thought you might like to see a hard copy. The first run was very successful—with an eighty percent improvement in long-term prognosis on kids over twelve. Brendan will be in the first trial of younger kids, but hopefully the numbers will fall in line with what they've seen. Of course, they'll continue observing to see if there are any cases of relapse. But this could be a lifesaver, to put it simply." I take a deep breath. "And just so you know, I talked to Brendan. All this fighting, it's hard on him. He blames himself. If he's going to get better, he needs both of you on his team."

Ms. Ruby grasps the paper, peering at him, her shoulders tense. She harrumphs, but tucks it into her knitting bag. "Well, in any case, I'm overruled. But I've got my eye on you, Saira Sehgal. And if anything goes wrong . . ."

"You can totally hold it against me, Ms. Ruby," I say, waving as we head to the door.

"Oh, you know I will," Ms. Ruby shouts back.

"She's quite a character, huh?" Arora says when we step outside. "'I've got my eye on you . . .'"

He laughs, and I frown. I mean, I get where she's coming from. "There's always such a risk involved," I say.

"Everything's a risk, Saira. You could die crossing the street, or asleep in your bed. Even breathing's a risk these days. Can't stop trying because of it. Can't stop living because of it."

I wonder if he's thinking of Howard and their conversation this morning. I wonder what they're going to do. She's at a critical stage in her career, one where she can't afford to pause for anything. Even love.

"Ready for the next?"

I nod.

"Good. Because I have some news."

My eyebrows do their thing, because he grins. "Patience, underling. Soon, everything will become clear."

I shrug again and follow him into Alina's room.

She looks much better than yesterday. There's a hint of rose to her cheeks, and her baby blues are brighter this morning. She's watching the *Bake Off* on her iPad again, and waves me over as soon as I walk in. Mr. Plotkin's half-asleep in the lounger but waves half-heartedly.

Bubbe hovers, a plate full of rugelach on the table in front of Alina. "From that show she keeps watching," Bubbe says. "Try it. You'll like it."

I take a cookie and nibble at it, and it's actually pretty good.

"You'll never believe!"

"What?" I say, and peer at the little screen as Arora heads off to a corner with Mr. Plotkin, now alert and ready.

"There's a half-Russian Jewish girl from Staten Island on the show! She's twelve. She's me."

Her face goes cloudy for just a second, and I know what she just realized: That girl is who Alina could've, would've, should've been. If not for the cancer.

The girl on the screen is a curly-haired brunette who looks nothing like my little Alina. But the accent is the same.

"Yep, that's you, all right!" I say. "How's she doing?"

"She held her own in the first three episodes, but this one is a big challenge—the POV episode," she says solemnly. "She's making trubochka, which is definitely no easy task." She looks at Bubbe, who frowns, realizing what her next assignment will be.

"Oh, I had that once with my friend Tasha at Hopkins—she's from Brooklyn."

"Yeah, there's some really good bakeries in Bay Ridge. Maybe . . ."

"We'll go one day," I finish. Gotta keep that chin up.

"In the meantime, I have some news," Arora says, returning from behind the curtain. "As you requested, Alina, Saira's been made the primary intern on your case. That means she'll help manage your day-to-day, and you'll go to her with any issues. If you run into trouble, you come to me."

I look at Mr. Plotkin. Surely he's got something to say about this.

"I agree. Alina has connected with you, Dr. Sehgal, and I think you are the best fit for her. You've gone above and beyond, I know."

"I'm on board if you're on board, Alina," I say, keeping my voice upbeat.

"One hundred percent!" she says, offering up her hand.

I grin, and we all high-five. Even Mr. Plotkin.

I try to let my smile falter, even when the weight of it all hits me. I've been tracking the GoFundMe, and while we can be optimistic, it's not a done deal. Yet.

Now I just have to make sure I do right by my patient.

CHAPTER 30

"Wait, wait, wait!" I say, directing Vish and my cousin Arun as they lift the flat screen onto the TV stand. We're redoing the patient lounge today—but it has to be done quietly, so no one notices. So we waited until after five, then started shuffling stuff down the hall on covered gurneys. I mean, nobody's usually down here, anyway. But we couldn't take any chances. "Let's move it to that corner instead."

The boys grunt and pout, but do as they're told. I wipe down the new coffee table, and look around the room, satisfied. José talked the janitor into an after-hours paint job and cleanup last week, so we've made some good progress. And just in time, too.

Today's the big day. Vish's got an edit of Link's video to show us, so I suggested (read: ordered) him to help me finish setting up the lounge, and he roped my cousin Arun into it, too. There are two recliners José swiped from the nurses' lounge, a new mini fridge my dad helped me sneak in after hours, along with a massive supply of actual treats: namkeen and chips, a stash of Girl Scout cookies we ordered from my neighbor, the contraband Korean beef jerky that Link likes. The boys brought in a bunch of beanbag chairs, and then smuggled in the flat screen on a movable bed. Luckily, Davis and her buddies have been too busy to notice.

There's a knock at the door, and we all nearly jump out of our skin. Or, well, I do at least. The boys pause, though, surprised.

The door opens, and Link's standing there, grinning. He's got his guitar with him, and his ubiquitous IV cart.

"Hey!"

Vish finishes setting up the Wi-Fi on the flat screen, then does a little swirly bow, like the Air India mustachioed man. "Just in time!"

Link plops himself down on the sofa and waves me over. I sit down, too—right next to him, so close my leg is touching his. If he notices, he doesn't let on. But I can't focus for a second. Or sixty.

Then there he is, on the big screen, beaming. I don't know what magic Vish has worked, but Link looks positively ethereal, the backdrop of the patient lounge dappled with sunlight as he sings a song about getting lost and finding his way. His voice shines through, a little rough and unadorned. After the musical segment, there's a section on Link's journey—how he got started singing in his mom's church choir, all about his old band, Linus, and how he thought music would be it for him.

"And then I found out I had cancer," he says on camera, and you can see the wetness of his eyes, the throb of his Adam's apple close up. "Acute myelogenous leukemia. Take two. And I thought that would be it. But music, it's what saved me. I wrote and played and sang my heart out, through chemo and radiation and losing all my hair and pretty much all my friends, too. And after eight months of treatment, I went into remission."

Vish pauses the tape, there, and I see Arun rub his eyes a bit, but I pretend not to notice.

"So I made two different versions," Vish says. "That's the short take. It sort of leaves out the second act of the story. Which might be just what you need for this—just enough to get you in without complicating things."

Link nods. "But that's not the whole story."

"Nope."

"And maybe it's better to be honest."

"Yup."

Link turns slightly to look at me, his arm thrown on the back of the sofa just behind me, and for a second, I can't breathe or think or do anything at all. He still smells like oranges and cinnamon (along with a hint of the lemony antiseptic that pervades the hospital), and I just want to stop time, and make the others disappear and breathe him in. But he's got one eyebrow perched, which means he's waiting for an answer.

"Well, wasn't it you who told me once that you didn't want to be known as the cancer kid?"

He nods.

"This version makes you the comeback kid. The other one, it'll be the charity case, right? And that's the last thing you want to be." I pause for a second. "The last thing you are."

"You're right," he says, and turns decisively toward Vish. "I don't even want to see it."

Half an hour later, the boys are still playing video games. I played a few rounds, then bowed out—I'm better at things like *Tetris* than these shoot-'em-up things they're obsessed with.

"This was the best idea *ever*," Link says as he kicks Arun's ass for the fourth round in a row.

Vish sits, about to replace Arun in the next round, but then Arun rises. "You gonna give me a ride to the pickup game?" he asks Vish, who shrugs.

"Wait," Link says. "Do you have a couple minutes?"

I frown. Will they never leave?

"Yeah, one more round?"

"No, I wanna add something to the tape."

Vish grabs his bag. "Sure." He pulls the camera out. "What'd you have in mind?"

Arun leans in front and shouts, "ACTION!" Then he says, "I've always wanted to say that."

Vish gives him that guy head-nod thing, and Link leans over me on the couch, reaching around to grab something off the floor.

It's a bag. He signals for Vish to shoot again, and then opens it.

"Two years ago, in September, I was told I was in remission. But in

July of this year, during what I thought was a routine follow-up visit, my doctors—including Dr. Sehgal here—told me that the cancer was back. And this time, it was worse. But the story's not over. Far from it. And I've never been a quitter. So I'm about to fight this thing. Again. And kick its ass."

He pulls a electric razor out of the bag and hands it to me. "Dr. Sehgal, will you do the honors?"

Vish cuts the camera. "Wait, what?"

"Shave my head."

"You don't have to do this, Link," I say. "There are options, other meds, and your hair—"

"I want to do this, Saira. To spite the chemo. I have control of this, and I'm going to win. And I want you to help me. Won't you help me?"

I nod.

"Good." He waves toward Vish, who steadies his camera again.

I take the razor from him and stand behind him as he takes his seat on the sofa again. "Ready?"

"As I'll ever be."

I take the electric razor and slide it over the top of his head, watching as the wispy dark strands slip easily and fall to floor, the buzzing in my ears getting louder and louder. Ten quick strokes, and it's all gone. His head is pale and perfect, with a small brown mole sits right below his left ear, a kala tilak to ward off the evil eye. I hope it works.

He grins up at me, then at the boys. "Well? How does it look?"

Vish smirks at me, then gives Link his cue. The little red light tells me the camera's still rolling. "Pretty damn sexy."

"Definitely rock star–worthy," Arun agrees with a shrug. "Works for you." Then he turns to Vish. "Dude, you ready?"

Vish nods and starts packing up the bag. "I'll bring you a new edit tomorrow," he says. "I know exactly what to do."

"Thanks."

"Anytime. Literally."

CHAPTER 31

The boys shuffle out, dusty and tired, and suddenly we're alone, Link and I. Alone. Together.

"You tired? Want me to call José?" I ask, trying not to notice that he's leaning on me a bit on the sofa, that our thighs and our hips and arms are touching. That if I lowered my head just a few inches, it would be right there on his shoulder.

"I'm okay." He's quiet for a minute, except for that ragged edge to his breathing, and I realize mine is echoing it, inhale, exhale, inhale, exhale. I bubble-face for a second, holding my breath so that my cheeks fill with air, and then pop the bubble with my finger, letting all the air out in a whoosh. He laughs, and I shrug. "Just something my sister and I did with my dadi at bedtime when we were little. It sort of stuck."

"I like it," he says, and bubble-faces back. But then his face is serious, intent. And there's our breath again, in and out, in and out, in unison, like the chorus of a Dashboard song.

"Jerky? Popcorn? Movie?" I ask, pointing to the new DVR. "I've got the new Shah Rukh Khan." And then I hold up another. "And a DVD version of the classic *Anne of Green Gables!*"

He grins but shakes his head. "Okay if we just sit?"

I nod. "Did I tell you that my sister wants to be a reality TV star, too? She's got her own FoodTube channel."

"Yeah? What does she make?"

"Like, healthier versions of Indian food. But I can't abide by tofu mattar instead of paneer." He grimaces. "But her paranthe are improving.

She's also going to be in *Hair*." I take a deep breath. "You know the one where they're all naked onstage?"

He covers his mouth, faux-scandalized, and I laugh.

"Starshine," he says, and I blush.

I take a deep breath again, but my heart is racing even faster than it does on the highway. "So, it's good. That you're doing it. Even if it's hard. Or whatever."

"Did you and Vish, like, ever actually hook up?"

I'm so shocked, I almost don't answer. "What?"

"I mean, was he ever really your boyfriend?"

He's leaning in toward me, looking at me, waiting for me to look at him. But my cheeks are aflame—the erythema, as usual—and I can't bring myself to meet his eyes.

"When I was younger, before I knew he was gay—before he accepted it himself, I think—we kissed a few times. I mean, I love him. I'll always love him. But I don't think I've ever been *in* love with him."

He slumps a little, his body resting against mine. Tired? Relieved?

"I don't think I've ever been in love, either," he says, in a voice so low I have to strain to hear it, even though he's barely inches away. "I wonder if I'll get the chance."

"Of course you will." I hope. "You've never been in love?"

He shakes his head. "I thought I was. This girl, Risa. I met her when I was taking guitar lessons, back, like, in seventh grade. We hung out for two years. She wanted to be, like, Lady Gaga. Which was a lot to take sometimes. But we thought we'd start a band and take over the world together. Or something."

"And then . . ."

"And then I got cancer. Like, at first, it wasn't a big deal. But then it spiraled. I mean, you know. From my file. Anyway, the thing is, she didn't bail. Surprisingly. But it was like *we* got cancer. She was all, 'We're going to live through this and be stronger in the end.' But she wasn't going to live through it. I was. For her, it was just something to write about."

"Ouch."

"Yeah. Like, last time, she'd be here for all the radiation sessions, talking to the nurses incessantly, hovering, being the 'good girlfriend.' It was too much for me." He's staring at his hands, his fingers moving involuntarily, like on a guitar fret. "So I broke up with her. Before the treatment even ended. Maybe it was unfair. And she still texts or whatever. But I have to do this solo."

Solo. "And you didn't love her?"

"No, I don't think I did. My mom liked her, though." He laughs. "Actually, she kind of reminds me of your friend from the mall."

Tall. Blond. Pretty.

"Loud and a bit self-centered."

"Hey." But then I giggle. And frown. "We had a big fight. Lizzie and me. She hasn't talked to me in a week." I sigh. "But she's still running your social media outreach."

He smirks. "Oh, that's who does it? I thought it was the hospital folks."

I shake my head. "They choose not to acknowledge. But you have ten thousand followers now. And soon you'll have more."

"Why?"

"Because of *Rock Star Boot Camp.*"

"No, I mean, why don't you talk to Lizzie anymore?"

"Oh, that. High school stuff."

He raises an eyebrow, which makes me laugh. "You're so beyond that."

"I mean . . ."

"I wonder who you'd be, Saira with an *i*, if you weren't Dr. Sehgal?"

I shrug. Sometimes I wonder, too. The know-it-all in the front row, maybe, who asks for extra credit and runs the debate club. When she's not in trouble for her distracted doodling.

"That day we first met, I thought I knew," he says. "I thought you were just like me."

"What do you mean?"

"That kid with all the plans." He swallows hard. "The one who doesn't know quite how to deal when the c-word takes over, destroying everything in its path."

I nod, staring as he drums his fingers on his thigh—which is still touching mine. "I'm not that kid. But I know her."

He grins. "Sure, Dr. Sehgal."

"My best friend Harper—"

"The one who died."

I nod. "The one from the picture. I was the one who diagnosed her. Sort of. Here. And then I watched her die. And I couldn't do anything about it."

"That explains so much."

I nod. "Yeah. We used to hang out right here." I wave my arms around. "In this same old dusty room. And watch *Anne of Green Gables* on scratchy VHS, and play Monopoly for hours. Just us."

He smiles. "There are a lot of ghosts here."

"I missed a lot of school in those last few weeks and months, and none of the other kids got it. Not Lizzie, for sure. I think Vish had to convince her to even come to the funeral."

"You think?"

"We don't really talk about it anymore." I take a deep breath. "We don't talk about a lot of things."

"Because she's still so high school, and you're so not?"

I shrug. "She's still trying to figure herself out."

"And you're all set, huh?" He takes my hand, tracing the lines on my palm. "It is written and all that?"

"There's nothing wrong with knowing what you want."

"But you're sixteen," he says, his fingers stroking the inside of my palm. There are goose bumps all over my skin, but he doesn't seem to notice. "So it's okay if you don't yet."

I pull my hand away, setting it uselessly in my lap. "But I do. And it's okay if I go after it, too."

"It is okay. But you can also take your time, you know."

"You don't know that."

He nods. "Do you ever think you might have missed out, not going to high school?"

I shake my head vigorously.

"Sometimes I wish I could just go back to that—mundane everyday, homework and basketball and making music with my friends. SATs and prom and college applications. You know, I didn't even fill any out? I don't even know where I'd start." He shrugs.

"Vish is going to USC."

"Long distance? That's tough."

"We'll have 'broken up' by then." I grin. "And his boyfriend will be there with him."

"And Lizzie?"

I shrug again. "Last time it was Yale, Tisch, maybe UCLA. Who knows now. She changes her mind every ten seconds."

"Good for her."

I frown.

"Oh, come on, Saira with an *i*. She's a kid. So are you. And you wouldn't know since you're so above it and all, but high school's great training for the real world."

This time I raise a carefully groomed brow.

"I mean, look at this place." He waves his arms around. "It has cool kids, wannabes, geeks . . ." He grins at me. "And I mean the doctors."

I jab him with my arm, grabbing his wrist. It's like the world has stopped, but his heart is racing. Or maybe that's mine again. He's looking at me, and I try to look away, to focus on anything but him and the moment that's unfolding. So this is what it's like, my heart hammering, my skin hot with anticipation, my eyes reflexively closing as our bodies turn in toward each other, leaning closer and closer until our noses are touching, our mouths sharing the same air.

We can't, though. He's sick. He can't share my air, my germs, my thoughts, my heartbeat. He can't—

"I can't." He leans back into the sofa quickly, his head falling back, his arms lifted to cover his eyes, like the light hurts.

216

"No."

"I mean, I want to kiss you, Saira. Believe me I do."

"Me too." Too quiet. I don't even know if he heard me.

"But . . ."

"You're sick."

"Yeah. And I'm not taking anyone down with me."

"And I'm your doctor."

"That, too."

But then he sits back up, turning to me, pulling me closer. His forehead is pressed to mine now, the only space between us the few millimeters that separate our mouths.

"So we can't," he says again, then closes the gap. His mouth is salty and sweet, a grapefruit sprinkled with sugar. His arms curl around me, his embrace stronger than I expected. My arms wrap around his neck, and I lean back onto the couch, taking him with me, until the tug of his IV pulls him back a bit, a warning.

"Sorry," he says, his breathing shallow and forced. "I didn't mean to do that."

I nod.

He stands, unraveling the tangle of the IV stand and bag. "I should go."

I nod. "Or you could stay."

He's grinning down at me, and I know he wants to. Stay. But I can tell today has taken its toll, too, in the short, quick breaths, and the wary stance.

"We can't," he says. And it kills us both a little, I think.

I nod again. "But just so you know. Whether you're eight or eighty, you only get so many chances at a real connection." Then I grin. "A friend once told me that."

I watch, a bit sad, as he grabs the IV cart. But instead of walking out, he locks the IV and untwists it from his wrist, disconnecting it. Freeing himself.

"That's better," he says. "Three's a crowd."

CHAPTER 32

It's past nine when I get home, and my mom is waiting for me at the door when the car pulls up.

I wonder if she can tell what I've been doing. If my lips look as bruised and used and happy as they feel. If the heat that warms my cheeks will give me away. But she just seems mad.

"What took you so long?" she says. There's worry in her voice, but it's also laced with annoyance. "I even had you paged. And Dadima made muttar paneer. She left you a bowl on the kitchen table."

I nod. "Patient drama, but thanks, Mom. I'll warm it up after I change into my pj's."

Vish texts then. He's done with his edits. *Should I send you the cut?*

I text him back: *I'll be right over.*

I go upstairs, wash up, and change into pj's, pulling a sweater on over them. It's hot for September, but the AC is still blasting—I know to Papa's chagrin—and it's freezing upstairs. I brush my teeth, splash water on my face, and stare at myself in the mirror. My eyes are bright, like I'm about to cry, and my cheeks are still flushed, from the heat of the shower and the linger of Link's kisses.

When Vish and I kissed a few times, it was nothing like today. It didn't make my heart go thump thump thump or that little kernel of want grow in the very center of me. It didn't make me want to forget everything else and just spend every waking moment kissing him. And doing other things, too.

"You didn't eat." Mom's peering in the door. She's in her pajamas, her usually straight bob curling. It's late. She's usually in bed, reading, by now. And Papa's usually out cold. Unless he's watching Bollywood films.

"Can I go to Vish's?"

"Now?" She looks at me like I'm a fool for even asking.

"Please."

"No. You have work tomorrow. Vish will have to wait." She pulls the bathroom door closed, and I hear her putter toward her bedroom.

I text him back: *Can you come here?*

Ten minutes later, he's at the back door—signaling with pebbles like he used to when I was a kid. I open it, lifting a finger to my lips to shush him.

"They're all asleep."

He frowns. "You didn't tell them?"

I shake my head. "But there's muttar paneer."

I fix him a bowl, too, and we sit in the breakfast nook, where he sets up his laptop.

Two minutes later, Vish hits play on his computer.

It starts with Link and his guitar—Lucy, he calls it—and some solo riffs and singing. Then some narration that documents his time with his band, Linus. And then him walking down the hall, his constant companion, the IV stand, in tow. "I may have cancer," he says, "but it doesn't have me."

Then there's more playing and some video—that Vish must've shot when I wasn't around—of Link and Arun playing video games in the lounge, him laughing with José, him and a few of the younger oncology patients making crafts. Then him and me—in my lab coat—talking seriously.

"That's it! Hit send. It's great," I say, and I can't stop grinning. "I mean, like really, truly brilliant."

"I knew you were smitten, but man, watching you watch this makes me realize just how gone you really are," he says, laughing, too loud. I poke him and he hushes. "You don't even know."

I wonder if I should tell him about tonight. But it feels a tiny bit like a betrayal. Even though it's not. Not really.

"So you guys made out?"

"How did you know?"

"Man, Arun and I were taking bets."

"That's really gross."

Vish laughs again, but then looks serious. "Is that, like, safe for him or whatever? You can't . . ."

I bury my head in my hands. "Oh my god, stop!"

"But, like, germs?"

"If he was severely immunocompromised, it would be an issue. But he's not. Though that's really not any of your business."

"But it is yours, as his doctor."

I frown at my bowl, which is nearly empty now. "Yes."

"Just be careful, Saira."

"Okay, Uncle."

"No, really, I mean it. Like, of course be careful, if that's something you're thinking about. But be careful, too. With, like, your heart."

"I am."

"You never got over Harper. This would be way worse."

"He's not going to die."

"You can't control that. Never could. Though you always try."

"Can't you just be excited for me?"

Vish then takes my hand. "I am. Truly excited. You are my favorite, Saira. I want you to have everything you want." He sighs. "But what you want is always the most impossible thing."

I frown, nibbling my lip. "I know."

He nods. "So please. Be careful. For both your sakes."

I stand, clearing bowls and spoons, when Dadi comes marching into the kitchen, her footsteps quiet as a cat.

"Yeh ladka yahan kya karahe?" she says, loud enough to wake the dead. Or even Papa.

"Shhhhh, Dadi."

"Why is he here?" she says, as if he's not standing there. As if he can't hear her. "You, boy. Go home. Saira. This is not done."

"Dadi, it's okay. We're working on a project."

"No, it's not." She gathers the dishes, slamming them around in the sink. "Go now." She points to the door, and Vish mad-dashes out of it. "You, upstairs. Now."

I nod. Dadima's livid, in her own seething way. Which means Mom is definitely going to hear about this in the morning.

CHAPTER 33

I check my phone one last time as I get into the elevator, hitting the button for eight. I texted Lizzie eighty times last night, and not one response. But she's been all over social, posting pics from acting camp—some new director dude—and pointedly responding to every comment but mine. At least she hasn't completely unfriended me. Yet.

As the elevator pings open on eight, I shove my phone into my pocket. Time to focus. It's bright and early on a sweltering August Tuesday, and as much as I want to head straight to Link's room to see him, I know I have to play it cool. He was breathless and exhausted when I finally walked him "home" last night. Even if he's not neutropenic—with a problematically low white blood cell count—all that kissing couldn't have been good for him. It could increase the risk of serious infection, like bronchitis or pneumonia, which could weaken his system right now. But every time we stopped, well, we didn't. I've never felt anything like this before, so reckless and out of control. We have to stop. We have to. And as a doctor, it's my responsibility to take charge of the situation. So no more making out.

I'll just have to focus on other things. Dadima made palak pakore with chai this morning, so I bought a stash of the spicy spinach fritters to the office for José and Alina. The brown paper bag is streaked with grease, and as I bustle into the room, Mr. Plotkin looks at me warily. Alina peers over from her massive bed. She looks smaller every day, which worries me. José's bustling around her, adjusting the bed, checking her IVs, prepping the files for me.

"What do we have today?" he asks, taking the thermos of chai from me immediately. He's grown accustomed to a morning cup of Dadima's adraki blend in the a.m., claiming it clears out his sinuses.

"Pakore," I say, opening up the bag. He reaches in tentatively and grabs one. "Chickpea-battered fritters, usually veggie. These are spinach and onion." I hold the bag out toward Alina. "You want?"

She shakes her head, looking a bit green. She rarely refuses food—and loves trying new things—so I'm a bit startled. But I pour her a mug of chai and offer it. She shakes her head again. José grabs the mug instead. "Don't mind if I do."

He perches on the lounger for a second with chai and pakore but shoots me a look that says we have a problem.

"Guys, maybe take the snacks to the lounge and offer them to the others, too?" I say, pointedly. I need to talk to Alina alone—and that means shuffling Mr. Plotkin out of here, too. "I'm sure they'd appreciate it."

José nods, and then grabs Mr. Plotkin's arm. "You haven't been to the patient lounge yet, right? They just refreshed it—come on, I'll show you."

I busy myself updating Alina's vitals for a minute, checking her fluids and heart rate, doing a quick analysis on her meds. Then I perch on the edge of the bed for the most important part.

"How are you doing, Alina?"

She shrugs, not quite looking at me. Her color is a bit more yellow than usual, and she's definitely lost weight.

"José noted that you've been rejecting meals?"

"I can't eat. Nothing tastes good."

"You have to eat. Or—"

"Feeding tube." She swallows hard. "I know."

"You don't want that."

She shakes her head, looking down at her hands.

I offer her a cup of orange juice. "Drink this. You need the nutrition."

She sips tentatively, grimacing at the taste.

"Sour?"

"Everything's sour."

I nod. "It's the meds. Maybe we can readjust—"

"I'm going to die this time, Saira. I've already accepted it. I just wish everyone else would." She takes a deep breath. "But if I talk about it, they panic. Especially Bubbe. And this isn't just killing me. It's killing my family. They sold the house, but it's not enough. There's so much debt now, my mom's gone for days at a time, my sisters have missed weeks of school. And for what? The miracle isn't coming. Not this time."

"You can't say that, Ali. You're young, you're strong, and we're doing everything we can."

"It's not enough. And it's too much. I don't want it."

"Alina, your family loves you. They want the best for you. They want you to get better, to live a long life. To live your dreams."

"But what about what *I* need? I can't eat. I can't sleep. I'm uncomfortable all the time. This is not a life worth living. And even if, by some miracle, we can get rid of it this time, it'll always be with me, looming, like a shadow. I'm ruining everything. I don't want to live like that."

I don't know what to say. And I didn't when Harper said the same thing, all those years ago. I just knew I needed her not to disappear on me. And now, here we are again.

"I know you're doing everything you can, Saira. And I'm grateful for that. But I need you to do one last thing for me. Take care of them when it happens. They'll need someone. They'll need you."

No, they need *her*. She has to fight.

But I've heard these words before—from Harper. Children can be so wise. But in the end, they're just children. They can only fight so much.

So I just nod. And pray for a miracle.

I walk out, staring down at her file. Her bills are still overdue, despite the GoFundMe, which covered a large chunk of the outstanding expenses. And honestly, the prognosis is not strong. But we have to do everything we can to save her.

Right?

We meet in the oncology office to do our updates. Davis is raging today—I can tell by the way she's pacing and plotting.

As soon as we're seated, she dives right in.

"I don't know whose idea this was," she says, though she's looking right at me, "but I'm really upset that Dr. Charles and I were not consulted before Brendan Jackson was enrolled in the trial."

"I actually mentioned it to Dr. Charles before filing the paperwork," Arora says, looking sheepish. "Yes, I should have set up a paper trail—that was my error. But what's done is done."

"And Brendan's showing a lot of improvement, thanks to the drug trial. It's only been a few days, but already his white blood cell count is up," Howard says. Ms. Ruby asked that she be the primary physician on the case, and for once, Ericka agreed. "It's no guarantee, but he seems to be improving. We're monitoring him closely and reporting in to the trial physicians on a daily basis."

"We're going to have to pull him," Davis says, unflinching. "It's just too controversial a trial, and for the university to secure ranking, we need to be as clean and lean as possible. This type of 'progressive' action could ding us in the long run."

"The patient's condition is improving." I bite my tongue for a second, regretting the interruption. But it's true. "Why would you stop a course of treatment that shows all signs of being successful midrun? That doesn't make medical sense."

"It's in the best interests of both the hospital—and the patient," Davis says. "The boy's grandmother Ruby Jackson has filed a complaint, citing reckless endangerment in our course of treatment."

"Ruby Jackson is an old fogy who just wants her 'wisp of a boy' to die in peace," Cho says with shocking ferocity. "The mother has signed off on the trial—and in fact, she was the one who suggested it."

I nod. "This seems like personal family drama playing out in an unfortunate mess, but both Dr. Howard and I vetted early trial results before we applied."

"Saira's right," Cho says, and my jaw nearly drops. "Brendan Jackson's condition is markedly improved. To take him off of the trial now would be effectively killing him. Grandma's gotta step down."

"We can look at other options long-term, but as of right now, I'd recommend continuing the current course as we research other options," Howard says firmly. "They only take a hundred patients, and this opportunity won't come again for Brendan Jackson."

Arora clears his throat. "I think my team is right, Dr. Davis, and I stand by them. If you and Dr. Charles insist on reversing this course of treatment at this stage, I'll have to take this to the medical advisory board."

Davis's eyes blaze. "Moving on. Plotkin payments are still not quite up-to-date, but we have continued to administer treatment," she says. "Sehgal?"

"Her condition is deteriorating despite our interventions," I say. "I think the family is well aware. But they have asked us to continue to do everything we can. Which means, it seems, that she'll need a feeding tube next."

Nurse José nods. "I've been tracking her intake, and it's reduced by about seventy percent in the last few days," he says. "I've started TPN, but the lack of nutrition is not doing her any favors."

"Sehgal, talk to the family about the feeding tube and other possibilities if she continues on this path," Arora says. "Reiterate that getting her to eat is critical, or these 'options' will become necessities."

I nod, making notes in Alina's file. "She has voiced reluctance to receive the feeding tube. But her parents insist on following through with necessary next steps."

"And Lincoln Chung-Radcliffe?"

"His condition is holding steady as we hunt for a donor," Cho says. "We've reached out to local organizations, ethnic media and other, to get the word out. It's happening, slowly but surely."

"Good," Davis says. "It's a long shot, but keep at it. Odds are slim, so getting the word out is critical in a case like this."

"Well, I think I know something that will help," Arora says, his voice smiling even though his face is serious. "As of this morning, Dr. Sehgal has been reinstated, unofficially, as part of Team Chung-Radcliffe, at least for social media. She's been helping Lincoln's mom Maggie with his social media, and they are making big strides on spreading the word."

Watching Davis scrawl her notes with a heavy hand, the weight of what Arora says hits me. Lincoln's now my patient. Officially. I don't know whether to be thrilled or terrified.

"And last but not least, Pinky Sharma," Davis announces.

"The mom finally signed the paperwork, thanks to an intervention from Dr. Sehgal," Arora says. "Ah, that would be Sehgal Senior. Surgery is scheduled for Friday at seven a.m. It'll be all hands on deck. Except for you, Dr. Sehgal." He pauses. "Be prepared. This is a big one."

The others nod gravely. I swallow hard. Pinky needs this surgery, but she's so little, who knows how her body will handle it. I just know I have to be there, no matter what.

GOFUNDME:

Alina Plotkin

Two years ago, at the age of 10, our happy-go-lucky
daughter Alina was your average fifth grader—she loved
going to the beach, baking with her bubbe, and cheering
on the US gymnastics team at the Olympics. Then she was
diagnosed with cancer.

In the two years that she has faced the disease, Alina
has had to give up a lot. She's missed her baby sisters'
birthday, starring in the school play, and countless homework
assignments. She's missed going to her fifth grade
graduation, the start of middle school, and lots of other big
moments in the life the average 12-year-old.

Alina was diagnosed with leukemia, which has taken its
toll. She's hopeful that with the right care and continued
treatment at Princeton Presbyterian, she'll be headed back to
school next fall.

*She keeps her spirits up by reading messages from you, and
watching the "Kids' Baking Challenge," which she hopes to
audition for once she's out of the hospital.*

$176,170 of $250,000 goal
Raised by 1,104 people in 2 months

CHAPTER 34

I head straight to my mom's office after the meeting. She was super casual about things this morning—didn't mention Vish at all. Which means she doesn't know. Or she does and has just decided to torture me.

But I need some light to clear out the darkness that's settled into my head. And I definitely need some chai. So Mom's it is.

"Hey, beta," she says as I push open the door. "Sit," she commands, and I do.

The electric kettle yelps, and she switches it off, pouring steaming hot water into a mug along with some of that instant chai mix she keeps here for lazy days.

She passes me the cup. "How'd it go today?" The weariness has settled onto her shoulders and the corners of her eyes. She's exhausted, and I can see her eyes taking me in, observing the same slump in me. "You look tired."

If Dadi said anything about Vish and yesterday, Mom isn't letting on. Which is probably worse.

"Yeah, I could use some chai," I say, taking a big sip. I grimace. It's pretty terrible, but it'll do in a pinch. And this is a pinch. "Mom, do you know a patient named Alina Plotkin? She's twelve. The same kind of leukemia that Harper had."

Mom shivers a little, and I know what she's thinking. But she pulls herself together. "I don't see most of the oncology kids," she says, "just the ones that come through my office. Which, luckily, there haven't been many of. Why?"

"The family is pretty gung ho. And—"

"She's not."

"No."

My mother frowns. She doesn't like where this is going.

"Yeah, that's too bad. But that's the thing with oncology, the losses, while statistically small, are staggering nonetheless. It's tough for any physician to deal with, let alone a new one. Especially one who's sixteen."

"There's something amazing about it, too—I have a real opportunity to make a difference," I tell her, and mostly myself. "To save lives. Except this time maybe . . . I can't."

My mother sits and takes a sip of her chai. She's thinking about the right words to say to me, as both her daughter, and as a doctor, albeit a baby one.

"Before us, after us, there is always the cycle of life and death. We're mere drops in the ocean, Saira, but it's hard to remember that as we fall." She takes a deep breath. "Anya is so very worried about Pinky. I wonder if she'll make the wrong decision."

"What do you mean?"

"To cancel the surgery."

I take a deep breath. "She can't. You can't let her." The surgery may not save Pinky. But without it, all that's left is a death sentence.

"She's two, baby."

"I know. And I'd like to see three. And four. And ten. And beyond."

"You know, and I know. But her mother—that's her child. It's a hard thing to put a child through that, even to save her life."

"Mom, should I talk to her?"

My mother laughs ruefully. "Not unless you definitely don't want Pinky to have the surgery."

"She has to have it, Mom. She has to have a chance."

"Right. I hope you remember that for all your patients."

I swallow hard. She's right. I'm too emotionally involved. But I don't know how not to be.

Mom heads behind the desk, and I feel like a patient, waiting for my diagnosis. But instead of sitting down, she pulls open a drawer and removes a big, flat box—one I've never seen before. She comes back around and takes the chair next to me, the box on her lap. She uncovers it and inside lays an album, a weathered black leather cover. "All these files take up so much room," she says with a sigh. "But this is my real patient record."

She hands me the album, and it's heavy with overstuffed pages. "There's a picture of every NICU baby I ever treated right here, in this book," my mom says, running her fingers over the pages lovingly as I flip through it. "From the very first, to Mrs. Mehta's daughter last week. It's the one thing I request of my patients right from the beginning. You see, so much of medicine is statistics and fear and harsh, cold realities," my mom says, and her eyes are misty, though I've never seen her let tears fall. "But there's also this: life and joy. The best of it all. That is what I would like for you."

Maybe Mom is right. Maybe I'm making this too hard on myself.

"But, beta, know this," she says, closing the book and tucking it back into the box. "You have to make your own choices. Some of us pick an easier path, and some of us are strong enough to handle the pain. In any case, beta, I'd advise you to tread carefully if oncology is the path you choose—learn how to detach."

"Easier said than done," I say, thinking of little Pinky, and the life-changing surgery that awaits her. And Alina. And Brendan. And Link.

"Then think about what's right for you. No specialization is easy—medicine is, of course, about life *and* death. But there can be joy in it, too. That's why I chose my specialization. I get to work with parents and children. There's a lot to love about that."

I nod. I know I have a lot of choices ahead of me. And not all of them will be right.

But there's one thing pulling me, no matter what.

Lincoln's not in his room. His mom is there, and she smiles at me when I poke my head in. "He's been talking about you," she says, and I wonder if she notices the blush. "About how well it's going. With all the posts and stuff. I think it's smart. With your reach, it could really make a difference."

"I'll do whatever I can," I say, the heat still flaming my cheeks. I feel like she can see the traces of fire his kisses left. If she knew how selfish I am, how I'm endangering her son in spite of all I know, she'd never forgive me. I can hardly forgive myself.

"Well, I won't tell if you don't," she says. "Anyway, you know where to find him. And thank you."

My feet carry me there automatically, as if the soothing strum of his guitar, Lucy, is beckoning me. I hear the muffled melody seeping out from under the door, the familiar cadence and rhythm embracing me like an old friend.

I lean against the door, savoring the words, even as half-formed as they are. *"There it is again, the space between us. / There it is again, the great divide. / There it is again, the space between us. / An endless cycle. / Like time and tide."*

It's a bit mournful, though the riffiness—is that what it would be called?—still makes it sound catchy. Like something that would do well on *Rock Star Boot Camp*. Which reminds me . . . I knock on the door to give him a warning, even though it feels a bit awkward, and then push it open.

He's sitting on the couch, the guitar in his lap, and he grins at me when I walk in.

"Hey."

"Hey."

Do I wave? Sit next to him? Kiss him hello? I don't know what to do with myself, because my body automatically starts dictating things.

But I have to do what's right for him, so sharing germs is definitely out. Maybe.

He pats the couch next to him, though, so I take a seat. Not too close. Like, there are still several inches of space between us. Or there were. Because then he leans and kisses me on the nose.

"You okay?" he says, looking at me funny. Then crossing his eyes. "You look dazed."

"I just, uh, I'm part of your medical team now." I'm his doctor. For real.

"I mean, not really. But we'll figure it out."

I nod. "Vish sent me the updated video. Want to see it?"

Link shrugs. "Tell him to send it. I trust him. And you."

"You sure? He added the last part, you know." I gesture to his head.

His hand flies to his now bald head, and he rubs it with his palm. And it's like an invitation, because I can't help but reach over and touch it, too. It's smooth, but the peach fuzz that's already cropping back up is like tiny little spikes. "New growth," I say, reaching to rub his head, and he grabs my arms, pulling me nearly into his lap. "That's a good sign."

"You're a good sign," he says, then kisses me.

But I pull back, shaking my head.

"We shouldn't. We can't."

"Touch is good for kids with cancer," he says with a smirk, and I laugh. But when he leans forward, I shake my head again.

"Nope."

He sighs and leans back into the sofa, his face a bit sulky, his mouth a bit pouty. Which makes me want to kiss away the tension. But I don't let myself. Even though his hand has inched its way over to mine, tracing my palm like he did before. Even though every cell in my body is screaming with the need to touch him back. It's just hormones. And chemistry. And maybe something more.

But I can't. We can't. For so many reasons.

"Wanna play me your song?" I ask, and he turns to me and grins.

"Okay," he says. "But not here."

"What?"

"I have my car." He grins at my confusion. "Come one. There's someplace I wanna go." I frown. "We can tell my mom if you want. But I'll be under doctor's supervision."

His mom probably *would* have let us sign him out. But apparently, Link wants an adventure, because he'd rather sneak out the back hall, which is still dark and a bit abandoned. He's disentangled himself from his IVs, and borrowed a pair of shorts from José.

The minivan is big and green with a giant white stripe. Hideous and homey. "We used to use it for the band. Back before the cancer." He unlocks the door and waits expectantly.

"Well, get in."

"Nope," he says with that familiar smirk. "You're driving."

"I can barely drive a car," I protest. "This thing—"

"Is so old, it doesn't matter if you crash it. And I'm dying of cancer. So you're good."

"You are not dying."

"And driving won't kill you."

"I dunno. It might. It might just kill both of us."

"I'll take my chances."

He pushes me up into the seat, then gets in on the passenger side. I look around, panic setting in, especially when I see the stick shift.

"Hands on the wheel, two and ten. Pull the gear and press the gas at the same time. Practice that. Yes. Again. And again." He laughs. "Okay, now turn the actual key in the ignition. We're about to blow this joint."

He makes me turn left, then right, then left again, then straight up the ramp. And all of the sudden, we're on the highway.

I try not to panic, but my hands are clammy, and sweat is dripping right down my face.

"We're gonna die."

"Yes, eventually." He grins, his eyes on me, and then the road, and then me again. "Just breathe and look forward. The rearview will warn you if there are any problems. But stay in this lane and maintain your fifty per hour, and try not to worry too much about everyone else." He laughs at that last line, realizing he's just asked the impossible.

But I do what he says, and he hums his song as we go, soothing and sweet. And twenty minutes later, we're pulling off the highway and into the salty sea air, with gulls swooping overhead.

The parking lot is empty, so I park the van across three spots and climb out, exhausted and drenched in sweat.

The sun's about to set as we walk toward the water, our shoes abandoned in the van, the sand squishing underfoot. I'm carrying Lucy, the guitar, and we settle on top of a blanket, just a few feet from the waves.

He starts playing a song, and it's something I haven't heard before. "Gin Blossoms," he says. "My mom used to listen to this song on repeat, back when I was younger. When I first got sick. It was one of the first ones I learned by heart, because there was a line that always stuck with me. 'My fear, pretend, that I'll never be in love again.'" He takes a deep breath. "That's me. That's pretty much all of me."

I stare at him as he stares at the water, his bare legs bruised as they stretch out on the blanket in front of him, the waves just barely reaching his toes. Light glistens off the water and him with his bright eyes, blinding me here and there, and all I hear is his voice above the crash of the ocean.

"When they say everything happens for a reason, it's a lie," he says. "Children don't suffer and die for a reason. I don't know how anyone can even begin to justify their pain." He turns to look at me then and takes my hand, tracing sand into the lines that mark my palm. "Sometimes I think about the nevers. I'll never go to Greece. Or have those tacos again from that little town in San Diego, on the border of Mexico. I'll never go to college. Or get to see my parents be happy again. Maybe I'll never even get to see the ocean again. And I used to

235

worry that I'd never fall in love, or realize that's what it was, anyway, until after it's gone. But I think I got that, Saira. Maybe this is it, this moment, here with you."

I swallow hard. This can't be all there is. But right now, for me, it might be enough. I hope it might be for him, too.

"Maybe I won't be your last love, Saira. And sometimes I think maybe I'll be okay with that. But you could be my last love."

The thought triggers something painful in me. The realization that it's too much to take on, as much as I want to. *No.* That's a distinction I refuse to wear like a badge of honor. I can't carry that weight around with me like I do Harper's ghost. I won't be able to breathe. But I can't let go of his hand, either. I clasp it tight, afraid of something, of everything. "It's a bit cold," I say, shivering as the water curls up around our ankles. "Maybe we should get moving."

He shakes his head. "It's not time yet." He's staring at the ocean again, his hand still in mine. "There are things—moments—that will never be. And there are things that always are. Just there. In the back of my mind. In some cycle of forever. We don't ever actually have to live them. We just know they're there, they exist, these moments. Like this one." He turns to look at me now. "If I'm gone, that's where I'll be. Okay?"

I nod. I think I know what he means. Like those moments, twirling in the sun with Harper. All those years ago. Long gone. But they're still right there. I can touch them. I can reach them when I need to. And that's when I know. No matter what happens to Link, I'll be okay. We'll be okay. Because at least we get to have this.

"Okay."

He pulls the guitar onto his lap and strums, slow and serene, and I watch the pain melt away, the edges all soft, like it's just him and music and his audience of one. Me. Quiet and lovely, like maybe we have all the time in the world.

CHAPTER 35

The weekend looms large ahead of me, like a dentist's appointment (yes, even doctors hate going to the dentist) or driver's test (and no, I haven't been practicing, thank you very much). I've committed to going to New Brunswick to see Taara, and what's worse, took New Jersey Transit to get there. And the train was late. Now we're in Taara's tiny dorm room, and instead of going to get nachos at Old Man Rafferty's, she insists on cooking on the tiny burner she's illegally set up on top of the mini fridge.

"Is that Vish?" she asks when my phone pings again. It's Link. We've been texting nonstop when he's not in therapy. He gets the weekend off. And I'm stuck here.

"Yeah, he's got a lacrosse game this weekend."

Taara frowns over her omelet pan. "Oh, were you gonna go?"

I shake my head. "He knows I'm here."

"Maybe he can come up next time."

I shrug.

She flips the omelet, then tops it with pepper jack. "All set." She cuts the omelet in half and serves it up on two plates with toast and chai on a large tray. "I love breakfast for dinner, don't you?"

"Or nachos would be good, too." I can't help it.

"Maybe tomorrow." She points to the computer on her desk. "Or I can make you tofu mattar. I just posted the recipe. Fourteen thousand views and counting!"

I nod and start shoveling omelet into my month. I know I'm being a brat. This weekend is taking up precious moments I could spend with Link. But the temptation is too much. So this is better. But I have to stop taking it out on Taara.

"I'm glad you're here," she says. "This place can be a bit lonely sometimes."

I can feel my eyebrows jump. Taara's stunning and super fun. She has a million friends. In fact, no less than four people have knocked in the past hour, asking if she wants to hang. She's turned them all down. Even the Greek biochem study buddy.

"You know what I mean. Like, everyone thinks they know you. But no one really bothers to really know you. It's all so shallow."

"Whatever you say."

"What was college like for you?"

"Like high school was for you, I guess. I mean, I got up, Dad drove me to school, I went to class, you or Mom picked me up. And that was it. I was eleven."

"Yeah. Must've been weird."

"It was fine."

"Do you ever regret it?" she asks over a biteful of omelet.

I think about Link, and the kissing, and how for a lot of teens, that's just a part of everyday life. Even for Link. But for me, it's one of a million moments I would've missed. Despite Lizzie. Despite Vish. Despite my dad's insistence that I be a "normal kid." Before, I realize with a start, I would have dismissed it as no big loss, as just a sacrifice to make, not thought about it too much. Because I knew—I know— what I wanted and what I had to give up to get it. But after that day at the beach, maybe it's not so simple. Maybe I didn't really understand just what I was giving up, exactly. But how do I begin to explain that to someone else when I can barely unravel it myself?

So I give the easy, satisfying answer. "Nope," I say. Because I don't think Taara would understand. Because nobody really does. "I mean, I got what I wanted. I gave up what I had to." Even though it's hard. Maybe too hard.

One sharp, refined brow rises ever so slightly. "I don't buy it." She takes her last bite, gathers our paper plates, and tosses them all in a plastic bag. "I mean, I feel like I barely had a normal childhood, and I'm not the genius."

"What do you mean?"

"I feel like our whole life shifted—for all of us—when you diagnosed Harper and Dr. Charles said they had to 'pursue your talents,' or whatever. And it was hard enough, in a family of doctors and engineers, to find any breathing room. But it got a whole lot worse after that."

I still don't get it.

"Not everyone wants to be a doctor, Saira."

"I know."

"*I* don't. Want to be a doctor."

I nod. She's said this before.

"The question is, what am I going to do about it?" She sits back down on the bed and stares at me, hard, for a minute. "I dropped premed."

"What?"

"You heard me." She sighs, picking at nothing on the bedspread. "I dropped it. I signed up for film and TV, and also culinary arts classes at an institute in New York. I've been going there twice a week."

I'm so floored, I don't know what to say, what to do.

"Can you switch back?"

She waves a hand in front of my face. "What are you not getting? I don't want to. I'm happy."

"Happy is overrated."

"It most certainly is not," she says. "And you know it. I don't know what it is, Vish or work or whatever, but you're happy, too. For once. Be honest with yourself."

If only it was that easy. I open my mouth to say something, anything, a confession or a denial, but I never get to figure out what it will be, because both our phones start buzzing at once. And this time, it's not Link.

It's Mom. "Dadima heart attack. Princeton Pres. COME NOW."

We both stand, my chai cup sliding off the tray and crashing to the floor, but we don't have time to worry about that. We've got to get to the hospital, stat.

Greek Boy drops us off, and we bypass admitting, thanks to my ID. It feels surreal to be here now not as a doctor, but as family, like it was with Harper. But I push that thought away as we get in the elevator, shuffling to six, the cardiac ICU.

Mom and Papa are in the hospital room, sitting in chairs on either side of the bed, the exhaustion racking their faces the way guilt no doubt mars mine. Dadi and I haven't really spoken since that night with Vish, though she still feeds me and makes me chai and does all those perfunctory Dadima things. And as far as I know, she hasn't mentioned it to Mom, either. I would hate for it to be a secret she takes to the grave. The thought gives me chills.

Dadima's asleep when we get in, and she looks frailer, even tinier than her usual four foot eleven. She's wearing a hospital gown, which she'd find terribly indecent, and there are IVs and pumps and monitors attached to every part of her.

"Congestive heart failure," Mom says as Taara and I perch lightly on Dadi's bed, trying not to breathe. "The fluid filled her lungs, but they've started the diuretics."

"And they're watching?" Taara says. "It won't come back?"

"There's a risk of respiratory failure," I say, watching the monitors, "but she seems to be doing okay right now."

"Yeah, they're keeping her in the ICU to monitor her for the next few days," Papa says, and his voice is small and shaky, like a little boy's. "But they—and your mom—assure me she should be okay."

Taara nods, stands, and wraps her arms around my dad. "She's definitely a fighter," she says.

"Don't we all know it," Mom adds.

We all stand around, staring at each other, realizing how incomplete our family picture would look without Dadi in it. I rub my shoulders, fidgeting and flummoxed by this foreign wing of a hospital I've come to consider home.

"Maybe we should go make chai and bring it back," I suggest. "Can Dadi have chai, even?" Cardiology is like a different language, one I'll never quite learn how to speak. Like offering up your sixth-grade Spanish in Italy.

Taara shakes her head, and there's a streak of tears on her pale cheeks. "Actually, I need to tell you guys something," she says, and I worry that she's going to announce a pregnancy or something that might just put my dad in cardiac arrest. "Saira knows." *Oh.* She stares at the hospital bed, where Dadi's chest goes up and down, up and down. "And so does Dadi." *Oh!* Taara takes a deep breath. "She told me to tell you. So I have to. Now. Before—"

Mom takes her hand. "Dadi will be okay, beta. But you're scaring me. What's wrong?"

"I quit. I quit premed. I can't do it."

Mom looks shocked, but Papa looks like he's about to crack up.

"I want to study nutrition and TV production."

"Is this about your FoodTube channel?" Papa says, unable to hide the glee.

"How do you know about that?"

"Your dadi is *terrible* at keeping secrets," Papa says as Mom continues to look baffled. "At least from me."

"But—nutrition? TV production? What about biochem?" Mom says. "What about pediatrics?" Mom looks truly shattered, like she just realized her dream is dying. And maybe it is. But that's not Taara's fault. Not really. It's mine. I'm the one who actually bailed. "Did everyone know about this but me? Did you all decide among yourselves, who cares what Rana thinks—"

"Mother, not everything is about you. Or Saira. Or how the family feels. I don't *like* medicine. I don't want to spend eight years studying something I hate to do a job I'll suck at. So I dropped it. I would have failed." Taara hiccups through her tears. "Not all of us are cut out for medicine. As hard as we try."

"But you could have at least talked to me—" Mom starts. "First Saira with the oncology, and then—You girls don't care what I think at all." Now there are tears slipping down Mom's cheeks, too, ruining her makeup and smudging her mascara, but she does nothing to stop them. I've never seen her like this. I want to do something, anything, to stop it. Volunteer to do pediatrics, even, but before I can open my mouth, Papa cuts in. Thank gods.

"Taara, beta, no one will force you to do anything," he says quite sternly, probably so Mom will hear it as much as Taara does. "Your papa is a very reluctant engineer, and if I had it to do over again—"

"What, you'd be Anil Kapoor?" Mom says in an irritated tone. "Singing and dancing instead of—"

Papa looks offended. "Amitabh, of course." He grins. "But working for the Port Authority?" Papa says with a grumble. "Damn straight I would do something else."

"And what would your dear mother say about that?"

"She'd say good for you," Dadi says, popping up in her bed, like a vampire up from her day's rest. "Better to do what you love. That's what I told Taara. And Saira, too."

"She did, actually," I say, then run over to hug her, like she's truly back from the dead. "I'm so glad you're okay."

"I'm fine. It will take far more than heart failure to kill this buddhi." Then she has a big coughing fit. "Now go get me asli khana. Go." Papa and Mom shuffle out, eager for a break. Taara and I stay put as Dadi drifts off again.

Taara dozes in a chair while I sit next to Dadi's bed, holding her hand until she awakes half an hour later, coughing. "Pani. Pani."

I rise and grab a cup of ice chips off the tray. "Ice hai, Dadi," I tell her. "No liquids. Yet." I look over at Taara—she stirs but doesn't wake.

She nods, and I use a spoon to feed her a chip or two. I don't realize when the tears start trickling—she notices them before I do. I was so worried about silly stuff, secrets, and here she is, suffering. "Nah, bache," she says, trying to sit up. I press the button to raise the bed a bit. "I'm fine. I'm strong."

"I know."

"Good."

We sit in silence for a few seconds, and then she says it. "You're strong, too. More than you know. You are a brave girl."

"No, I'm not."

"Hanji, you are. You are your mother's daughter. And your dadi's pothi. And your sister's bhena. You come from a long line of ziddi auraten. Stubborn women. Just ask your papa."

I nod, and try to smile. It doesn't work; tears seep into my open mouth.

"But I'm tired now," she says. "And I don't like all these machines." She looks at me, pointed. "Here it's always intervention this, intervention that. Next time, beta, I want to rest at home, in my bed." The doctor comes in then, waking Taara, but Dadi stares at me intently. "Got it?"

I nod.

I tell Taara I'm going to get coffee, then head to Link's room. He's in bed, watching videos, and sits up, surprised to see me. And especially the tears.

"What happened? What's wrong?" He climbs out of bed, his little IV cart following him, and wraps his arms around me, even though someone might see.

"My grandma's sick," I say, sobbing into his thin hospital gown. "She's in the ICU."

"Oh no! Is she going to be okay?"

"Yeah, my mom's bringing her daal and roti in a bit." I try to breathe. "Even though she's supposed to be on a liquid diet."

"Well, daal is liquid. Sort of."

I grin up at him, and he kisses my forehead. Then I realize someone could walk in any second.

"Get back in bed."

"Okay, Dr. Sehgal."

Two days later, Dadi is finally discharged. We've all been hovering—especially me—and she's sick of us. And starving. "For real food. Your mother is a terrible cook. How does one mess up kali daal? I don't understand."

Mom frowns at Dr. Perkovich. "You sure you don't want to keep her?"

"No thanks," the doctor says with a laugh. "But she did promise me some samosas when she's better, didn't you, Mrs. Sehgal?"

It sounds weird to hear someone call Dadi that. But I guess she is the original.

In the car on the way home, Dadi runs off a list of things she wants to make. "Bhartha, chole, pakore, mattar paneer—"

"I can make you tofu mattar," Taara says, and we all groan.

"Tofu?" Dadi says with disdain. "These are my last few meals. I want them to be good."

"These are not your last meals," Mom says as she pulls in front of the house. "You have plenty of years ahead of you."

"But you won't if you keep eating crap," Taara adds. "I can teach you how to lighten up some of your recipes."

"You mean butter instead of ghee?" Dadi says with a frown.

"Not exactly," Taara says. "But it's a start."

"Okay, but first learn how to make some decent chai."

Yup, Dadi's full speed ahead.

We get her tucked into her bed, and Papa makes the chai, since he knows what she likes.

"When I was a girl," she says, "men never made tea. They didn't even know the rastha to the rasoi. But these days, your mom has trained you all. Even that boy. Vish. He made me chai once. Trying to impress. Or keep up. That's what happens when you're a working woman."

"Dadi, you're a working woman, too," I remind her. "Just inside our home."

"Arrey jah. I'm not the maid. I do things out of love for you all. And because it's what I know. But sometimes I wish that I, too, could have done more. Not a doctor like you, Saira, but something."

That catches me off guard a bit. Dadi always pushed my mom and dad to let me take it easy, be a kid. "You have so much freedom," she says to me, pointed. "Sometimes it's easy to take it for granted. But I'm glad you get to be someone. You too, Taara. Whatever you want to be. But sometimes, beta, it's nice to just sit, have a cup of chai, gup-shup, and while the days away. That's what I was doing at your age. I wish that for you sometimes."

Me too, I realize with a start. Me too.

CHAPTER 36

There's a group of us gathered in the lounge—me, Arun, José, Vish, little Alina, and the man of the hour, Link. He's so far away from me—with both of us on our best "nothing's going on" behavior—that it might as well be a hundred people. But it's a big day. So we have to play along. For now.

Today they announce the top-twenty finalists on the new season of *Rock Star Boot Camp*—by showing the videos. Vish submitted the tape, and Link was one of two hundred asked to submit, so he has about a 10 percent chance of getting a slot. And the odds narrow further from there. If he gets chosen, he'll have to fly out to Los Angeles. Which he is probably, likely, definitely not well enough to do. But that's a long shot, anyway.

He's sitting on the couch, surrounded by people, and chewing on his cuticles, a habit José complains about endlessly. "Not getting enough nutrition?" he says now, smacking his hand away and laughing.

"Nerves," Link says, staring at the screen, his eyes glassy. Tired?

"Me too," Vish says, planting himself on the floor in front of Link, and passing around a bag of masala popcorn. "But your video is good."

"Enough to get me in the top twenty?" Link says. "I dunno."

Arun leans forward, turning up the sound. "All right, guys. They're starting."

First there's a blond girl from Utah—one of ten sisters from an overly strict Mormon family. "This is her ticket out," José says. "Belt it, girl!"

Then there's some generic LA and New York types, who kind of remind me of Lizzie. Who still isn't answering my texts, though she responds to Vish's immediately.

"I like that guy," José says as a Filipino country-star wannabe shimmies around, singing a Taylor Swift song. "But so far, most people have done pop hits. Did you do an original number, Link?"

He shrugs. "I am who I am," he says with a wink. "We'll see if it worked for or against me."

They count down five, then ten, then fifteen. Still no Link. Maybe it's not happening. Which would be the worst.

"The suspense is killing me," Alina says, her voice quiet. She's struggling, but she insisted on coming, tubes and all, so José is monitoring her closely. "I almost wish it would."

We all turn to look at her, appalled.

"I'm kidding," she says with a choked laugh. "Can't you guys take a joke?"

"Not funny," I say.

But then we're distracted. Because there he is. Number three. Link.

"I may have cancer, but it doesn't have me," he's saying on the screen, and then there's me behind him, shaving his head. "I'm going to keep making music until my last breath."

The announcer cuts to a short outtake—me, talking right to the camera. "Which won't be anytime soon. Not if we have anything to do with it," I say on screen. "I'm Dr. Saira Sehgal. You may know me as Dr. Girl Genius. I'm the youngest doctor in America, and Link is one of my patients. We're doing everything we can for him here. But he needs your help. He's looking for a marrow donor, specifically one of Korean and Dutch descent. Could that be you? Contact us at Princeton Presbyterian, or via Be The Match's Link Rad page. We need your help. Link needs your help—right now."

When I look back up at him, amid all the high fives and whoops from the boy, he sits in silence, a single tear slipping down his hollow cheeks. But then catches me staring and shoots me a thumbs-up.

With any luck, we're halfway there. With any luck, the matches will come pouring in now.

We've got Alina and Link tucked back into bed when it starts. The rage. I can feel it before it's actually there, in the physical form of one Dr. Davis. Who is livid. Dr. Arora races in right before her, as if trying to stave off the worst of it, but she's right behind him, and shouting.

"How dare you!" she's shouting. "This time you've gone too damn far. Sehgal, I'm about to fire your—"

"Dr. Davis," I say, trying not to duck. "So nice to see you, too."

"You think you're so smart. Girl Genius. See how smart you feel when your ass is grass."

Arora's physically holding her back, as if she'll claw right at me, like a cranky cat.

"Yes, Saira may have gone forward without consulting us, but if you look on the bright side of things—"

"There is no bright side!"

"Actually, there is," says a calm voice. It's Cho, standing in the doorway, his tie bearing pumpkins in August, his face a bit contorted, like he's confused to be coming to my defense. Dr. Charles is behind him, grinning.

"We've had three thousand people send kits in the last forty-eight hours—just from the activity on the show's website," Cho says, excitement building in his voice. Before he was even announced as a finalist. So we're going to see way more than that in the next few days, now that he's in the top twenty. And we'd only gotten five hundred in all our campaigning over the last two months. That's a significant increase. They'll be pouring in. That means Saira's plan is working. The more kits we get, the bigger the chance that we will find a match."

"Which means we will continue to utilize this very special resource we have found here at Princeton Presbyterian—in the form of Dr. Sehgal—to our advantage, won't we, Dr. Davis?" Charles says. He can't hide his glee. "In fact, I've gotten four calls just tonight from major media, asking to feature Link—and Saira." He looks at me. "You game?"

I nod, trying not to beam. "Of course."

"Great. Be ready tomorrow morning at ten," Charles says. "And make sure you get your eyebrows done. Because, Dr. Sehgal, this just might work."

Ah, I think, smiling to myself as Davis storms off. I can see why my mom and Dr. Charles get along so well.

CHAPTER 37

We're in the parking lot, Link and I, in the hideous minivan. It's become a go-to now that the recently refreshed patient lounge actually gets some traffic. Luckily, Link's mom covers for him—us—well. I think she likes me.

"Turn right. Right. No, your other right," he says, and I can hear the smirk in his voice, though I don't dare turn to look at him. There are enough casualties at the hospital as it is. "Do you want to try parallel parking?" I shake my head, but he ignores me. "Okay, pull behind that ambulance there." *No way.* "Yes way."

"You want me to run over people instead of curing them?"

"That thing is out of commission, hasn't moved in weeks," Link says, putting one hand over mine on the steering wheel. "Okay, now, turn the wheel the opposite way. It's a bit counterintuitive, but . . ." I can sense him frowning. "Up a little, no back a little, no wait, wait!"

Oops. I'm nearly in the space, but just tapped the bumper of the ambulance in front of us. Not hard. But definitely a tap.

Link's head drops to the dash, and he moans. "You're killing me here, Saira."

Then he realizes what he's said, and we both sit in silence for a minute.

I unbuckle my seat belt and open the door, ready to bolt, but he grabs my arm, pulling me back into place. I'm shaking, and I'm not quite sure why. But he can feel the tremors, and he pulls me toward

250

him, right out of my seat and into his. He leans his forehead against mine, so we're breathing the same air again.

"Now who's the specter of death?" I say, too loud, still shaking, or maybe he is, too.

"Sorry," he says, twisting his mouth. "But you are. You're almost as bad as my dad."

That's saying a lot. "Well, beef jerky is probably carcinogenic."

"I already have cancer."

"I know."

"Well, don't you let me forget it."

I give him a small kiss on the nose and start to turn back toward the steering wheel, but his arms don't let go.

"What?"

He grins, then gestures toward the back seat.

I frown. "I told you. No more kissing."

"And I told you—I might just die anyway." He smirks. "So shouldn't I enjoy living while I can?"

I sigh. He leans, slow, letting his lips brush mine. It's not the first time, but there's something different now. An urgency that wasn't there before. Like a small flame that's about to blaze.

He leans in again, and this time it's more assertive. His mouth smashing mine, teeth clashing, tongue pushing into my mouth. I want to stop it, but I also don't want to at all. He starts tugging me toward the back seat, and I pause to breathe.

This is irrational. Irresponsible. Irresistible.

We're in the hospital parking lot. Granted, there's no one in this part of it—it's pretty much abandoned. I grin, then scramble over the center dash into the back, and he's right behind me, arms around my waist before we even hit the seat. Our kisses skip tentative altogether this time, instead lingering long and slow but somehow super urgent, mouths soft and open, tongues salty and slippery, his hands wandering up my shirt and over my breasts and roaming the waist of my jeans, a question.

"Too much?" he asks between kisses, and I shake my head, pulling him closer. The thrum of energy between us is steaming up the windows of the car, which makes me giggle a bit.

"What?"

I point. "I thought that only happened in the movies."

He writes his name and mine in the fog. I draw a heart around it.

Then we're kissing again, and it's even more intense this time. He's on top of me, the weight of him more solid than I thought, my legs wrapping around his waist, his hands traveling. Every so often, he pauses between kisses to ask, "Is this okay? And this? And this?"

And it is. But then I can feel his heart racing, and while mine is, too, the jaggedness of his breathing makes me stop for a second.

"What?" he asks. "You okay?"

"I am," I says. "But are you?" I reach for his wrist again, but he leans back away from me, pulling it away.

"Stop playing doctor."

"I'm not," I say. "I just—"

"Can't relax."

"Was worried." I frown.

"What?" he says, frustration marking his voice. "I like you, and you like me, and we're just—"

"I mean, your heart is racing."

"So is yours. And I thought that was a good thing."

"But you're sick."

"Okay, Dr. Sehgal. But as you know, sexual activity—and certainly touch—can be beneficial to patients undergoing chemotherapy and other cancer treatments," he says, as if reciting from the manual. I giggle. "I feel good right now. I may not tomorrow. So let me enjoy it while it lasts. I'll know if and when I'm overexerting myself. So can you just stop overthinking everything?"

I look at him for a minute, completely floored. "I . . . I don't know how."

He grins down at me again. "Let me help you," he says, kissing me. I sit up, though, and start straightening my clothes a bit.

"It's just, I—this all new to me."

He looks at me for a minute, as if he's seeing me for the first time. "You mean . . . ?"

"Yeah, come on. You knew that."

He nods. "I did. In a way. But I just realized something." He sighs, silent for a moment.

He turns toward me then, putting his arm around me, his hand in my hair. Like he's going to kiss me. But he doesn't. "Listen, Saira." He takes a deep breath. "I think that this could be it. Love. Or the closest I'll ever get to it."

The shock hits me like a lightning bolt, synapses fried, unable to react.

I'm supposed to say something back. Because I can feel it. Right there. But then he's talking again.

"But I can't do this if . . . It's just . . . I won't let myself be the one who breaks your heart."

How do I tell him that it's already way too late to fix that? Don't fall. Don't fall. Don't fall.

But there they go. The tears.

"See?"

"No."

He looks confused. Or amused. Or I don't know what, exactly. "You're already getting attached."

"And you're not?" I mean. "You just said you think you love me."

"Yeah, and that makes me really happy. Happier than you'll ever know." He takes a deep breath.

"But—"

"But I've got nothing to lose." He takes my hand, strokes my palm, along the life line. "And you've got your whole life ahead of you."

"So do you."

"Those odds are dropping fast, Saira with an *i*."

Yeah, they're far closer to 20 percent now. A long shot. But I don't say that.

Our knees are knocked together, our breathing in sync, as usual. But he feels far away now. "Listen, I know the odds. I mean, I'm a doctor, for Christ's sake. But I want to be with you. Whether that's for a moment or a month or more, I don't care."

"All I'll leave you with is our moments."

Then let me have this one, I want to say.

"It's not enough. And too much. It'll break you And I can't do that," he says, pulling his hands from mine, disentangling. Disengaging. "We should go."

I nod, trying my best not to cry again, to prove him right. "But this isn't over."

"Oh, don't I know it," he says, laughing. He opens the car door, offering me his hand as I climb out. "You're like a toddler with a toy, refusing to let go."

"So best to give in," I say, looking up at him as he closes the car door. He takes my hand again. "Stop making everything so hard."

"I will if you will," he says, grinning.

We separate at the curb, going our different ways, and as I watch him leave, it occurs to me that we didn't really resolve anything. My heart drops for a minute, thinking about everything that could go wrong here. But I refuse to let it.

Wednesday morning dawns bright and early, and Papa's rapping at my door before my eight a.m. alarm even goes off.

"Time to get up," he singsongs in that familiar, horrifying way. Papa was the one who'd go with me to genius camp and all my other academic stuff on the road. He'd always wake me up the same way—with his singsong and a cup of white-people chai from the local Starbucks (better than nothing) and an almond croissant. I can almost smell it now. "Saira, come on."

I rise, bleary eyed, and crack the door open a smidge. "Papa."

He's holding a tray with chai and Nice biscuits, the sugar shimmering like glitter.

"No excuses."

"But I'm so sleepy."

"Then you shouldn't stay up until three in the morning, texting."

He's got me there. "Give me twenty minutes to shower."

"Teek hai." He passes me the tray and waltzes off, singing to himself.

It feels weird to be in a car with anyone but Link now. We've gone back to that old lot about a hundred times since last week. Okay, well, not a hundred. But it might as well be. And while we have been, uh, making out, there's been some actual driving, too. He's a good teacher, turns out.

Papa? Not so much.

"Take a right here. Slow, slow, slow, slow." Papa leans his hand on the dash, as if that will stifle the car's forward momentum. "Your turns are still too wide. Wait, wait, here! No, go tighter. Too wide."

He puts his palm over his chest, tapping it to imply palpitations. "Saira, kya yaar."

"I'm trying, Papa."

"But you're getting worse rather than better." How can that be? "Such wide turns."

I shrug. "So?" The streets are plenty wide.

"So you don't want to accidentally turn into the wrong lane."

"Oh, that."

"Yes, that."

He points to the curb. "Acha, now try parallel parking here."

Oh gods. Again? This is the worst. It's a wide space at least—two car widths between driveways on a cul-de-sac. Vish's cul-de-sac, actually. Hmmm . . .

"How's it going with Vish?" Papa asks, as if on cue. I hit the brake—literally—and we both jerk forward. Papa sighs. "That good, huh?"

I stare straight ahead as I begin the tedious process of trying to parallel park. "Vish's fine. We've both been busy. He's got college apps, and a senior project, and I've got—"

"Yes, I know all that. But I mean, like, what are your plans? He'll be leaving soon, nah?"

I shrug again, pulling the car over. It's crooked and about three feet from the curb. I frown, pulling out again. "He's planning to apply to some places in California. But he hasn't told his parents yet." I turn to give Papa an urgent look.

"Don't worry, beta. Your secret's safe with me." Papa points. "I never could stand that Sweetie Auntie of yours. Wait. A little closer in the front. Now back. Now up a bit." The car jerks forward, then back, then forward again, and it feels like we're not making any progress. "Okay, veer a little to the left. Now right."

Papa takes a small bow in his seat. "Voilà!"

I frown.

"Look, just like that, you have parallel parked."

He's right. It worked. Who knew? And I didn't even hit anything. Yet.

"You know, Saira," Papa says now, drumming his fingers. "You both have all these grown-up decisions to make. So sometimes, it can be easy—for all of us, I think—to forget that you are still a kid."

He clears his throat, and I turn to look at him.

"But you are. Still my kid."

I nod.

"Sometimes I feel like you don't really have the luxury of being a child. And I wish that wasn't the case. I wish you could just grow up playing gilli dunda and eating snow cones like I did."

I frown. "I know, Papa. But I have fun."

"You have chosen this path, and you are a brave girl. But you're only sixteen. So just remember, Mom and I—and Dadi, as cranky as she can be sometimes—are here if you need us." I wonder if she said something to him. About Vish. About that night. "For anything."

"I know, Papa. And just so you know—"

"I know."

I nod. He nods. "Chalo. Let's go home. I think Dadi is making aloo puri today."

"Okay," I say, and take my foot off the gas. The car lurches forward. "Slow, slow, slow, slow . . ."

**Papa's Bollywood manifesto
on what you can learn about
life from Amitabh Bachchan films**

1. Channel your anger at the world's injustice into something good.
2. Humor goes a long way in building—and mending—relationships.
3. There's nothing quite like a mother's love.
4. Two Amitabhs are always better than one.
5. You can't make an omelet without any eggs.

CHAPTER 38

We all gather at five a.m. on Friday morning to prepare for our first
official surgery—my baby cousin Pinky's. We won't actually be able to
perform the surgery of course—that will be done by the neurosurgery
team—we're here to prep and support Pinky and her family through
the process. Which will pretty much be the scariest thing I've ever
experienced.

If it happens at all. Because we're less than an hour away from the
scheduled slot, and Anya Auntie is panicking. "She could die," she
keeps saying, shaking and crying, as my mother tries to brace with
strong arms to keep her from collapsing. I watch from the hall, unwel-
come but compelled nonetheless to be here. "Right there in that room,
on that table."

"But this is the very best shot she has to live," my mom says, half
doctor, half sister, working hard to maintain her own composure as she
tries to convince this woman to let the people who know how to save
this child's life do just that.

Howard looks like she's thinking the same thing—her face is pale,
her hands are fidgety, her demeanor slack and unusual. She's looking around the room instead of going over the prep plan with Arora
and Cho, who are discussing the process step-by-step Ramesh Uncle,
the picture of composure. "Once the portion of the skull is removed,
Dr. Stevenson and his team will be able to go in and remove the tumor.
They'll continually monitor brain function with our team so they know
that they're not doing any long-term damage as they cut."

"Are you ready, are you ready, are you ready?"

A child's voice cuts through the sterility of the surgical prep area, shocking us all out of our stupors a bit.

It's six o'clock, and Pinky has arrived.

She lifts her chubby arms up. "Pick me up, pick me up," she says, her cherub voice on the verge. But she runs right past me, straight to Cho. He lifts her up and twirls her once, and then she points to his tie, which is a Dr. Seuss Cat and the Hat number today. "I do not like green eggs and cheese," she says to him, then roars with laughter—and he does, too. "I do not like them, thank you, please."

"Today's your big day, Pinky," Cho says to her in the most soothing voice I've ever heard come out of his mouth. "You ready for your short nap?"

"Just a little one," she says, nodding to confirm. "And then the new books?"

"Yes, a whole stack of them. Have you ever met the Berenstain Bears?"

He walks off, Pinky still in his arms, José following to help scrub her up.

"Did you just see what I just saw?" Howard says.

"I thought maybe I was hallucinating," I say, and we both grimace. It's hard to laugh today.

Then Dr. Arora walks over, his face grim. "Howard," he says. "Call Stevenson's team now. It's off."

Howard nods, but I rise, pulling her back. "Wait, what?"

"The mom won't agree. She's panicked. And unless she's on board, there's nothing we can do."

"But she'll die." Howard says it, but we're all thinking it.

"Our hands are tied."

"No," I say, though I don't really quite know what I mean. He's right. Legally, the parents have to be on board.

"Your mom tried," Arora says with a sigh. "But the mother just won't sign off. And I get it. I mean, that's her baby." He turns back to Howard. "Let Cho and José know, too. They're in pre-op with Pinky."

As Howard heads off to make the calls, I pace the hall. There has to be a way to fix this. There has to be a way to convince Anya Auntie that Pinky *needs* this. It's her only chance.

Before I know it, I'm standing in front of the family waiting room, peering in through the window on the door. My mom's there with Anya Auntie and Ramesh Uncle, their voice muffled.

"She's my daughter, too," Ramesh is saying in a cracked, heavy voice. "You can't just sentence her to death."

I open the door without thinking. And I know that the last face Anya Auntie wants to see today is mine. But I have to try.

"I don't want—" She's about to start in again on me, I can tell. And so I get my hackles up, ready to fight back. But then I watch as my mom takes Anya Auntie's hands, which are shaking. Way worse than mine. And in that moment, I'm kind of sorry for all the angst I put her through—the fights, calling her Dragon Auntie. She's scared, like every parent that walks through these doors, I can't blame her. I wish there was something I could do to set her mind at ease. But for now, if I have to play the punching bag, I can at least do that.

"I'll be here if you need me," I tell her. "And I can be gone, if you'd rather."

Anya Auntie, shocked, doesn't know what to say to that. But Ramesh Uncle takes my hand, nods, and says, "Dr. Arora always says you're an asset to his team. And there's no one I'd trust more to look out for my baby."

"Auntie," I say, in the quietest, most respectful voice I can manage. "I know today is going to be hard. But you can look at it one of two ways. It can be the day you lost your daughter. Right now. If you say no to this. Or it can be the day you—*you*—chose to give her a chance at life."

Anya doesn't speak, her whole body still shaking. "But she could die. Today. At least if we don't—"

"Yes, you might have her for a few months, if you're lucky, a few years," my mom says, still rubbing Anya Auntie's back. "But if you give her this chance—if you make this choice for her now—she could live a long, fruitful life. That's what you want, right? That's what we all want."

Anya Auntie nods. But I know she's not ready.

"I know you don't think I'm capable," I say. "And that's okay. But I promise you this: The team here is. And they'll take care of Pinky like she's one of their own. Because she is. Did you see the way she connects with Cho? Even I couldn't believe it. So you don't have to trust me. But trust them. They can do this. They can help her."

There's a long silence before she speaks again. "Okay," she says. "But I do want you to be there. Not as Dr. Sehgal. As Saira Didi. Watch over my baby. Make sure she's okay."

My mom nods, and Ramesh Uncle pats me on the back, his hands shaking.

"I will," I say, giving them a hug before I step away. "I'll let them know to start prepping her again now. I'll be back as soon as there's news."

A full three hours later, José and Cho roll Pinky's bed into the surgical suite. She already looks a bit sedated, but her little hand has a hold of Cho's tie, and he leans down to give her a quick hug.

It's so weird, standing in the galley, Dr. Cho by my side, watching the monitors and the surgery through the windows. Like watching a scene on *Grey's Anatomy* or one of those other doc dramas my dad likes—"It's like I can see inside your head," he always tells me, even though I've told him a thousand times how not real they are—except hopefully things here will be way less dramatic.

And things go smoothly for a while. Dr. Stevenson makes the incision into the base of her skull and then begins to drill. I can barely watch it, but I force myself to be present.

My task is simple. Keep my eyes open, my mind sharp and focused. Learn and be useful, so that one day, I can save someone's life, too. This is what I've been training for. This is why I chose to do this.

He's drilling right into that tiny little skull, and part of me wants to cry, to rage. How is this fair? But I know we're giving her a fighting chance.

Then there's a wave of frantic activity, and I can't figure out what's happening.

"Her pressure's dropping," Cho says, worried. "There's definitely a bleed. They have to catch it fast." A bleed could cause Pinky's little body to start convulsing, ruining any chance we have at removing the tumor—and causing further damage.

But just as quick as it started dropping, her pressure stabilizes. And for what feels like hours, Cho and I stand there, rapt and frantic, and watch the surgeons cut and cut and cut and cut. And then, in the end, there, on the little metal tray, sits the tumor. The size of a walnut, really, a bloody, pulsing thing. A tiny monster that would have, could have, taken a child's life. But it won't.

CHAPTER 39

It's past one p.m. when they finally walk out of the surgical suite, triumphant. And exhausted. And starving.

The prep nurses help us scrub down, but they can't move fast enough. My mom embraces me as soon as I step into the galley, and Howard does, too. We're a weeping, grinning mess, and my mom just keeps repeating, "She's going to be okay. She's going to be okay," into my hair. I'm not quite sure if she's talking about me or Pinky.

We head as a group to the family room—and it's filled with people. Anya Auntie, Ramesh Uncle, my dad, Dadi, Taara, a troupe full of aunties and uncles and cousins. All holding their breath.

"Mr. and Mrs. Sharma," Cho steps to the front, and he can't help it. He's beaming. "Pinky's going to be just fine, as far as we can tell. We got every last trace of that sucker, and if I have anything to say about it, it's never coming back. She'll be sleeping for a while, but should be awake and alert within twenty-four hours. If you'll come with me, we can get her settled into the PACU and you can see her in a bit, though she'll still be sleeping."

But Anya Auntie's not listening anymore. She's thrown her arms around me and Cho, and has latched on, soaking his Seuss tie and designer shirt with her tears as she sobs. "Thank you, thank you, thank you, thank you, thank you . . ."

Cho pats her back, gently, and lifts her away a bit. Howard offers a tissue.

Arora steps forward. "I think you should be aware. There was a

moment of tension during the surgery. Things could have gone awry."
He clears his throat, knowing he's treading worried territory. "But you
made the right decision by letting us operate today. You really did save
Pinky's life."

"No, you and your team did," Anya Auntie says. "I'm just glad that
I could bring myself to listen, at least this once." She turns to me, and I
must look panicked, because she laughs. "And that Saira could be there
today, as both a doctor and as family. We needed her."

I nod. That's a lot, but coming from the woman I used to call
"Dragon Auntie," I'll take it.

"Now," my mom says, "who's hungry? Because I ordered Pizza Hut."

I'm eating a slice of pepperoni, peppers, and onions when the lady I
recognize as Davis's assistant shows up in the family lounge. Uh-oh.

"Ms. Sehgal," she says, tapping me on the shoulder.

"Dr. Sehgal," my mother says testily, glaring at her over her veggie pie.

"Dr. Davis has requested your presence in her office."

This can't be good.

Mom raises a brow, an offer to come with me. But with Davis,
that's just about the worst idea ever.

I follow the lady—Ms. Clayton—to Davis's office like a prisoner
being led to execution—in silence, focusing on the clack, clack, clack
of her heels against the linoleum. When we get to the office, she waves
me in, bustling off to find her next victim, no doubt.

I stand in front of the door for a minute, composing myself, trying
to prepare myself for whatever wrath is about to descend. Maybe it'll be
good news, magically. Like, maybe she heard about me helping move
things forward on Pinky's surgery, or about how well Brendan's doing
on the trial, or that Alina's doing, well, okay at the moment.

But somehow I doubt it.

I take a deep breath and rap on the door.

"Come in, Sehgal."

I push the door open, and Davis is sitting at her desk, tapping away on her keyboard. She's grinning to herself, too, which worries me to no end.

"Have a seat."

I sit.

"So I've noticed that there have been some updates to the patient lounge."

"Yes, doesn't it look lovely? The patients are already enjoying it."

"I told you that was a no-go."

"But I didn't use hospital budget or resources to do it—and everything was done after hours, so it wasn't even on the clock. And Dr. Charles said it looked great."

"Strike one."

I nod. I should've seen it coming. "Won't happen again," I say, and rise to go.

"We're not done here, Sehgal."

Oh. I take a seat again.

"I also noted that your team proceeded with the second phase of Brendan Jackson's trial, despite my reservations."

"Yes, but that was a decision made by Dr. Arora. We all thought it'd be best for Brendan to continue, since phase one was clearly so successful for him. And Dr. Arora thought—"

"I don't want any justifications, Sehgal."

"I just—"

She puts a finger to her lips to shush me, like I'm a misbehaving toddler. I do my best not to suck my teeth. Because that would just prove her point.

"Strike two."

"Okay. Noted." I start to rise again. But the smirk playing on her lips tells me we're far from done.

"So you are suspended."

I can't help it. I stand up and lean forward. "You can't do that. You have no justification."

"Oh, don't I, though?"

She gestures with her finger—again, like a pre-K teacher beckoning a four-year-old—for me to come to look at her computer screen.

It's an email file from custodial services.

"I don't get it."

She happily clicks on the file attached, and a photograph pops up. It's grainy, blurry, and hard to decipher. But then I see the ambulance. And the van. Link's van.

Gleefully, she zooms in close up, and you can just barely see two figures inside the car. Not what they're doing or anything. But that doesn't matter. Because I know exactly who the two figures are. And exactly what they were doing.

"So now, Sehgal. Here's your opportunity to deny."

I open my mouth to say something. Anything.

"But I wouldn't, if I were you. Because there's plenty more where that came from. And I'm not afraid to use it."

All I keep thinking is, *Please don't tell my mom.* But of course, I can't say that.

"Strike three, Sehgal. Which means you are most definitely out."

"Please, Dr. Davis—"

"You're not very bright, Sehgal, for a purported genius. Sloppy, even. You've got absolutely no regard for authority—a genetic trait, I'm presuming—and that's going to cost you this time. A lot."

"He wasn't my patient—"

"And now I know why. But I do question why you'd 'hook up,' as the kids call it, with someone who doesn't care about ruining your career. I didn't understand the initial complaint, to be honest, but for sure, things make more sense now, knowing what I know."

"I don't—"

"Save it, Sehgal. You are suspended without pay until further review. I've already set up a meeting with Dr. Arora and Dr. Charles. And trust me, there's plenty to review."

I nod.

"Well, don't just sit there, Sehgal. Get your stuff and go. And if I see you on the hospital grounds during your suspension, I'll have no choice but to make it permanent." She grins with glee one last time, then waves me off.

I stand, trying to stop my knees from locking. Focus, Saira, focus. Get yourself together. Don't cry, don't cry, don't cry.

But as I walk away from Davis's office, aware of all the curious eyes on me, I can't stop the tears from falling.

CHAPTER 40

The hardest part of this: explaining to my parents exactly why I'm suspended.

The car ride home was absolutely silent, and now we sit in the tearoom, Dadi puttering around, serving up chai and pakore, oblivious. Or maybe not. "Ki hoa?" she says every so often, but no one has said a word to her. Yet.

My body's still shaking with sobs, but I try to compose myself. Taara, who was already headed home to check on Pinky, rubs my back every so often, and Papa paces while Mom analyzes the situation.

"Yes, so the clinical trial, the lounge and Anya's antics, but what of it? There's nothing there that would warrant this," my mother says again for the third time. "Something does not add up."

My hands shake, and my heart has sunk into my toes, and I can't quite quell the tears. But I have to get it together. I take a deep breath. It's better they hear it from me, right? Taara nods, encouraging. "There was an incident," I say tentatively. "With a patient."

"What kind of incident?" Papa asks, his voice wary. "Did someone say something to you? Do something?"

I shake my head. "There's this boy," I start, and Papa's already frowning. "Link. Lincoln Chung-Radcliffe."

A little light goes off in Mom's head. "The one who's tape you got onto the reality show? That was smart thinking, no? They should be thrilled with your proactive nature," she says.

"Yeah, but . . ."

"But what?" Papa says. "You were not on the case, and you still went above and beyond."

"Way beyond," Taara cracks then, and both my parents to turn to glare at her.

"What do you mean?" Papa says, and I can see him working to control himself. "Did that boy . . . you and that boy?"

All my words come out in a whoosh. "We were caught kissing in his van. Someone took a video."

"Kissing?" He looks so confused. "In the van? A patient? But what about Vish?"

Then it really hits him. The implications. Exactly what kind of girl the world will think his daughter is.

Papa stands, and I kind of expect him to slam his hands on the table, like Amitabh fighting some injustice in *Coolie*, but instead he just sits again. And glares at the mug Mom puts in front of him, the chai masala swirling in the cup like a little hurricane.

I melt into a puddle of shame. I know what he's thinking. I'm his too-American, pushy, loud, and decidedly disobedient daughter. Log kya kahenge? How will he ever explain this to his brothers, the rest of the family, all the people at the gurdwara. Vish's family? His daughter, the Girl Genius he was always bragging about, has been banished from her hospital for hooking up with a patient. A patient.

And just wait till Dadi actually finds out what happened.

"How could you do this to us?" Papa says, once, twice, repeatedly, in a daze. But the look on my mother's face silences him with a warning. I will be dealt with, make no mistake. Maybe she's just seething with anger and saving her explosion for later. The thought makes me shudder.

She looks at the box of stuff I've brought from my locker—my white coat sitting on the top of the box, gleaming white and pristine, unblemished. Unlike my actual medical career.

"She's young," my mother says, her voice eerily calm. "She has made mistakes. We all do. But my concern, beyond the boy—which was certainly ill-advised, Saira, and will be addressed—is that Dr. Davis has had a clear agenda against you from day one. And I do think that no matter what else may have happened, she has created a hostile work environment."

I nod, but I'm just waiting for my mother's wrath. But she's still focused on Davis. "Taara, open your laptop." She does as instructed. "Saira, we need to note every single altercation you've had with Davis, and include the names of coworkers who may have witnessed the incidents, as well as patients."

My mother takes my hand, which is still shaking. "Beta, I know you have made your mistakes and you will no doubt atone for them," she says. "But this is your career at stake—and something like this, if not addressed appropriately, can kill it. Do you understand me?"

I nod, although I can't imagine Davis will change her mind. She seemed pretty determined to tank my career, and she didn't even have to fight dirty. My actions with Link—which were completely wrong, and I knew it—gave her just the ammunition she needed.

"Once we have documented that, Saira, I will call a meeting for you with the board, where you will apologize—and you *will* apologize—take responsibility for your actions, and lay out everything you have contributed to the hospital in your short tenure there. Because it has been a lot, and I know the patients—including Lincoln's family—appreciate it." She squeezes my hand. "Get ready, my girl, because it's time to fight. And I will fight with you."

I still can't stop crying, but luckily, my mother is by my side, her face worried and fierce, ready to lead me into battle. Even if it takes down both of us.

CHAPTER 41

When it finally happens, the confrontation with my mom, it's not at all what I expected. Rage, fury, screaming. None of that. It's the silence, first. She'll talk to me about the work stuff, about getting my suspension annulled, about figuring this Davis thing out. But no casual chats around chaitime, no discussions of new medical innovations or going to med school in India. No real conversation. At all. For days that turn into weeks. Until I can't stand it anymore. Until I'm the one who triggers it.

"Don't you want to know what happened?" I ask her one night, leaning into her bathroom door as she rubs her Olay into her skin.

Her eyes are trained on me in the mirror, and they are cold as she shakes her head. "I don't think I'm ready yet. I don't know if I'll ever be ready."

"But I want to tell you." About the way he sends those lightning bolts of electricity shooting up my skin, about the little gap between his teeth. About the way he hums when no one's listening or everyone is, the way he talks about life like he's lived so much of it, even though he's only sixteen. The way he calls me Starshine.

But that would be a whole 'nother can of worms. Or whatever that phrase is.

"Well, Saira Sehgal, that's one decision you don't get to make," she says. "You don't get to tell me what could make you do something so very foolish, Girl Genius, that you almost ruined everything. Everything you've worked so hard for all these years. Everything *we've* worked so hard for all these years. No. You don't get to confess and be forgiven for that. Not now."

Maybe not ever. That's the part she doesn't say.

But she closes the door then. And I'm left standing there.

Not only am I suspended, but I'm grounded to boot.

Like, really, truly grounded. With no phone, no outside contact, no aloo ke paranthe, even.

I've spent my minutes, hours, days, staring at the walls, pretending to study for the boards, and thinking about Link. I don't know if he's texted me, because my mom took away my phone. I don't even know if he knows what happened. My cousin Arun told Vish, though, so maybe he does. Vish told Arun his parents are taking the "rumors" super hard—because he still hasn't told them the truth about us. Or about himself. Maybe he should. But he has to do what's right for him. Even if it makes me the bad guy. Right?

The only reason I know any of this at all is because of Taara, who's been trying her best to feed me information. And spending way too much of the beginning of her fall semester here at home instead of at school, where she should be.

I'm like a bird in a cage. And Dadi's done with me. She's banished me upstairs until lunchtime, because otherwise I hover in the kitchen and ask her a million questions. And she still hasn't asked me that one that's been lingering in the air for the past week: What did you do?

I wouldn't know how to begin to answer.

I'm staring at my oncology textbook, pondering radiation ratios, when I hear the doorbell, and then Dadi chattering for way too long for it to be the UPS guy.

"Want parantha?" I overhear her say from where I'm standing at the top of the steps. So I know exactly who it is.

Lizzie.

I thunder down the stairs, and Dadi shoots me a look. Not only am I grounded, but that was the height of inelegance. I couldn't help it, I'm just so excited to see Lizzie. But when I storm into the foyer, I freeze, unsure of what to do with myself. Do I hug her? Tell her how much I've missed her?

"Start with hi," she says. She's not smiling, but she's not frowning, either. Her skin is golden—apparently Yale is a good place to get a tan—and she already looks fall-ready, a denim jacket thrown over her flowery summer dress, and little boots on her feet.

How does she always know?

Meanwhile, I'm in my pj's and unshowered. For, like, the second day in a row.

"Vish told me what happened," she says. Dadi perches an eyebrow, looking from me to Lizzie and Lizzie to me, then decides to go make snacks.

"Namkeen thay chai landihiyan," she tells me, and I usher Lizzie to the tearoom.

"I've been craving Dadi's snacks," Lizzie says, sighing quite contentedly.

Why didn't you answer any of my one thousand text messages? I ask in my head. The question hangs. She doesn't answer it.

"I've missed this place," she says, setting herself down on the sofa a bit too prim and proper, like a stranger. I sit in the armchair on the left side, also quite formally, deciding to follow her cues. "Connecticut doesn't have great Indian food."

I nod. "Most places don't."

"Well, not like Dadi's anyway." She stares at the table for a minute. "So I went to go see Vish when I got back. He told me what happened."

I wonder what that means. Like, me and Link? The stuff with the hospital?

"All of it." She's still staring at her hands, as if her nail polish will magically change colors. Or something. "Even you and him."

It's like the ground drops from under me. He told her. It feels like a sock to the stomach, like a betrayal. Even though I knew it would happen eventually, and that eventually was soon. It was always his secret to keep, but it was something that lived just between the two of us, something we shared. And now it's not.

"I would have understood, you know. I would've played along."

"It wasn't my decision to make."

"But you went along with it," she says. "Kept it from everyone. Even me. Even though I was your best friend."

I shrug. She's right. That's true. But it was Vish's secret, and I had to protect him.

"You didn't tell me about Link, either." She looks at her hands. "Even though I was there for you. I was helping."

And she did. Continued to help me, and Link. Even when I ruined everything.

I open my mouth to speak, but nothing's right.

She wasn't talking to me. It was complicated. I didn't know what to call it. It was all a mess anyway. I'm a mess anyway. Always have been, always will be.

"It's been months—even years—since you've bothered to make time for me. You say you want to be a regular kid, but every time I try to get you to do regular kid stuff, you blow it off. You blow me off."

She's right. It's true. But lately, it hasn't been like it used to be. "You're always just so focused on Cat and the other kids. Like they're your world."

"They are my world. I'm seventeen. I'm in high school. It's senior year. They'd be your world, too, if you were still in school." She takes a deep breath. "And in any case, I wanted you to be part of my world. Like you've always been."

"I didn't feel like I could." The words tumble out in a rush, like the first few hiccups when I've eaten something too spicy. "There were so many things I didn't feel like I could say to you anymore. For too long."

"Since Harper." The name sounds wrong coming from her mouth. Like she's talking about a stranger. "You always held that—held her—against me. It's like she lived in this massive space between us, even though she's been dead so long." I know what she's thinking: growing like a tumor. One that can't be cut out.

Tears slip down my cheeks now, but there are too many to stop them. "You could have stayed. She needed you. I needed you."

"I was just a kid," she says. "But you held it against me forever. Every single thing. Collecting them all, like a list in your planner. Compiling them to pull out whenever things didn't go your way." She sighs and hands me a tissue.

Then she stands, as if to leave, even though Dadi hasn't brought the chai yet and would be devastated.

"Don't go," I say, grabbing her hand.

She sighs. "There's no reason to stay."

"I'm sorry," I say. I'm looking down at the glass coffee table, and I can see the tears about to spill in my reflection. "Things changed so fast, and I wanted us to be the one thing that could stay the same."

"But they're not the same. You're Saira Sehgal, a doctor, Girl Genius, big-time. Everything's all set for you. I'm just a high school kid who's about to graduate, trying to figure myself out, and scared of everything. When I tried to tell you about my fears, you scoffed at them. So I stopped trying."

That sounds familiar. Like something Taara said recently. Or even Vish. "Maybe we're all just scared. Even me."

She sighs. Maybe that's a cop-out. But I don't know how to fix this. Not this time. "Anyway, I'm going to Yale next year. I applied early decision, and Madame Yulia is going to write me a recommendation, which means it's a done deal. Even if I am a generic white girl."

"That's amazing!" I want to hug her, but I don't. "Congratulations."

"And, well," she says, waving her arms a bit, "this is a big mess you've made. But I know you, Saira. You'll figure it out."

I want to ask where we go from here, but that's the thing: We don't know.

"We'll figure it out," she says. "But you know, it's okay if it's not the same."

It has to be, because it's already different.

"We're not the same as we were at eight or fourteen or even two months ago. We've always been different people, and we need to accept that," she says, sounding way smarter than me. "Sometimes it works, sometimes it doesn't. Sometimes you have to let go to stay together, in whatever little way you can. And that's okay. Sometimes growing apart is part of growing up."

That's when Dadi brings out the chai, and Lizzie pastes on her too-perfect actress smile and pretends things are just the same. Or maybe, somewhere in her head, they sort of are. They're the way they have been, for her at least, for a long time now. And she's okay with that, maybe. It's not *all* a show, I know. But it pinches still, to know how much of her I've already lost.

To Whom It May Concern:

It has come to our understanding that Saira Sehgal, MD, an intern in pediatric oncology at Princeton Presbyterian, has been suspended by the hospital's administrator, one Dr. Hannah Davis, for a reported patient conduct violation.

Per the documents attached below, note that (a) Saira Sehgal, MD, was not on the medical team that supervised the care of Lincoln Chung-Radcliffe, the patient in the reported potential violation notice. However, she was on the publicity team formed by Maggie Chung-Radcliffe and Dr. Abhishek Arora, and therefore, frequently met with the patient, including off hospital grounds, to facilitate a successful media campaign with Be The Match, in association with the TV show "Rock Star Band Camp." And (b) that "evidence" of any such interaction between Sehgal and Mr. Chung-Radcliffe was from a meeting they had off hospital grounds for social media strategy purposes. Therefore, the hospital's monitoring and documenting of the pair's interaction constitutes a violation of privacy, and, as the suit below clarifies—filed on behalf of Mr. Lincoln Chung-Radcliffe—will be acted upon accordingly, if Dr. Sehgal is not reinstated in good standing immediately.

Signed,
Lily Ahn-Chung, Esquire

Chung & Bradford, Associates
Princeton, NJ

CHAPTER 42

This September Monday dawns cool, crisp, and full of import. I have a meeting at the hospital today to discuss my suspension and whether it will become permanent, I'm guessing.

At breakfast, after two full weeks of being suspended—and grounded—my mother finally lets me have my phone back. Except it's not *my* phone. It's a new number, a kid's line with limited data and texting, and it's got all of these monitoring settings on it. Like something a twelve-year-old might use.

"We thought you were grown up enough," she says over breakfast, as Dadi bustles in silence, annoyed to be left out of the discussion once again. "You know, being a doctor and all. But clearly we were wrong. So think of this as a new beginning."

Taara's face is grim as she watches. She's been busy rearranging her film/TV/nutrition schedule, second-guessing every little thing. Which can be annoying. But mostly it's been nice having her home. Like right now. She takes a sip of chai and squeezes my hand under the kitchen table.

"With new rules," Papa adds for good measure.

Among their other rules:

6. My curfew is now eight p.m., and I must report to them my whereabouts at any given time—the tracking app on my phone will ensure that.

7. My schedule is posted in the kitchen for everyone to see.

8. I am to focus on studying for the boards and investigating research opportunities, since the stank from "the incident" will likely take a while to wear off, meaning I won't be glowingly recommended to fellowship opportunities at Princeton Presbyterian or elsewhere.

"These terms, if you choose to accept them, will demonstrate to us that you are ready, willing, and hopefully able to behave professionally and thoughtfully."

"And no more seeing that boy." Papa is adamant. "Or any boys."

"Even Vish?" It's Dadi who asks this, shocking all of us.

"Yes, even Vish."

"No, Pash. I think you are wrong to say that," Dadi says, and Papa's jaw nearly drops into his piping-hot sevian.

Taara nods. "He's family, Pop. You can't just cut off an arm like that."

"I don't trust him, and right now I don't trust you," Papa says, shutting Taara up. "He clearly knew about this. And so did you." Even though she didn't. "So no, Vish will have to reearn his place. And I'm just not sure he can do that right now."

Mom nods, but I can see she's already more pliable on this. Though it'll take a minute. "Vish has his own things he's dealing with right now, as I'm sure you know, Saira."

That catches me off guard. What does she know?

"He probably could use your support," Mom says. "Although I don't think Sweetie Auntie is such a big Saira fan right now. And your papa's right. If . . . and that's a big if—you are going to see him, it will be here, at home." She takes a sip of her chai. "Now, if you're done with your breakfast"—she turns to Papa—"and you with your lecture, it's time for us to go. You know how Davis hates it when we're late."

The conference room is full when we get to the oncology office. Ms. Clayton asks us to have a seat, and Mom and I strain to hear what's being said inside, but it's no use. I can tell it's Davis, Arora, and Charles, and there is some heated discussion going on.

The phone on Davis's desk buzzes.

"You can go on in," Ms. Clayton says. "Good luck!"

Davis welcomes us with a glare. There are two empty chairs, thankfully between Charles and Arora, but that puts us right across from her warlike gaze. My heart flutters like a bird in a cage, and I feel like it'll escape right up and out of my mouth in a second if they don't say something soon.

"So, let's start with the good news, Dr. Sehgal, and, uh, Dr. Sehgal," Arora says. "I'm happy to say that Saira's been reinstated at work."

"On probation," Davis adds with what passes for glee on her. "We're going to be watching your every move."

Charles clears his throat. "No, well, *not* watching every move. At all. Of course not. But I am pleased to say that your efforts on the case of one Lincoln Chung-Radcliffe, with the video and the social media campaign, have increased the marrow match submissions for him by some four hundred percent. That's pretty astounding."

Mom looks pleased. And I'm floored. That's even better than I expected.

"Does that mean he's found a match?" I ask, and I can feel my eyes glistening, though I will them to stop.

"Not yet. But it's likely. And thus, we have a favor to ask of you, Saira," Charles says. "Obviously, for, uh, reasons, we can't allow you to get medically involved. It's just not ethical. You have a vested interest. And that's . . . understandable. In most cases, I would remove you from the case completely. But Lincoln Chung-Radcliffe's parents have asked that you continue to work on this case in a consulting capacity."

Dr. Arora nods. "The phone has been ringing off the hook—the media wants Link. And they want you, too." He turns to my mom. "I understand, Dr. Sehgal, if you are uncomfortable with this in any way. Saira is, after all, still a child." He looks a bit forlorn, almost pleading—exactly how I feel, actually. "But if she did some media interviews this could truly be the thing that helps us find a match and save Link's life."

My mom doesn't say anything for a long time, just looks at her hands, resting on the table. Then she looks up at me, and Charles.

"I think this is a case where Saira should follow her heart," my mother says. "And I'm pretty sure I know exactly where that will take her."

Davis harrumphs, but Charles and Arora nearly get up and bhangra. "Thank you, Dr. Sehgal. I know this an awkward situation, and we always tell doctors to stay detached. But sometimes, the emotional investment is what makes medicine work. I think this is one of those cases."

"Dr. Sehgal Junior," Arora says, picking up a folder from his desk. "If you're prepared, I'd like to reinstate you today. Unfortunately, Alina Plotkin's case needs some immediate attention, and I'd like to get you looped back in. Shall we?"

I nod and rise, as do the others. My mom grins at me, then mouths, "Seven p.m.," pointing at her watch, just so I'm clear that curfew's still on.

And as I walk out the door with Arora, I can feel Davis's eyes burning into the back of my head, the heat nearly curling my freshly blown-out hair.

Arora gives me the rundown on the patients on my rotation—Pinky's progressing well, and her scans are still clean. Brendan Jackson's second round in the trial has been nearly as successful as the first, so they're monitoring it closely to ensure he remains eligible to continue, especially with Davis on the prowl to make cuts there. Link's gotten nearly eight thousand marrow submissions from potential matches—and of those, twenty or so more closely echo his ethnic background, so while the odds are still slim, he has a chance. Be The Match is working as quickly as they can to process them all. "And *Rock Star Boot Camp* has requested his presence in Los Angeles," Arora says. "But unfortunately, the effects of the heavy radiation cycle he's receiving right now mean he's not well enough to go."

"What do you mean?"

"Your mom didn't tell you?" Arora says, startled. "I thought you knew."

"What?"

"He's neutropenic now. It's not looking good."

He looks at my face, and I know he can tell.

"Go ahead," he says, a hand on my shoulder, steadying. "Meet me in the lounge at noon and we can go over the rest and reactivate your ID."

José is in the hall, updating files on one of the computer floaters, and he catches me as a I race down it.

"Saira," he says, arms wrapping tight around me. "I'm so glad you're back. I have so much to tell you. I—" He sees me distracted and says, "Yeah, I tried to text you, but it kept saying message not sent. I guess your mom . . ."

I nod.

"He's okay. In good spirits. You know him. But it's hard."

"Can I go in?"

José nods. "He's resting, and I just gave him a dose of morphine, so I'm sure he'll be happy to see you."

The room is quiet but bright. Link lays motionless in the bed, on his side, his back to me. Monitors track every breath and heartbeat. I walk silently over to the machines and stare, the feed of numbers and lines and leaps telling me everything and nothing all at once.

It's too much. I can't stop looking, all the data scrambling together in my head, spilling truths and a future I can't begin to face.

All I can do right now is find that heartbeat. I take off my shoes, carefully, quietly, and climb gingerly onto the bed, curling my body around Link's like a big spoon, my arm slipping around his waist, my hand clasping his. For a few moments, all I focus on is breathing, our chests rising and falling together, the rhythm soothing my worries, at least for now. I lay there for a few moments, my head against his chest, his heartbeat in my ears. He plants a kiss on the top of my head, which is tucked just under his chin. "Morning, Starshine," he says, and that does it. The tears spill, fast and furious, soaking the small space between us. "Hey." He hugs me tighter. "It's okay. I'm okay. Or I will be. I told you, things get worse before they get better. And this is the worse." He swallows hard. "The worst."

I nod, and my head bops into his jaw. "Listen, to me, though, okay? I think that it's best for the both of us right now to let this just simmer for a minute."

I sit up in the bed, tangled in blankets and wires and Link's IVs. "What does that mean, simmer?"

He sits up a bit, too, but the IVs hold him back. "I told you, Saira. I won't be the one who breaks your heart." He's looking down at his hands, which look weathered and worn, like they belong to a sixty-year-old, not someone who's sixteen. "I refuse."

"That's not your decision to make," I say, and I can hear my voice rising, sounding rash, even to myself. And besides, it's way too late.

"Yeah, it is." In his eyes there's a warning, and I know exactly what he's capable of—of banning me from even breathing the same air as him. He's done it before. "I'm not saying we can't see each other at all. I'm not." He takes a deep breath. "But it can't be like this." He waves his arms around. "I can't do it. To you. Or to me."

In that moment, I want to disappear completely. I want to rip a hole in the tired linoleum, the earth to just shatter and swallow me whole. I want to rewind time to my first day here at Princeton Presbyterian and make it so I never ran into Link at all that morning, a few minutes ahead or behind, whatever, to stave off the sharp, stabbing feeling that's shooting through me right now. I want the heat that's blazing on my cheeks and my neck to combust, to take me out in a giant inferno, instantaneous and irreversible. Anything to just stop the pain, excruciating and familiar, but this time a thousand times worse.

Link sits up farther. "Listen to me, Saira. This isn't fair to either of us."

"Because life isn't fair."

"Right. And not everything happens for a reason, despite what they always say. So we have some choices to make. My choice is this: I need you to be my friend right now."

I'm shaking my head before I realize it. "I can't," I say. "I can't."

"You have to," a voice says. It's Link's mom, standing just behind the curtain, and I can see the salty streaks tears have left behind on her pale skin. "He needs you. Please."

She walks up to where I'm standing, and for a moment I'm really afraid she's going to hug me. If she does, I won't be able to hold it together. I barely am right now. But instead, she takes my hand and leads me out of the room, into the hall, where the lunchtime traffic is bustling and loud. José appears—Link no doubt pressed the button—and he reaches for me, but I shake my head.

"Saira, I know you're not technically on my son's team," Link's mom is saying, but I can't quite focus—I'm still back in that room with him, watching his face as he told me he doesn't want to be with me. "But what you've done, it's had a profound impact on the chance he has at surviving this. And I don't just mean the videos, or *Rock Star Boot Camp*. I mean being there. Caring. Giving him a reason."

I smile. But it's hollow. Because the pain that comes with it is too much. Maybe Link's right. I can't live through this again. I can't be the one who survives and carries the weight of memories forever.

"It's a lot to ask, Saira," she says. "But he needs you. Please, don't bail on us now. Even if he pushes you away. Because you might be the light that gets him through this."

I don't quite know when my heart got so very loud. But it's ringing in my ears like an incessant alarm I can't quite reach, a warning about nothing and everything all at once. All I know is that I have to get out of this place right now, this place that takes and takes and takes and maybe only ever gives just a little bit. "I can't." I don't even realize I've let the words escape, but she looks stricken. "I have to go."

I run off before she can say another word, José hot on my heels. He catches up to me at the intern lounge, and I worry that he's going to trip me up with words, reasons, rationales. But instead he just hugs me, and lets me cry, and so I do.

CHAPTER 43

I have to get myself together. José sits next to me on the couch in the intern lounge, patting my back tentatively every so often, and handing me a fresh tissue now and then. Aside from the occasional sob, we are silent. But I can almost feel the words waiting to burst out of him.

"I know."

"You know what?" he says. He's suppressing a smile, and I kind of want to throw something at him.

"I know I need to get it together."

He nods.

"Because it's my job."

"And because, when it's all said and done, no matter what, Link's your friend."

I feel a sob rising. "My friend."

"Saira, he needs you. More than you know."

"I don't think I can."

"I know you can, niña. And so do you. You've known since you were tiny. You're a healer. Even if it hurts."

"Even if it kills."

José gives me another hug, then holds me at arm's length and gives me a once-over. "You chose this life. Because you knew you could handle it. And we all believe in you—me, Dr. Arora, Dr. Charles, your mom. Link's mom. You can handle it. And he needs you."

I nod, but the shivers from my sobs still shake my body. I don't know if I can handle it this time. But I know I don't really have a choice. Because I can't give up on him. Not now.

"Okay, let's get you cleaned up and ready for your first day back," José says, handing me a tissue. I look at my watch. I better hustle. "It's going to be a big one."

I look at him sharply—there's something he's not telling me. "What?"

"Look, just take it easy this time, okay?"

"What's that supposed to mean?" I ask, heading over to the coffee machine for a cup. I dump several glugs of creamer in, along with three sugars. I take a sip and grimace. Perfect.

"I mean, a lot has happened while you were gone. Some of it good, some of it, not so much," he says. "But you're still on probation, so don't put your fists up right off the bat. Go easy."

"Davis been talking to you?"

José peers down at me. "Listen, a lot of people have had it rough—even rougher than you, little girl," he says.

That pinches. "What do you mean?"

"I mean, what you think you see is not always the truth. Sometimes it's worth digging a little deeper."

I frown into my coffee cup.

"Davis has been doing this for longer than you've been alive, Saira. Way longer. She knows the system inside and out. Yeah, it's made her cold, a bit. But she also knows how to work it so that things balance out as much as they can."

"I can't believe you're taking her side," I say, and I can feel the pout coming on, as much as I try to stop it.

"Look, I wasn't gonna tell you this, but she's the one who asked me to start the fund for Alina. You know, the one that's been paying for all of her medical bills?"

I nearly spit my coffee, I'm so surprised. I thought it was Dr. Charles.

"It was her." He's smiling, like he got me good. And maybe he did.

Maybe I've had her wrong this whole time. Like a fairy god-doctor behind the scenes, making magic happen. Or maybe not. "I mean, she's still super rude to all the interns, especially me."

"But, Saira, you're rude AF to her, too, sometimes. Have been from day one."

I frown again.

"And like I said, she's had it rough. She lost her wife recently. To cancer. So go easy."

Oh.

José wasn't kidding about today being intense. Five minutes before we start our rounds, Lily Sanchez from hospital PR shows up in the lounge, bursting with news.

"I hope you brought something presentable, Saira," she says, giving me a once-over. "Because ABC News will be here at four—they want to shoot you and Link for a segment on *Nightline* next week."

José shakes his head, then slips my phone from my pocket.

"What are you doing?" I say, trying to snatch it back.

"Texting Lizzie. She'll know what to bring," he says, and Lily nods with satisfaction.

"No prints," she adds, her four-inch heels clacking as she marches off. "And maybe get a blow-out."

"And you need those eyebrows done," José says, texting.

Cho steps into the lounge then, and frowns. "What'd she want?" he says, then sees me. "Oh, you're back."

"Yup," I say.

"Did you hear about the *Nightline* segment?" José says, a little too excited.

"For Link?" Cho says. "We shoot at four, right?"

"Yeah, and they want Saira in it."

Cho frowns. "Of course they do. But she's not even his doctor," he says, his mouth a straight line. He shrugs. "Whatever. If it'll get us the match we need, that's all that matters."

José and I nearly sputter in shock. That was definitely not what we were expecting.

Cho frowns. "I talked to Be The Match. Some close calls, but nothing usable so far. And we've got more than twenty thousand samples."

I swallow. We only need one. But it has to be the right one.

"I can help with your hair." It's Howard, who's just walked in—late. "I have curlers in my locker."

"That would be great," I say. She smiles at me, but she looks how I feel. Tearstained and worn out.

In the end, I don't have time to do anything but change—and let José powder and lip-gloss me up. The afternoon is a blur of intake updates, new patient introductions, and a full half hour of scoldings from Ms. Ruby Jackson, who was "so very disappointed" that I disappeared without informing her. But now that Brendan's cancer is nearly gone thanks to the trial, she's pleased that I'll be returning full-time. "Just get your license now, baby, and you'll be all set."

I wonder if she's been talking to Dadima.

The last appointment on my schedule for this afternoon is with Alina Plotkin. Howard and I visit her together, and it's weird, because despite her peace offering this morning, we've barely talked. It's all just perfunctory but cordial—"Pass the test tubes," or "Would you suggest upping the dosage on the IV?" I worry that Alina will sense it, but I'm armed with the jalebis Dadima sent as a distraction.

When I walk into her hospital room, though, I realize Alina's far beyond fretting about our intern drama.

She's passed out cold in the bed, wires and tubes attached to every visible patch of skin. Her arms and legs are bloated, and her face—what little I can see of it past the feeding tube—is puffy with water weight. That means her kidneys have started to shut down.

Mr. Plotkin leaps out of his chair when he sees me, and offers a hug, crushing me with his urgency.

"I'm so glad you're back," he says. "Alina missed you a lot. She was just talking about it the other day—back when she was still up. And José said he texted you to check in, but that your phone was shut down. She kept waiting for you to show up, but—" He breaks down then, sobbing on my shoulder as he towers over me, and I stand absolutely still, unsure of what to do.

José puts an arm around him, tugging him away gently. "It's okay, Mr. Plotkin," he says. "Let's give Saira a minute to reacquaint herself with Alina's situation."

Howard updates me, rattling off a litany of cancer-related ailments that have made Alina's system start to shut down. "She's got reduced liver function and circulation, and the feeding tube has been in place pretty much since you left. What we're really worried about, though, is congestive heart failure due to the overload of fluids in her system."

I nod. "But they don't want to intubate her yet."

"It's too much," Mr. Plotkin says, his voice cracking, "She didn't even want the feeding tube. All that pain. She's still breathing. Let her breathe." He looks at me. "Right?"

Howard glares at me from across the bed. I know what she's telling me, silently. That might just be what kills her.

CHAPTER 44

The patient lounge has been set up with all kinds of lights and these weird umbrella things, like it's going to rain or something. I can't really get excited about it, but Vish is thrilled. He keeps talking to a production assistant who's helping set up, following him around and asking questions. "So the silver thing is to divert the reflection?" he says, and I giggle. I've never seen him actually flirt with anyone. He's almost as bad at it as I am.

"Look this way," Lizzie says again. "No, up, like you're looking at the ceiling." She coats my lashes with another layer of mascara, and I fight the urge to rub my eyes. The only thing I know how to do makeup-wise is kajal and lip gloss, so José was smart to call in the expert, as awkward as it was at first. She also stole a cute red button-down dress from Taara's closet, which adds a nice pop of color under my lab coat, even though we had to pin the top to make sure my boobs don't manage a great escape.

"I'm glad you're here," I say as she glosses my lips.

"No talking!" she says. But she's smiling down at me.

"We're almost ready to go," the PA announces, and looks around. "Where's our star?"

Vish hovers on the edge, taking everything in. He's still banned from the house, and I haven't really had a chance to talk to him—to tell him I didn't tell anyone anything. That his secret is still his to share. But this isn't the right place or time. So I just let him bask in the glow of the TV lights. He's earned it.

Cho hustles forward, marking himself as the man in charge. "They're just cleaning him up. He'll be here in a second."

"Dr. Sehgal," the producer says, "I think you and Link can sit right here on this sofa, and we can put his guitar to the left here. Link will tell his story, you'll give us a bit of medical background, and together you can tell viewers how to submit a sample for Be The Match—"

That's when José wheels Link in. They've powdered his face a bit to cover some of the bruising along his jaw, and his head is freshly shaven. He's wearing a leather jacket over his hospital robe, and despite the smile on his face, he looks exhausted.

He scrambles out of the wheelchair and to the sofa, taking a seat next to me, and the production assistant gets right to work mic'ing him. Vish hovers, Lizzie frowns, and Link grins at them. "Glad you're here, guys," he says. Then he turns to me. "You too."

My heart leaps for a second, but I remind myself that this is work, business, or whatever.

"I promised your mom," I say, and for a moment his smile falters, and the little stab of pain he feels pricks me, too. But I can't let myself fall back into that easy rhythm with him. It hurts too much. And it will hurt even more later.

Within minutes, the cameras are rolling, and the host, Lara Ahn, from the medical reporting team, starts the segment. "We're here today with Lincoln Chung-Radcliffe, whom *Rock Star Boot Camp* fans will remember as the top-twenty finalist with an endearing rasp and definite front-man potential. But before he could take his shot at the top spot, his run on the show was curtailed by a longtime nemesis—cancer."

She turns to Link, and I can see the interest in her eyes—even though he's way too young for her, right? And, like, succumbing to cancer. I can see Lizzie glaring at Lara from behind the camera lights.

Diagnosis: Cougar baring teeth.
Prognosis: No way she's gonna get this prey.

"So, Lincoln," Lara says, leaning in a bit.

"Link," he says with that bright smile, showing off the little gap between his front teeth. "Link Rad, if you will."

She laughs. "This is not your first encounter with cancer, right?"

"Leukemia. I was diagnosed when I was thirteen, but we caught it early, blasted it with chemo and radiation, and I was in remission for a while. I almost remembered what it felt like to be a normal kid. Played basketball, made music—"

"Had a girlfriend?" Lara asks with a smirk. "What? Inquiring minds want to know."

Link blushes and laughs. "Yeah, had a girlfriend. Hi, Risa." He waves to the camera, and I pretty much die. That's cold. "Then I signed up to do the *Rock Star Band Camp* thing—and made it right through to the second round."

"And that's when Link found himself back here at Princeton Presbyterian for follow-up testing. Am I right, Dr. Sehgal?" Lara asks.

"Yeah," Link says, before I can speak. "I met Saira with an *i* my first day back—and I thought she was a patient, too." He's grinning at me now, but I'm having a hard time playing along. "Turns out she's a sixteen-year-old doctor."

Lara turns to me, and I want to knock that practiced smile off her face. "Saira, they call you the Girl Genius—and thanks to your campaigning on Link's behalf, there have been more than twenty thousand submissions to Be The Match in the last month, right?"

"Well, we're far from in the clear. So please, get tested. If you'd like to get tested, you can go to BeTheMatch.com to learn more now. There are so many people waiting. You might just be the one who can save a life," I say, thinking carefully about my words. "And Link still needs to find the right donor so he can go on being amazing and making music. Anyone who's watched him on *Rock Star Boot Camp* knows just how talented he is."

"So we've heard," Lara says, grinning at him. "Link, your mom told me you're working on some new material. Care to play us a tune?"

Vish helps him get the guitar out of the case and onto his lap, and Link winces as he readjusts the strings a bit. Then he starts to strum, humming along at first, the melody swirling and familiar—a riff on the song he's been toying with in this very room for months.

"There will come a time / when all I leave behind / is the melody of your name. There will come a day / when the words we used to say / will all but fade away. / Will you still remember / the moments we spent together / all those times we swore forever . . ."

I'm looking at my hands on my lap, fidgety, restless, as he sings, but I can feel his eyes on me. I can almost feel his pulse racing next to mine, the familiar rhythm beckoning, as if we were alone right now, and not being recorded for a million witnesses. When I finally lift my eyes to look up at him, though, he's looking right at the camera, and not at me at all.

The whole room claps, and the host gushes some more, rattling off information about Be The Match, and asking me something else, but it's all a blur. All I can think about is the fact that whatever was there—if it was there at all—is gone now. At least for him.

And then José is wheeling Link away, just like that, and it's all over.

"You okay, Guddi?" Vish says. "That was great, right?"

Lizzie comes up then, rubs my shoulders. "Great, but rough." She throws an arm around me, and the other around Vish. "So come on, guys. I think it's time for some Pizza Hut."

In the Jeep, driving, he finally brings it up. "That was weird, wasn't it?"

I'm sitting in the passenger seat, with Lizzie in the back, and it feels so familiar and comfortable, like an old sweater that still fits.

"Every single minute of it," I say, and it's like I can finally breathe again.

But Lizzie's suddenly livid. "Yeah, who the hell is Risa?"

I don't want to cry, so I don't say a word. But they won't let it go.

"It's like you barely knew each other at all," Lizzie says.

"When that song was totally about you," Vish adds, his voice low. "Like, for real."

The tears will come if I don't do something now. So I pivot. "Did you talk to your parents yet?"

He nearly smashes the brakes at the red light. But he can't avoid the conversation forever.

"I'm not ready."

"I won't say anything. Until you're ready. But you do know that this makes me the bad guy?" I ask. I'm always the bad guy these days.

"Villains are the most interesting characters," Lizzie says with a grin.

"Especially when their motivations are true," Vish adds, taking my hand. "And yours definitely are."

But that doesn't make this one bit easier.

CHAPTER 45

For two days now, I've been going through the motions. The *Nightline* segment featuring me and Link is supposed to air tonight, and everyone at the hospital has been talking about it incessantly. But I don't even know if I'll be able to bring myself to watch. But José's planned a screening in the lounge for anyone who wants to show up. I kind of don't want to, but probably should. Even though Link and I haven't talked since then. I wouldn't know what to say. So I just won't say anything at all. But he hasn't texted me, either. I wonder if he has my new number. Unlikely.

I'm updating files in the intern lounge when the alarm goes off. It goes off all the time— we're in a hospital, of course, so there are always patients coding. But this time, it's one of the machines me and Howard are logging. Alina's machine.

"Code blue! Code blue!" We all rush forward at once, waves crashing on a shore. Alina's pressure has dropped severely by the time we make it to the hospital bed. She's already in some unreachable place, and unwilling to be called back.

I get to her first and amp up the oxygen line, carefully placing a mask over her mouth, her thin lips gone blue, the limp coolness already settling into her limbs.

Dead weight.

I try to push the thought out of my head, but there it is. She feels like one of the countless cadavers I've sliced open on my journey to this very room.

"Pulse dropping, BP base-lining, we've got to get moving!" Howard's shouting. "Now."

Diagnosis: Acute cardiac arrest.
Prognosis: We're going to lose her this time.

There's nothing in my endless years of education that could really have prepared me for this moment. Not all the lectures, or the many months spent poring over twenty-pound tomes and patient files. Not the summers at genius camp or by my mother's side in her office, delivering babies and stitching up new moms. Not the MD degree—with highest honors—or the many surgeries on soulless bodies I had to do to get it. Not all the months I've spent by Arora's side here, observing and taking notes and assisting. The history books might mark me as the youngest doctor ever to practice medicine in the United States, a teenager, Dr. Girl Genius.

But in this moment, that means nothing.

Because it all comes down to this: A narrow hospital bed, a monitor flatlining, a little girl whose bright spirit is slowly seeping away, right here, right now, and there's nothing I can do to fix it. Nothing. And I didn't even get to say goodbye.

I stare at the small body lying there, skin pallid and cool, the fading heartbeat's every movement marked by machines and recorded as evidence of our failure to save a life. Her life. The monitor's beep burns into my brain, flat and dull, like my dad's car when I forget the seat belt, a warning, a threat.

"Start the IV thread," Arora's voice says, and he sounds murky and faraway, like we're all floating underwater in a dream, and any minute we'll surface and laugh, and this will be over. "Up the dosage to the highest level, we're losing rhythm fast. Go." His voice rises, and all the nerves in the room are firing, splitting, burning.

I hear the words. I know what they mean. But my body doesn't move. Sweat beads down my neck and dampens the back of my scrubs.

My papery mask is soaked through with sweat or tears or maybe both. "She's flatlining! Start compressions *now*."

José dabs my forehead with a pristine white towel, preventing the salty sheen from blinding me. "Focus, Saira, focus," he says, bringing me back to earth and this moment, the one that's slipping away much too quickly. The one that's not like anything I really expected, despite everything they've told me. He runs from one end of the body to the other, rubbing feet, checking IVs, shouting instructions to the galley nurses. "Come on, niña. We've got to move."

But my hands are shaking, useless by my sides, and the tremors are catching like the slow build of a Southern California earthquake, starting on the edges and working its way to the center. "Saira, you've got this." José's voice is a low rumble in my stomach, a warning that this is about to all slip away if I don't do something now.

All right, slow down, breathe. *Please.*

José tries to hand me the paddles, but I reject them, trusting my hands instead. I lean over the body and pump over her chest—one, two, three. Nothing. I stop for the same count—one, two, three—and then do the compressions again. Still nothing.

"The defibrillator, Saira. We don't have time," Cho shouts. "We have to!"

All eyes are on the monitor, and the rhythm is falling, flattening. My hands are not enough to save her, but she made me promise to let her go. If it came to this. Which she knew it would.

"Nothing's happening," José says, his voice roaring with stress. "Defib, now!"

I nod, and he rushes off, rolling the machine over.

"All right, set up, hurry," Howard says. "You know where, right, Saira? Let's go."

Cho's already setting up the pads on the girl's chest, moving forward, with or without me. Even now, he has to win.

"She doesn't want it," I say, and can't believe the words have escaped my mouth. "She told me so."

Howard stops cold for a second, and she looks like she might smack me, she's so livid. "It doesn't matter what she said—her chart says all means necessary, not DNR," Howard says. "And she's not an adult. She doesn't get to make that decision. And we need to do this."

"She's a human being!" I say, and realize too late that I'm shouting, my words bouncing around in my head. "Of course she does."

But Howard's plowing ahead, too, prepping for the charge. The machine's even more frantic now, beeping wildly, and the rest of the team storms in to see what's wrong.

"Code blue, code blue!" The words echo through the room over the dull, flat extended tone of the monitor, the steady rhythm flatlining into a long, low moan. "We've gotta do this now," Howard says. She's staring at me.

"You guys keep fighting it out," Cho seethes, his voice acid. "We'll just stand here and watch her die."

Howard checks the IV streams, aligning numbers, her eyes steady. "Her chart clearly states all means necessary." She looks down at the pages and up at me, the creases in her forehead aging her fast, making me feel like the child I am. Cho reads over her shoulder, nodding. "We're doing this, Saira. With or without you."

"We're gonna lose her," José says, carefully applying gel to the nodules, where the paddles will go. "I'm going in."

"No," I say, finally stepping forward. "It . . . She's my responsibility."

Slowly, carefully, I place the electrodes in careful alignment across the girl's chest, one just to the right of her heart, one to the left slightly below it, as I've practiced so many times. Her skin is cool to the touch already, her eyes flutter, once, twice, the pupils dilating, then rolling all the way up, as if she was looking for another view, a better place than here.

But despite the endless conversations we've had about dying and dignity, and knowing when to let go, I plow ahead, feeling the weight of a million prayers on my shoulders as I ramble off directions to José—monitor the rhythm, check her fluids—and prepare the paddles for what I hope will be a miracle. Even though, as a scientist, I've been taught not believe in those.

"Two hundred. Ready? One, two, three," I shout, and the defibrillator fires up and she shakes on the bed. "Clear. Charge two fifty. Charge! Clear."

Arora counts this time, and we go again. "She's not reacting. Is the EPI in? Charge three hundred. CHARGE!" Arora's face is lined with worry, his eyes red from endless hours on night call and countless shots of caffeine. I wonder if mine looks as worn. His exhaustion flattens his voice as he looks down at his watch and says the words I've been dreading. "I think we've done all we can. José, mark it down. Time of death, eleven forty-three p.m., Friday, September twenty-first."

It can't be. Just a month before she'd be thirteen. A teenager. Like me. "She's got a strong heart, and so do you," I keep reminding myself. But as the lines flatten and fade, tears spill down my cheeks fast and furious, and I'm wondering what I've gotten myself into.

Maybe I'm not cut out for this. Why did I ever think I was?

Cho removes his mask, staring down at the body in disbelief.

Howard's already scrubbing up and preparing herself for the worst—telling the family—but I can't let this be over. Not yet.

"We're going again," I tell José, even though he's already starting to shut down the electrocardiogram machine and detach the IVs. "One more time. Now!" My voice rises in a way I didn't know it could, and I'm already prepping the defibrillator by the time he gets back to the gurney. "I need another dose of lidocaine, and fast. Three hundred! Charge again," I shout. "Charge again."

I'm not giving up. Not this time. I will fix this. I won't let her die.

But it's not up to me.

CHAPTER 46

I can't stop crying. I can't stop shaking. I feel José's arms wrapping around, me, and Howard's chin on my head, and even Cho patting my back, whispering that it's okay, it's all right, we did the best we could. "She's in a better place now," he keeps saying, and I stop cold for a second.

"We don't know that," I say, and the truth of it hits me so hard, like the dirt they threw on top of Harper's tiny, kid-sized coffin that day all those years ago at the funeral, that day that has haunted my sleep ever since. "We don't know anything at all."

But Cho takes my hand then, and looks straight into my eyes. I wait for the zinger, but it never comes. Instead, he says, "Saira, I promise you two things. She knows how hard you tried. She knows. And wherever she is, she's not in pain anymore."

The wave of shudders start again then, and the sobs follow, blurring my vision, and taking the others down with me. Then Arora is standing there, looking like the only grown-up in the room, and reminding us that, as hard as this is, it's about to get a whole lot harder.

"I have to go talk to the family," he says, and there's a crack in his voice, even though he's learned how to mask it. "You guys should get yourselves together. I think they'll probably want to see you, too, given how close you all became to Alina. Especially you, Saira."

I nod. But I can't let him go alone.

"I need to come with you," I say.

"I don't think that's such a good idea," Arora says, but he's looking at me like he already knows it's a waste to argue.

"I have to do it," I tell him.

He nods. "Clean yourself up. I'll be waiting outside."

Mr. Plotkin and Bubbe are in the family room waiting, and for a minute I think back to the last time I was here—just after Pinky's surgery, and how we all celebrated that moment. How that little girl got to live. This time, we've come to break hearts, to offer a grief that has no salve. They sit on the sofa in the far corner, CNN droning on the TV just above their heads, Bubbe's frail hand sitting just on top of Mr. Plotkin's, a small comfort during this endless moment.

As soon as they hear our footsteps they rise, impatient for news, and I can tell from Mr. Plotkin's lined, worn, exhausted face that he knows the worst is coming. He's known it for weeks and months and years now, and I remember that small relief from when I experienced it myself with Harper. The lifting of pain and the horror of loss, encapsulated in the same unforgettable, unforgiving moment, the one that will stay with you forever after.

He hugs me, the gesture more of a command than a comfort, and his hand is on my face when the words spill out. "She's gone," I say, and I'm sobbing again, and Mr. Plotkin's tears are soaking my hair. And it's okay, because I know he knows I understand. And I know he knows I'll miss her forever, too, and carry her with me for always.

The tears are still streaming when we leave, Bubbe, and Mr. Plotkin and mama Tina and the children all gathered, all needing the comfort of being alone with Alina one last time. I almost can't bear to part from them, knowing that the thing that connected us for so long has been ripped away now. But I have to go, to let them have this moment.

Arora's arm is around my shoulder, my tears soaking his lab coat, as we walk back toward the oncology office.

"I feel like a failure," I tell him through tears, and he smiles sympathetically at me. "And I can't stop crying."

"Honestly, I'd be worried if you weren't crying. And trust me, Dr.

Sehgal. This will be the first of many failures you'll have as a doctor. A wise woman—I think it may have been your mother, no?—once said to me, back when I was a lowly resident doing my pediatrics rotation, that where there is life, there must always be death. They're a pair. Better to learn that quickly." He looks at me for a moment, all Yoda in his wisdom. "Although I think you know that already."

"They don't call me a genius for nothing, Dr. Arora," I say, and manage to crack a smile.

That's when José comes racing down the hallway, like his scrubs are on fire or something.

"They found it! They found it!" he's shouting to everyone in sight— then he grabs me, twirls me, and does a little salsa, right then and there.

"What are you saying?" I ask, the tears starting fresh. "What are you saying?"

Arora jumps in, impatient. "Link?"

José grins. "They found a match."

Arora looks truly stunned, and I'm sure he's pondering that thing he just said about life and death.

"Well then, Dr. Sehgal. Would you like to deliver the news?"

I almost say no. How can I? It's too much.

But José's nodding and pushing me along down the hallway, and then there we are, standing in Link's doorway, with Link's mom and Dr. Radcliffe looking at us expectantly.

But I walk right past them all and to Link, who sits up, weary, tired but curious, in his bed.

"Hey," he says, that smirk on his lips again. But when he sees my tearstained face, it fades fast.

And then I grin. "They found one," I tell him, sitting by his side. "A match. They found one."

And for a minute, he just looks at me, floored, his eyes shimmering, but steady on me. Then he leans forward and kisses me, in front of his parents, José, and even Arora. And it's okay. Because at I know, in that moment, that I will take every last kiss I can get.

STATEN ISLAND SUMMIT—SEPTEMBER 24

PLOTKIN, ALINA K.

Passed on September 21, in Princeton, New Jersey. She was 12 years old, and succumbed to complications related to leukemia. She was survived by her bubbe, Marina Plotkin, 83, father Alfred Plotkin, 48, mother Tina Plotkin, 44, and twin sisters, Anna and Amelia Plotkin, 8. The family resides in Staten Island, New York, and funeral services will take place at the Rosewood Cemetery on Saturday at 4 p.m. In lieu of flowers, the family has requested that donations be made to the National Pediatric Cancer Foundation.

CHAPTER 47

It's been a week since we got the news. And after that kiss, Arora decided that perhaps it would be wise for Link and I not to see each other at the hospital, in any sort of "official" capacity. Especially since he's immunocompromised. Which sucks. But makes sense. In any case, he didn't tell Davis, and he didn't report it to Mom. So I still have my job. And my head. Two good things to have.

Link's procedure is Monday and I am banished—how very *Romeo and Juliet*—from the hospital until Tuesday, just to be safe. Which is well and good, because today I have a major hurdle of my own to overcome. My driver's test.

Papa knocked at my door bright and early this morning, and this time he wasn't about to let me get out of it. "The next Saturday available is not for six months," he warned, offering up a kachori as enticement. It worked, because here I am. The last place I want to be. Well, almost.

"You ready?" Papa says as we inch up into the queue. There are four cars ahead of us, and the waiting is excruciating. There's a horrible pain in the pit of my stomach—nerves, maybe, or just the sadness of losing Alina, which has been relentless in its constancy.

I nod.

"You'll be relieved when it's done, beta."

I lay my forehead down on the top of the steering wheel. "It won't change anything."

But I know. It'll change everything. Because that's it. When I get my license, the last vestiges of my life as a kid—as brief as it was—will be gone. I'll officially be Dr. Sehgal. A grown-up. An adult. A certified mess.

Rap, rap, rap. I look up, and the driving test administrator's knocking on Papa's passenger side window. It's time.

Papa gets out, making small talk about cool September Saturdays with the man, who's balding and gray, like Mr. Plotkin if he was fast-forwarded to old age. Which he will be. That familiar lump—the one that used to belong just to Harper—pops up in my throat. I'm so not ready for this. But it's too late now.

The man takes a seat and clears his throat. Maybe he misses someone, too. "I'm Mr. Calvin. Ms. Sehgal, is it? First time?"

I shake my head. I've tried and failed more times than I can remember now.

"Well, maybe this one will do the trick," he says. "Pull up to the intersection there, and we can begin the exam."

"Yes, sir," I say, feeling more like a child than I have in months.

"Okay, Ms. Sehgal," he says, and I wonder if I should correct him. Dr. Sehgal. But it's not worth the drama. "Let's go straight down this path, and then make a left at the four-way intersection four blocks down."

I do exactly what he says, then make a left, slim and trim, remembering Papa's warnings about too-wide turns.

"Good, Ms. Sehgal. Now let's come to the next four-way. How do we proceed here?" I can see him from the corner of my eyes, making small notes about my actions—the way my hands land on the wheel, my use of blinkers and signals, my timing as I turn. It kind of makes me want to laugh, but it also makes me want to cry. Life and death, my mom said, two sides of a coin. Cancer kills. But people die on the roads every day. Is it better to go fast, not knowing? Or slow, living through every punishing moment?

"Ms. Sehgal?" he says again, sounding irritated.

"Yes, sir?"

"Parallel park, please. Here, at the curb. You already passed the other spot."

Shit. That means I've probably failed already. Should I just call it quits now? Might as well. I'm not ready for this, anyway.

But then I remember Link's words in the car that day. No, not the "I refuse to be the one who breaks your heart." Though I'll never forget those. He said something about parallel parking, how it's a little give, a little tug, meeting in the middle. I veer the car right and touch the curb a teensy bit. Oops. But not all is lost. I reverse, pulling back, the way Vish showed me, and manage to align the back wheel to the road, about six inches away. Now it's just bringing the front into alignment, right? What was it Taara said? Turn the wheel in the opposite direction for surprising results. Just like life. I do it, and it works. The wheels align like magic. The car is perfectly parallel to the curb.

"Interesting methodology, Ms. Sehgal," the man says, grinning. "But it worked." He scrawls something on the paper. Oh gods. I failed. I know I failed. Again. "Pull out and drive back to the starting point, please."

Oh well. What's one more failure?

"Congratulations, Ms. Sehgal. You passed."

"What?" I say. Papa's already rapping on the window, grinning, waving his arms in curiosity.

"You passed. Congratulations."

"Thank you, but it's Dr. Sehgal," I say to the man, then abruptly erupt into sobs.

He looks shocked. So does Papa, who opens the door, nearly pulling the man out by the arm. The guy scurries off, slip in hand, looking worried.

Papa jumps into the passenger seat. "What happened, beta? Why are you crying?" He's rubbing my shoulders and my back, wiping tears from cheeks like he did when I was little. "It's okay. You can take it again."

"I passed." I sob some more. "I passed."

"It's okay, beta," my papa says, stroking my hair. "It's okay. I know we've all been very hard on you this year. Too hard, maybe."

I can't stop crying long enough to say a word. So Papa just continues. "But honestly, bachoo, you are so much stronger than we give you credit for. And maybe we underestimate you. I always talk to your mom about all this—the medical school, the internship, oncology, and tell her it's too much. But she's the one who knows, and she says you can handle it." That shocks me out of my tears. Because that's definitely not what my mother said to me. "And she's right. You're a strong girl; you can handle it. Maybe it's why God introduced you to Harper, and to Alina, and even to Link." He frowns a little as he says Link's name. "Because you were meant to do this work."

I nod.

"Now let's go get that license."

I drive my dad home, and Dadi's full speed ahead, as if the hospital stay never happened at all. Thank gods. She's got the kathoris hot and ready with chole and thari wale aloo, but I have something else on my agenda.

"Papa, can I take the car?" My dad's shoulders jump when he hears the words.

"I knew it'd be coming. Just not so soon," he says, thumping his chest like the dramaebaaz he is. But then he gets out, and waves. "Be safe, bachoo."

"Okay."

I turn the key in the ignition, and set the GPS for Rosewood Cemetery, for Alina's funeral, even though I'm wearing a blue summer dress. She would have approved. This will be one of the hardest things I'll ever have to do. My first solo ride will not be a bright one, but that's what being a grown-up's all about, right?

CHAPTER 48

I get to work early on Tuesday morning, hoping to sneak into Link's room to see how he's doing—even though Vish and José texted me, like, every three minutes yesterday and gave me the play-by-play, and by all accounts, he's doing fine, still asleep, doesn't even know what day it is.

But once I'm there, I'm thrown into the thick of the chaos—new patient intake, file updates, rounds. It's two o'clock before I even manage a second cup of coffee. Then I'm paged over the speaker—not unusual—and my heart sinks for a minute. This could be bad. But when I get to the nurse's station, José tells me that there's been a meeting called, and my presence is demanded, along with Howard and Cho. Uh-oh.

We gather around the conference table, and Dr. Stevenson—the head of neurosurgery—is there along with Arora, Charles, and a few people I don't recognize. This doesn't bode well. Howard, Cho and I exchange anxious glances.

Charles raps on the table to get everyone's attention, and we all sit up a little straighter in our seats.

"It's with some dismay that we've called today's meeting to announce to you that Dr. Davis is taking a—perhaps permanent—leave of absence," he says, his face grim. "Unfortunately, some evidence has come to light, including information shared by patients, nurses, and Dr. Davis's own assistant, that demonstrates to us that she has not been able to make the wisest choices lately. We feel the trauma she faced after losing her wife last year has caused her to make some shaky decisions, and she agrees that a break to seek professional help is smart. She's cleaning out her office today and will be gone as of tomorrow. We wanted you to hear it from us, rather than through the office grapevine."

"Grapevine" is such a funny word. But wow. Davis is out. I'm not quite sure whether to laugh or cry, though all signs point to me crying pretty much all the time lately. Cho looks shocked, and Howard a bit relieved. I should be, too, right? But I just feel exhausted.

Arora clears his throat, as usual. "I know some of you have struggled in building a secure, trusting relationship with Dr. Davis, and this, uh, explains a lot. As you know, I am always here if you want to talk, and if there is anything that concerns you regarding this matter, please do not hesitate to reach out. In the meantime, I will be looking over the HR files Davis left behind on all of you, and reevaluating what needs to be included." He looks at me for a minute, and I look down at the table. There could be some pretty incriminating things in that file, I know. But I have to own them, for better or for worse.

I'm shocked to find myself knocking on Davis's office door, just a half hour after the meeting. She answers herself—the assistant is gone and doesn't look very surprised to see me.

"Sehgal," she says. "Come in. Here to gloat?"

I shake my head, standing, like a kid at the chalkboard, waiting for a pat on the head.

"Well, you should. So few opportunities to truly win these days. You were a worthy opponent."

Nemesis. She means nemesis. "I'm sorry to see you go, Dr. Davis. And even more sorry to hear about your wife."

She nods curtly and sits behind her desk, looking around the office like she's memorizing it. "After Leela died, this was my home," she says, but there's nothing bitter in her voice for once. It sounds different without that hard edge. Almost lovely. "I was grateful for it. I mean, you know, grief does funny things to people. I couldn't handle it. So I started spending all my time here, and I didn't understand why others weren't doing the same. Sorry if I was hard on you, kid."

"It was a learning experience."

She grins. "Good for you. That's certainly a way to look at it. And you'll have others. Worse than me. Heck, I've heard similar things about your mom—not an easy boss, that woman. Not an easy mother, too, I'm sure."

She's right, though there's no way I'm giving her that one. "What will you do now?" I ask instead.

"Oh, my daughter Kavya—she reminds me of you, actually—she's in California now. She does cancer research at UCLA. She said she can use me as a lab tech. Haven't done that in about twenty years. But you can't yell at a test tube, so I should be okay." She shrugs. "I'll tell you this, kid. You did what you could. And you did good. For Alina. And the others. Especially Link. Maybe a bit of vested interest isn't a terrible thing." She's looking at the photograph on her desk when she says it, stroking the image of her dead wife. "Maybe I could've, should've done more." She looks up at me. "You would have liked Leela. She was a spitfire." She grins. "Like you. Always causing trouble."

I try to shrug it off but smile instead. Might as well embrace it.

"We met at this very hospital thirty years ago. Your mom was a resident then—you should ask her. Caught Leela and I making out in the intern lounge once. Never said a word. I always liked that about her. No one suspected two women back then. And she kept our secret for us, until we were ready to share it."

"Anyway," she says. "I've been hard on you. But with good reason. You've got so much potential. Grow into it. Don't waste it on impulsive choices. And weigh the risks you take. That trial worked for Brendan—and thank god for that. But not everyone does," she says, looking down at the picture again. "I mean, maybe Alina would have lived if I made different choices. Or if you had. We all make good decisions, and bad ones. Got to learn to live with both. That's the hard part. But I think you'll be okay. And I don't know what Dr. Arora has planned, but you've got my vote, if it counts for anything."

She looks up, smiles one last time, and waves me off. "See you, Dr. Sehgal."

And I try to hide my smile as I walk out the door, still in shock.

Of course, my feet carry me straight to Link's room. It's dark, the curtains drawn, the lights dimmed, the hum of the machines the only sound. Except for Howard, sitting in the chair, knitting quietly as she watches his vitals.

"Hey," she whispers, putting down her knitting.

I walk over to the bed, and I can't help it, even though she's there, watching, I put my head to his chest, just to confirm it's still there, that familiar heartbeat.

"He's okay. I think, honestly, miraculously, that maybe he'll be fine," she says, her breath catching. "Though it's too soon to tell."

I nod. "I wish I could have been there."

"I wish you could have, too," she says, and her voice sounds a bit mournful. "But also, I'm glad you weren't. It would have been so, so hard. It still will be, because he has a long road ahead. But he's got a great team, and his family. And you."

I sit in the chair next to her, then stand, rethinking it. There are so many things I want to ask her. So many things I want to say. Like how could you do that? And I sort of totally get it. But instead, I say, "You know, if it's real, you and Dr. Arora, you should figure it out. Because someone very smart once told me that it's rare, and you can't control it. Finding something real like that. You love who you love. And you only get so many chances."

Howard looks down at her knitting for a long moment. "I know," she says. "But things . . . This is more complicated than that. I think it could be real. But it's too soon to tell. And Abhi's got himself all sorted out, and I'm just starting. I can't drop everything I've worked so hard for just to figure that, us, out. I have to focus."

Yeah, focus. That's been the hard part. "But you don't have to choose just one thing."

"Sometimes, though, you do. I mean, in all logical sense, you should. I should. We're modern, smart, feminist, strong. Of course, we need to chase our dreams. Right?"

I nod. But I don't buy it. Not completely. "I still think I'm right."

She sighs. "Well, you are the genius." Ouch. That hurt. "But, I mean, it's not so simple for all of us. I worked for a decade to get here. Georgetown, Yale, my own nonprofit. This is my shot. I'm not going to throw it away because maybe he makes my heart leap a little bit."

I mean, I get it. I do. And the old Saira—the one who got here on that blazing hot day in July, before the world shifted under her feet—would have said exactly the same thing. But this new Saira. Maybe she's wiser that that Girl Genius. Just a little bit.

"Anyway. I'm quitting." I nearly knock over the jug on the table, as I flail in shock. Howard grins. "It's just too much. Too weird. Sticky. Him. Here. I already told Abhishek. I'll be here through December, and he'll look for another intern in the meantime. I'll go to St. Jude's. It's not too far away, so we can still see each other, but it won't be tense like this." She waves her arms. "Then he and I can figure out what's real."

I nod. "I'll miss you."

"You will and you won't," she says. "And that's okay. But I will miss you. And you can always text me. Especially when the Cho-splaining becomes incessant." She picks up her knitting and leaves then, looking one last time at Link's vitals.

I scoot my chair close to the bed, rest my head near Link's, and lie there like that, in the dark, for what feels like forever, maybe, and just watch the rise and fall of his chest. Maybe he knows I'm there, feels my presence. Maybe he's just gone, in that limbo space they always talk about. But for now, his breath, his heartbeat, they're all here, all real.

CHAPTER 49

Late. Again. Mom and I rush to the elevators, and I punch the button for eight, checking my watch again. It's nearly ten. And today, my eyebrows are impeccable.

"Reshma did a good job," Mom says, approvingly, as the elevator doors close. "See, the others are a waste. In any profession, you really want someone who knows what they're doing. And someone who will really give you what *you* need."

I hit the button again, but instead of moving, the elevator doors open again. Sigh. So. Very. Late.

When the door opens, there stands a young man: brown skin, wire-rim glasses, lab coat, longish curly hair that always got him in trouble. Grinning.

"I thought I heard your voice," he says. "Is that Saira Sehgal, Girl Genius?"

I do a double take. Yep, it's him. My nemesis, if only he weren't so swoon-worthy: Varun Khanna, MD. The second-youngest doctor in America. "Dr. Arora told me I might run into you here," he says, stepping onto the elevator. He namastes at my mom. "Hi, Auntie. How are you?"

I frown. "What . . . what are you doing here?" Mom looks confused. Or is it amused?

"Oh, haven't you heard? I thought Dr. Charles would have told you by now. Or your mom." Mom shrugs. But she's not good at lying, even silently. "I'm here doing paperwork for my internship. I start in January."

He grins again, too pleased with himself, and when the door opens on eight, does this whole faux-courtesy thing, waving his arms. "After you," he says. And I can feel his smug eyes on me, boring into the back of my head, as I trip over nothing on my race to the pediatric oncology wing. Because I'm late. Again.

Today's the day. After two months, one week, four days, and thirteen hours, Lincoln Chung-Radcliffe has been declared officially in remission. The bone marrow transplant worked. "All of which is to say, Link, that you are officially discharged," Cho says, his grin nearly swallowing his face. "You're cleared to go home—although, as your mom mentioned, you'll do one more round of chemo for good measure, and then the follow-up survival care."

Link was grinning, too—until he heard that last bit. "Another round?" he says, his frown accentuating the dent in his cheek. "I thought that was the last of it?"

Link's mom looks a bit worried as she turns to Dr. Arora, who is all nonchalant, as if he didn't just have a meeting with my nemesis. "Is it really necessary, Dr. Arora?" she asks, looking from Cho to Arora. "It takes so much out of him."

I want to tell them it's 100 percent necessary—an ounce of prevention versus a pound of cure, or whatever. But I'm not allowed to talk. I'm here only in official "friend" capacity. So I compose my face to neutral, not negative, not positive, just observing innocently. Then I say: "You should do it. Just in case."

"Just in case it doesn't stick?" Link says, his eyes on me, a bit amused at my major failure to not speak. But his mood is dour, for someone who's just been given a sort-of clean bill of health. "It never sticks, is what you're saying."

Arora looks thoughtful for a second, rubbing the scruff on his chin. Then he does that half-smile thing I've gotten so used to. It's a diffusing method. And it works. "I'd advise that we do the last round, Link. We want to come out of this fighting strong. Let's face it, finding that marrow match was pretty much a miracle." He grins at me. "We don't want to waste this shot."

Howard steps in, paperwork in hand. "We all set?" she asks. She reads the room, her face worried. "What's up?"

"Link's pouting because of chemo," I say, and he glares at me. But I grin. "But he's overruled. Doctor's orders."

Link's mom sighs. "I guess that means mother's orders, too," she says, putting her hand out for the paperwork. "Now, where do I sign?"

She scrawls on the sheet Howard lays on the table, and that's it. He's out. He's done. He's free.

Which means we're free. Finally. This has been the longest almost three months of my life. First, he was just so tired, barely awake, and completely not himself. But the marrow transfer was working. The new cells were growing, multiplying, devouring and replacing the malignant old cells. I looked at some of the slides under the microscopes—thanks to Howard, who'd sneak me the samples—and it was a like a real, true miracle. Science at work. The marrow and the medicine together were rebuilding a better, stronger, faster Link. One who's standing in front of me now, grinning, worn for the wear, but alive and well and healthy.

"I can't believe it," I whisper to Link as the rest of the doctors follow his mom off to the conference room, leaving us behind—though José's still hovering, fluffing pillows, adjusting the bed, his eyes on us. I can tell he wants to be nosy, but is working very, very hard to give us some space. "You're okay."

"Yeah." He grins. "And you didn't get fired."

"Probation," I remind him. "But yeah."

"And so, Saira with an *i*, I ask, will you do me the honors?"

I shrug. "What?"

"Well, now that I'm cancer-free, alive, and well, I'm feeling a little reckless."

I don't get it. But José's grinning.

"Wanna drive me to the beach?"

I can feel my perfect brows perch high.

"This boy truly has a death wish," José says, laughing.

I grin, then get my purse. "Okay, sure, I'll tell the boys to meet us there."

Link frowns. The boys? "Not quite what I had in mind."

I wave a packet of papers in his face. He frowns harder. More paperwork?

"It's the first day of the rest of your life, Link," I say. "And you already have plans." He looks around the room, then at José, who shrugs. "Vish and I sent *Rock Star Band Camp* a tape from the ABC News shoot—he used it for his USC app, remember? Anyway. You're in the top ten, if you want it. But that means you're headed to LA next month. And you've got a month of rehearsals to catch up on."

Link looks shocked, but a slow grin spreads across his face. "Always with your plans, huh, Saira?" he says, leaning down to kiss me. "That's kind of what I love about you." Then he adds, "But tell the boys *Rock Star Band Camp* can wait. First, you and I are going to make up for lost time. And get out of this damned hospital." He hands me his keys. "To Pizza Hut! Our chariot awaits."

Together, we walk away from the cancer wing, knowing, certainly, that we'll be back. But in the meantime, we've got a lot of life to live.

ACKNOWLEDGMENTS

I sat down to write these acknowledgments so many times. After all, no author gets to *The End* alone. But every time I did, I cried. Because so many people contributed their hopes and hard work to this book.

First and foremost: To all the little brown kids—the dreamers, the schemers, the overachievers and especially the underachievers. I see you. This story is for you. I write so that maybe you can see yourself, too. To Kavya, to Shaiyar, to all of you: You can be whatever you want to be. It's okay. Thank you for chasing your dreams and changing the world.

Thank you to my team at Imprint—the brilliant Erin Stein, Weslie Turner, Nicole Otto, and the much-missed Rhoda Belleza, another small brown girl with big dreams. There's also the visionary designer Natalie Sousa, whose poppy, bold cover is sure to make *Symptoms* a standout on the shelf—and who gave Saira Sehgal those signature, impeccable brows that even her mama can't complain about. To Katie Quinn and Alexandra Hernandez, for both their hustle and their flow—thank you for your patience and your efforts! Dawn Ryan, Raymond Colón, Avia Perez, and Elynn Cohen—this book could not have existed without you. And thank you to the rest of the Imprint crew!

To my early readers: the brilliant Jackie Hsieh, MD, and kickass writers Candice Montgomery, Sayantani DasGupta, Rajat Singh, Kat Cho, Olugbemisola Rhuday-Perkovich—thank you so much for all your help with this book. You are all amazing, and your insights were priceless.

And thank you so much to cheerleaders Nisha Sharma, Preeti

Chhibber, Samira Ahmed, Melissa Albert, Dahlia Adler, Ericka Souter, Ellen Oh, Lamar Giles and the We Need Diverse Books team, my Deb Ball queens, the wonderful folks at WORD Jersey City, and the community of kidlit and YA writers I'm proud to be a part of. And to my neighbor Samantha Howard, thank you for letting me swipe your name.

To my awesome, assertive and ever-ambitious agent, Victoria Marini. Your vision for me, for CAKE, and for the future is always brighter and bolder than anything D and I could dream up. (And we love you for that.) To Dhonielle Clayton, my partner in crime and CAKE. You are truly a sister. Thank you for your patience and practicality. You know how my brain works, and that is huge. Thank you for always being in my corner, for always aiming bigger, for dragging me along kicking and screaming (or sulking). You are a blessing, and I am forever grateful.

And to the amazing CAKE team—Sasha and Sarena Nanua, and Clay Morrell! Thank you for all you do! We could not do it without you.

To Pizza Hut, for all the moments over all the years. And to my big, fat, bustling, noisy, and amazing clan—the Bhambris, the Charaipotras, the Dhillons—for sharing those moments with me. There is so much of your life scattered throughout these pages, and I hope I've done you justice. To Vishal, Arun, Sonia Mamiji, Raju Mamaji, and everyone else I've borrowed from, thank you. And to Divya Dodhia, you are amazing. Thank you.

And last but certainly not least: To my heart and soul, my family. You are my favorites, and so very loved.

Thank you to Mum and Pappari, for unknowingly letting me steal their names, among other things, and for raising the best man I know. Thank-you to Navreet, Simrit, Joshvir, and Seerit for being exactly who you are.

Thank you, Lisa, for the joy you bring. And to my first and forever collaborators, Meena and Tarun. Love Zona, always.

To Navdeep, Kavya, and Shaiyar, my beloved little band of storytellers. Thank you for always being patient, always being present, and reminding me to do the same. I can't wait to see the stories you will share with the world.

And to Mommy and Papa. I know my path wasn't exactly the one you were hoping I'd take. But everything you've taught me has led me here. Thank you for believing in dreams, and in me, no matter what direction I went off in. (And even though I still can't drive.) I hope I can make you proud.